PASSIONATE PRINCES

Billionaires & Royals Box Set #2

Scorsolini Baby Scandal

Her Off Limits Prince

The Maharajah's Billionaire Heir

Lucy Monroe

Lucy Monroe LLC

PRAISE FOR LUCY MONROE

Lucy Monroe captures the very heart of the genre. She pulls the reader into the story from the first to the last page. ~ NYT Bestseller Debbie Macomber

Lucy Monroe writes smart, sensual, emotional books for intelligent women. ~ NYT Bestseller JoAnn Ross

Thank you for writing those alpha heroes I love. ~ NYT Bestseller Lori Foster

A Lucy Monroe book is a treat not to be missed. ~ NYT Bestseller Lora Leigh

Lucy Monroe is one of my favorite indulgences. ~ NYT Bestseller Christine Feehan

Monroe writes with a flourish the type of lovemaking and desire that women can truly appreciate. ~ RT Book Reviews

Lucy Monroe excels at creating authentic erotic romance. ~ Romance B(u)y the Book

Just when one thinks this author has written the best of her best heroes, she releases another story and we are proven wrong. ~ The Road to Romance

CONTENTS

SCORSOLINI BABY SCANDAL

Lucy Monroe

Lucy Monroe LLC

For everyone who has ever felt like they didn't fit their own world or lived up to the expectations of the people that matter to them. You are exactly who you are supposed to be and do not need to chip away at your edges to fit into someone else's mold for you. No matter how well meaning. Hugs!

CHAPTER ONE

Rio: A Prince in the Piazza

I am Principe Vittorio Micheli Scorsolini, third in line to the throne of Isole dei Re and trained from the cradle to be self-possessed even in the face of country-wide catastrophe.

Yet, when the most compellingly beautiful woman I have ever seen walks by, I trip over my own feet.

Twenty-five years of training kick in, and I stop myself from falling, pivoting to follow the vision of loveliness crossing Palermo's Piazza Pretoria. The view is as beguiling from the back as the front, although her hat's wide brim obscures most of her hair.

What I did see is rich brown with golden highlights, falling in silky waves to her shoulders and framing a face worthy of a Botticelli. If Botticelli's Muses had worn Chanel sunglasses and backless white sundresses with a plunging neckline.

There's too much of the tanned skin on her back on display for her to be wearing a bra.

My dick engorges to semi-hardness in a single heartbeat.

Wanting another glimpse of her mouthwatering cleavage, I quicken my steps to catch up with her.

Her strappy sandals add three inches to her already statuesque height, but she walks with elegant grace, her hips swaying enticingly.

My beauty stops in front of the Fontana Pretoria and lifts her phone for a selfie giving me what I want. Another view of her appealing curves from the front. Papa would throw a blanket over my sister if she wore something that revealed so much flesh.

As Crown Princess to the throne of Isole dei Re, Elena would never think to wear a dress like the one gracing the delicious figure of my obsession.

Primal satisfaction courses through me that this woman is not hampered by the same expectations.

Frowning, the beautiful woman shifts her position and takes another selfie, but shakes her head.

Never slow to take advantage of an opportunity when presented, I step forward. "Would you like me to take a picture of you in front of the fountain?"

I sound so damn formal. I've tried relaxing my speech, but it feels like I'm pretending to be someone I'm not. People will accept me for who I am, or not at all.

The English is a calculated risk though. Most tourists speak at least some English. Though with her perfectly oval face, defined cheekbones and narrow nose, the other option I consider is Castilian Spanish.

She drops the hand holding her phone and eyes warm with humor meet mine through the light tint of her sunglasses. "You noticed my pathetic attempts to get both me and the fountain framed in my shot?"

"*Sì.*" I manage a passably coherent affirmative, mesmerized by the soft contralto of her tone.

"That's a Sicilian *yes*, not Spanish." She cocks her head to one side, looking at me with curiosity.

"It is. I would be happy to..." I offer again, waving between her, the camera and the fountain.

Lightly glossed, bow shaped lips curve in a smile. "That would be great!"

The response isn't anything out of the norm. However, the breathy quality in her voice and the way she leans toward me without seeming to realize she's doing it tells me this instant and overwhelming attraction is not one-way.

I put my hand out for her phone.

After a brief hesitation, she gives it to me, careful not to brush my fingers with hers. "Just tap either of the white dots."

"I'm sure I can figure it out."

Slipping off her sunglasses, she puts one foot in front of the other at a slight angle and poses unselfconsciously in front of the fountain.

Eyes the color of storm clouds connect with mine in a look so compelling, it's me leaning forward this time.

Tia Maggie always claims she fell in love with *Tio* Tomasso at first sight, but it had taken him a lot longer to catch up.

I always thought my aunt was being a fanciful romantic until this moment. This overwhelming reaction cannot be love, but it is *something*. Something I can neither ignore nor deny.

The object of my newfound obsession shifts her position in a natural rhythm that seems almost choreographed and I take several shots in quick succession. "Are you a model?"

"Nope, just a student." But there had been an odd flicker of reaction to the word *model* in her grey gaze.

I take my time getting the perfect shot, using the opportunity to chat her up. Her name is Tanzi Menendez. So, my guess on the Spanish heritage had not been off.

I tell her that my name is Vittorio Scorsolini, making no mention of my connection to the royal family of Isole dei Re or my title. Scorsolini is a common enough name that unless she's familiar with my small island country, she will not realize who I am.

I'm not the brother whose face made it into the tabloids. That is Adamo.

For some reason, Tanzi knowing Vittorio the man, not *Principe* Vittorio is important.

She's in her last year of university in New York, which makes her two to three years younger than me. She's in Sicily with friends for Spring Break, but she's only in Palermo for the day.

Tanzi puts her hand up to keep her bright white sunhat on when a small gust of wind threatened to send it flying. "I'll be finished in June if my dad doesn't talk me into going for my MBA."

"Not interested in climbing the corporate ladder?" I ask.

Her lips twist in a moue of distaste. "No offense, Rio, as clearly that's your thing, but no. My bachelor's will be in psychology."

"What gave me away?" I force myself to banter, having a strange reaction to her shortening my name. No one does that. "The suit?"

"Well, it is custom tailored Armani. And probably the only reason I handed my camera over to a stranger to take my picture."

"It could be a knock off, and I could be trolling the square to steal unwary tourist's cameras."

She shakes her head. "No chance. That's definitely Armani and it fits you like a glove."

"You're very sure of your designers."

"It's in my genes. I don't think my mom knows there are clothes made without a fashion house label attached."

I laugh. "She sounds like my sister."

Elena might be forced to dress more conservatively than other women her age, but her closet is well acquainted with the world's leading designers.

"Why businessman and not rich playboy?" I've never been entirely sure how people can always tell my brother Adamo is the "fun" one.

He got his MBA just like I did, but he did it cutting a swath through the female population at our university. And he still managed to graduate Summa Cum

Laude right beside me. He's moved on from coeds to super models, but he still spends a lot more time entertaining than I do.

"The tie," Tanzi says, answering my question. "I bought one very similar for my dad. They're both from the Oleg Cassini line designed for the power broker businessman. Too expensive for your average office drone and too serious for a rich playboy."

For the first time in memory, I'm not feeling serious, or intently focused on my day's "power business" agenda right now. In fact, I'm tempted to do the unthinkable.

Take a day off.

I could text my assistant with instructions to reschedule the rest of the afternoon. It would be entirely out of character and seriously considering it is absurd.

And yet, my fingers itch to tap out the message.

"I think that's enough pictures." She smiles, even white teeth flashing, clearly unaware of the revolution of thought going on inside my head. "Thank you for taking them."

"Are you visiting the palazzo?" I ask, referring to one of the more commonly visited sights in the city.

"Actually, our tour group is supposed to head to the cathedral next."

I consider possible scenarios to stay in her company without coming off like a stalker.

She flicks a glance down at herself and grins. "I brought a shawl so I could go inside."

"Too many tourists don't give deference to Sicilian conventions. I like that you do."

She shrugs, like it's not a big deal. "I grew up splitting time between Southern California and Spain with my parents. Two very different cultures. They expected me and my brothers to respect each culture and adapt to the norms of both." She flashes that brilliant smile again. "Besides showing respect for the culture in which you find yourself is just good manners."

"Agreed." Though it isn't merely good manners for the son of a monarch; it is imperative. "Have a coffee with me and I will give you a personally guided tour of the cathedral after."

"You're an expert, are you?" she teases

"My family were originally from Sicily." Generations ago, before the country of Isole dei Re was founded by my ancestors. "We still have business interests here."

She bites her bottom lip, clearly considering whether she wanted to break away from her tour group to spend time with a stranger.

"You said you are here with friends, *sì*?"

"Yes."

"Invite them to join us."

The concerned furrow on her brow smoothed. "You don't mind?"

"Not at all." Would I rather be alone with my beautiful goddess?

Certo. But I understand her reluctance.

"Let me text them." She lifts her phone and points it at me before tapping the screen. It clicks, indicating she took my photo. "I'm sending your picture too. What's your mobile number?"

I rattle it off, surprised at my own willingness to do so.

She dials. When the phone in my suit jacket inner pocket buzzes, she nods with satisfaction and sends her text.

"I approve your caution."

Perfectly shaped brows rose, her expression turning wry. "How nice for you."

I laugh. "Yes, well, I have a tendency to think my opinion matters too much. At least, according to my sister and brother."

"Younger, I bet."

"My sister is twenty-five minutes older, my brother fifteen."

"And *you* boss *them* both around?"

"Boss is a strong term. I make suggestions." Not that either Elena or Adamo appreciate my advice when I give it.

They both might be older by minutes, but we were born on the same day and of the three of us, I am the most practical.

"You're a triplet?" she asks with obvious curiosity.

"*Sì*." And my entire life is overshadowed by that fact.

The youngest triplet of the royal family. Not the heir. Not the spare. But I refuse to melt into the background like a distant relation to the throne.

My siblings and I share our family's business responsibilities, but I am the one who took over those that kept my father away from the palace. Our family's business *is* Isole dei Re. If our company does not thrive, neither does our economy.

So, I travel extensively. Add that to my increasing diplomatic duties on behalf of the Crown and I spend only scattered weeks throughout the year with my family.

"My older brothers are twins. There's a bond that they don't share with me." For a moment, she looks sad.

And I understand. Being the heir and the spare, Elena and Adamo share a bond outside of our multiple birth that I'm not part of.

"Being a triplet isn't always amazing," I offer. "We aren't identical, but we look enough alike there is never a question we are siblings. And we tend to be judged as one entity."

Their roles as future queen and her heir (until Elena has children), set my sister and brother apart. However, there has been very little in their life I have not done right along with them. That can both be beneficial and incredibly stifling at times.

Especially when I am forced to train for a role I will never inhabit, nor do I wish to.

While our royal parents see only the benefits to our multiple birth, Adamo and Elena share my sometimes ambivalent feelings.

Each of us has our own way of establishing our individuality.

Tanzi carries on texting while we talk. "It beats being the only daughter with older twin brothers and parents with huge expectations any day." She reads her latest text and smiles. "They're coming."

"Good." If I touch the sun-kissed skin of her naked shoulder, will it be as smooth and silky as it looks? "Trust me, expectations can be just as entrenched when you have siblings to share some of the burden."

Even when you aren't destined to wear the biggest crown.

Chapter Two

Tanzi: Her Royal Tour Guide

Seeing the cathedral with a private tour guide (and a sexy one at that) and two of my friends is cool. I like it better than being part of a big group, but I still can't believe I let the gorgeous Sicilian pick me up in the *piazza*.

Even if he did invite my friends to come along.

With a Spanish billionaire for a dad and former super model for a mom, I've been raised to be about ten times more cautious than the average person.

Only there's something really special about Rio. Mom always said I would know when I met *that* guy – the one I cannot resist. The one I crave spending time with from our first *hello*.

I've dated. A lot more than dad would like and less than mom encourages me to.

But Rio? He's catnip. He got to me with a single smile in ways other men haven't managed to after months of going out.

Okay. Yeah, he's gorgeous. Like stop you in the street and nearly get hit by a car good-looking.

Even in my heels, he's at least three inches taller than me. His body is *to die for* and the way his tailored suit fits shows off more muscles than any businessman has a right to possess.

He's got these aristocratic looks that go perfectly with the arrogance I realize pretty quickly is innate too.

I want to reach up and muss his perfectly styled black hair. Just to see how he'll react.

And maybe to spoil that perfection a tiny bit. To make it easier to *breathe*.

It's his eyes that really get to me though. Espresso brown, they glow with appreciation for *me*. Like I'm all that *and a bag of chips*.

Which feels weird because he's over the top, alpha of the pack impressive. He can't be more a few years older than me, but you can tell he's already one of the "important players" as dad calls them.

And he's fascinated by me. He barely looks at my friends and Joni *is* a model. She's the one men stop to watch when she walks by. But not Rio.

He only has eyes for me.

And I'm basking in all the alpha male approval. It's heady stuff.

After the cathedral, we spend an hour at a *trattoria*, talking about everything and nothing at all while Joni and Dylan played tourists with their cameras nearby. Palermo is a beautiful city with bits of history and art everywhere.

And rather than wallowing in *it*, I'm lost in another kind of attraction altogether.

"I feel like I've known you forever," I admit when there's a lull in our conversation.

His dark eyes spark with something almost feral. "Me too."

"It's weird, right?"

Shaking his gorgeous head, he grins. "Not weird. Amazing."

"It's kind of scary, though." Even more terrifying is how fast the minutes are counting down until I have to tell him good-bye.

"We need to get a taxi to catch up to the group if we don't want to miss this afternoon's tour." Dylan stands beside the café table and I don't know how he got here without me noticing his approach.

Dylan is nearly as big as Rio and not a silent guy.

"Yeah. You need to stop mooning over the pretty Sicilian and get a move on, Tanzi." Joni's commiserating grimace takes the sting out of her words.

A fist of panic squeezes my heart.

This reaction is ridiculous, but I can't ignore the sense of dread skating up my spine at the thought of never seeing Rio again.

He smiles, relaxed and confident. "I am happy to continue in the role of tour guide and I believe my Mercedes will be a more comfortable ride than a tour bus."

"Only if one of us drives." Joni crosses her arms, her expression set in stubborn lines.

That's my friend. She's taken classes at my dad's school of caution.

No way will Rio agree to that, though. And no matter how desperately I want to stay with him for just a few more hours, I can't. Not without my friends.

Rio fishes in his pocket and then hands a key fob to Joni. "Have at."

He offers his hand to help me from my chair. Which I'm totally capable of doing on my own, but I take his hand anyway.

Pulling me up, he leans down and whispers. "Please tell me she's at least a passable driver."

"Joni's a great driver." Not that she's gotten to do much of it this trip. "Are you worried about your car?"

"No, but your safety is paramount to me."

Warmth spreads through my insides.

His car is parked only a couple of blocks away. Joni points toward it with the fob and presses the unlock.

She opens the door and slips into the driver's seat, giving Dylan a superior look. "Not all men are such Neanderthals they think women are lesser drivers."

"I don't think you are a bad driver," Dylan defends himself. "I just feel better when I'm the one behind the wheel. It's got nothing to do with you being female."

"I didn't see you insisting on driving when it was Rio offering to take us around."

"Unlike you, I'm not going to demand someone give me *his* car keys."

I slide into the backseat to the sound of their good-natured bickering. I'm used to it.

Rio shocks me by taking the other side of the back seat and leaving the front passenger seat for Dylan.

"Wouldn't you be more comfortable in front?" I ask.

He shakes his head. "Not unless you're the one driving."

"I hate driving." Especially in New York.

Though I doubt I'd like it any better here. The streets in Palermo are narrow and packed with cars and pedestrians.

We buckle our seatbelts and Rio takes my hand in his, lacing our fingers. "What's on the tour for this afternoon?"

My heart stops and then starts beating double-time at the small touch. I have no answer for him. I can barely remember my own name right now, much less what was on the itinerary for the afternoon.

Rio's expression says he knows exactly what the chaste physical connection is doing to me. Then he starts caressing my hand with his thumb, the brushes back and forth never stopping.

I had no idea that holding hands could be so sexual.

Dylan isn't so hampered, and he rattles off the two places we are supposed to see.

"If you trust me to set our agenda, I can promise you a more comprehensive and interesting tour." Rio's asking all of us, but his gaze never leaves mine.

"Cool," Dylan says.

"Just give me directions," Joni agrees. "But tell me how to turn on the nav system so I know where we are."

It's a good thing my friend has her caution cap on, because mine is long gone and Dylan is the risk taker in our group. He's always up for the unexpected.

Rio gives directions and a really fascinating tour commentary of the city. It's a forty-minute drive to our first stop and he keeps up the interesting tidbits of history and local color, never once taking his hand from mine.

I'm so wound up by the time we reach Piana, I'm ready to explode. The bulge in Rio's slacks says he's not unaffected either.

Of course, Dylan insists on getting cannoli. "We can't come to Cannoli Village without eating at least one."

"Did you have to tell him the nickname for the town?" Joni mock whines. "He's going to insist on trying several to see who makes them best."

We all know it's not Dylan that won't be satisfied with tasting only one of the cream-filled tubes of pastry. Joni's the one with the sweet tooth.

But we all try different types of cannoli at three different bakeries. My favorite is filled with pistachio cream.

Probably because after I eat it, Rio swipes a bit of cream from the corner of my mouth with his thumb and then licks it off. My mouth tingles like he just kissed me.

We're all too full from cannoli to get lunch, but Rio insists we try food at every stop. Fresh fruit so juicy and sweet I wish I could take some home. Arancini so deliciously seasoned, I ask the vendor for the recipe.

"You send me an announcement of your wedding I will send my *bisnona's* recipe as a gift to bless your marriage." The old man speaks in Sicilian, but it's close enough to Italian, I get his drift.

My cheek heats with a blush, but Rio grins and offers his hand to shake on it.

Eventually we make our way back into the city.

"Come to dinner with me," Rio says as we draw up outside the tour hotel.

It's ridiculous. Impulsive. But every instinct I possess tells me I can trust this man. Those same instincts insist I will regret walking away right now.

And it's not just the sexual need buzzing through my body like a whole hive of bees. "Yes."

Joni about has a conniption, and she insists on getting Rio's phone number. When she tells him to put her contact in with *find my friend* privileges, I put my foot down.

"Knock it off, Joni—" I start.

But Dylan interrupts. "While you were busy driving, I looked the guy up." He and Rio share an enigmatic glance. "He's safe, alright? Not only do I know where to find him here in Sicily, but where his family business is headquartered."

"Do you want to know those things?" Rio asks me, wariness in his tone.

I shake my head. "Dylan knows them. That's enough."

The truth is, I don't want to tell Rio about my parents and I'd rather get to know *him*, not his background.

Chapter Three

Tanzi: I Never Do This

Rio pulls away from the hotel. "Would you like to freshen up at my apartment before we go to dinner?"

Not sure how much freshening up is going to happen, I agree. I'd rather get messed up than more presentable right now.

"Send my address to Joni."

I nod and do what he says along with a picture of the front of the apartment building in a well-maintained area of Palermo when we reach it.

Her return text is filled with scathing commentary about my common sense and severe admonishments to be careful.

My reply is a little short, but seriously? Does she remember those first couple of weeks with Dylan? Joni was *not* the soul of caution then.

Her next text arrives as Rio parks in the underground garage.

Joni: *I'm sorry. You're smarter than anyone else I know.*

And a few seconds later.

Joni: *Have fun and get you some of that.*

Joni: ::wink emoji::

Joni: ::melting face emoji::

Joni: ::eggplant emoji::

Joni: ::taco emoji::

Unable to help it, I burst out laughing.

Rio opens my door and offered his hand in a move I associate with men like my father, not young professionals. But I like it. There's a lot about Rio that fits with the old-world manners my dad drilled into my brothers and me.

He indicates my phone with a dip of his head. "Do I want to know?"

"I don't think so." I know I don't want him to.

He pulls me toward him, keeping me inside his personal space as he pushes the door shut behind me and arms the car's alarm.

"Oh...I get the feeling, maybe I do." His smile is wicked, his dark eyes teasing.

I duck around him. "She told me to be careful and that I didn't have the common sense of a flea."

He leads me to the elevator and waits for the doors to close before saying, "That's not what made you laugh."

I grin and shake my head. "Sorry. Not telling."

He grabs for my phone, which I not so smartly am still holding.

Laughing, I pull my arm back to keep it out of reach. "No. You are not reading my texts."

One strong arm pulls me into the hard body, and his other hand stretches for the phone.

I gasp. Our bodies are connected from chest to hip and the last thing I'm thinking about is my phone right now. Humor is replaced by fierce sexual energy.

He bends toward me, his mouth coming perilously close to mine. "I did not bring you here for this."

"Didn't you?" I ask, breathless.

He shrugs, the European male answer to numerous communications. "Maybe I did, but I *thought* my intention was to take you to dinner."

"Not very self-aware, are you?"

The elevator stops and the doors open.

His gaze stays fixed on mine. "Everything with you is different."

"That's a pretty broad statement."

"Are you saying you don't feel the same?" He steps out of the elevator, his hand on the door to stop it closing on me.

"I..." I swallow and then say quietly. "No. I do feel it."

Whatever this thing is between us, it's powerful and we both feel it. That's good, right? I'm not in this alone.

Only knowing he's experiencing every bit of the intense attraction and unexpected emotion is also kind of scary. Neither of us is going to put the brakes on.

"So, you expected this?" He leads me out of the elevator with one hand on the small of my back into a nice, but not overly large apartment.

Curiously impersonal, the décor is a lot like a suite in a high-end hotel.

I turn to face him, very aware of the hand against me, remaining on my back, causing me to step closer and have to tilt my head back to see his expression.

"Not when you asked me to dinner." Not exactly, I amend to myself.

I knew once we were alone here that the chances of leaving again quickly were slim though. If he doesn't make a move, I will.

And I'm not a sexually aggressive person. Or at least I never have been in the past.

Like at all.

"So, this is not the norm for you?" He oozes masculine arrogance, clearly satisfied by that thought.

I want to claim I do this sort of thing all the time just to wipe the smug look from his face, but I tell the truth instead. "I don't have sex with men I just met."

I've hardly had sex at all. But I went a little nuts with freedom my freshman year, when I was allowed to attend university without a twenty-four-seven bodyguard presence for the first time in my life.

So, not a virgin.

But not really experienced, either.

He takes my hat from my unresisting fingers and tosses it onto an armchair. "Even on your last hurrah from university?"

"It wasn't part of the plan, no."

He examines me, like he was trying to read the honesty of my statement. I should be offended, but I'm not. I'm trying to read him too.

Is he a player?

My gut says no, but can I trust any body part of mine knowing how much I want this guy?

I have nothing to hide, so I let him look his fill. "What about you? Do you pick up tourists for sex often?"

"I never pick up tourists at all." There's a ring of truth to his words I can't ignore.

"Good."

Rio's gaze turns heated, scorching me with unmistakable sexual desire. "I am going to kiss you."

"Are you?" I whisper.

"I do not think I can help myself."

"Good," I breathe against his lips before they connect with mine.

I've been kissed before. Hello kisses. Goodbye kisses. Let's-make-out kisses. Even I-want-to-have-sex kisses.

But I've never been kissed like this.

His mouth conquers mine with a confidence none of my fellow students have even come close to. Rio doesn't just know what he's doing, he knows why he's doing it and where he expects it to lead.

His lips tell me exactly what is going to happen between us with devastating intensity, as his tongue takes possession of my mouth in imitation of what our bodies will be doing soon.

He might be only a few years older than me, but Rio is light years ahead of me in experience and sexual self-assurance.

And I like it.

A lot.

I move backward, his body guiding mine while his lips continued their annihilation to my self-control. Not that I want to hold back.

It doesn't make sense. This sexual being is not who I am, but I have every intention of taking Joni's second bit of advice and getting me some of that.

Rio is unlike any guy I've ever met.

I didn't even *know* I could respond to someone's kiss this way. That it could light up every nerve ending in my body and send them skyrocketing into the stratosphere.

Even if this is a one-off for him, I don't care. I want this. This feeling. This intensity.

If it's the only time in my life I feel this way, I'm going to revel in every second of it.

For the first time, I understand how the desire for sex could drive totally illogical, and even bad decisions.

He pulls his lips away and my eyes flutter open. "What?"

Did I do something wrong? Did he just remember he has another engagement? If that's the case, I'm slashing his tires before getting a cab back to the hotel.

Chapter Four

Tanzi: Insatiable & Irresistible

"I'm not sure I want to know what that fierce look means." He brushes my hair back from my face. "Care to tell me anyway?"

"Why did you stop?" I counter.

No need to let him know the risk to his Mercedes' tires if he's not planning to stop completely.

"Do you want this?" he asks.

Is that a trick question? "Yes."

He doesn't ask again. Just grabs me and tugs me through to his bedroom.

Dappled sunlight filters through privacy panels casting a soft glow over the room. The huge bed in the center of the room should scare me maybe, but all I want is to be on it...naked, with him.

"You are so beautiful, Tanzi." He makes a sound of frustration. "There should be better words, but there aren't."

Growing up the daughter of a former international supermodel, I have been taught that appreciation for my physical beauty counts for very little. So, why does hearing Rio tell me he finds me really attractive feel so wonderful?

There's no time to ponder it before he's kissing me again, this time accompanying it with small, barely-there caresses along my back, over my buttocks, and down my arms, before skimming the top of my breasts.

It's more seductive than any direct onslaught could be. I crave every new touch and ache for more direct stimulation.

He's long since discarded his suit jacket and tie, leaving the way clear for me to undo the buttons on his shirt. My thumbs brush over hot masculine flesh with each one I undo.

Unlike a lot of guys at school, Rio doesn't shave his chest. Soft whorls of dark hair tease my fingers. Giving up on his shirt, I slide my hands over his muscular pecs, enjoying the sensation of warm skin and silky curls under my palms.

I find tiny twin bumps and he moans as I swipe my forefingers back and forth over his nipples.

Heated lips move from my mouth down my neck and along my collarbone, leaving hyper-sensitized nerve endings in their wake. He undoes the closure holding the halter style bodice on my dress together.

The white fabric falls below my breasts, revealing my invisible halter bra.

Rio runs his fingertip along the halter straps and under the cups stuck to my breasts with washable adhesive. "Clever. I thought you were braless."

"If I had been, my nipples would have been on display all afternoon." I was that turned on.

And also, white dress.

He unsnaps the front closure and peels the molded silicon cups away, proving the truth of my statement as my hard nipples come into view.

Rio inhales a harsh breath, his gaze feral with sexual desire and drops to his knees in front of me. His hot breath washes over my left nipple before his lips close around it.

Sensation erupts in the tender flesh, sending tingles of ecstasy straight to my core.

I drop my hands to his head, tunneling my fingers in his dark hair. "Suck harder."

Is that me? Demanding more? Telling him exactly what I want?

I don't care if it makes sense, I trust him to listen. To do what I need.

And he does. Not only does he suck harder on my already engorged nipple, but he gently bites down with his teeth and pulls.

Shards of bliss spear my breast and hot wetness dampens my underwear.

I swear I'm going to come from this alone.

His hands are busy on the back of my dress, undoing the invisible catch and zipper so the skirt slides down my legs and I'm left wearing only my sandals and baby pink La Perla panties with the French lace.

His mouth pops off my swollen nipple and he leans back to see my nearly naked body. "Beautiful."

"Mom says foundations make the clothes." Why am I telling him *anything* about my mom right now?

"I'm sure your father appreciates her attitude."

I grin. "They're still crazy in love. It's sickening."

"My parents as well, as uncommon as that is in our circles."

"That's what I want." I bit my lips together.

Too late. The words are already out.

His gaze locks on mine. "Me too."

"One-night stands aren't going to get either of us there." No matter how much pleasure they bring.

He leans forward and nuzzles my heavy breasts. "Who says this is a one-night-stand?"

"What else can it be?" My thighs press together, but the ache between them doesn't diminish even a little.

"Anything we want."

Does he mean that? Do I want him to?

Yes. So much yes. Diving in headfirst with no idea how deep the pool is, I trust.

I tug on his shoulders. "Come here. I want more kisses."

He surges up to his feet and draws me close with arms as tight as steel bands. His kiss starts out soft and dreamy but within seconds his tongue is demanding entrance to my mouth.

Parting my lips, I give it eagerly.

Wanting more of his skin, I yank at his shirt, pulling it out of his slacks. He helps, undoing cufflinks with deft fingers before letting them drop to the carpet, his shirt fluttering to the floor after.

Our bodies press together, naked skin sliding along naked skin. He touches me everywhere, cupping my breasts, teasing my nipples, squeezing my backside and tracing the heretofore unknown erogenous zones along my collarbone and down my sides.

I moan into his mouth, my pleasure so intense I'm drowning in it.

Refusing to be an inactive participant, I return kiss for kiss, caress for caress.

We're both panting, light sweat forming on our exposed skin when he pushes me toward the bed.

I let myself fall back, sprawling in unmistakable invitation.

He makes a primal sound, his face set in almost scary lines of desire. "You are something, Tanzi."

"Something good I hope," I quip, but my voice is low and breathless.

"Very good." He removes my sandals before stepping back to finish undressing.

His sex is so hard it bobs upward when he shoves his boxers and slacks down. It's also big. Like he should be a porn model big.

My vagina pulses in anticipation.

Gloriously nude, he joins me on the bed, crawling over me like a predator inspecting his prey, the very impressive proof of his excitement brushing along my body.

Leaning down, he whispers, "You're still wearing your panties."

"Going to do something about that?" I challenge.

The sound of silk tearing is my answer.

I gasp as he yanks the remains of what used to be my favorite underwear away from my body, his gaze so hot it turns the blood in my veins to lava.

Our bodies move together in familiar patterns, but they cause wholly alien sensations. I've never been so excited. Or needy. I want that big, fat erection inside me.

He wants to taste my skin. Everywhere.

When he reaches my most intimate flesh I spread my thighs wide to give him room.

His face buried between my legs, he inhales deeply and gives a low rumble of approval.

My hips cant up of their own volition and he accepts the invitation with his tongue.

He knows exactly how to build my pleasure, showing no hesitation in the level of intimacy he's willing to give me with his mouth. He presses inside my greedy vagina with his tongue, teasing me.

It feels so good, but I need more. I need him.

When I say that, his fingers replace his tongue as he moved his mouth up to my clitoris, hardening the tip and using it to stimulate the already excited bundle of nerve endings.

Undulating against his mouth, ecstasy spirals tighter and tighter inside me. Rio reaches up with his free hand and pinched first my right nipple and then my left. Then he goes back to the right one and rolls that hard little bud between his thumb and forefinger, proving there is a direct line between my nipples and the aching depths between my legs.

My climax crashes over me without warning. My body arches up like a bow, my womb clenches and my inner walls contract around his fingers.

He surges up over me, reaching for something.

A foil packet tears.

A condom.

I hope it's extra-large, or that puppy isn't going to last through what's coming.

He rolls it down his engorged sex and it fits, surprising me a little. He's very turned on.

Not allowing my body to settle back to anything like normal after my orgasm, he thrusts inside me, filling me as I have never been filled before.

Unbelievably, that feeling of impeding orgasm coils tight inside me once again as he pistons in and out of me, a litany of praise dropping from his lips to shower over me, giving me nearly as much pleasure as his sex joined to mine.

It's an age old rhythm, but it feels so new. I've never known anything so incredible, never felt so completely connected to another human being.

"Rio!" I can't hold his name inside. "Please, don't stop..."

"Not stopping," he growls. "We were made for this, Tanzi."

"Yes." I believe he means it. I know I do.

This is too special for just sex, too intense to be taken for granted. This is not a last hurrah; it is a glimmer of what I've always craved.

A window into what my parents have, full of profound potential and possibilities.

With a deep, animalistic shout, he comes first, but his thumb pressed against my clitoris pulls me right over with him and my cry joins his.

We make love until the sunlight turns to shadows and then he takes me into the shower and makes love to me again.

Afterward, we manage to wash each other without succumbing to another bout of lovemaking only because my stomach growls and he insists we get dinner.

He makes a call and food that smells like it comes from a Michelin starred restaurant gets delivered. We devour it before devouring each other. Again.

We touch and sleep and touch some more, pushing our bodies to exhaustion, but unable to hold back from the pleasure that exploded between us with the slightest caress.

CHAPTER FIVE

Tanzi: Just a Spring Break Fling?

The first text comes an hour after I return to my tour group. It's a picture of a conference room filled with men and women I've never seen before. Then a message.

RIO: *Miss you.*

I send a picture of the interior of our tour bus. It's not nearly as swank and there's not a tailored suit in sight. We're students, after all. Even if some of our parents employ enough people to populate a small country.

TANZI: *Me too.*

We text each other at least a dozen times a day. Sometimes a dozen times in an hour. He calls at least once a day, but sometimes twice.

He surprises me at the ferry terminal in Civitavecchia and insists on driving me to Rome. This time we don't have chaperones in the car.

That's when I learn he travels *a lot* for his job.

We spend the night together in his hotel suite and when he drops me off at the airport way too early for anyone to be awake, but especially me, Rio parks his car to walk me inside.

"You could have just dropped me at departures." I yawn, barely getting my hand up to cover my mouth in time.

Yep, way too early.

"No. Even if I did not want to spend every last second with you, and I do, I would never simply drop you off like that."

"Somebody trained you with impeccable old-world manners." Maybe he's got a billionaire dad who grew up in a traditional European family too.

Still reluctant to know all his secrets because that means sharing mine, I don't ask and I don't Google his name either. Dylan already did and I trust my friend to tell me if there's anything I need to know.

He doesn't answer, but swings me around and kisses me. Right there in the arrival terminal. Okay, so not so old-world.

It's my last coherent thought for several very pleasurable minutes.

When he draws back from me, someone claps. Another person whistles. I'm pretty sure it's Dylan.

I ignore it all. So does Rio, his eyes fixed on me and me alone. "I'll be in New York in a couple of months."

"For me?" I ask, disbelieving.

He grimaces. "For business, but I really want to see you."

That actually makes me feel better. If he promised to come just for me, I don't think I would believe him. It's enough that he wants to carve time out of what I now know is a seriously busy schedule.

"Okay." I don't play games.

I won't pretend to be busy when I'm not, but I won't rearrange my schedule for him either. Maybe.

Back at college, my friends tell me not to expect my Spring Break romance to last into summer.

Everyone but Joni, surprisingly. "If it's meant to be, it's going to happen. That's how love works."

I haven't used the L-word yet. Not even in my head. Neither has Rio. Out loud anyway. I don't know what words he uses inside his mind.

It's coming though. For sure for me. Maybe for him too.

I don't tell him my dad is a multi-billionaire. He doesn't tell me anything about his family's finances either. Stuff he says makes me think we have a lot in common in that regard.

We talk about the truly important stuff though. I know how he felt growing up a triplet. He doesn't like being the last born. He refuses to call himself the youngest. Which I totally get.

He doesn't give off youngest child vibes at all.

I don't either. Even though I'm the youngest and only girl, my parents expect as much out of me as my brothers. Dad is convinced I'll use my psychology degree to make me a better C level manager one day.

Mom says do what I need to be happy, but she doesn't get *normal* either. And that's all I want to be. Not a supermodel like mom. Not a corporate shark like dad. Not at the top of any pyramid.

Rio gets it. He says I need to follow my own path or who I am will get ground to dust on someone else's. He sounds like he knows what he's talking about.

When I ask how, he says their family have certain expectations of each child. He is supposed to play a support role, but he's blazed his own path in business and that's how he likes it.

I tell him how much I love my small extended family and even the highlights of my mom and her twin's bizarre story. He reveals that his own family isn't nearly so small, but they're just as close.

Despite the role they expected him to fit into, he doesn't just love his family, but he really likes his parents, aunts, uncles, grandparents and even his cousins.

That's something we have in common.

We discuss the belief we both harbor that neither of our parents meant to put such pressures on us, but life doesn't always allow for personal autonomy and choices.

No, I don't know the precise details of his background, but I know what matters and he knows what matters about me.

The fact my dad makes the big tech billionaires look like small fish in his shark-infested waters isn't what matters. The fact I adore my dad? Yeah, that does.

That he wants me to follow up my Bachelor of Science in Psychology with an MBA so I can take over part of his global empire? Is too problematic for me to deal with, much less share with anyone else.

Regardless of what the future holds, I miss Rio with ridiculous intensity.

Yeah. The L-word is definitely sneaking around the back of my brain getting ready to pop out of my mouth.

Chapter Six

Rio: Keeping a Promise

The uptown location of the well-maintained apartment building is not a surprise. Tanzi comes from money but I haven't had her investigated.

I'm not the heir to the throne. I can have a girlfriend without impeccable bloodlines and political affiliations. She doesn't have a criminal record and she's not front-page tabloid fodder.

That's as deep as I want to go into her background right now. And with a name like Menendez, it will take a security dive to find out more. It's nearly as common as Smith. Or Jones. Or Rossi.

Whoever her parents are, they've done a good job of keeping her out of the press.

They might be wealthy, but they aren't well known either.

Not like my parents. Except apparently, she's never heard of Isole dei Re because she has no idea I'm a prince.

And I like that. A lot.

Leaning on my rented Lambo, I text her.

RIO: *Where R U?*

TANZI: *Studying in my room. Miss you.*

I grin.

RIO: *Come outside.*

TANZI: *What? R U HERE???!!!*

RIO: *Come outside and find out.*

Scant minutes later the front door of apartment building bursts open. Tanzi's wearing a pair of sleep pants and tank top with tiny straps, no bra.

Of course I notice, but I'm pretty sure my dick notes it before my brain registers the way her curves sway under the thin cotton as she sprints toward me. Because I'm already painfully hard.

"Rio!" She launches herself at me.

I catch her with a laugh that breaks the tight bands that have been constricting my chest for the last three weeks. This is where I'm meant to be. With this woman in my arms.

It takes more self-control than it should not to yank her against me. My gaze fixed on the lips that haunt my dreams I pull her close with careful hands. "*Porca miseria*, Tanzi. I've missed you."

She nods, her eyes suspiciously bright and I have to kiss her.

It's a risk showing her affection in public like this, just like the time in Rome. If pictures of us together hit the tabloids, my family will erupt with more devastation than Mount Vesuvius.

Father has plans for me. Plans he only made me aware of this last week.

Plans I have *zero* desire to follow through on.

Those plans are why I moved my business trip to New York forward by five weeks.

Whatever duty might dictate and regardless of the repercussions of discovery, I cannot let Tanzi go. Not even if a whole horde of reporters shows up.

She is necessary in a way no woman ever has been.

"How long are you here for?" she demands after the first fervid kisses.

"I have business in New York for the next week."

"A whole week?" Her beautiful gray eyes glisten with an emotion that wraps itself around my heart.

"*Sì, amate.* A full week."

Tanzi melts against me, hugging me tight. "I love you too."

"What?" I've never said I love her.

I do. *Dio mio. I do.*

"Even if I wasn't fluent in Italian, beloved is almost identical in Spanish, *amado.* Unless you didn't mean it?" She tries to step away from me.

Not happening. I tighten my arms around her. "*T'amu.*" Leaning down, I kiss her tenderly. Our first *almost* chaste kiss. "*T'amu,*" I say again.

It's Sicilian, but close enough to both the Italian and Spanish words, there's no mistaking my meaning.

She sighs, contentment pouring off of her. "We're going to make this work."

"Somehow." No matter what my father's plans are for my future.

I am not giving this woman up.

She nods against my chest. "But right now, we're just going to enjoy each other, right?"

"Right." She does not graduate for another month.

That is time enough to start looking for solutions, for me to tell her about the part of me that is Principe Vittorio. Time enough to meet each other's families.

Perhaps it is selfish, I am not yet ready to share Tanzi with my family. And I cannot be entirely sure they will meet her with open arms, considering what my king wants from me.

Despite two of my aunts being American when they married my uncles, my father has made it clear he expects his children to marry from within our extensive circle. Preferably a woman of Sicilian or Italian heritage. A woman from our own country of Isole dei Re would be even better.

Like the woman he wants me to return to the palace to spend time *getting to know*. In other words, negotiating marriage contracts.

Not happening.

My arms tighten reflexively again. I will not let this woman go. She is the other half of my soul.

However, now is not the time to dwell on the problems of the future. I have one week to spend with the woman I love and I'm going to make the most of it.

Chapter Seven

Rio: Playing Tourist in NY

"I can't believe you come to NY at least four times a year for business and you've never been to Central Park." Tanzi's gray eyes judge me.

"The *for business* is the big clue there, *dolce bella*."

"You can't be in meetings all the time." She grins up at me. "We've gotten together every day this week."

"That's because I've rescheduled and canceled more meetings this week than I have in the last year." I would never tell another woman something like that.

It reveals the depth of my affection for my beautiful girlfriend. And yes, the intensity of my need.

A prince isn't supposed to show vulnerability.

Tanzi scoots around me until she's smiling up into my face, her expression filled with soft affection. "Every time you say something perfect like that, I fall harder for you. So, maybe stop?"

"No chance." And once again, I take the risk of being photographed kissing this beautiful woman in a public place.

None of the rules apply when it comes to Tanzi Menendez.

We continue to explore the park, but when Tanzi wants to take the path up to Belvedere Castle, I balk. "It's not a real castle."

"Of course not. It's too small for one, and this is New York City, for two. No royal residences here. But the views are amazing."

"You've been here before?"

"Of course I have. I'm not a heathen." Her raised brows and sarcastic look imply I am.

"We've already been over this."

"But today, you're not in meetings. So, come on." She grabs my hand and drags me up the path.

I let her. No other person would be so brash with me, but she doesn't know that. And I don't care that she doesn't. I do. And I like how she treats me like a regular guy.

"Oh, it's open," she breathes with rapturous delight. "We can go up to the terraces."

"You have the sweetest reaction to life, *amore mio*." I know she's from wealth.

Her clothes, manner and apartment are all dead giveaways to that. But her enthusiasm is a strong wind, blowing away my jaded view of tourist attractions and pretty much everything else.

She gave me a whole new view of the Statue of Liberty when we went to see it, telling me a story about a friend's great grandparents who were processed on Ellis Island for immigration. Tanzi's emotional reaction to the story drew forth my own.

"Is that why you call me sweet girl?" she teases.

Bella literally means beauty or pretty, but we use it colloquially almost interchangeably with girl or woman. Tanzi's so conversant in the language, she gets that.

"I call you sweet beauty because you are the sweetest thing I have ever tasted, and you're beautiful inside and out." So beautiful, it almost hurts to look at her sometimes.

Her eyes go all soft once more. "There you go saying perfect stuff again. Does that mean you're being literal when you call me *dolce bella*?"

"It means that you are a sweet, sweet girl and *my beauty*. My woman."

She bumps my arm with her shoulder. "I'm okay with that."

But I know she's more than okay. Tanzi loves when I call her *dolce bella*.

Which I prove to her a couple of hours later in my hotel suite.

Naked, her beautiful body sheened with sweat, she rides me with a slow, sensual undulation of her hips.

"That's right *dolce bella*. Just like that." I squeeze her thighs, brushing my thumbs toward her center, but not touching.

Her slick vaginal walls tighten around my erection. Yes, she definitely likes being called sweet girl.

Tilting my pelvis upward, I spear deeper into her welcoming heat.

Her mouth drops open. "*Ahh*," she cries. "Do that again."

I do. Over and over again as her breathing grows more ragged and the roll of her hips turns erratic.

"Rio! *Amato*, do something," she pleads.

I could flip us and drive us both to shattering ecstasy but that's not what either of us wants.

"What do you want, *dolce bella*? Tell me," I demand.

She does one better.

Grabbing my right wrist, she drags my hand up to her rosy tipped breast, placing my palm right over the hard nipple. "Play with me."

I'm already kneading the soft curve and I move my palm in small circles, stimulating that sweet little morsel.

She moans and grabs my other hand, shifting it until my thumb presses right against her swollen clit.

"Tell me what you want," I demand again, refusing to move my thumb and keeping the pressure light on her bundle of nerves.

"I want you to rub me there. Make me come, Rio," she orders.

Satisfaction surges through me. "*Brava ragazza.*" I press harder on her clit before pinching it between my thumb and forefinger.

Screaming, Tanzi's sex tightens around me as her body arches in climax. I'm not sure which sends her over the edge, the extra stimulation or calling her good girl.

But I draw out her orgasm with soft circles on her swollen bud.

Her eyes wild, she grabs my wrist. "Too much."

"Come for me again. I know you can," I tell her in the same voice I use to coax more speed out of my favorite stallion when I am riding.

Her head twists back and forth. "No, I..."

My thumb traces the intimate flesh stretched around my still hard dick. She gasps.

"You can do it *mi brava ragazza*. Show me your sweetness and how very good you are."

This time I'm sure it's the words that spark her climax and unable to hold mine back any longer, I join her, thrusting my hips upward and pumping my seed into her tight channel.

I damn well love going without condoms.

I never have before. Neither has she, but she told me she started birth control when she got back to New York. I was surprised she wasn't already on it.

She told me she only had two sexual partners before me and now I know she had no intention of having another one anytime soon.

Mi dolce bella might have been intimate with two other men, but she never gave them her trust like she gives it to me. I know because I don't let myself go with other partners like I do her either.

I'm her exception just like she's mine.

No other man will ever get the chance to see if he can be one too.

CHAPTER EIGHT

Tanzi: Ready to Meet the Parents?

Sexually replete, but emotionally fragile, I curl into Rio's side.

He flies back to Europe tomorrow and of course I don't want him to go. Or I want to go with him.

But neither option is even remotely possible.

At least not for a few more weeks, when I graduate. Does he even want me to follow him? Will my dad go ballistic and hire a hitman if I do?

Even dad wouldn't be that over-the-top protective, I don't think. But the ballistic part? That's a good possibility.

The past week has been the most amazing one of my life. Even better than Spring break because I get to spend the entire time with Rio. When he's not in meetings and I'm not in class, which is still a lot of time every day. And we spend every night, all night, together.

We don't go out much. Our trip to Central Park is the exception. Neither of us wants to share the other with strangers, or even with friends, in my case. Or business associates in his.

Watching first-run movies in his suite and eating takeout from Michelin star restaurants, we wallow in the intimacy of being the only two people in the room.

But tomorrow it all ends and I don't know how soon I'll see him again.

"Will you come to my graduation?" pops out of my mouth before I realize the words are even in my brain.

Rio goes still. Not like he was moving a lot to begin with, but the hand trailing lazy patterns along my arm stops. It feels like he's not even breathing.

"You don't have to," I rush to offer him an out.

What am I thinking? Yes, we love each other, but our relationship is still barely a minute old. Besides, I know how busy he is.

Which doesn't bode well for you seeing him a lot after graduation either, the voice of reason says.

Or you know, my brain channeling my mom.

I haven't even told my parents about Rio. And I'm not sure I'm ready to either. Not yet.

But here I am, inviting him to graduation which means *if he comes* that he will definitely meet them. And my brothers.

My dad's picture is in the dictionary next to *over-protective*. I don't want Miguel Menendez unleashing his people on Rio, doing a background check that makes the invasiveness of the paparazzi seem downright friendly in comparison.

I don't want to learn things about Rio from a dossier. I'm more determined than ever to get to know him the old-fashioned way, and so far that's working really great.

We know the important stuff about each other. We're in love. And when the time is right, we'll bring families into it.

That time being exactly three weeks and four days from now.

A pit forms in my stomach. "Yeah, you probably can't come, right? You said you only visit New York a few times a year. You won't have to be back that soon."

"Not for business, no." In a quick, powerful move, he shifts us so I'm lying on my back with him hovering above me. "I'll come back to share that milestone with you though."

"Are you sure?" I bite my lip, not sure if I want him to say yes or that he's just kidding.

"I am sure, Tanzi. But if I'm going to meet your parents, you have to meet mine."

"Why does that sound like a threat?" I ask.

He doesn't answer me. Just kisses me until I forget all about graduation and meeting his parents, much less him meeting mine.

CHAPTER NINE

Rio: Back in New York

Going on less than five hours of sleep I managed to get on the jet, I walk swiftly away from the helicopter that landed on a business ally's roof in New York.

Never have I been so grateful for my diplomatic status as today when it streamlined customs, made even faster by the white glove treatment my position as a Prince of Isole dei Re affords me.

Tanzi graduates in less than an hour, which is cutting it too damn fine.

But I'm in the City and even if I have to walk to the graduation venue, I'll make it in time. If traffic is good and I can take the car waiting for me in the parking garage, I'll get there a little early.

I've spent the last week putting out fires with business interests in Central Europe so a planned venture with the Royal House of Volyarus can go through. It almost didn't happen, but unwilling to miss Tanzi's big day, I gave the two companies causing trouble an ultimatum.

Shape up or forfeit the contract. My refusal to negotiate even one more point got through to them and everything is a go.

If only my private life was as easy to wrangle.

I dial Tanzi's number.

She picks up on the first ring. "Are you here?"

"I'm in New York. I'll be there before the ceremony starts." Bodyguards she didn't see the last time I was in New York trail behind.

I dismissed them in Sicily, but when my father found out, he *ordered* me not to do it again.

As both my king and my parent, the order carries some punch. I still don't like it.

Things that never before irritated me about my status are annoying the hell out of me lately. Probably because I have no idea how Tanzi is going to respond to learning I'm a prince and what that entails for us.

"Um..."

"What's wrong?"

"Nothing. Not exactly. Look, Rio, I really want you here today, but is it okay if you meet my parents someplace less stressful? Less public," she adds in a mutter. "The whole family is going to be here. I'd rather introduce you to them at my grandfather's house tomorrow."

She sounds stressed and if agreeing will take some of the tension out of her voice, I'm good with it. "No problem."

Not being with her family in the audience to the graduation means you won't be linked to her in the news if anyone sees you, too.

I want to ignore my inner voice taunting me, but I can't. My easy acquiescence has as much to do with me as it does with her comfort and that pisses me off.

At myself.

"You'll know I'm there for you, even if no one else does," I remind both her and that sarcastic voice in my head.

"Yes." There was a wealth of emotion in that one word. "So, Mom and Dad understand I want to celebrate with my friends tonight."

"Sì?" Does she want to drag me to a college graduation party with her friends?

I've only ever met two of them and I wouldn't mind seeing Joni and Dylan again, though I'd rather have Tanzi all to myself. Yes, it's selfish, so I don't say that out loud.

But it's been three long weeks since I touched her.

"Only, well, I'd rather just spend it with you."

Relief and pleasure are a heady mix, but I ask, "Are you sure?"

"Absolutely. I don't want to share you with anyone the first time I see you after three weeks."

It's so close to what I'm thinking, my self-castigation stops. This will give me the chance to tell her what I need to about my own family. Something I did not want to do over the phone, or even a video call.

"It will be my pleasure to help you celebrate your achievement," I assure her.

"Sometimes you're so formal," she says with a nervous sounding laugh. "Um. ..tonight, Rio...we need to talk."

"I agree."

"You do?"

"I know what I feel. It is not going to change." Some things were meant to be. "It is time to settle our future. And I give you full warning, I expect you in mine."

"I'm really, really happy to hear you say that."

CHAPTER TEN

Tanzi: Oops! Unexpected Revelations

I'm relieved when Rio agrees to meet at his hotel. I don't want to have this discussion in a restaurant. I don't want a bunch of strangers around me when I tell him what I need to.

He opens the door on my first knock.

"You're eager, I like that." I grin up at his handsome and yes, beloved face. "You had to be waiting right by the door."

"I've been checking the hall every few minutes." He reaches for me.

I let him draw me into the room and into his arms. "I can't believe you just admitted that."

"Neither can I." He kisses me.

And like every time his lips meet mine, the world just sort of melts away. I don't know how long we stand there, kissing and holding each other, but every passing second helps calm the riot of butterflies that have taken up residence in my stomach.

It's going to be okay.

Rio isn't going to yell or act like my situation is nothing to do with him.

When we break the kiss, he holds me tight, his eyes dark with desire. "It would be stupid to pretend I didn't miss you after working so hard to get here."

"You look tired." There are faint shadows under his eyes, but that doesn't decrease the animal magnetism of his presence one iota.

"I am a little, but not too tired to give us both what we need." He starts moving back toward the suite's bedroom without releasing me.

It would be so easy to get lost in the moment, but that wouldn't be fair. To either of us. "Wait, we need to talk."

He stops and looks down at me, his eyes reading my face. "Would you feel better having this discussion on the sofa in the living room?"

"Yes." I shake my head. "No, not really, but I think we should."

With a contemplative look, he nods. "Alright."

He pivots our bodies and guides me to the sofa. I sit down at one end, but he sits right beside me, giving me no space. And instead of making me feel crowded, I am comforted.

His arm slides around me and he tugs me into his lap where the evidence of his arousal presses against my hip. "I think I know what you want to talk about."

"No, no, I really don't think you do."

The look he gives me is skeptical.

"You think I want to talk about us continuing to see each other and bringing our relationship into the real world."

His eyes narrow.

I'm quick to add, "Which I do." Oh, man, do I.

"But?" His tone is wary now.

And I hate that.

I grab the small, clear plastic bag out of my pocket and hand it to him so the side of the white stick with the little window and its two blue lines shows.

He looks at it and then at me, a question burning bright and clear in his dark gaze.

"We're pregnant," I blurt.

If there's a way to soft sell that statement, I don't know what it is.

He stares at me, his mouth opening and closing, but no sound comes out. I think I broke his brain. But mine was pretty fractured the first time I read the results too. And the fifth time, after the *fifth* test came back positive.

He takes the stick, and now he stares down at it. "Two blue lines means pregnant?"

"Yes."

"How?"

"I don't know. My doctor told me that only eight couples in one-hundred get pregnant while using the patch." Because of course I had to have my doctor confirm it and boy did I have questions for her.

"That makes us one of the lucky 8% then." He smiles at me, his joy blinding and unmistakable.

Tears burn my eyes and choke my throat, but I hug him and kissed him so hard our teeth clack together. "I love you so much, Rio. I didn't know how you were going to take this."

I knew he wouldn't blame me, but I didn't expect this. For him to be so obviously, openly happy. And that allows me to let my own delight burble up inside me.

No, this isn't how I planned to start my post-collegiate life, but I'm excited to be a mom. To be a family. With Rio.

Whether or not we get married, we're a family now.

"It was not planned, but every baby is a gift," he says sincerely.

Maybe that's a Sicilian thing, because I'm pretty sure my parents aren't going to be so calm or nearly as happy as he is about this. "My dad is going to freak."

"Because you are pregnant?"

"We aren't married. Not that I expect you to marry me. We can take our time, make this work. He might not understand, but I do." I will make Rio be there for moral support when I tell my parents though.

I'll return the favor with his.

"Why should we take our time?" He sounds genuinely confused. "I have known I wanted you for the rest of my future since you walked away from me that morning in Palermo. I thought I was going to throw up from missing you before your tour bus even left the parking area."

His emotional honesty overwhelms me. "How could any guy be more perfect than you?"

His bright white teeth flash. "Well, this perfect guy has the perfect solution."

"What?"

"We elope. Tonight. My family has a house in the Caribbean and the local priest and magistrate are indebted to my family. The island has no waiting period on a marriage license. We can be married by tomorrow afternoon."

"Isn't that crazy?" But excitement is already filling my veins like champagne.

"Isn't love?"

"But—"

"If we don't elope, our families will get ahold of this, and it will become a circus. It will stop being about us, about the family we're starting and be about the families we come from."

He is so right about that. Relief-driven euphoria and adrenaline poured through me. "Yes, let's elope."

I never wanted the huge wedding, dreading the day my mother and father got their teeth into that milestone event. "You know I always wanted something small on the beach. No reporters, no business or political allies. Just me, the man I love and our immediate families."

His espresso gaze says my dream sounds wonderful to him. "We'll share our happiness with them *after* the event."

"Yes."

I'm so glad I prepped my family for meeting Rio in a couple of days, not tomorrow like I led him to believe. I knew we needed time to formulate a plan. Now we have that time to elope before dad sends the troops after me.

Chapter Eleven

Tanzi: A Caribbean Wedding

My toes dig into the sand on the beach outside Rio's borrowed Caribbean villa.

It's golden, fine and moister than what I'm used to in Southern California and it's *nothing* like the pebbly beaches of Spain's eastern coastline.

A gentle breeze, heavy with humidity lifts my hair and I'm glad I left off the sun hat I wore the last time I had this dress on.

I'm getting married in the white Oscar de la Renta sundress I wore that first day I met Rio in Palermo. It feels right, like we're coming full circle, even if it's with the speed of carnival ride in high gear

I'm also wearing a white gold diamond teardrop necklace and earrings my parents gave me for graduation. It's a little like they're here. In spirit, if not in person. And as much as I adore them, that is more than okay with me right now.

Because wearing their gifts is a lot less stressful than having them here to witness me speak my vows on a beach to the man I am fully, irrevocably in love with, but whom they have never met.

It's fast. I don't even try to deny that truth to myself, but there's another undeniable reality. My feelings are as deep as the ocean beyond the reef.

Rio's barefoot too and he left his suit off for once. He's wearing Calvin Klein chinos and a white Spanish style shirt of fine lawn, embroidered in traditional patterns around the hem and neckline in white silk thread.

When I asked him to wear the shirt my dad left behind on a visit, Rio gave me a strange look. Honestly, maybe it is strange. Maybe it's pregnancy hormones, but I really wanted him to wear it.

"It's a connection to my Spanish heritage," I told him. "It will make my parents happy to see it in the pictures later."

And just like with everything that matters to me, he made it happen. "I will wear it. Our future will hold a multitude of inescapable opportunities for us to bow to my own heritage."

I don't know why it's so important to feel like my parents are part of my wedding when I'm really glad they aren't here. If they were, the wedding wouldn't be happening.

Dad would insist on investigating Rio to the nth degree and forcing him to somehow prove he isn't marrying me for my father's money.

Miguel Menendez would never believe that Rio doesn't know anything about my family background. But I'm careful to keep details about my family vague. Just like Rio is.

My last name is pretty common and one of the reasons I went to university in New York was to maintain my anonymity. So, unless he had my background investigated, he doesn't know that Miguel Menendez my father is also Miguel Menendez, multi billionaire.

Rio told me once that he wanted to get to know me like a normal person. I believed him and his words struck a resounding chord inside me.

This relationship is about us, not our families.

My chaotic thoughts grind to a halt when the priest begins the vows.

As is traditional, the priest begins with Rio. "Prin—"

"Father," Rio cuts him off with a serious glower.

Which is understandable. The priest nearly got Rio's name wrong.

The begins again, his voice more nervous now. "Vittorio Micheli Scorsolini, will you take this woman..."

The vows are traditional, but I feel like the first woman in the world to hear the promises uttered in such a determined and rich masculine voice. Rio's words are thick with a Sicilian accent I never hear outside of lovemaking.

Although I speak my vows in English because that is the Priest's first language, I say them over again in Spanish in my heart.

"I, Constanza Elena Menendez, take you, Vittorio Micheli Scorsolini for my lawful husband." I look directly into Rio's eyes, meaning every syllable of the promises I speak with every fiber of my being. "To have and to hold from this day forward."

I pause and wait for the priest to lead me through the final vows. "For better. For worse. For richer. For poorer. In sickness and health, until death do us part."

The old-fashioned verbiage speaks to something deep inside me.

When Rio slides a diamond encrusted platinum band on my finger, it's accompanied by a second ring with a diamond that rivals mom's for size, set in a gorgeous cluster of rubies and more diamonds.

I stare up at him, wondering how he managed to produce such a dazzling wedding set for our unplanned elopement when we haven't been apart since I arrived at his hotel suite.

"I had it flown in," he mouths, reading my mind.

Which doesn't explain where such an exquisite set came from in the first place.

The priest gives us a disapproving look but continues with his blessing at a nod from Rio.

Dipping my head, I hide my smile and the happy tears filling my eyes. My ring for him has a ruby too, but it is set in antique gold. It's an heirloom my grandfather gave me for my future husband when I turned sixteen.

I've kept it with me ever since.

Both rings have the stones of passionate love and I think that's a good sign for our future.

That passion is in delicious evidence when we returned to the primary suite in the villa. Rio can't keep his hands off me and I don't mind at all.

We are naked in every way as he poises to slide inside of me. No condom, no security of birth control. Just him and me. And the baby we made together inside me.

His expression is so intense, it sends a shiver through me. "We are a family now."

"Yes."

His deep and powerful thrust sets off fireworks inside me, the sensations different in an undefinable way.

"Oh, yes," I moan.

I don't know if it's that we're married, committed to a lifetime together, or that I'm pregnant, but laced with the overwhelming passion is a primal and profound connection we've never achieved before.

Although he makes love to me with consuming sexual urgency, there is a new tenderness and care to his movements.

We climax within a second of each other. I have no clue which of us comes first. It doesn't matter. Our bodies just consecrated our union with as much power and worship as the priest's final blessing.

"And the two shall become one." Still inside me, Rio's words prove our thoughts are in the same accord.

"Forever," I promise.

"Amate."

Beloved. I am his and he is mine.

CHAPTER TWELVE

Rio: Reckoning Part I

Bright sunlight filters through the gauze covered windows, illuminating every perfect, beautiful line of my sleeping wife.

Saints above. *My wife.* And *the mother of my child.*

My family is going to have a royal conniption.

Queen Therese, who also happens to be my mother, known so well for her patience and calm, might even yell. A prince simply does not elope. Not even the prince who is neither the heir, nor the spare.

For his own grandson to do so? No doubt a criminal offence in the old king's eyes. His and my father will be furious, but father cannot claim I did not tell him I had no interest in his plans for my matrimonial future. He's certain I will change my mind and *do my duty.*

But my greatest duty is to the woman I love and the child she carries.

So, even knowing the storm I face – *we* face – I will never regret that so very precious ceremony on the beach.

I move to caress her shoulder with a barely there touch, not to wake her, only to feel the satin smoothness of *mi amate's* skin under my hand.

A thunderous pounding on the villa's front door in the other room aborts the movement, my fingers a centimeter from Tanzi's shoulder.

A furious, deep voice shouts in Spanish.

The windows open to allow the cross breezes also allow the voice to penetrate all the way to the peace of our bedroom.

Tanzi sits straight up in bed, her eyes going comically wide as she turned her head side to side. "What? Who...papa?"

"Constanza Eleanor Menendez, open this door *immediamente* or I will break it down!"

There's the mumble of a woman's voice, but I cannot make out her words.

"I will not call her Scorsolini. I have not even met this man who dares to steal my daughter away!"

There's no difficulty hearing that.

"He's loud," I observe.

"And he'll only get louder if I don't calm him down." Tanzi leaps out of the bed, rushes around the room grabbing clothes, but gives up on trying to get her wedding dress on and grabs the sheet off the bed instead.

Leaving me with no covering at all.

Wrapping the sheet around herself, she runs for the door. "Papa calm down, you're upsetting mom. You know you are. She hates it when you yell."

Oh, no. *My* wife is not tearing through the house to appease another man. Not even her father.

I jump up and grab my chinos, dragging them on as I follow Tanzi at speed.

I reach her just as she goes to open the door.

Grabbing her arm, I shake my head. "Go back and dress. I will let them in."

Pure panic glows in her storm gray eyes. "No. You don't understand. I need—"

Another loud knock sounds on the door accompanied by a demand for it to be opened.

Tanzi's sound of distress convinces me to open the door, not her father's clearly increasing ire.

I gently pushed her backward so I stand between my new wife and the furious man on the other side. Then I unlock and open the door in one movement.

The group of people are so eerily familiar, they could be a contingent of my own family. A tall man who is clearly Tanzi's father vibrates with incandescent fury. Beside him stands an older, stunning version of the woman I married – Tanzi's mother. On either side of them are two men about my age and a full contingent of security.

We are significantly outnumbered and it does not matter. I draw my royalty around me like the suit I'm not wearing and step back. "Come in. *Signore e Signora* Menendez, I presume."

I could use their Spanish titles, but that would establish a different power dynamic than the one I want. The one in which they recognized *me* as the primary man in Tanzi's life now.

Tanzi's father glowers, making no move to enter the house after all his demands to be let inside. "And you are?"

His wife slaps his arm. "You know very well who he is, Miguel. He's your daughter's husband and if you don't want to alienate her, I suggest you get your temper under control."

Miguel's gaze slides past me to Tanzi and a slight tightening of his mouth says maybe his wife's warning has been heard and heeded.

Tanzi's brothers stand there with identical looks of disdain on their faces. I return it with interest. They are upsetting my wife and it is their job to protect her.

Full stop.

"Mom," sounds from behind me, the single word expressing happiness, anxiety and *desperation*.

It's the tiny quaver that has me turning around to see my wife. Tanzi is blinking back tears and looking too damn vulnerable.

Ignoring the people behind me, I reach for her. "All will be well, *dolce bella*. We knew this moment was coming."

We just didn't expect it this quickly.

"Don't make my daughter promises you may not be able to keep," Miguel threatens.

My arms firmly around my trembling wife, I turn back to her parents. "Any promise I make to your daughter I will honor; all vows I have made to her are permanent."

Some of the fury in Miguel's eyes banks and I realize the man had been worried *for* his daughter. But why?

"You two need to get dressed immediately," he says, his tone only marginally more civil. "I convinced your father to allow me to collect you, but you are facing a storm of epic proportions when we reach the palace. I will not allow my daughter to be hit by its lightning. You understand me?"

"Palace?" Tanzi asks. She tips her head back to meet my eyes. "Rio, what is my dad talking about?"

Miguel replies before I can. "Tanzi, meet your husband. Principe Vittorio Micheli Scorsolini."

"You're a prince?" she asks in shock.

"And you are a billionaire's daughter." My brain is firing on all cylinders and I recognize Miguel Menendez from the financial news.

Incredibly, she blushes. "Um, yeah about that."

I shake my head. "No. It doesn't matter. I fell in love with you, Tanzi Scorsolini." I use her new last name on purpose, to drill home to her family that she is mine now. "And you fell in love with me, not my title."

"But you're a prince?"

"Heir to the throne of Isole dei Re," her father answers again.

Earning a blistering look from me. "I'm capable of speaking for myself."

"Really? Then why is it that my daughter is not aware that one day she will be queen?" Miguel looked at Tanzi, one brow raised. "And you had issues with taking over my company."

The temptation to clock the billionaire has my hands clenching into fists.

"Don't," Tanzi said softly.

I smile down at her.

"Of course not and you won't be queen." I glare at her father again. "I am third in line to the throne. *An* heir, not *the* heir. That would be my sister, Elena."

"But the news said—"

"Don't," Tanzi's mother says with enough force her son stops speaking.

His meaning is clear though. Somehow, our elopement is already public knowledge. The curses running through my brain are not nice.

I focus on *mi amate* again. "I was going to tell you, before—"

"Before you found out I was pregnant with *your* heir?" she asks with a rueful smile.

Her mother gasps. Her father lets loose some creative invective in Spanish.

Tanzi ignores them both. "Before you whisked me off to marry you so no one, not even a king, could stop us?"

She understands. Relief flows through me in a near debilitating wave. "*Sì*. I was going to tell you everything today."

"You do not think you should have told her before you married her?" Miguel demands.

"Forgive me, please," I say to Tanzi, refusing to acknowledge the Spanish billionaire.

"Yes, Rio. I love you and there is nothing to forgive. We both wanted to be loved for who we are, not where we come from. Our future is a little more complicated than I thought though."

"A little." I smile down at her, letting my love shine in the eyes only she can see.

Her return smile tells me everything coming is worth it.

"We do need to get back on the plane. The royal family's PR team is working with ours, but we need to face this news with a united front." Surprisingly, that comes from Tanzi's mother.

"Amber, as always, you are the voice of intelligent reason, *mi amor*."

"I'm going to be a grandmother," the voice of reason says in an emotion laden voice to her spouse.

"They're kissing. That should give us enough time to shower and dress anyway," Tanzi says dryly, looking past my shoulder.

Chapter Thirteen

Tanzi: Reckoning Part II

With its soaring turrets and quintessential castle façade, the royal palace of Isole dei Re impresses me from my first glimpse through the limousine's window.

But it's the royal family, gathered en masse in their private reception room that intimidates me. Like seriously.

Rio didn't even flinch when my whole family showed up on the villa doorstep this morning, but I'm ready to throw up faced with his less than welcoming relatives.

And there are a lot of them. Grandparents, parents, aunts, uncles, cousins and siblings. Every single one of them royal and not one looking particularly friendly.

The prevailing emotion doesn't seem to be anger so much as utter shock. Which is something, I suppose.

Apparently, Rio is the responsible one, the guy everyone counts on to do the right thing. And in their eyes that right thing in this case is *not* marrying me. No one has come right out and said it, but the feeling is there in the tense air around us.

He hasn't left my side though. Not for a second. Not even to greet his parents, making it clear where his loyalty lies.

My parents and brothers stand behind us, dad's top two security guys flanking them.

It feels a lot like the Capulets and Montagues.

I'm not sure which is which, but I don't want to be enemies with Rio's family. I catch myself from turning to my dad for help and squeeze Rio's hand instead, seeking comfort and trying to give some.

This is the Rio and Tanzi show. Not the Miguel Menendez show.

King Claudio looks a lot like his son, except for the grey at his temples and the chill in his dark eyes as they take me in.

"So, you are the woman who has convinced my son to marry you in some elopement, abandoning his training and obligation."

He makes our beach wedding sound sordid, not private and special like we both wanted it to be. Or was that just me? *Did* I somehow convince Rio he needed to abandon royal protocol and elope?

"She is the woman I love." There is ungiving steel in Rio's tone.

Woah. That's not a voice I want directed at me. Ever.

"You love her so much, you did not think enough of her to introduce us?" The queen sounds more upset and confused than angry, her lovely Italian features wreathed with concern.

Rio's arms tighten around me like he's worried I'll take his mother's words as truth. "I had every intention of introducing you when the time came."

If anything, King Claudio's expression grows darker. "The time would have been before you asked her to marry you."

"Because you think you should have a say in who I marry?" Rio demands, sounding every inch the prince I know him to be.

"Your wife has an important role to play in this country. An inappropriate match could do damage to our political and economic standing."

Not wanting to offend my new father-in-law right off the bat, I stifle the derisive laugh that wants out. Rio marrying the daughter of Miguel Menendez is no hardship for Isole dei Re.

My father's voice says almost those exact words in a frigid tone I have rarely heard in my life and never directed at me. Not even this morning.

The king looks nonplussed for a moment, though nowhere near cowed.

Queen Therese interjects calmly, "The point is we were not given the opportunity to know her before the deed was done."

"The deed can be undone easily enough." The king glares at both me and Rio. "But not without scandal."

"No one is undoing my marriage," I say with my own version of my dad's frigid tone.

King Claudio shakes his head. "You did not marry merely a man, young lady, you married a prince."

"She married *me*," Rio argues, his hand releasing mine so that he can wrap his arm around my waist. "If Tanzi is deemed unsuited for the role of my wife, I will abdicate my place in the succession to the throne and give up my role in the company."

Rio should sound upset saying something like that, but he doesn't. He sounds absolutely sure of himself.

The entire room erupts into arguments and exclamations, but I don't care how anyone else is taking his announcement.

I turn and look up at the man who married me and claimed our child without hesitation. "You would do that for me?"

"*Sì. T'amo.* You belong to me, and I love you. That means your happiness is paramount to me. Above duty. Even above the others in my family."

"Are you sure you are not using my daughter to justify abdicating responsibilities you do not want yourself?" Dad's tone is scornful.

For the first time in my life, I want to kick him. But mom's furious admonishment is even better. Especially when she steps away from my dad and moves to stand on Rio's other side.

The look on my dad's face is worth admission. The expression on the king's not so much. I guess it's okay for him to deride his son, but not my dad.

I'm not thrilled with either of them.

"You will apologize, Miguel," Tanzi's mom demands.

"It is a legitimate question," the king says before my dad can decide if it is worth it to defy the love of his life.

So, that look isn't for my dad, but his son? Oh man, I want to just hug Rio because while I didn't know his dad was a king, I do know how much Rio cares about the older man's good opinion.

This time the giggle escapes. It's not a sound of scorn, but amusement. Maybe even hysterical laugher, but really? The whole situation is taking on farcical proportions. If it were not for the pained expression on my beloved's, I would burst into real laughter.

"*Amate?*" Rio's beautiful dark eyes say he does not see the humor in this situation.

At all.

Unexpected exhaustion washes over me, but I grin up at him tiredly. "Our dads are like two peas in a pod. It's almost scary. Bet you want to kick yours too."

"If I did, I would not say so. Threatening the monarch is against the law in Isole dei Re." Which is as good as an admission.

"Vittorio!" His father's chiding bark says he knows it too.

I narrow my eyes at the king. "If you don't want your son feeling some kind of way toward you, then maybe don't say awful things about him."

Nausea swirls in my tummy and I don't think it's from this situation, but then again, I doubt the stress is helping it either.

"You look pale, Tanzi." Rio turns to face me fully, his expression deeply concerned. "Are you all right?"

"Maybe a little tired." She lean heavily into him, suddenly not so steady on my feet.

"Take Tanzi someplace where she can rest," mom orders Rio firmly.

King Claudio frowns. "We are not finished with this discussion."

"Can you not see the girl needs a break?" Rio's grandfather admonishes, getting an immediate top spot on my *favorite relatives of my husband* list.

Rio told me on the plane that for the sake of his health, his grandfather abdicated in favor of Claudio several years ago.

"What do you call an ex-king?" I wonder aloud, things going a little sparkly at the edges.

"Vitorrio!" Queen Therese barks at my husband, sounding very different than the calm woman she was only moments before. "Now."

"Excuse me—" King Claudio starts only to be interrupted by my mom.

"Excuse me, your highness, but my daughter is carrying your first grandchild and she has had a very stressful few days between graduating university, telling the father of her baby about their coming joy and flying off to marry him on a Caribbean beach. And this morning only added to that stress when she was summarily summoned to a palace she didn't even know was in her future. You will save the rest of your questions, harangue and attitude for later."

Oh, man, my mom can do icy disdain with the best of them.

Even my dad knows to back down when mom gets this angry. Apparently, the King of Isole dei Re isn't a complete dunderhead either, because he keeps his mouth shut.

There's no surprise on his face at the news of his impending grandparenthood. There's no expression there at all.

Rio shows he knows when to take an order too, lifting me into his arms and carrying me from the room. Although, honestly, I think I'd be in the same position right this second without our moms and his grandfather putting their oars in the water.

Did my mom really have to spill the beans like that though?

Mom and the queen follow us, giving advice, expressing concern and watching over us all the way down the long corridors, up marble steps and down another plush hallway until Rio stops outside a set of double doors.

Queen Therese gracefully moves around her son to open both doors to a luxurious suite done in dark wood and navy blue. Rio carries me inside it, crossing the outer room without pausing and going directly into the bedroom. There, he lays me down after mom pulls back the bedding.

Everything feels fuzzy around the edges and I have no problem being babied. Especially by Rio.

He tucks me in and then pours a glass of water from the carafe by the bed. "Drink this, *dolce bella*."

I take several sips, before resting back against the pillows. "I don't know what's wrong with me."

"Stress. It can be debilitating in early pregnancy," the queen says softly.

"Mama, you must talk to him," Rio warns. "I don't care if he wants to yell at me, but he'll treat Tanzi with tender care, or I'll take her away."

Queen Therese nods. "I will speak with him, but I'm confident *Signora* Menendez's announcement will have already gone a long way toward bringing your father back from his anger and his confusion. He is only hurt, you understand? That you did not introduce us to the woman you love. He thinks you are ashamed of us."

The way the king talked, I think it's more he believes Rio should be ashamed of me.

Rio snorts in own disbelief. "Father is too arrogant to believe that."

"You forget his love for his family is greater than even his arrogance," the queen chides gently.

Rio doesn't look convinced. "That was not on display just now."

"Remember, he is both king and your father."

"King first, father second." Rio's tone has no give in it.

"That is not true. He loves you so much, Rio." The queen's eyes are dark with emotion. "He's worried about you."

"So, he accuses me of using Tanzi as an excuse to dismiss my responsibilities?"

Mom climbs onto the bed to sit beside me. "That was my husband."

But it wasn't just dad, and we all know it.

"He didn't mean that," Queen Therese says with conviction. "While it does not happen very often, you know your father can say things he regrets later if his emotions are too high."

Rio gives a grudging nod.

"Remember the man who taught you and your siblings to swim, refusing to leave it to paid instructors. Claudio took time from a schedule most would not in order to be a dad to you children as well as your royal father."

Rio sighs.

And I reach out to take his hand. "He loves you and I know you love him. We knew this wasn't going to be easy, but having the wedding we wanted was worth it, right?"

Rio kneels on the floor by the bed, taking my hands in his, his gaze snagging mine. "Absolutely."

"Then we'll both have to practice some patience with our dads." I give him a weary smile. This pregnancy stuff is no joke. "Who knew they were so much alike though, huh?"

Both mothers give identical sounds of amused exasperation. Our dads aren't the only ones with a lot in common. Hopefully, that will make the coming days easier to navigate.

"I think we should return to your father and let Constanza's mother care for her." Queen Therese gives a rueful smile. "I think my pregnant daughter-in-law has dealt with enough royal drama for today."

"Oh, I'm up for the drama, but be warned, I might start a blog about it. *What it's like behind the doors of the palace.*"

Rio leans forward and kisses me right on the lips. In front of both our mothers. "You're going to be trouble, Tanzi Scorsolini."

"You're just figuring this out?" my mom asks.

"I believe your lovely bride will be exactly the type of trouble you need, my son."

After another sweet kiss, Rio accompanies his mom out of the room.

Her voice drifts back to me before they exit the suite. "Perhaps now that you are married to the woman you love and beginning a family of your own, you will spend more time here at the palace."

"Is that what you want?" mom asks me.

I shrug. "That depends on if the king gets over his anger about our marriage."

"If he really is like your dad, he'll get over it."

I hope my mom is right because I'm not giving my prince up. Not even for the sake of his royal family.

Chapter Fourteen

Rio: Confronting the Dads

I wait until Tanzi's brothers and the rest of my family go to their rooms to freshen up for dinner – another all family gathering...oh joy – to talk to the two dads in private.

Their glares indicate they do not appreciate how much restraint I have shown dealing with both of them so far.

"Let's go into my study," my father says.

I shake my head, in no mood to give into his power move. He has enough of an advantage having this discussion here in the palace. We aren't going into his private sanctum for it.

I lean back on the sectional. "I'm good here."

A flicker of respect glimmers in Miguel Menendez's gaze. Then he fixes it on my dad. "This is fine."

Father's mouth tightens infinitesimally, but that is all the evidence he gives that our refusal to fall in immediately with his plans displeases him. "You realize your actions have put our family in a difficult position. You were all but engaged to Giannetta Bellini."

"About that," Miguel butts in. "Explain how you were able to get my daughter pregnant while in a relationship with another woman and why I shouldn't beat you to the point of death for doing so?"

At least he's giving me the benefit of the doubt. His fury this morning is understandable in light of the tabloid stories circulating about mine and Tanzi's elopement.

Royal Heir Abandons Marriage Plans to Run Away with Billionaire Heiress
Prince Vittorio Follows in Playboy Brother's Footsteps
Prince cheating on fiancée before the wedding?

He made sure I saw the headlines while Tanzi was occupied consoling her mom about a lack of a formal wedding. I told him they weren't true, but until now, there has been no time to expound on that.

"First, I am not and have never been in a relationship with Giannetta Bellini." I glare at my father "I told you I wasn't interested in her. Any impression she, or her family had to the contrary is all on you.""

He's the one that pushed the idea and if those headlines hurt my wife, I won't forgive easily.

"Because of this girl just out of college?"

"She's exactly two years and eight months younger than me." There is no culture in the world where that is considered a significant gap after the age of consent. "And at twenty-two, Tanzi is a woman not a girl."

"Who you did not have the guts or the courtesy to approach me for her hand in marriage," Miguel slots in.

I refrain from rolling my eyes. Barely. "I won't tell her you said that. Tanzi isn't a piece of property for you to give away. Your daughter doesn't need anyone's permission to marry—"

"But you do," my father inserts.

"Perhaps, but as I said, if you attempt to exercise your power to dissolve the marriage, I will abdicate my place in the royal family and marry her all over again." Not that my father decreeing the marriage invalid would hold legal sway anywhere but Isole de Rei.

But I am making a point.

"Let's get back to the other woman," Miguel says.

"There is no other woman," I tell him between gritted teeth. "Even if I was not in love with your daughter, I would have no interest in marrying Giannetta Bellini."

"You never gave the idea due consideration," my father says with disapproval.

I don't like disappointing him. Or my mother. But I'm not living my life to please them either, so it is inevitable.

"I am not your heir," I remind him. "I'm not even the spare. Who I marry has no bearing on the throne of Isole dei Re."

"Is that what this is about? You not being the first or second born? Do you think you are less important to me and your mother, or to this country, as your sister and brother are?"

"Yes. And before you go all emo dad on me, I am okay with that. I prefer a life over which I have more control."

Emo dad? Miguel mouths.

I grimace. My father locks it down well, but he's a passionate man and every bit as capable of over dramatizing as my grandfather. It runs in the family. Something Tanzi has to look forward to.

"A life away from your home." My father's already unhappy visage goes darker. "Do you think we have not noticed how much time you spend away from the palace?"

"It's normal for an adult child to move out on their own. You and mom may live in the same palace with your father, but your brothers and their families don't." Whoever demanded their presence for this confrontation didn't do me any favors.

My guess is my grandfather. My father would have preferred to keep the situation under wraps until he heard my side of the story. But none of us was given that opportunity because of whoever leaked the story to the press.

My marriage is still a secret as far as the media is concerned, but me taking Tanzi to the Caribbean on one of our private jets is now common knowledge. Losing their job will be the least of their problems for whoever told a reporter about the trip.

How many of my brother's exploits got blown up in the press the same way? We thought we plugged the leaks, but we were wrong.

"You are as much a part of the crown as your sister or brother." My father's return to an earlier point while ignoring the valid one I made is textbook negotiation tactics.

The problem here is that there is no negotiation. I'm not giving Tanzi up. Ever.

"Not true. Elena is your heir. She is the Crown. And until she has a child, Adamo is her heir. Pivotal to the Crown. I am a prince of this country, but progeniture of the Crown is not dependent on me." And if it was?

Tanzi and I are ahead of the curve. We're already pregnant.

Being the youngest of triplets is a pain in the ass. Because there is no actual difference in ages, but the birth order dictates behavior in a big way. But the single benefit is that *I am not key to the Crown.*

"You had to know that eloping would cause more trouble than it resolves," my father changes the subject again.

Good call. Pushing to prove his point requires him being willing to acknowledge there could come a time that neither of my siblings is around to become monarch. And my dad is never going to speak that thought into existence.

"That is not possible," I assure my father. "No matter what the fallout, Tanzi and I deserved a private wedding that was about us."

Yes, more for Tanzi's sake than mine, but I'm not giving my dad any ammunition against the woman I love.

"Our marriage is not about her dad's billionaire empire." I give my father-in-law a harsh look. "And it's not about my family royal lineage. *Our marriage is us.*"

"Do not be naïve, son. Royal marriages do not happen in a vacuum. Marriage alliances are arranged for a reason."

"That reason isn't good enough to justify arranging them any longer," I say urgently. "Just because you and mom started off as an arranged marriage, and turned out for you because you fell in love, that doesn't mean your children want, or should be forced, to endure a marriage of convenience."

My dad winces and there is a memory lurking in his gaze he's never shared. The press treats my parents' marriage like a love match, but it wasn't one. I don't know when they fell for each other, or what came before, but I doubt it was anything like my instantly intense relationship with Tanzi.

"Think about it," I urge my father. "Elena deserves to pick out her own husband."

"That is not—"

I interrupt my father in a way I i never do. "She is not a fool and would not marry someone who would make a poor consort to the queen."

Honestly? I would not blame my sister for following in my footsteps and keeping a relationship secret from the family until she is ready to make it permanent.

Living under the microscope of being a modern royal is not easy. Yes, there is a reason I spend so much time away from Isole dei Re. Because I am not as well-known as my siblings outside of it.

My sister because she is heir to the throne and my brother because he can't seem to stay out of the tabloids.

I can live the normal life of a corporate shark when I'm away from the country that only sees me as a prince.

CHAPTER FIFTEEN

Tanzi: A Fly in the Royal Honey

The following days are filled with frantic activity.

A diplomatic reception that's been in the works for over six months is suddenly a party to announce our marriage.

There was no more talk about my suitability as Rio's wife, or ending my marriage before it has even really begun. Which I'm glad about, but the amount of work involved in spinning the story of the elopement is daunting.

Rio makes sure I rest, and I make sure he decompresses.

My brothers leave to handle business, one for California and the other goes to Spain. I understand the necessity, especially with mom *and* dad insisting on staying in the small island country until after the reception.

We're waiting to announce our pregnancy until I reach my second trimester. It's not an uncommon practice, and will hopefully minimize speculation on the reason for our elopement.

The PR teams are spinning it as a whirlwind romance that culminated in an even more whirlwind marriage. Which it kind of is. The best PR is based on parts of reality.

At least that's what my parents always say.

I guess the palace's public relations department agrees.

King Claudio hasn't warmed up to me exactly, but he's stopped glaring at me like Public Enemy Number One. I'm taking that as a win.

I'm not worried. The more I see of him, the more he reminds me of my dad.

The king will come around. He just has to do it in his own time. My own dad isn't exactly all sunshine and approval with Rio, though he is showing a little more tolerance every day for the man who had dared to marry his daughter.

A lot more worrying is Giannetta Bellini, the daughter of one of Isole dei Re's top diplomats. And apparently a very good friend of the family.

Also the woman who expected to marry Principe Vittorio Micheli Scorsolini, if I don't miss my guess.

Rio told me his dad had someone in mind for him that he refused and I'm pretty sure it's Giannetta.

She'd been helping Queen Therese plan the reception already and has managed to insert herself in the middle of the transformation to formal wedding announcement and reception. Rio's mom likes Giannetta. A lot. And relies heavily on her.

But Giannetta does *not* like me.

She's made several oblique comments that imply she thinks the wedding announcement is premature.

But this morning? She is in top form.

"Perhaps we should consider keeping the elopement completely under wraps until a traditional wedding can be planned. No public relations effort will prevent speculation if the nature of the prince's liaison with Ms. Menendez comes out."

We? Giannetta is not a member of the Scorsolini family, no matter how much she wants to be and she's sure as heck not part of mine. Neither is she on the PR team in charge of the announcement.

"Unfortunately, that will not work," Queen Therese says. "A wedding would take a minimum of a year to plan."

"Two would be better," is my mom's unsurprising contribution.

I dread my five-year anniversary because no way will Amber Menendez pass up the first milestone opportunity to host a formal wedding with a renewal of vows. She'd do it at our first-year wedding anniversary if she wasn't firmly on Team Tanzi.

She says being a first-time mom is one of the hardest transitions I will ever make in my life. I believe her and I have no desire to add a huge, stressful event into the mix when my baby is only a few months old.

Shock washes over Giannetta's face. "She's *pregnant*?"

"Yes, but we are not announcing it until later. We don't want everyone saying Vittorio and Constanza only married because she is pregnant." Queen Therese smiles at me. "No one who spends even ten minutes with the two of you could doubt your love, but the press in unforgiving."

If looks could kill, I'd be dead on the floor from the one Giannetta is sending me right now. But when the queen looks at her, she's all smiles and assurances.

When I tell Rio about it, he shakes his head and laughs. "If my own parents, the reigning monarchs of my country, don't get a say about who I marry, friends definitely don't."

I don't think Giannetta is his friend and I'm positive she's not mine.

CHAPTER SIXTEEN

Tanzi: Setting the Record Straight

I wear a strapless vintage Alexander McQueen gown (that mom convinced the design house to pull out of their vault) to the reception.

My jewelry is just as stunning. Mom and dad paid a favorite jeweler vast amounts of money to create a diamond and ruby choker and earrings fit for a princess that match my engagement ring in time for the party.

The complimentary ruby and diamond tiara placed carefully amidst the gold and brown curls swept up in an elegant pile on my head is a gift from the king and Queen. And it's not recently made.

According to Queen Therese, the tiara was favored by King Claudio's third-great-grandmother.

"You look like a princess, even if you never expected to be one." Rio's eyes are hot with admiration.

I grin up at him while we wait at the bottom of the grand staircase of the cavernous ballroom with both our parents to greet the guests. "Thank you. I like the prince togs too. Who knew epaulets could be so sexy?"

He laughs, looking amazing in the formal suit of Isole dei Re royalty.

One of the first guests is a tall man who could give my husband a run for his money in the whole *too gorgeous for words* category.

Only this guy's eyes? Are cold like January in Upstate New York.

"Prince Vittorio, may I extend our most sincere congratulations on behalf of Volyarus and my family?" Hottie McHotterson extends his hand to shake Rio's.

Rio introduced me, revealing the man is the Crown Prince of Volyarus. Goose-bumps chased up my arm when the imposing man bends over my hand.

The Volyarussian prince moves on and I fan myself. "Wow. Who was that guy?"

"I introduced you." Rio's jaw is taut.

"Yes, but he's kind of intense, isn't he?"

"He's the perfect prince. My father only wishes I was as dutiful and committed to my country's welfare."

I don't like the sound of that. To my knowledge, Rio and his father never talked about the accusation our fathers made during that first volatile meeting after the wedding.

"So, you were just in Palermo on vacation?" I ask a little loudly after greeting another guest.

"No. I was on business, I told you."

"For Isole dei Re." Again, I speak louder than normal so our parents can hear.

Am I rubbing his and my father's noses in the message I'm trying to get across? Why, yes, yes I am.

"Yes, he was," his father answers for Rio. "We run many interests to support our island country's economy and Rio has taken a key role in some of the hardest but most lucrative for the country."

I'm perfectly happy to loop his dad into the conversation. "Huh. So, Rio must have taken a long break after university before diving into the country's business though, right? Travelled. Dated beautiful women. Played with the other young royals of the world."

Rio does another introduction before laughing drily. "Not a chance. I started working for the country's interests long before I graduated with my MBA from Harvard."

I give his father and mine a narrow-eyed glare before smiling up at my husband again. "I'd say you're pretty darn dutiful and committed to the best interests of your country then."

Rio doesn't reply, but he's smiling when he performs the next introduction.

And his mood is buoyant for the rest of the night, which we spend dancing with each other and our families, but also *important* people that expect the privilege.

Just like it would have been at our wedding if we'd had one.

For the millionth time, I'm glad we didn't.

Chapter Seventeen

Tanzi: Flypaper

Two days after the reception, I have my first ultrasound.

They can't tell the baby's sex, but everything looks good. The doctor questions the dates, saying the baby and my uterus are measuring a week smaller than they should be.

"Is she okay?" I ask, worry I can't help dripping from my voice. "Why would she measure small?"

"The baby might be a he," Rio teases.

But I don't smile. I'm scared. "You know when I got pregnant and we were apart for the weeks after, so there's no question about the due date. There must be something wrong."

"Do the measurement again," Rio insists immediately.

When he does, the doctor smiles. "Baby shifted and now he *or* she is measuring exactly right."

Relief pours through me.

Rio isn't relieved. He's furious and gives the doctor a dressing down about upsetting his patients. "We will change obstetricians," he assures the man.

"You only did that because you want me seeing a woman OB," I accuse when we get into the car.

Rio shakes his head. "No. If you had bonded with this doctor, I would not allow a change but his incompetence scared you. I will not allow that."

"He wasn't incompetent. The baby shifted, changing the angle of the measurement."

"He should not have frightened you," Rio insists stubbornly.

Since I *didn't* bond with the doctor, I don't argue about finding a different one.

Giannetta *helpfully* made this appointment for me with her OB/GYN.

No wonder it wasn't the best experience.

I'm surprised later that afternoon to be called into the king's office. Rio is already there, nothing in his face indicating why we're here.

So is Giannetta, which I do not take as a good sign.

My husband guides me to a chair before sitting down in one he drags next to mine.

"It grieves me to have this conversation with you," the king says. "But Giannetta has brought something to my attention that cannot be ignored."

Showing good instincts, Rio slides his arm around my waist. "What might that be, dad?"

King Claudio's lips tilt slightly at the familiar address.

"Giannetta has informed me that your ultrasound," he shifts his gaze to me. "Measures a week smaller than dates provided by you and my son would indicate."

"But you already knew—" Rio starts, but his father shakes his head just slightly.

I don't know what's going on, but I do know I'm tired of Giannetta being in my business. "Yes. Now, can someone please explain to me why this woman is privy to my medical records?"

"Precisely," King Claudio says, giving Giannetta a frigid stare.

"But you said you were concerned too. You can't believe she's telling the truth about Vittorio being the father of her child. She just wanted to marry into royalty. You need to demand a DNA test."

"No one is performing a DNA test on my unborn child." For the second time in my life, my tone emulates my dad's when he's ready to start taking people apart, or at least their departments.

Huh. Mom always says we're more alike than I want to admit. She might be right. That doesn't mean I want to run part of his empire though.

"Of course not," Rio says, his hold on me reassuringly tight. "Our child will never be put at risk if I can help it."

"Because you are very protective of your family," King Claudio says, as if he's trying to give his son a message.

Which I'm sure he is. My dad sucks at apologizing too.

"I am." Rio's voice doesn't bode well for anyone who might try to put me at risk.

But then, he's kind of perfect like that. No wonder I love him to the moon and back.

King Claudio clears his throat. "You are an excellent prince and more importantly, you are a son to be proud of."

"Thanks, dad." Rio clears his own throat and I grin.

Letting the smile slip from my face, I look straight at Giannetta. "I'll leave it to the king to find out how you got confidential information about me, but let me warn you that my family make very formidable and dangerous enemies. Think very carefully before you make the mistake of trying to take me on again."

"Precisely," King Claudio agrees. "I could not have said it any better. Tanzi's family is both formidable and dangerous. As the head of *that* family, let me tell you what is going to happen. Your father's diplomatic assignment is going to be changing."

Chills run down my spine when King Claudio claims me as his family.

Giannetta's face drains of color. "It is?"

"*Sì*. He will be assigned to Volyarus. It is another island country, though not in nearly such warm climes. He should do well there."

"But they're Russians!"

"Descended from Ukrainians actually, but I'm sure your father knows that. He is a good diplomat. You will accompany your father to Volyarus."

"You're kicking me out of Isole dei Re?"

"For your father's sake, I am not pressing charges for this reprehensible breach of protocol and privacy. However, you will not be welcome back into this country for a minimum of five years. It is entirely your father's discretion whether he keeps you with him in Volyarus. He will however be informed of your attempt to do harm to my daughter-in-law."

"But what about—"

King Claudio turned to Rio. "Vittorio, do you have any doubts about the parentage of your baby?"

What an odd way to ask the question, but then maybe not. Maybe that was a message from the king to Tanzi.

"None."

It's the answer I expect, but I like hearing it all the same.

"Nor do I." The king spells it out. "Tanzi you are a welcome and trusted member to our family."

"Thank you."

I ignore Giannetta's continued squawking as the king rises to come around his desk to give me and then his son a tight hug. "Welcome to the family, Tanzi."

Blinking back the moisture in my eyes, I smile and kiss his cheek. "Thank you. I think you and my father are going to have a lot of fun being related."

The king gives me a mock shudder and Rio laughs before pulling me from the room.

CHAPTER EIGHTEEN

Rio: Happily Every After

I pull Tanzi into my lap on the leather sofa after leading her to our suite. "I'm sorry you had to endure that."

"I'm not." Her lovely grey eyes reflect her bone deep honesty. "I think Giannetta tipped your dad over to our side."

"He was coming around anyway."

She shrugs. "But this was faster."

"Are you going to be okay?" I ask, not sure how to articulate my worries.

"With being a princess? With facing people like Giannetta because there's always someone out there who wants what I have?"

"Yes, that."

"Tell me something, Rio."

"No one but you calls me Rio." And I guard that intimacy jealously.

Adamo called me Rio once after hearing Tanzi say it. After my visceral and somewhat violent reaction, my brother will never make that mistake again.

She sighs happily. "I know."

"So?" I ask.

"So, when the doctor said I was measuring small for the due date, did you doubt for even one minute that you are the father of my baby?"

"Not for even a millisecond," I assure her. "I love you, Tanzi. It happened crazy fast, but you're it for me and I'm it for you."

She laughs. "No lack of confidence on your part."

"Not about this, no."

"Then stop worrying about how I'll handle being a real live princess. It's part of the package."

"It doesn't have to be. I've discussed it with my father and I can abdicate my position in the lineage to the throne without giving up my job taking care of my country by growing the business that supports so many of them."

"I love that you talked to your dad about it because I know how much being a prince means to you."

She knows me better than anyone. Even my own family.

"It does, but you mean more." I kiss her, getting lost in the press of our lips together immediately.

Some time later, we snuggle naked on the bed because a leather sofa and nude bodies is not a great mix.

Tanzi traces patterns on my chest and after a second I realize she's writing out the word *amado*. "I want to be your wife, your other half, whatever that entails."

I believe her. "And I want only to be the other half of your soul for eternity."

Her lips are her only answer. One kiss follows another and we whisper words of love between them.

We'll still be saying these words when we hit the twilight of life because two hearts that beat as one cannot beat without the other.

Love at first sight is supposed to be a myth, but our story isn't going to end the way most myths do.

We are going to live and love happily for the rest of their lives, which I promise her before affirming that vow with our bodies.

THE END

Eight months later when Rio and Tanzi's daughter is born, the spitting image of the grandmother the prince never got to know, Isole dei Re rejoices. But no one more happily and loudly than the royal family.

If you enjoyed SCORSOLINI BABY SCANDAL, please consider leaving a review, or rating. Thank you!

To access all my free bonus content, sign up for my newsletter on my website: https://www.lucymonroe.com/

If you want to read Therese & Claudio's story it can be found in *The Scorsolini Marriage Bargain* and Amber & Miguel's story can be found in *Taken: The Spaniard's Virgin*.

And if you love alpha heroes with an edge, try my new spicy mafia romance series, Syndicate Rules.

Her Off Limits Prince

Lucy Monroe

Lucy Monroe LLC

For my writing buddies, Carrie, Traci, Aleksandr, Rachael & Pippa. Because you all have made writing fun again and during the hardest times, we've been there to cheer each other on. Good friends are one of the greatest gifts in life and I am so pleased to be able to call each of you friend.

You enrich my life and fill my heart and make me
laugh on a regular. Thank you!

Dear Reader,

You may notice some similarities between this book and The Cost of Their Royal Fling. That is because I wrote this one first, and yes it was originally intended to be the final book in my Princess by Royal Decree miniseries. However, my editor at Harlequin wanted me to delete 3/4 of the book and go from there. I loved the story too much to gut it like that, so we agreed I would keep rights to this title and would write another story to finish the trilogy, with some of the same elements.

Those elements are also popular tropes you will find in hundreds of other romances. Friends to lovers, friends with benefits turning into something more, etc. However, the things that I wanted to keep, that were so important to me as the author necessitated a whole new story for Harlequin. The most important (to me) of these is Tor's journey to becoming what we consider the alpha hero. We get to see the path as he takes it, not in flashback, or backstory, but in the present as he transforms from youngest prince to a man who sets his own rules.

Equally important to me was dealing with Blythe's infertility as something that did not magically disappear at the end of the book. I've heard from so many readers over the years that wanted their story told, that of acceptance and adoption. So, I told it. It is also my story. Though I had no difficulty getting pregnant, carrying my children was extremely difficult on my body. My husband and I decided to take permanent steps to prevent further pregnancy. However, we wanted more children and ended up adopting as well. We also opened our home to several teens over the years, but that's another story.

If the similarities between the two books disappoints you, I am truly sorry. However, I hope that like me, many of you will find satisfaction in reading this story and the very different ways that Tor & Blythe handle the situations they face.

Warmly,
Lucy

CHAPTER ONE

Prince Tor, youngest son of the House of Asgersen, stood silent, his expression grave, but stoic, as his oldest brother, King of Tapt Oyer spoke vows to his bride.

Reflecting the old Norwegian roots of the country, the centuries old Lutheran church was filled with royal guests, dignitaries, and representatives from some of the most wealthy and powerful families in the world.

Young distant cousins, one from Tapt Oyer and one from their family's branch in America, dressed in white robes like the pastor, but without the vestments, approached the large brass candelabras on either side of the altar to light the candles as part of the wedding ceremony.

The small island country of Tapt Oyer was getting a new princess.

However, in that moment, Tor's attention was *not* on the royal couple, but it was fully fixed on the woman standing as maid-of-honor.

Blythe Whitney-Jones, Travel journalist with a Vlog and her own show on a small cable channel. Best friend to the soon to be crowned princess, Blythe was also undeniably the sexiest woman Tor had ever seen.

Five feet, eight inches tall, she wore her brown hair long and wavy. No perfect curls or updo, even for the wedding. Just silky, brown waves Tor itched to run his fingers through. Could it be as soft as it looked?

Unlike a lot of the women who made their living on the small screen, she wasn't rail thin, but had lush curves with gorgeous breasts and a sumptuous bottom. Neither were the result of augmentation. Blythe was too natural for that.

She might make her living in front of the camera, but she was not one of the plastic people.

And Tor liked that. A lot.

His world was filled with people who did whatever was necessary to present the perfect façade. Amidst all that *fake*, Blythe Whitney-Jones was real.

From her tendency to tease his dignified brother to shutting down anyone who even thought of criticizing her best friend, she was a breath of fresh air blowing through the palace every time she visited.

Her cerulean gown not only brought out the clear sapphire blue of her eyes, but also clung to the curves Tor longed to caress.

When they got within six feet of each other, Tor's hands sometimes literally shook with the need to touch her. At first, he hadn't liked how strong her effect on him was, but he'd gotten used to the sexual heat that surged through him in her presence.

Now, he craved it. Craved her.

At twenty-two, he had yet to have full on sex, though he knew all sorts of ways to give and receive pleasure without actual intercourse. He'd never met a woman who made him crave joining their bodies, not merely seeking pleasure from one another.

Not when that act could come with so many complications.

He was a prince and that was a fact he could never forget.

Blythe wasn't on the make, looking to catch herself a prince though. Even if she had not been so vocal about how little she wanted what she called her friend's *fairytale*, Tor would have instinctively known that Blythe was not one of the women who would trade sex for royal status.

She just wasn't the type.

And that was rare in his life.

"Stop it." A feminine voice hissed in his ear.

He looked sideways at his best friend and spoke without moving his lips. "I'm not doing anything."

Tor had grown up knowing Else Kirkson. Her family had emigrated to America with his great uncle three generations ago, and had been instrumental in building the connections between the two countries that brought with them military, economic and technological benefits to this day.

In exchange for first rights to buy from the rich oil reserves of his country, of course.

It worked well for both nations.

Many assumed that since they got along so well, he and Else would one day marry. That was so not going to happen. They were more like siblings than friends.

She got a kick out of treating him like a little brother, even though she was only two months older.

"You're drooling, Tor." And she liked to tease.

He refrained from glaring down at his friend and knew better than to speak his denial out loud.

Eyes were always on him. He'd taken a risk responding to her first sally. To be seen talking to Else during the ceremony could lead to gossip and speculation that could run the gamut from him proposing to Else to him being unhappy with his brother's choice in brides.

"I'm surprised she can't feel the weight of your salivating stare from here," Else said in a subvocal, barely moving her lips as she'd learned long ago to do, just as he had.

Privacy maintenance skills. They had them.

Tor's gaze caught on sapphire blue eyes looking straight at him. Instant erotic heat zinged through him, and he was grateful for the cut of his tuxedo.

Blythe's beautiful lips parted on a puff of air and in that moment, no one else existed for either of them.

He was sure of it.

"I told you," Else hissed. "She's into you too. You better do something about it, Tor."

Blythe's gaze shifted to Else, a slight frown marring her beautiful features and then she returned her full attention to the bride, groom and priest.

Refusing to acknowledge Else's words, he wondered what had caused that frown.

Blythe smiled, watching Janice, new Crown Princess of Tapt Oyer, rush off to meet her new husband as they escaped their wedding reception early.

It was sweet, the way the King had arranged for them to leave for their honeymoon without the fanfare that Janice would rather avoid. He might be a king and part of the oligarchy, but that man understood romance.

Even if the marriage proposal had been anything but. A member of Tapt Oyer nobility, Janice had grown up knowing that if things played out a certain way, she could one day be a princess, or queen. Blythe shuddered at the very thought.

She had no desire toward what many would call a fairytale ending. She'd seen the cost that came with the title of royalty. Poor Janice had had to change careers to something that worked for the palace.

Blythe could not imagine giving up her travelog to marry anyone, much less a stuffy king like Holger.

"Did my brother and new sister-in-law abandon their guests?"

Blythe knew that voice. The sarcastic tone was all too familiar.

"Tor." She turned to face the youngest Asgersen prince. "Don't say anything."

"You think I would?" he asked, affronted. "I live under the same microscope my brothers and father do."

She forced down the totally inappropriate attraction she felt to the younger man. Seven years her junior, he was too young for her.

Not to mention, he was a prince. Another serious strike against him.

"Your brother is a king; I don't think the microscope is on the same setting for you." Blythe tried not to wince at how disparaging she sounded.

She didn't mean to put Tor down. For a prince, he was a nice guy. Funny and caring about his family, even if there always seemed to be some kind of barrier between him and the rest of the Tapt Oyer royals.

Tor frowned, but shrugged. "If you say so."

That was another thing she liked about the younger man. His wasn't defensive or egotistical.

Which probably made her less careful than she should be with the stuff she said to him.

Regardless, she couldn't afford a lot of alone time with the prince that, in Blythe's estimation, was twice as sexy as his two older brothers. Combined.

"I need to get back to the reception." Blythe went to move around him.

"Why?" he asked, conspicuously not moving out of her way.

"What do you mean, why?"

"You're not a member of the royal family," he reminded her practically. Tor moved toward her half a step. "You aren't obligated to entertain the guests."

Blythe wasn't part of any family really. She'd figured that out when she was little, but she didn't appreciate having that fact shoved into her face.

And his nearness? Was dangerous to her self-control.

"Well, you *are* one of the hosts, as a member of the royal family, and I *am* part of the wedding party. We both have a social obligation to return to the reception."

He frowned, studying her like trying to figure her out. "I never thought you worried about that kind of thing."

"Then you thought wrong. Janice is more precious to me than a sister. Anything I can to do to make her life easier, I will do it."

"And being in there, talking to people you don't know, will do that?" he asked, his sarcasm in full throttle.

"Maybe I can keep people from speculating immediately on her and Holger's disappearance."

An expression, like he'd just considered that possibility, came over Tor's handsome features. "You're right, but we're going to talk later."

She didn't ask about what. She'd seen this coming since first meeting this man.

Because that inappropriate attraction she felt? It wasn't one sided.

Tor looked at her like she was a meal prepared by a Michelin starred chef and he was a starving man. When other guys looked at her like that, well never quite *like that*, but like they wanted her, it did nothing for her.

Tor?

Turned her on. Wildly.

And he was her best friend's new little brother.

Completely and totally off limits.

Tor waited until they were back in the ballroom to ask Blythe to dance.

"Dance?" she asked, like it was an unheard of concept.

"Yes. You know, that activity where two people move to the beat of music together."

"I don't dance."

"I know that isn't true." She liked clubs and dancing back in Seattle.

Pictures posted at least every other weekend to her social media proved as much.

Blythe waved her arm toward the couples moving on the dance floor. "I don't dance like *that*."

"Everybody can waltz. Just follow my lead." With that instruction, Tor pulled Blythe into his arms and started moving them toward the dance floor, whispering instructions on how to place her feet and body.

Blythe was naturally rhythmic and allowed her body to take a formal stance easily. Just as he'd known she would.

Tor was careful to let her catch the rhythm and his lead before spinning them in a gentle circle that landed them amidst the other couples.

"You're good at this." The surprise in her voice could have offended him.

It didn't. Tor liked surprising her.

He winked at her. "Eight years of ballroom dancing."

"Eight years?" she asked faintly.

"From the age of eight to sixteen."

"You don't seem like the ballroom dancing type."

"Is there a type?" Tor spun Blythe out and guided her back in.

Their movements weren't competition worthy, but they were good together.

Flushed a lovely pink, Blythe shrugged. "I just would have thought you'd have other hobbies."

"Dancing was never a hobby." No more than any of the things he had to study to be a proper prince had been. "My brother insisted on it as part of my curriculum."

Holger had told Tor that not only would ballroom dancing be a necessary skill for diplomacy, it would also help him in his martial arts training.

Tor's older brother had been right on both counts.

Holger was always right, and if there was a tinge of sardonic bite to Tor's thoughts, no one had to know that.

"Your brother? Not your dad?"

"When my mother died, my father used work to assuage his grief." At least that's what Tor had surmised.

It wasn't as if his father had ever admitted to any emotion, even grief, to his sons.

"So, your brother stepped in?"

"You could say that," he said noncommittally, the tendency to obfuscate now so ingrained, it was his natural response to any question of a personal nature.

"But he was still a child himself."

"Holger was eighteen when our mom died." And he'd seen how dismayed his eight-year-old brother had been at the effective loss of both his parents in one fell swoop. "He did not think of himself as a child, but a fully grown man."

Being raised as a prince, with the weight of the country on their shoulders, none of them had wallowed in childhood. Had there been play? Certainly, but always with a purpose. To teach Tor and his brothers strategy and diplomacy, etc.

"I never realized King Holger was more like a father than a brother to you." Blythe wore her compassion like he'd once worn a school uniform. No mistaking it for anything else. "Janice always talks about you like a good friend."

"She and I have become friends." Unlike his brothers or father, Janne texted him randomly.

She made time in her schedule to hang out. Even though it was his brother she was marrying, she'd made an effort to get to know the entire royal family personally.

"My brother is, and has always been, my brother." And his sovereign for the past 8 years.

When their father's health had forced him to abdicate the throne, Holger had been crowned their king and the new monarch had no longer had time to take a personal interest in his teenage brother's life.

At fourteen, Tor became the first prince in Tapt Oyer' history to be sent to boarding school.

His arguments against it were dismissed as a youthful lack of understanding of what was best for him. The only argument he won was to be sent to New York, rather than England to school. He'd spent time there every summer with the relatives descended from his great uncle.

But Else had been there two and if Tor couldn't be near his family, he wanted to be near his friend.

He had missed his family at first, but he'd learned to do without them.

Tor had drawn further away from the brothers and father he no longer trusted and had followed up his boarding school years with attending university in the States as well.

He no longer believed the old adage: *Når problemer kommer, er det familien din som støtter deg*. When trouble comes, it's your family that supports you. But he still firmly adhered to *Du må forsvare din ære. Og din familie*. You have to defend your honor. And your family.

Tor was still Holger's brother. Their relationship might be distant now, but they were still family.

CHAPTER TWO

B lythe looked at him musingly. "I suppose your dad stepped back into the parental role after he abdicated the throne."

"Do you?" Then she supposed wrong.

"That must have been hard for your brother, too."

"Perhaps. He has never said." Tor didn't want to think about his family any longer.

Not his father who might as well be a stranger, or his brother who was also his sovereign, or his other brother who had closed himself off from all of them on some level while following their father's example of becoming a workaholic.

"You're a very good dancer," he told Blythe, his smile filled with heat he made no effort to deny.

She stumbled and then laughed. "Don't say that, you're jinxing me."

More like she reacted as strongly to him as he did to her.

"We fit very well together," he said meaningfully.

"Don't, Tor."

"Don't what?"

"Say stuff like that."

So, she'd taken his double meaning. He smiled.

But then the song ended and Blythe went to pull away.

Tor held on though. "One more. You're just getting the hang of this."

She bit her lip, her beautiful sapphire eyes filled with confusion and attraction she could not hide.

"Please, Blythe. Just one more." He was a prince, he never pleaded for anything.

But for this woman? Tor would make an exception.

"Just one more," she finally acquiesced.

He pulled her a little closer and spent the next song teaching her steps which she seemed to enjoy very much.

His brother Geir tapped his shoulder and right then Tor could have consigned his entire family to a glacier wasteland.

Older brothers could be such a pain the ass.

But Blythe smiled up at Geir, like she *wanted* to dance with him, no convincing required.

Disgruntled, but undaunted in his plan, Tor relinquished his hold, giving his brother a look that warned him to keep his playboy hands to himself.

Geir's eyes widened, but he gave an infinitesimal nod to acknowledge Tor's warning.

Tor waited until the social niceties had been observed before tracking Blythe down again. Dancing with her had been amazing, but it had had a predictable effect on his body.

Since he did not want to walk around with a hard-on, he kept his distance from her.

But the major dignitaries had left, including his father, which meant that Tor could leave without being censured for it.

He found Blythe talking to a diplomat and his wife. It sounded like they were discussing the best spots for Spring travel. He wouldn't mind taking Blythe on a trip in the Spring, preferably someplace warm they could spend most of their time in swimsuits and with no paparazzi.

He tapped her smooth shoulder, left bare by the haler neckline of her gown. That small connection to her skin sent messages zinging to his libido. "Miss Whitney-Jones, I would like a word, please."

She startled as if he'd yelled rather than speaking in the moderate tone he'd been trained to since childhood.

Turning, she faced him, her expression guarded. "Of course, Your Highness."

Blythe was really good at remembering to use formal address in public, even if she called him Tor in private.

He led her out of the ballroom and toward a little used study he'd prepared for them.

"Where are we going?" Blythe asked, her heels clicking on the marble floors as she kept pace with him. "What did you need to talk to me about? Couldn't this be handled back at the reception?"

Tor opened the door the study and ushered Blythe inside. "No."

Though it was summer, he had a fire going in the grate.

Although the Gulf Stream made for a milder climate than the country his ancestors had come from, temperatures rarely rose above sixty in the summer. They almost never dropped below forty in the winter though.

There was a small table where he'd placed chocolate dipped strawberries and champagne.

"What is this?" Blythe demanded, stepping wide of him and what Else had assured him was a *romantic* repast. "Tor, what is going on?"

She wasn't usually slow on the uptake, so he had to wonder if the question was more for form than substance.

Either way, he answered it. "I thought we could spend some time together, getting to know each other."

"You said you needed to talk to me." She sounded accusing.

"I do." Couldn't she see that?

"No." Blythe took another step away from him. "Just no. This is not happening, Your Highness."

"My name is Tor." She was the one person he did not want seeing him as only a prince. Especially not the youngest prince.

Blythe grimaced, her kissable lips twisting. "Are you even old enough to drink that champagne?" she demanded of him.

"I am twenty-two." And she damn well knew it. Just as he knew she was twenty-nine.

A year younger than Janne. But what did their age matter? It wasn't as if she was old enough to be his mother, or something.

"I'm seven years older than you. We aren't dating."

"Why? What is seven years?"

"Life experience, for one. You've never even held a job."

"Are you kidding me?" he asked, offended. "I've had the job of being a Prince of the Royal House of Asgersen since my birth." All the time she'd spent with the royal family and she still didn't understand that?

"Yes, such a hardship," she said, her tone dry.

While Tor usually appreciated sarcasm, he did *not* appreciate her implication.

"Being a prince is a twenty-four hour a day, seven days a week job." He'd had that truth drilled into him since birth.

"On top of my studies for the past four years, I have had numerous diplomatic responsibilities as well as the job of maintaining our family's blog," he explained to her, wondering why he felt the need to do so.

Transparency to the masses had sounded great in theory, but since his father was too luddite and his brothers too busy, it had fallen to Tor to research and write the weekly *family news* since his junior year in high school.

All from America, where he had to get that news from the palace's press office, among other sources.

Blythe rolled her eyes, clearly unimpressed. "Yes, I'm sure it was hard rubber stamping whatever your PR team wrote for you each week."

"I wrote those articles," Tor said, disappointment in her reaction hidden, as he hid all his emotions.

Emotions were the luxury of others. Or so his father had told Tor time and again.

It was a good thing he didn't feel anything soppy toward Blythe. If Else had been right when she'd teased him about *being in love*, Tor might be bleeding inside right now.

He wasn't. He didn't bleed inside for anyone.

He stuck with what he knew. "We're attracted to each other."

"And because you are used to getting what you want, you think you can have me." The beautiful woman's voice just dripped with disdain.

Damn. She really didn't know him at all.

"I thought we could have each other." The words and tone were confident. He'd learned to put that kind of front up like a second skin, but inside rejection stung like a wasp.

"Cute, but no."

He stepped toward her, feeling the zing of mutual attraction that she tried to deny with that small closing of the distance. It was like the air between them rose several degrees, though the room around them remained the same.

"Are you sure about that?" he asked.

"Okay, yes, I'm attracted to you, but I'm not proud of that." She frowned. "You're too young for me."

"Age is just a number."

"Says the infant."

Tor stepped back, that wasp stinging agan. "I am no infant."

"No, you're a young man who thinks you can have whatever you want."

If only she knew how much he could not have because of his birth and up-bringing. "You do not know me."

"And you don't know me."

"Hence this." He indicated the room prepared for a *date*. "An opportunity to get to know each other."

"Oh, be honest. This is a scene for seduction." Her beautiful blue eyes sparked with challenge, daring him to deny it. "You want sex."

"Yes," he acknowledged without hesitation. He had no reason to lie. He was not ashamed of wanting this woman. "But I wanted your friendship too."

"Look, Tor, even if I wanted to date a university student, which I don't—"

"I graduated with my bachelor's a week ago." There had been no celebration this close to The Royal Wedding of the Century, but that didn't mean it hadn't happened.

"Right, but you've got two more years to get your master's."

"So?"

"So..." She blew out a clearly frustrated breath. "So," she repeated. "I am not risking my friendship with Janice for sex with you."

"Sex with me would *not* be risking your friendship with my sister-in-law. What happens between us is no one else's business."

"Until we break up," Blythe said with a frown.

He couldn't promise they *wouldn't* break up. Tor didn't know how their future would roll out, but he didn't like her assumption that was the inevitable outcome either.

"I am interested in the present, not what ifs." He thought it was a good argument.

Blythe's expression said she didn't agree. "You're taking a gap year, for goodness sake. You've got no concept of real life."

"Lots of people take gap years," he informed her.

"Between high school and university, to figure out what they want to do with their lives. Your future is already set."

He was well aware. Tor's future had been set before his birth. So, he wanted one year where he could travel and experience life as a man and not a prince, at least not in every aspect. That did not make him irresponsible.

He'd hoped to spend a good part of that year traveling with Blythe.

What a fool he was. Maybe he was the callow youth she seemed to think, because looking at those plans now, he realized he'd been daydreaming.

She might be sexually attracted to him, but just like the rest of the world, she only saw who she thought he was. And that person wasn't worth risking anything for.

His pride smarting, Tor pulled all emotion behind the armor he'd erected long ago to deal with loss he had no control over.

Straightening his shoulders, he said, "We are not friends."

Blythe bit her lip, but then her own expression hardened. "No, we are not. I am Janice's friend, not yours."

Tor nodded. "Then, in future, I would prefer you address me as Your Highness, or Prince Tor."

He sounded like an arrogant prig, but Tor did not care. Blythe had misjudged him because she had not cared to get to know him or learn about him at all.

She did not see him as a man, but only as a prince; so, she could address him as such.

He had misjudged her attraction to *him* as the potential for something more. He would never make that same mistake again.

Lesson learned.

"If that's the way you want it, Your Highness."

"Miss Whitney-Jones." He inclined his head in dismissal.

Chapter Three

The door shut with a heavy thud on Blythe's exit from the library indicating she wasn't much happier with how that had gone than Tor was.

That had not gone as he'd expected.

At all.

Apparently off the charts sexual attraction was not enough for a woman who saw him as little more than a child.

Tor's childhood had been curtailed at age six when his mother died and was completely over when his brother took over as sovereign, leaving Tor to navigate his world without any adult playing any kind of real parental role in his life. At twenty-two, he was hardly on the cusp of adulthood, and he felt far older.

His life had required maturity from him from a very early age.

How strange that the woman he'd taken such pains to learn everything he could about, knew him so superficially. It felt surreal.

Tor settled into one of the chairs in the cozy setting he'd arranged and wondered why he'd gone to the effort.

He didn't know how long he stared into the fire before a knock sounded at the door.

Thinking it might be Blythe coming back for some reason, he straightened his posture and said, "Come in."

But it was Else's concerned features that showed as the door opened.

She took in the untouched food and champagne and frowned. "She didn't even sit down and visit with you?"

They both knew who *she* was. Else was his best friend and knew things he'd never told anyone else.

"I'm too young. Too spoiled. Too unimportant to risk her friendship with Janne for."

"She said all that?" Else asked with disbelief.

"Yes."

"What a b-one-t-charlie. She could have just said she wasn't that into you."

"She didn't deny being into me."

Else winced. "Ouch."

"Want a strawberry?" he asked her. "You can tell me how your own doomed love life is going."

Else growled. "Mother and Father are all set on marrying me off as some kind of eighteenth century chattel making an advantageous match."

He poured his friend a glass of champagne, an idea forming. "Here, drink this."

"Gladly." She gulped down the five-thousand-dollar bubbly like it was water and shoved the glass toward him for a refill. "More."

Blythe felt like a mean girl for the first time in her life and she didn't like that feeling at all. She owed Tor a huge apology. She'd been fighting her attraction for him from the moment they entered the study.

Want him? She craved the blond hottie like a drug.

And that was not okay.

Blythe had once thought she wanted to be with a man whose kiss made her stupid. That was *before* she realized just how attracted she was to the youngest Tapt Oyerian prince. With his muscle honed body, gorgeous grey eyes and chiseled jaw that just screamed Old Norse royalty, he was definitely her catnip.

The kind that left her reeling and bumping into walls if she wasn't careful. This out of control feeling was *not* pleasant. It was scary.

Eight years her junior, he wasn't ready to settle down. Blythe wasn't sure she was either, but she had a feeling that she could fall in love with Tor, and there was no way they could ever have anything lasting.

Though she was sure he wasn't looking for long term.

He had too much living to do yet. He still had two years left of schooling to get his master's degree, as well as two years of military service for the Crown. Not to mention his gap year.

Blythe didn't know why she'd criticized him for wanting one. She'd been grasping at straws and said a bunch of stuff she hadn't meant. Just because she was way too attracted him.

But no matter how much she wanted Tor, how could Blythe risk her relationship with the only real family she had? Janice.

Because even if Tor wanted more, they had no future. Not with her limitations and his role as a prince.

So, the inevitable break-up *would* come, and Blythe could lose the one person she knew she could count on for family.

Yes, Blythe had parents. And they did an excellent job of putting on the façade of the perfect twenty-first century, enlightened family.

But the truth was, the only person on earth who genuinely cared about Blythe, was the new Princess of Tapt Oyer.

If Blythe fell off the face of the Earth tomorrow, her parents wouldn't even notice.

It had always been that way.

Blythe's childhood was filled with circumstances from the mundane to the tragic that proved how little her parents cared.

None of which justified her acting like such a jerk to Tor. Okay, so he was younger than her and she was right he'd never had a proper job.

But she didn't need to denigrate his role in the royal family. He was the youngest and she knew his brothers and father spoiled him, but she hadn't needed to point that out.

She'd said stuff she didn't even mean in her effort to keep emotional distance between them. And that was not okay.

She had to apologize, because as much as their current strained relationship worked in her favor, Blythe was not a cruel person.

And it was cruel to let him think she thought he was anything less than he was, even if she still had zero intention of becoming involved with him.

Blythe found the study after a couple of wrong turns in palace corridors and knocked on the door. Tor was probably long gone by now and she'd have to hunt him down.

Which she would do.

She owed him that much.

The door swung open and the scene that Blythe walked into was not what she had expected.

How could she have forgotten that Tor had brought another woman to the wedding as his date?

"You're busy. I did not mean to intrude." She gave Tor a look though, one that asked what the heck he'd been doing trying to seduce her when he had a date already?

The other woman surged to her feet in a tipsy rush. "Oh, hi. You're Blythe Whitney-Jones. I'm Else Kirkson."

"We've met." This wasn't the first time Tor had brought Else as his plus one.

"Oh, that's right." Else smiled and then she frowned. "You're mean." Then she hiccupped. "Tor is too good for you."

Utterly confused, Blythe looked toward the prince. He'd told Else about earlier?

Tor rolled his eyes and helped the young woman back into her seat. "You're drunk, Else."

"Impossible. I never get drunk."

"The bottle of champagne is empty, and I never got a glass."

"Oh." Else looked up at Blythe. "Tor is my best friend, the brother I always wanted and never had." She glared at Tor. "If you *had* been my brother my parents wouldn't be so stuck on marrying me off to someone. I'm only twenty-two. I don't want to get married."

Which did not surprise Blythe at all.

"I've got a plan for that," the prince promised his tipsy friend. Then he turned to Blythe. "Did you want something? As you can see, I've got my hands full."

"Can I help you get her to her room?" Blythe thought it might be just slightly less scandal worthy if she helped the younger woman undress and get ready for bed than if Tor did.

And by slightly, she meant hugely.

Besides the idea of Tor helping Else in that way did not sit well with Blythe.

Not even a little bit.

"You don't mind?" the prince asked warily.

"Not at all."

Blythe and Tor lifted the young woman between them and he led them down unused corridors to the guest wing of the palace. The prince was way too good at avoiding detection to have never done so before and she told him that.

"Making judgments again?" he asked instead of answering.

Blythe winced. "Point taken. I came back to tell you that I'm sorry. I shouldn't have said the stuff I did to you."

"You thought it. Why not say it?" All the vulnerability she'd seen in him earlier was gone now.

This man was one-hundred percent invulnerable prince. This Tor would *not* plead so charmingly for a second dance.

"Well, I didn't really think it. Look, I just didn't want to get involved with you and chose a poor way to express myself."

"You could have just said no." This was Else's slurred contribution.

"I did try. He didn't believe I meant it."

"Did he try to kiss you anyway? If you say *yes* I'll know you're lying. Tor wouldn't do that." Else answered her own question.

"No, he did not try to kiss me." Tor had been a perfect gentleman.

It had been her own desire and his honest reciprocation that Blythe had had to fight so hard.

"He kissed me once. I *asked* him too," the other woman stressed.

They were in her bedroom now.

Else giggled. "That's when I knew he was my brother, by another mother."

"No sparks?" Blythe asked, not able to fathom that.

If Tor ever kissed her, she was pretty sure she'd combust with the flames.

"Not a one. Too bad. He'd fulfill all my parents' requirements."

"I'll get some water and headache tabs to put by the bed," Tor said, heading into the en suite. "Could you get her in her pajamas?" he called to Blythe.

Blythe did just that, helping the younger woman get out of her designer gown and don sleep shorts and a t-shirt.

"Not exactly high fashion, huh?" Else asked with a burp. "My mom would be appalled."

"I'm sure it doesn't matter what you wear to bed."

"You're wrong about that. Everything matters to my parents. Everything. But you're wrong about lots of stuff, aren't you?"

Blythe wasn't used to being called out because well, she didn't often get it wrong and she *never* judged people the way she had Tor earlier.

"I can be, I suppose."

"Tor isn't spoiled."

Blythe forbore arguing that point. She was pretty sure Else saw the brother of her heart with rose colored glasses on that score.

"Everyone thinks he is, because he's the youngest, but they all abandoned him."

"Blythe's not interested in my life story," Tor said from behind her.

He reached around and put the water and medicine on the bedside table. "Take those and drink that whole glass of water when you wake up in the middle of the night feeling like death warmed over."

Else mumbled something and then turned over to sleep.

The prince turned off the lights and then exited the room, making sure the hallway was clear first.

"Won't the security cameras catch you leaving her room?"

"There won't be anything on them come morning."

"They erase that quickly?" That didn't sound very secure to Blythe.

But Tor just shrugged. "Goodnight, Blythe."

"Wait."

He stopped. "Yes?"

"I am sorry, about earlier. Really."

"All right."

When Blythe realized he wasn't going to say anything else, she said, "I don't think you're spoiled per se."

"Just spoiled by my position in life. I got the message."

"That's not what I meant."

"I think it is."

Maybe it was and maybe Blythe needed to seriously rethink her opinions about the young prince. She realized she'd formed them with her own self-protection in mind, so she'd let herself believe what she needed to about him to protect both her heart and her relationship with Janice.

"What did Else mean when she said they all abandoned you?"

"Nothing that would interest you."

"But I am interested."

"I am not interested in talking about it."

That told her. And she understood, but she didn't want to leave it there.

"I know I said I wasn't your friend, but I'd like to be," she said. "I understand if you don't want to though."

Blythe hadn't shown herself to be good friendship material for him up to this point.

He inclined his head. It was such a regal move, she wondered if he even realized how *royal* he seemed in that moment.

It was neither an agreement, nor a denial, simply an acknowledgment that she'd spoken.

"Okay, well, I'm off to bed too, I think. Goodnight, Your Highness." It was clear there would be no sharing of confidences tonight. Any friendship would have to built later, over time.

Blythe couldn't help feeling she'd dismissed an opportunity to get to know the prince that wasn't going to be offered again.

"Goodnight, Miss Whitney-Jones."

Blythe did her best not to wince at his acceptance of her formal address and just as formal response to it.

It was for the best.

She was still telling herself that hours later as she lay sleepless in her solitary bed.

Chapter Four

T or didn't see Else until lunch the following day. They were eating alone in the private gardens. She wore dark glasses, her hair pulled back in a sloppy ponytail.

"This is a different look for you," he teased. "Still feeling the effects of last night's champagne?"

She flopped into a chair and flipped him off. "My parents are spending the day shopping."

"So, you can get away with it, huh?"

"Exactly." She stared up at him morosely. "If they have their way, I'll have a husband soon to make sure I'm always up to their perfect standards."

"I have an idea about that."

"What?"

"I'm going to cancel my gap year and tell my family it's because I want to spend both years of graduate school with you." Which, in one respect was very true. If Tor wasn't going to spend his gap year traveling and pursuing a relationship with Blythe, he would prefer to have the company of his best friends for both years.

"I'm sorry," Else said, clearly knowing why he no longer felt the need for the time between university and pursuing his MBA. "But I don't see how that's going to curb my parents' enthusiasm for me getting my MRS."

"I am going to announce it at dinner tonight."

"So?"

"So... I'm also going to say that while you and I are not ready to make anything official, we have an understanding."

"That's brilliant." Else praised him, showing more animation than she had since finding him in their favorite secluded picnic area. "Not a lie, because we *do* have an understanding."

"Yes, we are never going to get married." He smiled grimly.

"But it will buy me at least a couple of years. You know once we get our MBAs, they are going to push for us to set a date."

"I know it's not a long-term solution, but if you want to continue with the pretense, we can tell them we don't want to set anything until I finish my two years of military service. Since, I will most likely spend the entire two years in a war zone, that it entirely practical."

While both his older brothers had done their two years of military service, neither the king, nor his heir could be risked in actual combat or the more dangerous peacekeeping assignments. As the third son, Tor, on the other hand, had served in a reservist capacity in the Tapt Oyerian Military since he was eighteen, attending weekly training during the academic year and longer sessions in the summers for both combat skills and officer training.

He would have six weeks of final training before deployment to a high priority location for their allies.

Else frowned, pulling her sunglasses off to glare at him with bleary eyes. "You're going in as an officer."

"I am." But he had no intention of hiding behind his position or royal privilege. His friend knew him well enough to know that too.

Else's grimace of acceptance said as much. "You're sure you're okay with pretending we have something between us?"

"I am." Tor had no intention of actually lying to his family.

It would all be implication. Which he had no problem with. Because if they knew him at all, or had listened to him talk about his best friend, they would know that implication could never be what it sounded like.

"It will benefit me too," he told her. "If I'm seen as taken, I won't have to spend as much time fending off social climbers, looking for princess status through marriage."

He wasn't so naïve he thought that the appearance of him having a girlfriend would stop all of that, but it would help.

"That's great for the women you *don't* want to date, but what if you meet someone you *want* to? What if Blythe changes her mind? She came back last night."

"First, if either of us meets someone we want to get to know better, we'll tell each other and do a subtle shift in our public relationship persona. Agreed?" Else was more likely to meet someone than Tor was, but he didn't tell her that.

He added, "As for Blythe, she wanted to apologize, not set up a date with me."

"An apology means she cared she hurt your feelings."

"She did *not* hurt me," Tor immediately denied. "She offended me. I realized that she does not know me at all."

"Well, to be fair, none of you Asgersen princes are that easy to get to know."

Tor shrugged. If Blythe had really been interested in him, she would have taken the time to learn at least some basic things about him.

She had not.

Which meant that no matter how attracted they were to each other, she wasn't interested in dating him.

He was *too young*. *Too spoiled*. *Too unimportant* in the scheme of her life.

"Whatever you are thinking, stop."

"Why?"

"You've got that look."

"What look?"

"The one you get when you start pushing everyone away. You did it after your mom died. You did it after your father's heart attack. You—"

"Stop with the litany of my life. We were six when my mom left. Don't pretend you remember what I was like."

"But I do."

"Right."

"People make mistakes, Tor. You do get that don't you? Mistakes they regret later."

Since he had never seen regret from anyone in his life who had relegated him to the designation of unimportant, Tor didn't agree.

Oh, he knew people made mistakes, but he was not convinced they saw the same actions as mistakes as he did, or that they regretted those actions.

His announcement at dinner went over about how he had expected it to.

At least with his father, who said he liked Else quite well and her parents were good connections to have.

Of course, the former king, approved. The Kirksons were not Tapt Oyerian nobility, but they were part of the royal *set*. Though Tor suspected Else's mother would be a lot happier if the family had a title attached to their name.

Tor merely inclined his head, not really concerned with his father's viewpoint on an alluded to, but fictitious relationship.

"I am surprised you're giving up your gap year," His brother, Geir, frowned. "You fought hard for that."

"I will be able to spend both years of graduate school with Else this way."

"I thought your interests lay in another direction." Geir did not look down the table at Blythe, who would be flying home the next morning. Tor's middle brother was far too sophisticated for that kind of obvious action, but the look he gave Tor was unmistakable. "I always thought you looked at Else as more of a sister."

"They're not even distantly related," their father slotted in.

Tor allowed the conversation to take its course without him. He neither confirmed, nor denied any of the opinions set forth by his father or brother. He was sure one, or both, would make sure Holger knew of this supposed development as soon as the monarch returned from his honeymoon.

Later, after being pretty silent throughout dinner, Blythe grabbed Tor's arm as soon as they all stood up from the table. "I need to talk to you, Your Highness."

She then dragged him into the small library nearest the palace dining room. He let her because he was curious what had her so agitated.

"What the heck was that in there?" she demanded as soon as the door was shut, practically vibrating with anger.

Though what *she* had to be angry about, Tor did not know.

He narrowed his eyes at her. "I do not know what you mean."

"You aren't going to marry Else."

She was right of course, but that didn't mean he would confirm her assumption.

"Excuse me, but what business is it of yours?" he asked, letting chill seep into his tone. "This anger you are exhibiting is misplaced."

"I don't want you lying to your family."

"I have lied to no one." That his father had made the assumption Tor knew he would was beside the point.

The expression on Blythe's beautiful face said she wasn't buying it. At all. "Yes, you did. You told them you're going to marry Else Kirkson and we both know you aren't."

Tor was pretty sure Geir didn't believe that either, but he wasn't worried about whether or not his brother bought the subterfuge. The only people he needed to believe the false hope of a future between him and Else were her parents.

She was the only friend, only person, he knew he could trust implicitly and he would protect her any way he could.

"What I do in the future, or the present, for that matter, is not your concern Miss Whitney-Jones. As you said last night, you are Janice's friend. Not mine. Not a member of my family." He didn't add the last to hurt her, but to remind her of the role she'd chosen in his life.

None at all.

She'd backpedaled some after helping him get Else to bed, but he'd seen the overture for friendship for what it was. A pity offer.

And Tor did not now, and never would, need anyone's pity.

"Is this about last night? I reject your seduction overtures and you're getting back at me by pretending to get engaged to your bff?" Blythe asked like she wasn't sure she believed that scenario herself.

That was some mitigation of the accusation, but not much.

Tor shook his head firmly and pointed out the flaw in her logic. "I am not sure how you think that my announcement at dinner would be getting back at you. How could it? That only works if you wanted to date me, and you don't."

"I knew it. This is about me telling you no."

Wow. Talk about being illogical. Who was the younger one here? Because Tor had honestly never even considered any sort of aspect to this that might be showing Blythe something, or even more ludicrously getting back at her for telling him no.

"Believe what you want, Miss Whitney-Jones, but I am not trying to *get back at you* in some immature attempt at revenge."

"Then you're doing it to protect her," Blythe said with more astuteness than he expected. "But Tor, don't you realize Else has to stand up to her parents on her own? You can't break trust with your family to make her life easier. It's not worth it."

"I have asked you to use a more formal address with me." For some reason his name on her lips made something in his chest tighten and he didn't like it. "Please remember in future."

"Fine, *Your Highness*," she emphasized. "But what I said is true."

"My relationship with my family has nothing to do with you. My future has nothing to do with you." By *her* choice, but he didn't add that. "Please, remember those salient facts."

He didn't care if she chose to take her beliefs to Janne, or even Holger. So long as the Palace Press Office never outright denied the relationship, Else's parents would stop hounding her to quit school and get married.

The royal family's policy was not to comment on personal matters unless necessary. They didn't bother denying the rumors that inevitably swirled around them, unless such rumors got in the way of the country's best interests.

Any coupling of his name with Else's in the media would not.

Tor swept from the room with every bit as much cool, not to mention arrogance, as either of his older brothers could have done.

Blythe would do her best to remember to address him more formally in the future, but in her head, she knew he would always be Tor.

Sitting in one of the dark leather chairs in the library, she sighed. She could have handled that better, but she just *knew* this whole engagement thing was not on the up and up.

She was disproportionately disappointed that he would lie to his family that way.

Going over what had been said at the table, Blythe realized that Tor had never actually said he and Else were getting married, or even dating. He'd said things that could be taken to mean that though and had not disabused his father of the notion he had so clearly taken.

And Tor had cancelled his gap year.

Despite what he'd said, she couldn't help feeling responsible.

Okay, so he wasn't dating Else to get back at Blythe. Talk about self-important delusions. Clearly Blythe had done a bang-up job of convincing him she was not interested. *At all*.

Which was not the truth.

Blythe had never met a man who she was *more* interested in getting to know...in every way. But he was off limits.

That was not the message she'd gotten across, however.

So, of course he thought she was being *extra*, accusing him of trying to get back at her.

Only she *was* jealous. Whether it had been intended to hurt her, or not. The thought of him and Else together did hurt.

Even knowing that Else and Tor had zero sexual chemistry, Blythe had wanted to stand up and say that of course they were *not* dating.

And dating, or not, Else got to be Tor's friend in a way he and Blythe never would be. Never *could* be.

Because as much as she said she wanted them to be friends the night before, she knew that even friendship would be dangerous to her.

She wanted him too much.

Chapter Five

Home from graduate school for the winter break, Tor watched his family opening Christmas gifts, a smile fixed on his face.

Janne was giving his brother Holger doe eyes over her gift. Their father was smiling and exclaiming over the contract Geir had had framed for him. Tor thought it must be one of the early contracts his ancestors had signed when establishing their sovereign monarchy and creating a business consortium to finance it.

Geir had enlisted Tor's help over the summer to do some searching in the oldest archives from when the archipelago kingdom was first created.

Though the details of what it was weren't that important. The fact his family was happy and together, that was what mattered.

It was all he'd wanted as a child. It was all he wanted now, though he'd never be so naff as to say so out loud.

His own Christmas gifts were few but thoughtful. Even so they showed very little understanding of the man he had become and more familiarity of the boy he had once been.

Nevertheless, his thanks were genuine.

He noticed that his father had gotten a rather personal gift for Janne's mother, Lady Ingrid.

She blushed when opening it, though the painting by her favorite artist was in no way inappropriate.

Which meant what?

The *feelings* behind the gift and in the receiver were more intimate than one might expect. He'd noticed his father and the countess spent a great deal of time together, but Tor had chalked that up to being thick as thieves planning The Great Royal Wedding.

Now, he had to rethink that conclusion.

Was his father having an affair with the countess? In a relationship with her?

Certainly, whatever was going on between the two was not for public consumption as no official, or even *family only* announcements had been made.

Blythe sat across the room, opening her own gifts. Her festive but stylish, dark red jumpsuit clung to her curves enticingly. She'd pulled her long brown hair away from her face with a clip. She was, as always, beautiful.

Not that he allowed even the slightest spark of that approval to show in his expression. Tor kept his gaze moving on to the rest of his family, though his mind stayed fixed on the Travel journalist.

He had been unsurprised to discover she planned to spend Christmas with them. Blythe seemed to prefer spending holidays with Janne rather than her own parents.

Tor knew there was a story there, but it was one he doubted he would ever hear.

"Just imagine Christmas morning when we have little ones to tear into the gifts." Tor's father rubbed his hands together in anticipatory glee and gave Janne and Holger a significant look.

"I used to love watching you open your gifts," Lady Ingrid said to Janne.

His father gave them all a benevolent look. "It was my favorite time of year when you boys were children."

"Whenever we have children, I will have a fine example of fatherhood to follow," Holger said with uncustomary sentimentality.

Geir added something similar.

Tor knew he was expected to echo the sentiment. He couldn't do it.

His father had abdicated that role when he was eight years old and although everyone in his family seemed to think there was nothing wrong with that, he couldn't voice some lie about how Prince Canute, former king, had set the prime example of fatherhood.

Tor was a grown man now and it did not matter anymore that he had no relationship with his father, but he wasn't pretending some perfect childhood either.

Standing up, he said, "I need to call Else and wish her happy Christmas."

He left the room before anyone could answer.

His phone call to Else was short, but she thanked him for making it. Their implied relationship had done what he'd intended and taken the pressure off her to look for a husband rather than focus on her education.

Her relationship with her parents was no warmer and he was sure she'd rather be here in the palace than in Vale, Colorado celebrating the holidays with her family's wealthy friends. But at least she did not have to have the same argument about her duty to them as their only child over and over again.

And he'd been right that their subterfuge would have the secondary benefit of operating as a buffer between him and women interested in becoming a princess by marriage.

Not that his wife would necessarily be named a princess. That was entirely up to his brother's discretion. Tor's wife *would* be a duchess by marriage and that was quite enough for some social climbers.

"You hurt your dad's feelings when you left that way." The censure in Blythe's voice was unmistakable.

He'd stayed in the library after the call, not really keen to return to his family's festivities and sentimentalities he did not share.

Tor was so lost in thought that he was startled to realize she'd joined him without him realizing it.

"At the risk of repeating myself. My relationship with my family is not your concern."

"Do we have to be like this?" she asked with a sad frown.

"Like what?" But he knew. He kept his distance.

She kept hers. The easy camaraderie they'd had when they first met was gone. "You are so combative with me."

He opened his mouth to deny her accusation, but then shut it. She was right. He'd been offended by her rejection and the assumptions she made about him.

A mature man would let that go.

Tor had no desire to act like a child.

"I apologize. I will endeavor for a higher level of civility."

"Thank you. I like you, Tor—Your Highness. I would like to be friends."

She'd said that before, but he had not believed her, and he'd seen no real evidence of that since.

Civility he would and could do. However, friendship was another thing entirely. "I trust my friends."

"And you do not trust me?" she asked, managing to sound both surprised and a little hurt.

Which he thought was odd on both counts. Why should she expect him to trust her when they agreed they were *not* friends? Whatever she might prefer now. And why should she be hurt when she'd taken the same pains to make sure he knew how unimportant he was to her?

"I am sorry if that offends you," he told her honestly. It was never his intention to hurt others, but he was not a man who lied to protect their feelings either. "But no."

She nodded, seeming to take his words at face value. "Okay. Why did you leave like that? You could have waited to make your phone call, couldn't you?"

She really did not seem to get the concept of the boundary differences between friends and acquaintances. "No."

She stared at him, like she was waiting for him to explain.

Which he had no intention of doing.

She bit her lip in that way he'd found so endearing before. "I'm sorry you feel that you cannot talk to me." Blythe stepped right into his personal space and laid her hand on his arm. "Your feelings matter to me, Tor."

He stared at her. Did she have any idea how mixed her signals were with him?

Right now, the openness of her body language, the way she touched him, it implied an intimacy, a *friendship* they did not share.

She looked up at him, her blue eyes fastened on his.

That fast, the air around them charged with sexual attraction.

Blythe made a breathy little sound. Then she whispered his name. "Tor."

Tor could not make his body move away from her. No matter how frustrating he found her mixed signals, he had never been so intensely turned on by another woman.

They both stood there in silence, not moving. But Tor could feel his heart pounding in his chest.

Blythe's nostril's flared, her pupils dilating with excitement, making her sapphire eyes look almost black with desire. And still neither moved.

"You want me," he accused, equally frustrated and excited by her hot-cold act.

"Yes." The word was barely a puff of air between them.

His own eyes narrowed. "You want to kiss me."

She nodded.

He waited for her to add a *but* that never came.

He challenged, "Then do it."

Tor still expected her to step away. To refuse.

Blythe shocked him. Putting her hands on his shoulders, she reached up on her tiptoes, needing the extra height despite wearing heels, and pressed her lips to his.

Need whooshed through Tor like a flash fire. His entire body lit up with sensation as the woman he'd craved for months kissed him.

He wrapped his arms around her, pressing their bodies together. She wound her arms around his neck, pushing upward and against him, a sound of feminine need coming from her throat.

The slow burn of desire he always felt in her presence went to four alarm status, his erection straining against the fabric of his slacks. The kiss was everything he'd ever imagined it would be with this woman, and more.

Their whole bodies were involved in it, undulating against each other. Her pillowy breasts pressed into him, nipples obviously hard. He wanted to touch, but settled for cupping her bottom, squeezing the ample flesh and groaning with desire sparked by finally having his hands on her.

Blythe hopped up and wrapped her legs around him, the silky fabric of her jumpsuit no barrier to the heat of her body as the apex of her thighs pressed intimately against his hard-on.

Without thought, he shifted one arm down to support under her bottom and started moving toward the wall. Once the wall was against her back, Blythe moved against him, her body massaging his erection through the layers of cloth separating them.

He thrust his tongue into her mouth, and she kissed back with equal passion, their mouths eating at each other. They were both breathing through their noses, but every few seconds they would break the connection of their mouths to gulp in air and then go right back to the passionate kiss.

Ecstasy arced through Tor, excitement growing to levels way beyond what a mere kiss should elicit. His balls drew tight and he knew he was close to coming. Blythe seemed to know and her movements grew more frenzied.

Like she wanted him to come as much as he did. Knowing she craved his pleasure tipped Tor right over.

He couldn't believe he was coming in his pants like an adolescent with no control, but the ecstasy was so great, it overshadowed any embarrassment he might feel.

This was right. Pleasure exploded out of him in a rush, her mouth swallowing his shout of completion.

His desire not abated even a tiny bit by that amazing release, Tor finally allowed himself to cup Blythe's breast, rubbing his thumb over the hard nub of her nipple.

She moaned against his lips, her body moving even more frantically against him.

Knowing the kiss was affecting her every bit as strongly as it did him amped his desire to new heights.

The sound of voices outside the door reminded him they needed to move this to somewhere more private.

Tor lifted his head only to find Blythe looking at him with something akin to horror.

"What are we doing?" she asked.

"If you don't know..." he teased.

But she frowned instead of smiling. "It's not funny. We can't do this, Tor. Put me down."

She pushed against his chest, trying to create space between them.

"Give me a second," he said with less patience than he probably should have.

But damn it, were they back to this?

He released her and let her down, stepping back only when he was sure Blythe would not topple over.

The tight expression on her beautiful features did not indicate appreciation for his concern.

"Relax," he told her. "It was just a kiss."

"You came," she accused. "I almost did. Oh my gosh, I cannot believe this." Blythe looked around wildly like, she hoped something would magically change about where they were, or what they'd done.

He was fully aware he had climaxed. The physical evidence was undeniable. He didn't need her rubbing his face in his untried response to something as simple as a kiss.

Damn it.

Hearing she had not achieved the same level of pleasure wasn't making him feel any better about it either, no matter how close she'd been.

"You cannot tell me after that...that *kiss*, that you are going to marry Else," Blythe said, her voice shaky. "You need to stop lying to your family."

Furious at how easy he'd been when she'd just been making a point, he demanded, "Is that why?"

"Why what?" she asked like she didn't understand the question.

"Why you kissed me," he clarified, angry with her and even more angry with himself. He should have known. "You wanted to prove a point."

She looked away from him, but didn't deny it. "It can't happen again."

"If you don't want it to, it won't," he promised with pure sarcasm.

She might have had an agenda, but Blythe had been as into that kiss as Tor had been. She admitted she'd almost come.

But despite his lack of experience, he would have known without her admission.

Just from the frantic way she moved against him and kissed him.

She hadn't been able to hold back either.

If they hadn't heard someone outside the door, they would still be kissing and most likely half naked by now.

His body gave a throb of need at that thought.

"Don't sound so smug." Her expression was accusing.

Like he'd been the one to initiate the kiss. But that first touch had been all her. She'd kissed him.

"Stop looking like that," she instructed him again when he remained silent. "You know I don't want this."

"Next time don't kiss me, I might believe you." With that, he turned to leave.

He wasn't sticking around to listen to her tell him how much she didn't want him when her actions said the opposite.

"Tell your family the truth about Else," she said as he opened the door. "They deserve it."

He stopped, his hand on the knob. "You mean like how honest you are about wanting me?" he asked sardonically.

No matter what Blythe claimed, he was not hurting his family with his pretense that protected Else from being pushing into marriage by her parents before she was ready. If his father and brothers were emotionally invested in a relationship between him and Else, then yes, they would be hurt.

But they weren't. They were not emotionally invested in him, much less who he was dating. He had a role to play in this family and he fulfilled it; that did not mean the minutiae of his life mattered to either his father, or his brothers.

Tor hurt no one in his bid to protect his one true friend.

Blythe made a wounded little sound that he forced himself to ignore as he opened the door. He had to take a damn shower.

And if he got himself off again remembering that kiss and the feel of Blythe's body against his? That wouldn't be anybody's business but his own.

Chapter Six

Blythe collapsed into a chair after Tor left. Déjà vu. Just like their last confrontation in here.

How could she have let that happen though? She'd kissed him! Not the other way around and she was fully cognizant of that fact.

She couldn't help the frisson of feminine pride that went through her at the thought she'd brought him to a climax with a kiss and some rubbing.

He was probably embarrassed, but Blythe thought it was the sexiest thing she'd ever experienced.

And that was just all kinds of wrong.

The fact that he wouldn't come clean about his relationship with Else to his family showed that they had very different priorities. He was so lucky to have a family that cared about him, and he was going to hurt them all when they found out he had no plans to marry Else.

He *couldn't* have any plans to marry the other woman. Not when he did nothing to hide how much he wanted Blythe.

Tor wasn't a player. He wasn't the type of man who would marry one woman while sexually pursuing another.

Was he?

Blythe simply couldn't let herself believe that of him, but was that her own emotions talking, or logic?

She couldn't understand why Tor would lie to his family though. What did he believe was so different about his upbringing than that of his brothers?

Yes, he'd lost his mother and his father had become something of a workaholic after, but she'd seen Prince Canute with his sons. He cared about all of them, like a father should.

It was one of the reasons Blythe adored the whole royal family the way she did. They had a dynamic missing from her own.

Parents that actually wanted the best for their children. Parents who actually *wanted* their children.

Not like her own parents, who would have let her die when she was eight rather than be inconvenienced with a medical procedure, who had not even known what degree Blythe had gotten at university, much less gone to her graduation. They'd both been out of country on business at the time, but she doubted it would have mattered if they hadn't been.

They had paid for it, of course. It was expected. And they always did what looked right to their peers, but it was never with any sense of caring.

Until she met Janice and her mom, Lady Ingrid, Blythe'd had exactly two birthday celebrations in her life, both milestones others would have noticed if her parents didn't do something for her.

When Blythe had learned that her father's inheritance had depended on him having a child, she'd finally understood why she'd been given life at all.

She'd fulfilled a will's codicil and that was all.

Her parents did not, and had never, loved or wanted her.

Tor had a whole family who loved him and wanted the best for him. That he would deceive them hurt Blythe deep inside.

It shouldn't.

He wasn't her friend, not really.

He for sure wasn't her family. Not like Janice.

So, why did she care so much if he did something Blythe couldn't approve of?

A knock on Tor's apartment door startled him out of his immersion in graduate level economic theory.

He lived in a secure building not too far from Harvard, where he was studying for his MBA. Not merely a building with a buzzer system, but one that catered to the world's wealthy and had a doorman and security guards on duty twenty-four-seven.

He had his own security naturally, living in the apartment next to his.

All of which, meant that whoever was on the other side of that knock had to be on the list of approved visitors, both for the building and his own security staff.

As far as Tor knew, none of his family were in America, much less Boston, and Else was in a study group for her class on sustainable business models.

The knock sounded again and Tor stood to answer it, still not sure who it could be.

He looked out through the peephole and sucked in a breath of shock.

Blythe Whitney-Jones stood there looking both impatient and worried.

If his first thought was maybe she was there to take up where they'd left off at Christmas, he squashed it fast. No doubt she had other reasons far more prosaic for coming to his condo. Though what she was doing in Boston, he had no idea. She'd been hiking through the Rockies the last time he checked in with her Vlog.

Which admittedly had been yesterday.

So, what was she doing here? Was something wrong with Janne? Why would his family send Blythe to tell him about it?

He swung the door open. "Miss Whitney-Jones, this is a surprise."

"Hi, Tor—Your Highness."

"Come in." Tor'd had courtesy drilled into him from infancy, but what he really wanted to do was ask why she was there and if his family were all okay.

However, the lessons of a lifetime could not be dismissed and he stepped back to allow her entrance.

When he'd shut the door and led her to the living room, he asked? "Would you like something to drink?"

She was dressed casually in some classic 90s chic. As a prince, Tor was required to know a little about a lot of topics. Current trends in fashion included.

While he took a full load of credits for graduate school, he continued to be tutored for his royal role in things ranging from politics to fashion.

Blythe's calf length crocheted vest over grey sleeveless top and matching narrow legged slacks managed to enhance rather than hide her curves.

Her mouth twisted in a not-quite-there smile as she stepped into his apartment. "Sure."

He went into the kitchen and found a can of her favorite seltzer water. Why he instructed his staff to buy that brand, he wasn't going to contemplate.

She was sitting in a chair by his gas fireplace when he returned to the living room, the seltzer poured into a glass with ice.

He handed her the fizzing beverage and she took it with a murmured thanks.

"Nice place," she commented.

Tor shrugged. "It serves its purpose."

Holger had purchased the luxury condo for Tor's use while he was in graduate school and would sell it and the furnishings at a profit when Tor graduated.

It was not a home, just an investment.

"I would have loved to have a place this nice when I was in school."

"You didn't live in penury," he replied mildly.

She might not have the warmest relationship with her parents, but Blythe had never had to do the starving student gig.

"No, of course you are right, but I bet you're the only graduate student in this complex."

He shrugged again, uncaring if she was right, or not. The few friendly acquaintances he'd made in the master's program lived elsewhere. Where any of the other students lived was of no interest to him.

"So, I got a disturbing phone call today."

"Did you?" And why was she telling him?

"Yes. I have friends in a lot of areas of journalism."

"Good for you."

She gave him a wry look. "Don't be a smartass, Tor, I mean Your Highness."

"You could call me Prince Tor."

"I could." She shook her head. "Look, that's not important. The friend that called works for a tabloid."

"And he's *your* friend?" Tor asked with disgust he made no effort to hide.

"Yes, *she* is. It's helpful to have friends in that part of the industry, especially when the woman I think of as a sister has a high public profile."

"If you say so."

"I do. And it worked in *your* favor this time."

"My favor?" he asked with disbelief.

"Yes, *yours*. Look, I don't know how to tell you this without hurting you."

"Hurting me?" he scoffed. "Not likely."

Blythe frowned. "Lisette, the girl you've been dating, she's offered an exclusive to the tabloid my friend works for."

Fury rolled through Tor, but he kept it locked inside. "Lisette and I never dated."

"Hooked up, whatever."

"We never did that either." Yes, he'd been thinking about it.

Tor had gone as far as to talk to Else about announcing that while they were still close, they would both be seeing other people.

"That's not what Lisette told the reporter."

"I see."

"I'm not sure you do. Because of your relationship with Else Kirkson, this could cause a really ugly scandal."

"Did you tell Holger?" Tor asked, trying to work out why Blythe was there and why he hadn't already gotten an irate phone call from his kingly brother.

"I came to you first."

That surprised him.

"We need to get the palace PR team on this right away." Tor scowled. "I knew she was trouble, but I thought I had it handled."

Which is what he told his brother, when he called Holger moments later.

For some reason, Blythe was still there and Tor, who hated exposing his personal life, did not mind her overhearing the conversation.

"I never dated her," he answered Holger. "But I did consider it."

"What about Else?" his brother asked in his most disapproving tone.

"I would have talked to her about seeing other people before I asked another woman on a date." Not that he was going to tell Holger he'd already done that.

Since he *wasn't* going to be dating Lisette, there was no reason to put Else back in her marriage minded parents' sights.

"If you're considering dating other people, maybe you should." Holger sounded like there was more he wanted to say, but held back.

Tor could only be grateful. He hadn't talked about anything real with either of his brothers in so long, he wasn't sure he remembered how.

"I called because we need to handle this story," Tor told Holger.

"You never went out with her, even for coffee?" his brother asked.

Tor stifled a sound of impatience. His brother didn't know him anymore, so he had felt compelled to ask.

"No. We're in a couple of the same classes." Which he now realized she had probably engineered. "Have attended some of the same group study sessions, but *nothing* else. I know how things can get misconstrued by the media."

"There must be some reason she thinks she can get away with making these claims." His brother's tone was not exactly accusing, but it wasn't perfectly neutral either.

Tor stifled his anger at his brother's assertion. If Holger had said he didn't go out with a woman, Tor would have believed him.

Full stop. Period. No clarification needed.

"I don't think she cares if she gets away with it entirely," Tor informed his brother. "Once the story is out there, she achieves the celebrity she craves. She wants status, to be *famous*."

And maybe a book deal. At least that's what he'd overheard her saying.

Blythe was looking worriedly at him and somehow Tor found her regard comforting. She wasn't looking at him like she thought he'd done something to bring this on like his brother was implying.

Blythe looked like she was worried about Tor.

Even if that was wishful thinking on his part, he'd take it.

"I'll get our PR and legal team on this immediately. We'll get her to sign a gag order, even if we have to pay for it," Holger said decisively. "Do you want a restraining order?"

Tor considered and liked the message that would send, to Lisette, to the media and to any other women thinking to capitalize on their vicinity to a prince. "Yes."

"We'll keep this quiet, but I need you to put any plans for dating someone besides Else on hold for a few months. We are in some delicate diplomatic negotiations right now."

Considering Holger was the one who had just told Tor he *should* date other people than Else if he wanted to, the request was annoying. However, not surprising. Once again, Tor's wellbeing, or what his brother considered that to be, was expected to take second place to duty.

Since Tor had no intention of dating anyone, he agreed easily though. "No problem."

"You deserve to be happy, Tor."

Right. As long as that happiness didn't impinge on what was best for the royal family as a whole, or Tapt Oyer.

Tor knew the drill by now.

He said none of that, simply reminding his brother, "You don't have to worry about me."

"I do though. You're my little brother."

"Not little anymore." And years on from needing his sovereign sibling to play the fatherly role, or even *big brother* role in his life.

They talked for only a few seconds more before Holger rang off.

Chapter Seven

"Why do you push him away like that?" Blythe asked before Tor got a chance to say anything to her, or even wonder how she'd taken what she'd overheard.

Tor frowned. "I don't push him away."

"I think you do."

"You are entitled to your opinion." Which he had come to realize she would give, whether asked for it, or not.

"You just don't share it." Blythe looked at him like she was trying to figure Tor out. "Why did you decide not to date Lisette?"

"You really don't get the boundary between friendship and friend of the family, do you?" he asked, presently more amused than annoyed by that fact.

Right now, he appreciated Blythe's nosiness and concern for his whole family too much to take issue with it, even in his own head.

"I think I bought the right to ask a few questions by coming to you first."

"You might be right," Tor acknowledged. "I overheard her talking to a friend." He'd gotten an earful and another lesson in trust.

Blythe made a continuing motion with her hand. "Go on."

He rolled his eyes at her. "You really are inquisitive."

"Tell me something I don't know, like what Lisette said that turned you off her," Blythe pressed, her blue eyes filled with curiosity.

"She'd mapped out our relationship before it even happened. The *scandalous* beginning while I'm still *with* Else, the tumultuous but short liaison, followed by selling her story to the highest bidder, her social media blowing up and making her an *it* girl and maybe even a book deal." If his tone was just a tad bitter while he sarcastically listed off Lisette's plans, Tor wasn't sorry for it.

He'd almost fallen for the act, believing Lisette hadn't known who he was when they ran into each other that first class.

The shy glances. The subtle flirting.

All of it.

And he'd been attracted to her, when no one else but Blythe had attracted him since meeting the Travel Vlogger.

"That's really disgusting," Blythe said with a moue of distaste.

"You think? I have always been, and will always be, a target. Letting myself forget that for even a little while was dangerous. Not to mention stupid." He would not repeat that mistake, however.

"You should be able to trust that people are in your life for the reason they say they are." There was a wealth of feeling in Blythe's voice Tor did not think was all for him.

"You make your living behind the camera," he reminded her, refusing to believe her world was any less cutthroat, in its own way. "You know that's not true."

Blythe sighed. "Yes, but it's different when I hear about something like this. She *targeted* you."

"And my family through me, yes I know." If Blythe hadn't caught wind of Lisette's plans, the schemer would have succeeded in her plans to gain fame via involving his family in a scandal that could have hurt them all.

"You can't be feeling guilty." Blythe surged up from her chair and then stood there like she wasn't sure what she wanted to do. "You did nothing wrong."

"Stupid. Wrong. What's the difference?"

"You weren't stupid either," she insisted passionately. "You were trusting."

"*Were* being the operative word."

Blythe reached out and touched his arm. "I'm sorry."

Predictably, Tor's body responded to that slight touch way out of proportion. It was all he could do not to growl with impatience at his own folly.

"Why?" he asked her. "You didn't do anything. Though I'm still a little confused as to why you told me about Lisette's plans before telling Janne, or my brother."

Blythe looked like she didn't understand the need for the question. "It was about you, you had a right to know."

"Sure, but *first*? I thought you didn't want to see me again."

"I never said that." She huffed out a breath. "I see you plenty, when I'm visiting the palace the same time you are."

"That's not what I meant."

"I know." She walked to the other side of the room and looked down at the book he'd been studying when she knocked. "Looks complicated."

He shrugged. Economic theory was pretty straight forward if you understood the parameters. "Not really."

She made a sound of disbelief. "Somehow I doubt that."

"Have you had dinner?" he asked her.

"No."

"Would you like to order something in?" He wasn't in the mood to go out and being seen in a woman's company wasn't smart right now.

Even his sister-in-law's best friend.

"I'm not sure that's a good idea."

"It's just dinner."

"Is it?"

He gave her a wry look. "Not everything is a big drama."

"I don't know," she said, sounding unconvinced. "I've spent enough time around your family to suspect it is when it comes to the House of Asgersen."

Her words startled a laugh out of him. "You could be right. I thought we were a boring family, but ever since Janne married Holger things have been pretty damn interesting. And to think everyone believed she would make such a perfect Crown Princess because of her quiet and laid-back manner."

Blythe laughed. "Janice has never hesitated to stand up for herself. It's why I was so startled when she agreed to marry your brother."

"It was expected of her."

"Yes, but she'd spent most of her life in America, not Tapt Oyer."

"Nevertheless, she is a member of the nobility. She was raised to put duty above personal happiness from birth."

"Were you?" Blythe's beautiful blue gaze searched his.

He shrugged. "Can you doubt it? I am a prince, my sense of duty is written into my DNA, I am sure."

Blythe abruptly moved back to her chair by the fireplace and sat down. "Yes. Dinner. Let's get some. I want pasta."

He wondered what had changed her mind, but didn't ask. He was curiously loathe to eat a solitary dinner, so he was simply glad she'd agreed to stay.

Tor pulled up his delivery app and found his favorite Italian restaurant. He handed her the phone. "Order what you want."

Her fingers brushed his as she took the device. Both inhaled sharply at the contact.

Neither spoke.

She tapped a few times on the phone and held it back to him. Tor made his order and then sent off a quick text to his security detail, letting them know food was arriving for him at their place.

It was just another security protocol he did by rote.

"We need to talk," Blythe said after he put his phone away.

"No, we don't."

"Could you sound more like a guy right now?" she asked with a wry smile.

"Newsflash, I *am* a man."

She rolled her eyes at him. "Talking about feelings is not an ancient form of torture."

"Says you." He was pretty sure sitting through another rendition of the *this is what's wrong with you and I'm not interested* speech would be tortuous.

"Look, Janice isn't just my best friend. She's the only family that matters to me."

"Harsh." Considering both Blythe's parents were still living.

"The truth often is." She looked at him, like she was trying to decide something and then she nodded to herself. "I'm going to tell you something I've only ever shared with her."

"Okay." He had to wonder why she would, but didn't ask because Tor was curious and didn't want Blythe changing her mind about telling him.

And Blythe had to know that any confidences she shared were safe with a prince who'd been raised to *never* gossip.

"My parents only had me to fulfill a requirement for my father getting his full inheritance." Blythe said the words like she was admitting a shameful secret.

If it was one, it certainly wasn't *her* shame. "I've heard of codicils like that, but it still surprised me they exist in this day and age." Especially outside of royal families where lineage and the future monarchy were not at stake.

"Yes, well, apparently my grandfather was a very old-fashioned sort of man."

"Apparently? You never met him?"

"He died when my father was still a child. My grandmother has never taken any interest in me, or her own son for that matter, so long as she gets her annual income from the company." Blythe's soft voice was flat, unemotional, but the expression in her chocolate gaze told another story. This part of her history hurt her. "I guess it came naturally to my father. I'm not sure how my mother came by her attitude toward her only child. Her parents were loving, if a bit reserved."

"Were?"

"They died when I was young. I remember them only in bits and pieces."

His own grandparents had been gone before Tor was born and his father had been an only child. His mother's only brother had left Tapt Oyer for university long before Tor's birth and had never returned to the island country.

So, Tor knew what it was like to grow up without any sort of close extended family.

"I used to be jealous of big families," Tor admitted.

Blythe smiled wryly. "I can still be jealous of families where the parents care about their children, but mostly I'm happy for them." She sighed. "Once my parents had me and control of my father's fortune, the only thing that mattered to them was the appearance of the perfect family."

"What does that mean, Blythe?"

"They didn't love me, they provided for me," she said baldly. "Both were wrapped up in their own careers and interests. Their relationship is a distant one, with little demands on either side toward the other. Which is probably the only way it could work for two purely selfish people."

"That's a pretty severe indictment." Though from her description, a fairly accurate one.

"You might think so."

"Not really, from what you've said so far."

She looked at him. "You don't think I'm terrible?"

"For looking at your parents with truth? No. You know them better than probably anyone else. If, as their child, you believe they are selfish, the probably are."

She nodded. "Not that everyone else would agree with you. It's so easy to dismiss a child's opinions. The grandparents I knew got very upset with me when I asked things like *Why don't mommy and daddy love me?* They had a very rosy view of their daughter, my mom. I'm glad in some ways they passed before the final proof came that would have changed even their minds."

"What happened?"

"I got leukemia when I was eight." Blythe sounded so prosaic saying those devasting words. "My nanny at the time insisted I see the doctor because of my lethargy and the *flu* that just never went away. I was always getting bruises."

Tor felt like all the air had been sucked out of the room.

Cancer could kill. It had killed his mother.

And that list of symptoms? Sounded way too familiar. Even though he'd been a small child when his mother was sick, Tor remembered how tired she'd always been, how her arms and legs were always marred with purple bruises from the slightest bumps.

He snared Blythe's sapphire gaze with his own. "You had cancer?"

"Yes." The confirmation was too matter of fact for what she was agreeing to.

Was Blythe in remission? She had to be. What was her long term prognosis? "Will it come back?"

She shook her head, silky brown waves swaying over her shoulders. "I've been cancer free since I was nine." She smiled then. "I beat it," she said with a very present sense of victory for that long ago crisis. "They consider you cured if you go ten years in remission. It has been eighteen years."

Relief washed through him, but he did not let it show. It was an out of proportion reaction to news from a family friend that her health was good.

"Do you blame your parents for not noticing you needed to go to the doctor?" he asked.

"No, of course not," she denied, looking at him like he'd lost his mind. "It's not a matter of blaming them for anything, but accepting the truth of our relationship."

"Which is?"

"We don't have one. I do not and have never mattered to them as a human being."

"That...I..." For once, he wasn't sure what to say.

"I was in and out of the hospital for nearly a year. Radiation and chemotherapy are hard. They hurt. They leave you feeling sick all the time. I was a child. I needed comfort."

"And they didn't comfort you?" He could not fathom that level of unconcern in a parent.

His father might have abdicated his role, but if Tor had ever been seriously ill, he knew the former king would have cared. He would have shown up at the hospital at the very least, but Tor still had enough memories of being tucked into bed by his father before he was eight to know that the man knew how to give comfort.

Just not when they'd both been grieving the loss of the same person.

"I barely saw them the entire time," Blythe said, like it was someone else's memory. Not a painful personal one. "They did not visit the hospital. They did not comfort me at night when I cried myself to sleep from the pain. They quite literally did not care whether I lived or died."

How could anyone not care whether this amazing woman lived, or died? Especially as a child. "No."

"Yes. I needed marrow stem cell replacement therapy. Both refused to even be tested for a match. Luckily for me, against the odds, there was a donor match in the database."

"They refused to be tested?" he asked with disbelief.

"Categorically."

He said an ugly word.

She nodded. "And in answer to whether or not they comforted me? No chance. They did not comfort me when I was terrified of the pain each new hospital visit would bring. Sure, my mom got a new charity to support to make her look good. My dad got the *sick kid at home* card when he didn't want to take a lateral transfer that meant moving to a smaller town."

"And you got the pain and the fear." He had the weirdest completely nonsexual urge to pull her into his arms.

"I had my nannies." Blythe shrugged, like this horror story wasn't any big deal. "Friends from school who supported me when and how they could, but until I met Janice, I never had someone in my life who would sacrifice their own comfort for my own."

Their food arrived, interrupting Blythe's story, but Tor was hooked.

So, after they dished up and sat down at his small, dinging table...so much cozier than even the family dining table in the palace...he wanted to hear more.

"How did Janne prove she would put your first?" Because he was sure his sister-in-law had done that in some big way for Blythe to be so loyal and protective of the relationship.

"We hit it off right away." Blythe smiled with some memory that clearly made her happy. "We both loved the same kinds of movies, were quiet studiers, not interested in the college parties every weekend."

"Sounds like a good fit for roommates."

"I got the flu our first semester in the dorm together. Because of my past, the flu was never just the flu for me. I was always afraid it was me coming out of remission."

"But this time it was just the flu?"

"Yes, only I didn't know at first. I was crying and Janice found me. She got me to tell her about having leukemia all the while fussing around me, making sure I was warm enough, that I had something to drink. Not only did she take care of me, without a single care for whether or not she came down with my flu, but she made me go to the doctor to make sure it wasn't cancer again and insisted on going with me, so I wasn't alone."

"And that felt good to you." He understood, if on a very different level.

As a young boy, Tor had craved Holger's questions about how school was going, if he'd taken his vitamins...the things that let a child know someone cared about them.

Blythe had never had that, until she was technically an adult and Janne came into her life.

"She's nurturing," he said, musingly.

"She is, and Janice always took care of me when I got sick." Blythe's smile was self-deprecating. "I guess I've got a weakness for that."

"She took me home to her mom and Lady Solomia loved on me like a second daughter."

Tor understood. "In every way that matters, Janne is your family."

"Exactly."

Blythe still looked so damned vulnerable, that Tor gave into his strange non-sexual urge to hug her, pulling her to her feet and into his arms.

Even odder, she let him.

He held her for several long seconds, neither speaking. She sighed, melting into him like she needed to be right where she was.

"She's not going anywhere," Tor promised. "And now, you are a part of our family too. You understand that, right?"

She laughed. "As if."

He pulled back and stared down at her, catching her gaze with his own. "Not as if. Did you see anyone *but* family there Christmas morning?"

"No, but it's not like Geir has any friends, much less a best one."

"That's not true." But Tor couldn't help smiling at her certainty.

He didn't think Blythe had ever forgiven Geir for not appreciating her best friend for the amazing person Janne was when Holger had set his sights on the now Crown Princess.

"Well, maybe he has friends." Blythe sighed and moved as if to step back.

His arms tightened around her of their own volition. "Stay."

She stared up at him. "This is dangerous."

"What?" He rubbed his hand up and down her back, so damn tempted to caress her perfect bottom. "Us being close?"

"Yes."

"You say dangerous. I say good." Too damn good to give up.

"Tor."

"Blythe."

Her lips parted, no words coming out.

The desire that was always there when she was around intensified to something he could not ignore. "I want to kiss you."

"I want..." she let her words trail off.

"Say *yes*."

<h1 style="text-align:center">CHAPTER EIGHT</h1>

Blythe licked her lips, so clearly wanting it. The question was: did she want it enough to overcome her reservations?

"I shouldn't."

"If I promise you won't lose Janne?"

"You can't promise that."

But he could. Even if they had the ugliest breakup in the history of breakups, Janne wasn't going to dissolve her friendship with Blythe. They were sisters.

It was time Blythe really started believing that.

"Nothing you and I do will impact your status with Janne."

"Says you."

"Would you reject her if she hurt someone you cared about?" he asked.

"I'd trust her to not have done it on purpose," Blythe answered without taking time to think.

"Don't you think she trusts and relies on you just as strongly?"

"Maybe."

"Anyway, this between us? It's just sex." It couldn't be anything else when Blythe didn't even know who he was.

She jolted, like his words had shocked her. "What?"

"I think the term is *friends with benefits*." Maybe that sounded better.

Else was always telling Tor he was too blunt and that he only got away with it because of his charm.

"Is that what you and Else have?" Blythe demanded, sounding annoyed.

"Else and I have never had sex."

"But..."

"Come on, Blythe. You were there when she told you we don't have any chemistry."

"But you told your family."

"Nothing that wasn't true. They drew their own conclusions." And he was pretty sure Geir still didn't believe Tor and Else were dating.

He didn't really know what Holger believed.

Their father clearly bought the idea.

"You realize that isn't fair to them?"

"In what way?"

"They're expecting you to marry her someday. Can't you see they'll be hurt when they realized you deceived them?"

"No. I do not see that."

"You are being deliberately obtuse."

"Do not speak to me like I am a recalcitrant child. I am a man." And he wanted her to see him as such.

Not a *boy*. He might be younger than her, but Tor was no boy.

She all but rolled her eyes at him. "Of that I am fully aware."

"Really? Then why question my choices like I'm a child?"

"This isn't about me seeing you as a child."

"Isn't it? You don't trust my judgment when it comes to my family."

"You're lying to them."

"I am not." Damn it, he was sick of having this conversation with her.

Tor grabbed his phone and dialed his brother's private line for the second time in an hour.

"Was there something you forgot, Tor?" Holger asked after the usual greeting.

"I am not, and have never been dating, Else."

"Oh. Well, that makes more sense. Janne said there was no way you were dating her, but well..."

"I led you and the rest of the family to certain conclusions."

"Yes. The question is why?"

"I wanted to get Else's parents off her back."

"So, I assume you don't want me sharing this confidence with our father."

"I would appreciate your discretion."

"Why did you feel the need to tell me now?"

"Someone thinks it would hurt you if I don't."

"Else. She's got a tender heart, but she needn't have worried. You've got plenty of time to settle down."

Tor didn't correct his brother on the name of the woman who had prompted the phone call.

He said goodbye to his brother and then looked with challenge at Blythe. "Happy now?"

"I..."

When she didn't continue, he said, "Holger said it didn't matter. I was right. He also agreed not to tell my father."

"He did?" Blythe sounded confused.

"I guarantee you Holger would not agree to maintain the subterfuge if he believed that our father not knowing the truth would hurt him."

"Are you sure about that?"

"Positive."

CHAPTER NINE

Blythe looked so lost.

Tor sighed. "Listen, Blythe, my family isn't perfect. My father can be ruthless when it comes to *encouraging* his sons down the path he wants them to take. He's not the warm-fuzzy father you seem to think he is."

"He cares about all of you. I've seen it."

"Really?" On what did she base such a rose-colored conclusion?

"Yes. He takes an interest in his children's lives." Blythe was so sincere in her belief.

Part of Tor did not want to burst her bubble of belief, but a bigger part needed her to understand that his relationship with his family was not what she so obviously thought it was.

He didn't know why that was important to him, but it was. "My mother died when I was eight."

"I know. I'm sorry," Blythe said, her tone ringing with sincerity.

"I lost my dad the same day."

"What? No. That's not true."

Even after what he'd told her at the wedding, when they were dancing, Blythe maintained this stalwart belief that Tor's father was also his *dad*. That it was true at one time, he would not deny, but it hadn't been true since his mother's death.

"Yes. It is. He stopped spending time with me, Blythe. Completely. The only time I saw him was during the meals he managed to show up for, and those were not usually family only. I don't think he stopped caring, but it felt like he did."

He used to think differently, sure his father had stopped loving him at all, but as Tor grew older he realized that Prince Canute had dealt with his own loss and grief in a way that didn't leave him available for his youngest son.

Tor didn't know if it was because he had been his mom's favorite, or if the questions and needs of a younger child were just too hard to deal with. Whatever the difference, their father had not cut himself off as completely from Tor's older brothers.

"That...I don't understand."

"I was a child and I didn't have a mom or a dad anymore," Tor spelled out for her.

"That's when Holger stepped in," she said, but then her brows furrowed. "You said your dad changed after the heart attack."

"No, *you* said he did and I didn't correct you."

"He didn't?" she asked, her expression concerned.

He didn't need her concern, or her pity. He just wanted her to stop feeding him a rose-colored view of his own life that was nothing like the truth.

"No. Holger was still the one who had to approve my choice of university and my major." And anything else to do with Tor's studies, or life.

"You said he pulled away when he became king."

"Naturally. He had concerns of much heavier import. I wasn't his responsibility. After all, he's not my father."

"But your father—"

"Wasn't interested in the role either." Prince Canute had thrown his time and energy into improving his own health and the duties that he had maintained on the diplomatic and business front as a past sovereign.

He didn't put the time into work he once had to preserve his own life, but that didn't mean he put it into his family either.

"Your family loves you." She said it like it was something she *had* to believe.

He had no desire to make her think otherwise. Only to stop assuming that love played out like the fantasy in her head. "And I love them."

"It doesn't sound like it."

"Doesn't it? Do you think love only looks one way?"

"I thought you were all so close."

Tor shrugged. What could he say? The first time he'd spoken to Holger since Christmas was tonight on the phone. Tor had met Geir for dinner once when his brother was in the States on business. That Geir had made the detour from New York, to Boston had meant a lot, even if their talk over dinner hadn't approached anything personal.

Tor hadn't spoken to his father at all.

That could be as much his choice now, as it had been his father's in the past. Tor did not reach out to the ex-monarch and only replied to communications from him that asked a specific question.

"We're not estranged by any stretch," he assured Blythe.

"But you don't think they care if they hear from you, or not."

She was right. He *didn't* think his family would be really bothered if they only saw him on the odd holiday. That didn't mean he thought they didn't love him, or that he in turn did not care about them.

"We have more in common than I thought we did," she said softly.

She was comparing his relationship with his family with hers to her parents. They were very different, but if he pointed out how, he would only hurt her.

So, he said nothing.

"Only I think if you were sick, your family would be lining up to get tested to see if they could be your donors."

He agreed. "As I would for them."

"So, not quite the same."

No, not the same. "I am sorry." He really was.

"That my parents are so disconnected from me? I got over that a long time ago."

If that were true, she wouldn't be so afraid of losing Janne.

Tor stepped back into Blythe's personal space. "You're so beautiful."

"I'm not."

"Agree to disagree."

"I'm no model."

He cupped her shoulders, pulling her almost close enough to touch. "Did you want to be?"

"Did I what?" Her eyes had gone unfocused.

"Want to be a model?"

"No," she said a little breathlessly, her gaze stuck on his mouth. "I like what I do."

Travelling and sharing her experiences with others. It worked for her.

"I like what you do, too." He leaned down so his lips were just a breath from her. "May I kiss you, Blythe?"

"Yes." Her head bobbed up and down like she needed him to know she meant her affirmative.

Tor didn't wait any longer, pressing his mouth to hers at the same time he tugged her body into full contact with his.

Sexual need surged through him, the kiss going from soft and careful to passionate in a single heartbeat.

He teased against the seam of her lips, wanting entrance, which she gave. But she didn't remain passive. Blythe kissed him every bit as enthusiastically as he kissed her.

Her hands were all over his body, caressing him with fevered movements. She cupped his growing erection, making a feminine sound of approval.

His hips jerked forward, seeking more of that touch.

With no worry about being interrupted, he began undressing her, needing to feel her naked skin under his fingertips.

Finally.

Blythe didn't object and started tugging his shirt up his body. He stopped kissing her long enough to yank it off over his head.

She shrugged out of her own top, revealing her rounded curves held in by a bit of sexy lace.

Without thought, he reached out to cup her breasts in both his hands. Soft and heavy in his hands, they were beautiful with pretty pink tips.

Lust surged through him at having permission to touch.

Watching with an undeniable fascination as they beaded and darkened with a rush of blood, he brushed his thumbs back and forth over the hardened peaks.

Reveling in her instant and unmistakable reaction to him, Tor's own excitement shot into the stratosphere.

Blythe moaned, letting her head fall back. "So good, Tor."

He smiled at the sound of his name on her lips.

He gently pinched those hardened nubs. She gasped. He did it again and again, sometime with a soft brush in between, sometimes with immediate gentle pressure and release one right after the other.

His beautiful brunette almost lover began to pant.

Reaching behind her to unlatch her bra, he fumbled on the small hooks.

"Here let me," she said, reaching behind her own back and undoing the clasp with a quick movement.

Heat that was not sexual desire crawled up his neck.

She noticed. Of course she did, but her smile was warm and sexy. "If you want the truth, Tor, I'm kind of glad to know you're not so experienced this is all blasé for you."

He said nothing, not about to admit that he was technically still a virgin. Call him arrogant, but he wasn't worried at all about being able to satisfy her. And while he'd never had penetrative sex, he'd had plenty of sexual experience.

But this woman and his reaction to her turned him into a novice.

Blythe reached out and pulled his hands back to press against her breasts again.

They both shuddered when his hands pressed against the now naked flesh, silkier than the lace bra she'd worn.

"You feel amazing." As he'd known she would.

"You do too," she said, her hands coming up to knead the muscles of his chest. She ran her fingers through his chest hair. "I like this."

From how preoccupied she seemed by it, he thought *like* might be a tad understatement. "I'm glad."

"You're very sexy, Tor."

"So are you." So sexy, he was in danger of coming like he had the last time they'd kissed, without even getting his trousers off.

Not going to happen.

Tor stepped back. "No more clothes."

She nodded, reaching to undo his fly without hesitation. He almost laughed. He'd meant they should both finish undressing, but Blythe had other ideas.

He decided he liked her plan and found the side zip of her fitted slacks. He had better luck with the hook and eye at the top than he had with her bra, then he slid the zip down, before pushing the grey fabric down her hips.

She stepped out of her heels and then her slacks, standing there in nothing but a tiny lacy thong, her generous curves on mouthwatering display.

He swallowed, his throat gone dry. "You are gorgeous."

"You're not so bad yourself." She was looking at his now naked, straining erection.

He would have laughed if just that look didn't have him even closer to coming.

Done with teasing and waiting, he swept her up into his arms, intending to carry her into the bedroom.

Her laughter was all warm sensuality. "In a hurry, Your Highness?"

In that tone? With that look, *Your Highness* turned from a formal address into something sexy and endearing.

"Aren't you?" he teased right back.

He could smell her arousal, see the proof of her desire in her beaded nipples, flushed skin, panting breaths.

"Oh, yes," she said throatily.

He made his way with more speed than finesse to the bedroom. He set her on her feet, then yanked the comforter and sheet to the bottom of the bed.

Without a second's hesitation, Blythe climbed onto the bed, shoving the pillows so two were in the middle and then settling back on them.

Looking up at him with pure provocation she shifted, her legs falling apart. "Come on, Tor."

He took a necessary breath before joining her on the mattress.

He wanted inside her so badly, he ached, but Tor wanted to touch her even more. So that was what he did, learning every silky inch of her skin, watching closely for what turned up her desire and what didn't seem to impact it as much.

He brushed over the pretty curls at the apex of her thighs, loving how she moaned and writhed.

"Feel good?" he asked.

She moved her hips, seeking more of his touch. "You know it does."

He caressed and then tasted every bit of skin he'd dreamt of since meeting this woman.

"I need, Tor! Please!"

He couldn't make his voice work, but he reached for the condoms in his bedside table, wanting to cheer when he got one on the first try.

In that moment, he sent mental thanks to his brother Geir for that embarrassing talk when he was an adolescent about using condoms to masturbate for easy and tidy cleanup. He'd never been without them in his bedside table since.

Then Tor was between Blythe's thighs, the thin barrier of the condom in no way diminishing the sensation of his erection kissing her most intimate flesh.

"Ready?" he gritted out, poised to join his body with a woman for the first time.

She grabbed his hips, pulling forward. "More than."

He took that for the challenge it was and pushed forward, sheathing himself in her tight, wet heat.

He said a particularly dirty curse in Norwegian. Words he would never say in public.

But this feeling? Her slick, silky heat surrounding him. It was so damn good.

Like she'd been made just for him.

Chapter Ten

"Tor." Her voice sounded like he felt.

Awed.

He pulled back and then pressed forward, glorying in every agonizing centimeter of slow movement when all he wanted was to piston his hips. "You fit me perfectly."

"You're big," she said, her voice strained.

He stopped, suddenly unsure she was enjoying this as much as he was. "Am I hurting you?"

"No!" She pushed up with her hips, taking more of him inside her. "Don't you dare stop. It's so good."

No matter how much he wanted to just thrust inside her, he could not dismiss her words. He was big. He needed to take it slow.

She was swearing at him and demanding he move by the time he rocked himself fully inside her again.

He liked it. Liked knowing he could turn her on so much that she lost her control.

He reached down to rub her clitoris.

Blythe screamed and arched upward off the bed, her climax taking her over and shocking Tor with its suddenness. He kept touching her, letting go of some of his control to pound into her.

She writhed under, another orgasm taking her over as he found his own release.

His shout shocked him as much her scream. He hadn't expected to lose himself so completely in that moment.

As their orgasms and the aftershocks faded, he wanted to just collapse down but was smart enough to know that wouldn't be cool.

Holding onto the condom, he reluctantly pulled out. "I need to take care of this."

No matter how much he would rather remain where he was, but as a prince, his sex education had included very strict instructions about birth control.

Blythe nodded, her eyes closed, her body lax.

He pulled the sheet and comforter up from the bottom of the bed to cover her before he went to the en suite to take care of what he needed to.

When got back into his bedroom, Blythe was sitting up in the bed, her expression not exactly relaxed with replete pleasure.

In fact, he'd go as far as to say she looked pretty agitated.

Picking at the comforter, her gaze set somewhere over Tor's shoulder, she said, "This can't happen again."

He did not agree. "Oh, it will happen again," he promised her.

It had been way too amazing never to experience again. Even again tonight.

His semi-erection wouldn't take much to become full on hard.

"It can't." She still wasn't looking at him.

Good thing, or she'd see how turned on he still was. For the first time, it struck Tor how vulnerable men were. That's not the way society painted the picture of sex between a man and a woman, but he had no hope of hiding his reaction to her.

He shook his head. "You really think that with how good it is between us, we're going to be able to keep our hands off each other?"

"If we try hard enough." She bit her lip, like she wasn't convinced by her own words.

"But why should we?" he asked. "Friends with benefits, right? We aren't starting the love affair of the century. Nothing to risk your relationship with Janne."

That had Blythe looking at him, her eyes widened when she noticed his growing erection.

"But..." She paused and then she fisted her hands on top of the comforter. "I don't like hiding things from her."

"So, you tell her every time you hook up?" He didn't believe it.

"No, of course not."

"Then, what is the problem?"

"This is a little more than a hookup."

He was glad she thought so. "We're friends too." Or they would be. He thought their talking tonight had definitely put them both more firmly in the friend than acquaintance category. "You don't have to hide that from her. That we're adding sex to the mix is no one's business but ours."

"So, you think friends with benefits could work for us?" Blythe asked, sounding hopeful.

"What else? You're not interested in a relationship with me." She'd made that clear enough.

"It's not that I'm not interested in you. We're just...too different."

"And it's not worth you risking anything, I got the message."

"You don't sound bitter."

"What would be the point?" He'd learned a long time ago not to rely on others emotionally.

The only one who had never let him down was Else. His life would be so much simpler if he could be as attracted to his childhood friend as he was to the woman in his bed.

But he understood friendships feeling like family because Else was like his sister and always would be.

"Okay." Blythe swallowed and then added, "But we need to be discreet."

"Not least of which because right now I cannot afford to be seen with a woman other than Else," he agreed.

Even once the Palace's PR team got Lisette's fake tell all story squashed, the rumor would be out there and if Tor was seen dating someone else, gossip would lead to scandal and embarrassment for the Royal House. Something Tor had never brought onto them and never planned to.

"That too," Blythe said with a nod. "But I don't want Janne finding out. She'll think we have something more than sex between us. No matter what I tell her."

And Blythe wasn't risking her best friend's opinion of her. Not for him. Not even for mind blowing sex.

Tor ignored the strange twinge in his chest that thought elicited.

She shifted restlessly. "I supposed I should get going. Spending the night would be too risky."

He agreed, but that didn't mean he was ready for her to go right that minute. "I don't know about you, but I'm not nearly done."

With that he returned to the bed and had fully penetrative sex for the second time in his life.

Unbelievably, it was better than the first time.

Tor's family was growing.

He watched his first nephew's baptism into the Lutheran Church, the official religious affiliation for the Royal House, smiling when the baby didn't even wake as the trickle of water was poured over his tiny head. A symbolic crowning would happen for the heir to the throne following the christening.

Prince Bjorn would have another adjacent ceremony when he turned twenty-one and became the Crown Prince, Heir Apparent, where he would actually wear the crown and hold the scepter of office.

Looking at the way Tor's father stood so close to Lady Ingrid in the church, Tor thought the House of Asgersen would expand by one more soon.

Blythe stood beside Janne in the family section, though that was certainly not protocol. The press had gotten used to seeing the Travel Vlogger with his sister-in-law and often referred to her as *a friend as close as a sister*.

Else was Tor's own *good friend* as far as the press were concerned. Every few weeks an article would come out speculating about when they were going to make things official.

The answer was never, but that wasn't an answer he'd be sharing anytime soon.

He caught Blythe's gaze and felt his insides heat.

By her decree, their friends-with-benefits arrangement never enjoyed those benefits when they were both at the palace.

She made the train trip from New York to Boston every few weeks and stayed the weekend in his apartment. They never went out. She never invited him up to New York, or to meet her on her travels. Discreetly, or otherwise.

Tor allowed the limits to their relationship because they worked for him too. His supposed interest in Else continued to protect her from family pressure and censure. Tor didn't want a bunch of speculation about him and Blythe either.

One day, their relationship, such that it was, would end. He had no desire to be the butt of jokes or speculation in the media about why she walked away from the prince.

And walk away, she would. Her attitude had not shifted about not wanting anything permanent or public with him. Though their friendship had grown into something deeper than he expected.

Tor wasn't interested in a lifetime commitment either. Not right now.

Tor was waiting for the sex to lose its appeal, but it didn't.

Physical intimacy with Blythe never got old, or stale. Tor craved her more, not less, as time went on.

She responded to him like her body had been created for his touch.

Else thought he *and* Blythe were both living in denial of what was between them, but that was because his friend had a romantic imagination.

With her tender heart that believed in fairytales, Tor worried for Else. Her parents were social climbing pragmatists with a sexist view of the world that would not allow them to see Else as her father's natural heir, despite how smart and business minded she was.

If Else was hoping to live out her romantic fantasies vicariously through him and Blythe, she was destined to be disappointed, however.

Watching the family's response to Janice's pregnancy and Bjorn's birth had cemented in Blythe's mind the truth that she and Tor had no future.

Even if he were interested in one, and ready to settle down with one woman, Blythe could not be that woman.

Her childhood cancer had not only revealed how little her parents cared if she lived, or died, but remission had come at a cost. Both the radiation treatment and the marrow cell replacement had taken a permanent toll on her body.

Blythe would never have biological children.

She had known it was possible side effect, but until she'd gone through puberty, the doctors couldn't know for sure. Having no need for a definitive answer, Blythe had never had the tests done, though her monthlies had always been irregular and very light.

As her feelings for Tor had grown though, she'd begun to wonder if maybe, just maybe, she'd been one of the lucky ones.

So, unbeknownst to anyone else, even Janice, Blythe had gone in for the battery of invasive and sometimes difficult fertility tests.

The results had not been what she'd been secretly hoping for.

Blythe's ovaries did not produce viable eggs and the lining of her uterus had been affected by the radiation. It was unlikely that even artificial insemination with a viable egg would result in a lasting pregnancy for Blythe.

If Blythe *were* the kind of woman who would excel at being royal, which she was pretty sure she was not, she and Tor could never have more than what they had right now.

Friendship with benefits.

She could never give him the children a prince was expected to have.

Feeling vulnerable and a lot sadder than she wanted to admit to herself, Blythe decided to seek out the person she knew could dispel those emotions.

Not her sister of the heart, Janice, but the man Blythe craved as much on an emotional level as a physical one now. Tor.

Blythe sent a quick text.

What are you doing?

Nothing important. Came back in seconds.

For Tor, that could mean he was studying for an exam, or working on his family's blog post for the week. She'd learned that she'd been dead wrong about him holding down a job. That his role as prince was in fact very demanding and that Tor took all his responsibilities seriously.

He never let anyone down, but he also had a tendency to downplay how hard he worked.

??? Came from Tor, interrupting her woolgathering.

Feel like visiting? She texted euphemistically. *Visiting* was their code for sex.

He was too vulnerable to scandal for them to get intimate with texts or emails. That wasn't to say they couldn't burn up the sheets with phone sex when they couldn't get together in person.

It was in fact, how they'd handled their time *apart* when they were together at the palace.

Even knowing that Tor always felt like sex, she waited with bated breath for his answer.

She'd been the one to put the moratorium on sex in the palace, where there was risk of being discovered by his family, but maybe he'd come to like having that boundary.

His lack of answer was starting to make her wish she'd never sent the text in the first place when a knock sounded on her door.

Blythe yanked it open and was being kissed within an inch of her life against it seconds later.

CHAPTER ELEVEN

Tor kissed Blythe like he was starving for sexual release.

Not like they'd just gotten together the night before.

They'd flown to Tapt Oyer together on the palace jet, which had been her excuse for meeting him in Boston.

His hands were everywhere, divesting Blythe of her clothes, touching her, ratcheting up her own desire to a fever pitch.

Never a very passive lover, Blythe returned the caresses and help undressing.

But when Tor started playing with her breasts, particularly her nipples, she forgot what she was doing and just *felt*.

Before Tor, Blythe had never had a lover who worked so hard to capitalize on her sensitivity there. He was enthralled with her generous curves and could spend an hour, or more, focused on her breasts, licking and tugging on her nipples until she came from that stimulus alone.

Before Tor, she'd thought that kind of climax was a myth.

She knew it wasn't now, but she wasn't in the mood for prolonged play. Blythe didn't just want a physical connection, she *needed* it.

Sliding out from between him and the door she headed toward the bed, walking backward. "Come on, Tor. I want you."

"I always want you."

The words were a balm on her wounded soul.

They might not have forever, but they were together now because they wanted each other to the exclusion of all others.

Tor had managed to get her naked already, so Blythe yanked the silk covered duvet back and climbed onto the opulent four-poster bed.

Nothing understated about the palace décor.

For just a second, it hit Blythe how much her life had changed since her best friend married a king.

Then all her attention was snagged by the gorgeous man in front of her.

Tor wore only his slacks, the fly undone. His sculpted chest covered in silky dark hair that ran down his trim stomach like an arrow toward the erection bulging against his trousers.

"Like what you see, *min skatt?*" he asked.

He'd started calling her that a while ago and she'd looked it up, wondering what it meant. Literally translated it was, my gold, but she'd learned it was like being called his special treasure.

She only wished she could be that in his life in a very true sense, but knew she could not.

"You know I do," she told him in a sultry voice no one else ever heard from her.

Not past hook ups or boyfriends. No one.

He dug in his pocket and swore viciously.

"What is it?" she asked, sitting up.

He looked furious. "I forgot condoms."

He'd been so enthusiastic about joining her, he'd left his palace apartment without grabbing protection. That was a lot more flattering than annoying.

"I can't get pregnant." Blythe blurted out her painful truth, feeling a release in the telling, even though she knew he'd take it to mean she was on birth control.

He stilled, his expression going from angry frustration to something she could not read. "You don't want to use condoms anymore?"

"Have you been with anyone since we started this?" she asked, rather than answer his question directly.

He gave her another indecipherable look. "No."

"Me either." She swallowed, not wanting to acknowledge just how much she liked hearing he hadn't either. "I've been tested recently and everything came back good."

"I have no doubt. My annual physical was two weeks ago. I am clean."

Nice that he didn't assume because he was a prince he didn't have to say.

"As long as this arrangement is exclusive..." Blythe let her words trail off.

"We can go without condoms," he finished for her, his expression turning feral with want.

She shivered, her own desire spiking. "Yes."

Tor shoved his slacks and those sexy body-hugging boxers he wore down his hips before joining her on the bed, entirely naked.

From the way he acted, she'd expected a passionate, quick coupling.

But that's not what happened.

Tor started with the most amazing kiss, moving his lips over hers in leisurely pleasure until they were both panting with need. Only then did he begin touching her again, caressing her breasts, her tummy, the super sensitive spot on her inner thighs.

Blythe thrummed with pleasure, orgasm close but not urgent.

This was about more than reaching the pinnacle of pleasure. It was about the connection. The ability to touch and be touched without boundaries or barriers.

Quivering with an intensity of feeling she did not want to acknowledge, Blythe pushed insistently against Tor until he was lying on his back.

Then she set about exploring his body as he had done hers, reveling in every groan and masculine sound of pleasure.

"Damn it, Blythe. It is too good."

She smiled, ready to make it even better.

Blythe scooted down so she had access his to his hardened sex.

She never did this with other men because Blythe did not like the taste of latex. She'd never done it with Tor and he'd never asked for it.

So, his shocked gasp when she licked up his steel-like shaft, was to be expected.

His sex jumped against her mouth and she smiled. "Like that?" she teased and did it again.

He groaned and lifted his hips off the bed. "Yes!"

Blythe took him into her mouth, laving him with her tongue and sucking gently.

He liked it. A lot.

So much that she had to stop after only a few minutes because she wanted him inside her when they both came.

Sliding up his body, Blythe positioned herself so his turgid erection pressed against her core.

"Ready?" she asked breathlessly.

His grey gaze was almost too intense to meet. "Yes."

She nodded, and then she took a man inside her for the first time without protection.

Her body stretched to accommodate him, filling her with a familiar pleasure, intensified by the knowledge there was no barrier.

Once he was fully seated, she paused and looked at him, afraid this moment wouldn't be as profound to him as it was to her and equally afraid it would be.

He stared back, his grey eyes dark with unnamed emotion, his expression intent, none of his usual humor evident.

"This is pretty profound for friends with benefits," he said, his voice harsh and low as she began to move her hips.

"Don't." She didn't want to talk about anything real.

What they were doing was real enough.

"I can't get upgraded to lover now?" he asked, his tone giving nothing away of how he felt about that either way.

In just the time she'd known him, she'd seen changes in the prince. When they'd first met, he'd been Tor, prone to joking and smiles. Charming and relaxed.

Or so she'd thought.

Blythe had come to realize that other Tor was a façade for the intense man he really was.

Acknowledging to herself she might know him even better than his own family gave Blythe a thrill she'd never admit to out loud.

"If you were my lover, I'd have to tell Janice about us." And Blythe would have to admit her infertility to Tor.

While she felt no guilt about not sharing that truth with a friend, a lover, who could potentially become something more? Would be different.

Something shifted in Tor's eyes, but he said nothing.

He reached down between them to touch her clitoris, driving all thought from her mind.

Blythe set a pace with her hips to give them both maximum pleasure and allowed herself to be immersed in sensation.

They talked, as they always did during sex. But only about what was happening between them, what they liked, what they planned to do with and for the other.

She felt her climax building and warned him.

He touched her exactly as she needed and pleasure detonated from her core, exploding outward until her entire body jerked in convulsions of orgasm.

Tor grabbed her hips, thrusting his own upward and came inside her with a shout.

She felt the heat, the extra stickiness between them and collapsed down as aftershocks pulsed through her body.

He wrapped his arms around her, holding her close as they never got to do post orgasm.

No condom to take care of meant they got to relax and revel in the nearness.

It also meant they could do it again as soon as they were ready.

Which was embarrassingly quick, really.

The lack of protection between them seemed to increase both their libidos to the extent they got very little sleep and had Tor sneaking back to his room after their final shower together just before dawn.

Tor and Blythe were back to their façade of casual friendship the next day.

He didn't chafe at the restrictions because he was still coming to terms with having sex with Blythe without condoms. With the fact he had done so not in a fit of passion, but having chosen to with full forethought and knowledge of the potential consequences.

As a prince who took his responsibilities very seriously, especially the one not to get a woman pregnant outside of marriage, Tor had been certain he would never do that with any woman but the one he married.

Now he had had sex, not once, but many times in a single night, without using condoms. Out of this world sex. Profound sex.

Sex that felt like a hell of a lot more than just two bodies coming together physically.

But it had been with a casual lover.

Friends with exclusive, but *secret*, benefits.

Tor could not regret going without condoms, even though it had been drilled into him from his first sex education talk that he must use them with every partner until he married. That he could never leave the prospect of pregnancy up to chance or even to the birth control his partner might be using.

And yet, he'd done exactly that the night before. Repeatedly.

Blythe had said she couldn't get pregnant and he'd believed her.

Even though there was no single form of birth control that was 100% effective, he had made the call to go without condoms without a second thought.

For a woman who made it clear she could not be part of his future.

Not that he accepted that, but he had his own reasons for accepting the status quo between them for the present.

And he was honest enough to admit to himself that if they had no future, he was going to enjoy the hell out of the present.

Prince, or not, he was still a man.

And this man craved Blythe Whitney Jones, Travel Vlogger, like he had never craved anyone, or anything, else in his life.

So, no, he did not regret making a choice he'd been sure he never would.

Because while Blythe had no plans for their future, Tor did have them.

And those plans alleviated any sense of irresponsibility in choosing to have sex without a physical barrier between them for him.

CHAPTER TWELVE

"I thought I'd find you in here." His sister-in-law's voice interrupted Tor's weightlifting reps.

Seeking privacy and a good workout, he'd come to the palace gym after lunch, when he knew no one else would be using it.

So much for his privacy.

So much for his workout.

Tor finished his reps and put down the barbell he'd been working with.

"Hello, *Princess*," he teased her with her current title, the one she'd barely gotten used to since marriage to his brother. "Did you need something?"

Janne grimaced. "Don't tease. You know your brother wants to make me queen." Janne's lack of enthusiasm for that eventuality dripped from her voice.

"I would be disappointed if he didn't," Tor replied honestly.

"Are you kidding me?" she demanded crankily. "Do you think I *want* to be queen?"

Tor had to stifle a smile at his sister-in-law's clear discontent. "I think that Tapt Oyer deserves a queen who puts the interests of our people ahead of her own whims."

"And you think I'll do that?"

He just gave her a look. They both knew she would.

Janne blew out a frustrated breath. "I didn't come looking to talk to you about your brother's harebrained ideas."

"I do not think anyone has ever accused my ultra responsible, reserved brother of being harebrained before."

She rolled her eyes. "Point taken. I think those traits run in the family though."

"Perhaps."

"I used to think you were the affable one, Tor."

"I am what I am." Tor could still use charm to good effect, but felt less inclined to do so as he got older.

The more people who tried to take advantage of him and his position, like Lisette, the more cynical he became.

"Oh man, I don't know how either of your brothers doesn't see you're every bit as emotionally repressed, not to mention as arrogant as they are."

"You believe your husband is repressed?" Tor said nothing about the arrogance. It was a family trait. Full stop.

"He was when we got married."

"Not so much anymore?" Tor asked, thinking he'd noticed a change in his brother but wanting confirmation.

After all, they were no longer close as they'd been when he was young. He could not claim to know Holger best and vice-versa.

Janne gave a knowing smile and then frowned. "I didn't come looking to talk about that either."

Tor just waited in silence for his sister-in-law to get to the point.

"There was a time you would have badgered me to know what I wanted to talk to you about," she said musingly.

They'd met many years ago, before Holger had taken on the role of Monarch and sent Tor to boarding school in America. Tor had still been an irrepressible teenager and hadn't yet been pushed entirely to the fringes of his family's lives.

"We all change," he said mildly.

"Yes, we do." Janne bit her lip, looking at him with concern. "I see the way you look at Blythe."

Tor just raised his brow, giving nothing away.

"You want her."

"If that is true, it is certainly between Miss Whitney-Jones and myself." Want her? He craved Blythe. Maybe even *needed* her, but what he felt for his clandestine lover was no one's business but his own.

Not even Blythe's. Not as long as she was insisting on their *secret* friends with benefits agreement, and refusing to acknowledge the label of *lover*.

"She's too old for you, Tor."

Janne's words surprised him. Coming from anyone else, even Blythe, they weren't as shocking.

But not only were he and Janne friends, she'd always treated him as an equal. And there was her own situation of course, married to his brother.

"You mean like my brother is too old for you?" he asked sardonically.

Holger was seven years Janne's senior. Blythe was eight years older than Tor; that single additional year made no difference to the circumstance.

"It's not the—"

"If you say, *the same,*" he interrupted. "I will seriously question your professed commitment to equality between the sexes."

Janne's mouth snapped shut.

When she added nothing more, Tor informed her, "In the context you are implying, the age difference between myself and Miss Whitney-Jones is entirely irrelevant. As is whatever you *think* you know about any attraction I *might* have for her."

"How can you say that?"

"I can say it because it is the truth. You are my sister-in-law. More importantly, you are one of the few people I consider a friend, but my life is still my own, Janne, and has been for a very long time."

"Look, I just don't want to see you get hurt." Janne's gaze reflected genuine concern.

"Thank you, but your worry on my behalf is unnecessary."

Janne frowned. "Holger said you told him the same thing."

"I have not discussed Miss Whitney-Jones with my brother."

"That's not what I meant. I was talking about that Lisette media scandal thing."

"There was no media scandal."

"Stop picking apart my words," she said with exasperation. "You told Holger he didn't have to worry about you then too."

"And he does not. I have been solely responsible for myself for many years now," Tor spelled out more precisely since she didn't seem to get the message the first time he'd said it.

"You make it sound like you've been on your own, but you have a father and brothers who care about you. You have me now, too."

"I did not say I have been on my own, but that I alone am responsible for myself. I am aware I have a family who cares, just as I care for you all. Okay?"

She nodded, but managed to look unconvinced.

He shook his head. Tor had no desire to get into his complicated relationship with his family.

So, he said, "You know I consider you a friend."

"I am glad."

"Friend, or not, I need you to butt out."

The Princess of Tapt Oyer did not look the least offended at his plain speech. Nor did she look like she had any intention of listening as her words confirmed. "Not going to happen, Tor. Blythe is my sister in every way that matters."

"I am aware."

"She supported me during the courtship and after I decided to marry your brother."

"And your point is?"

"Blythe might support me, but she's doesn't want to be me."

"Good. No one can live another person's life." And it would seriously suck if Blythe wanted to be married to a king.

Tor would never be anything but the prince he had been born.

"You know what I mean. She doesn't want to be a princess."

Tor was aware. Blythe had made it clear she didn't want any part of the false fairytale of being a modern day royal.

"And you do not want to be a queen, but I think that you will be one before my precious nephew celebrates his first birthday."

Janne glared at him. "Don't remind me."

"You married my brother. You knew it was a possibility," he said with no sympathy.

"He said he didn't want to make me queen."

"He changed his mind."

"Well, he can change it back."

Tor's money was on his brother in this horse race. And he said so.

"It seems really important to him," Janne acknowledged with an attitude of doom.

"As I said earlier, Tapt Oyer deserves a queen of your integrity and compassion. Holger is fully aware."

She made a disgruntled sound of agreement. "And you need to be fully aware that Blythe wants nothing to do with being a royal anything. I just don't want you to take her rejection personally."

For just a moment Tor had a taste of what Blythe kept saying was going to happen when his father found out that Tor and Else were not planning to marry.

Because this subterfuge about his currently casual relationship with Blythe was going to hurt Janne deeply if he and Blythe were not careful.

She thought she knew everything there was to know about her dearest friend.

Tor did not like keeping her in the dark, but he could not dismiss Blythe's almost pathological need to keep their sexual liaison a secret either.

Whether or not he agreed with Blythe's assessment of the outcome to them being honest about what they were doing, her needs superseded his sister-in-law's, or even his brothers' or father's needs.

That realization was not the total shock to him that he was sure it would be to Blythe.

She had her head buried firmly in the sand about anything remotely like real feelings between them.

And for now, he would let her keep it buried.

Six months later, Janne was crowned Queen of Tapt Oyer. Tor was happy for his brother and his country.

Nevertheless, he had enjoyed teasing his friend via text beforehand about how much she was going to love her new job. At one point she'd sent him an emoji flipping him off and he knew Janne was feeling the strain.

He'd called Blythe and told her he thought the sister of her heart needed her. Of course, Blythe dropped everything and flew out to Tapt Oyer.

Tor had been unable to get away from grad school to go with her to Tapt Oyer ahead of the coronation and he regretted that, as any time spent with Blythe was something to look forward to.

Even so, he did not balk minimizing their time together around his family.

Hiding the sexual chemistry between them was getting harder to do.

Blythe continued to insist on secrecy and referring to them as *friends with benefits* and refused utterly to ever talk about the future.

Tor's own long term outlook was uncertain enough with his military service looming that he allowed it without too much pushing. The pretense of him and Else dating was still standing as a buffer between her and her parents' plans for her future as well.

Though not nearly as effective as their first year of graduate school.

Things changed between him and Else at Janne's coronation as Queen Consort.

Else had been pensive and distracted since her arrival and Tor had taken her aside to find out what was wrong.

"You want to date this man?" he asked after Else told him about a business tycoon her parents had started throwing in her path the last couple of months.

"I think I do. He makes me feel all fluttery inside."

Tor didn't know about fluttery, but Blythe turned him on like no other woman, so he didn't mock his friend as he once might have done.

If he were honest, he didn't even see other woman besides Blythe as sexual beings anymore. His focus was entirely on the Travel Vlogger who shared his bed and refused to be counted as part of his life.

Bringing his focus back to Else, he did some quick scenario projections. They would be graduating with their MBAs in six weeks' time and he would be entering his military service only two weeks later.

"It's a good time to do our *breakup* announcement." She was less likely to receive any flack if they were already officially "not dating" when he went into the military.

It would not seem like she'd abandoned him, which would not have been the case. However, appearances were often at odds with the truth.

She looked at him with a vulnerability he hadn't seen on her face since their younger days, when she was still trying to effect warmer relationships with her parents. "I'm scared."

"Of dating?"

"Yes. Just look at you and Blythe. You're together, but not together."

"Just don't agree to a *friends with benefits* deal and you're safe."

Else grimaced. "No chance of that. I don't know what carrot my dad is offering, but I'm pretty sure marriage is the only option."

Although Else was on track to ger her MBA and had a brilliant mind, her father had not shifted one bit on his belief that a daughter could not take over his empire from him. He wanted a son-in-law who would provide grandsons. Heaven help both Else and the man she was interested in if they only had daughters.

"I'm going to have him investigated," Tor warned her, not even half-jokingly. "You know that, right?"

She laughed anyway. "He's a stand up guy...I just, he makes me feel stuff."

And for people like them, that was damn scary. Tor knew.

Their press release went out the day after they returned to Boston.

His father actually called to tell Tor he was sorry to hear about the breakup.

Tor kept the call short, hanging up as quickly as he could without being rude.

"You rushed him off the phone." Blythe sat naked in his bed, her beautiful brown eyes filled with censure.

He joined her on the bed, pulling Blythe into his arms. "You are surprised? If you had wanted me to talk longer, you should have put some clothes on and maybe stepped into the other room."

Blythe anywhere near a bed was temptation enough. Naked? He had no hope of ignoring her.

"Don't you blame me. You could have waited a few more minutes to rejoin me." The words were chastising, but she melted against him, responding to his touch as she always did.

"My father wanted to commiserate over a misery I do not feel," Tor said against the soft skin of her nape between nibbling kisses.

Blythe shivered, her entire body moving in an altogether enticing way. "I told you so."

"Told me what?" he asked before moving down to latch onto a nipple already sensitive from their earlier lovemaking.

"What?" she asked, her tone dazed.

He did not bother to answer, but focused on the pleasure he was giving her and ecstasy she returned to him.

Penetration without protection never got old. Every single time he slipped into her body skin to skin, Tor felt the weight of it and the pleasure that could not be topped.

They were snuggling in a sweaty, post coital haze of lingering pleasure when Blythe said. "I told you it would hurt his feelings."

He knew immediately what she was talking about. It was like that between them. They had entire conversations in silence that would erupt into speech that no one else would have understood.

But they did.

He didn't dwell on what that meant, but accepted that the friendship part of friends with benefits was as important as the sex to him.

"His feelings are not hurt. He thought mine were."

"Which hurt him."

"You're looking at my father through rose colored glasses again." He spoke with an indulgence he afforded few people in his life.

Blythe sat up, the view she offered sending a throb of sated pleasure through him. "I know he let you down, but he cares about you, Tor."

"I have never said he did not."

"But..."

"I will call him tomorrow and reaffirm my own lack of malaise of spirit if that will make you feel better."

"Really?" She looked at him like she was shocked.

He did not know why. If it was in his power to please her, he did it.

Thus far, he had not found anything *not* within his power and did not expect to.

"Consider it done."

"Thank you, Tor. I think both you and your father need that."

He didn't bother to argue, though he did not agree. He had more important things to do with his mouth.

Her cries of pleasure were his reward for doing them.

The call to his father went pretty much as he expected until the older man said there was something he'd wanted to talk to Tor about.

"Yes?" Tor asked warily.

He and his father did not indulge in confidences and the older man had abdicated voicing opinions about Tor's life choices years before.

"You may have noticed the countess and I enjoy one another's company a great deal."

"Yes." Despite there never having been any kind of announcement, Tor would be shocked if anyone in the family was unaware that his father and the countess were personally involved.

"It is more than a friendship."

"Good."

"Do you mean that?"

"Why wouldn't I?" Tor asked, genuinely confused.

"You were the youngest when we lost your mother."

"Yes?"

"Out of respect for your feelings, the Lady Ingrid and I have naturally been circumspect about our relationship." His father's words were stilted and tense.

If he was even half as uncomfortable with this conversation as Tor, no wonder. But his words also made little sense to Tor.

"For *my* benefit? I do not understand."

"Naturally, you would not want someone replacing your mother."

"Perhaps it has escaped your notice, Father, but I am a twenty-five-year-old man. What you do in your personal life is of no consequence to me."

It was not as if the countess would be taking on the role of his stepmother. His father's wife, yes, and welcome to the family as far as Tor was concerned.

But he was past the age of needing a mother.

"I did not want to hurt you," his father said, his tone inexplicably sincere.

"I do not understand why you would think you marrying Lady Ingrid would hurt me," Tor said honestly. "But let me set your mind at rest, I have absolutely no objection to it. We are talking marriage here, right?"

"Of course we are talking marriage. I should have made things official before this, but..." Uncharacteristically his father let his voice trail off.

"You were inexplicably worried that *I* would be upset."

"Not so inexplicable. You are my youngest son."

"But I am no longer a child."

"No, you are right. I think I just wanted my son's lives settled before I allowed myself to move on. I wanted to know *you* were settled."

And now his father knew that Tor would *not* be settling down with Else. He respected that the older man was not insisting the countess continue to wait on such an eventuality.

"But you deserve happiness," Tor said with absolute sincerity.

Blythe was getting ready and paused in applying her makeup to give him one of those looks. The ones that said he was a prince among men, and not just because of his title.

He smiled at her.

She blew him a kiss and went back the mirror.

"You can say that after the way I abandoned you after your mother's death?"

"You were grieving." Tor did not deny the abandonment. His eight-year-old self had been devastated.

But he'd been a man for a long time now and mature enough to realize his father had never hurt him purposefully.

"So were you."

"I had my brothers."

"They are good brothers."

"Yes, and you are a good father." If not always the father he had needed.

"That you can say that when we both know it is not true."

"I think the countess is already having a positive impact on you. I could not imagine having a discussion like this before you met her."

"You are right. She makes me examine my feelings as well as my actions." His father sounded bewildered by that, but clearly he'd been willing to do so.

"Father, nothing would please me more than to attend a wedding between you and the countess."

He said the words because he meant them, but the reward he received from Blythe for saying them after he got off the phone sent his senses into the stratosphere.

His father and the countess were married two months after Tor's elite unit was deployed to a high priority zone, as he had expected. While he refused to take leave when his unit was in a dangerous situation, Tor did attend via video call.

CHAPTER THIRTEEN

Tor got the 911 text from Blythe when he was out on maneuvers and had to wait six hours to call her on the satellite phone.

Six hours of imagining successively grim scenarios.

"Tor?"

When he heard Blythe's voice, his knees nearly buckled with relief. "What has happened?"

"Janne thinks I have a thing for you." Blythe's tone said that would be the end of the world.

So, it took Tor a moment to realize that her 911 emergency was not in fact an emergency at all.

"You are aware that I spent that last six hours imagining the worst?" he asked through gritted teeth.

"What do you mean? What could be worse?" she asked, doing nothing for his ego and even less for his temper.

"You could have had an accident and be lying in a ditch somewhere. You could be sick." He didn't say cancer because he would not give that nebulous fear a voice. "Someone could be seriously ill or dead."

"Oh...I...I didn't mean to worry you like that. Everyone is fine. *I'm* fine," Blythe emphasized. "But she *knows*, Tor."

"Unless you have told her something, at best Janne *suspects*," Tor reassured Blythe grimly, still not over six hours of thinking wildly negative thoughts.

"Knows...suspects...what's the difference?"

"The difference is one is fact and the other supposition. Whatever risk you imagine to your relationship with Janne, it will not be realized over supposition."

"I'm not imagining things."

He ignored that blatant attempt to pick an argument.

"What makes you so worried she suspects something?" he forced himself to ask patiently.

"She asked me if I had a thing for you."

"And you said?"

"That she was ridiculous."

"Nice."

"Don't. You know it's not about you." She gusted out a sigh easily discerned across the satellite connection.

"Worst case scenario, you tell her we are friends with benefits and to butt out." It's what he'd done when Janne thought to advise him on his feelings for Blythe.

"I would never!"

He was aware. And now that his adrenalin wasn't spiking that awareness that Blythe was so committed to keeping their liaison a secret wasn't filling him with peace and light.

"I guess I asked one too many times if she'd had any news about you." Blythe spoke like admitting a deep, dark secret.

That surprised him. "I don't know why you ask her at all. You are more likely to have heard from me than my family."

"What to do you mean?"

"I contact the palace once a month."

"But you text me almost daily. And email me..." Her voice trailed off in confusion.

He also had a standing monthly video chat with her arranged through a buddy's account so the media wouldn't catch wind of it. No wonder he confused her. Tor stayed in closer contact with Blythe than anyone else in his life.

They weren't engaged. They weren't even dating.

"I get worried on the days you don't text," she offered to his silent contemplation.

It was an admission of sorts. One that made his own actions less difficult to acknowledge.

"I am sorry, but some days it's radio silence."

"I understand. Of course, I do."

"Be assured if you have not heard from me, no one has," he reiterated.

"That doesn't make me feel better."

He could not fix that.

Tor was part of an elite team and their assignments didn't allow for daily communication outside the military. Prince, or not.

Tor had more freedom than most because he had a state of the art, secure satellite phone and computer. His sister-in-law had made sure of that.

Which is why he used it to contact his oldest brother once a month and speak to whoever chose to be available during that call.

"You should call your family more," Blythe said after a few seconds of silence.

"Should I?"

"Yes." He could just see her giving him that sassy look that turned him on. Every single time.

"You have very firm opinions for someone whose own family barely qualifies for the term."

"So, I know how *not* to be," she shot back. "It isn't right that Else and I hear from you more often than they do."

"Else does not."

Tor had very little time to spend texting or emailing, much less calling. His squad had constant assignments. Others spent a lot of time sitting around waiting to act, but not his elite group.

"But she's your best friend."

"She is my oldest friend." Else no longer had the distinction of being his closest friend.

That title went to Blythe, but he was sure she would get squirrely if he said so. So, he did not.

"I should tell you not to text me as much, to spend more time on communication with your family." Blythe said, sounding guilty but not convincing despite that.

"Is that what you want me to do?" he asked, having no intention of changing his behavior.

He relied on his connection to Blythe to keep him thinking straight, though he wasn't about to say so. It would reveal a weakness he was neither proud of, nor remotely willing to acknowledge out loud.

"No."

Unexpected relief washed through him that she was not asking him to cut back their communication.

"I like hearing from you." Once again she sounded like she was admitting something shameful.

"Good."

"You had no intention of changing regardless," she accused.

"I am not in the habit of letting others dictate my behavior." The chain of command notwithstanding.

"The older you get, the more you sound like Holger."

"He is a king. I am merely a prince."

"Sure. You just keep telling yourself that."

But it was true.

Now that his brother and Janne had their son, Tor had been bumped down to fourth in line to the throne.

A very different role than the one he'd known for most of his life.

It came with freedoms he wasn't sure even his family understood the extent of yet. As well as responsibilities. Like military service in a war zone.

"I hate to tell you then, but you've got all the arrogance of a king." Far from sounding annoyed by that, Blythe sounded impressed.

"As does my father and he has not carried that title for many years."

"It must be in the genes then."

Tor laughed. "Perhaps."

"I'm sorry I worried you with my 911 text."

"It is good to hear your voice regardless."

"It is. I wish..."

"What do you wish?"

"That I could see you, but I know that's not possible."

"Maybe."

"I know you're returning to the palace for annual leave in November. Janne is really disappointed you can't be there for Christmas."

"Will you be there?"

"I was going to, but now...I'm worried Janne will notice our sexual chemistry if we're together."

"And that would be a tragedy." Of course it would.

Blythe had never changed her mind on that point. Hence her emergency text today.

"Be there."

"You cannot boss me around."

Tor had stared death in the face several times since starting his military service. The action they had planned for December was more dangerous than any he and his team had been on so far.

All of it worked *because* he had time with this woman to look forward to. Whether on the phone, or in person...or even just texting.

"Be there," he repeated.

"You aren't being reasonable."

"According to you, I am arrogant, not reasonable."

"One does not have to preclude the other," she said with asperity.

"I can skip my trip to the palace and come to visit you in New York, if you prefer."

Her gasp was loud in his ear. "You can't do that!"

"I assure you, I can."

"But, Tor, they're *your family*!"

She was his woman, not that he expected her to acknowledge that truth. She hadn't in two years.

Their time was coming though.

Because Blythe was right about one thing. Tor had his own share of princely confidence. He knew they belonged together.

Convincing the prickly woman she was destined to be a princess would be a challenge, but one a hell of a lot less dangerous than the ones he faced currently.

"Be there," he said one last time.

Her sigh sounded her capitulation. "If Janne figures out we're sleeping together I'm going to blame you."

"Have you considered that hiding our relationship from her has more potential to damage your relationship with Janne than just telling her the truth?"

"We don't have a relationship."

Over her denials, Tor said, "I have to go."

"I didn't mean..." Blythe's words trailed off, like she didn't know where to go from there.

"Goodbye, Blythe."

"No, wait, please...Tor, I'm sorry, okay?"

"Okay."

"Of course we have a relationship. We're friends."

Janne and Else were his friends too, but he wasn't texting them as often as he could. Neither were upset when they didn't hear from him either.

Tor said none of that. "I will see you in November."

"I'll be there."

He hung up. It was two days later before he had a chance to check his phone again. There were about a half dozen texts from Blythe, none of them coded for an emergency.

HavePassportWillTravel: I don't like how we left things on the phone.

HavePassportWillTravel: You probably think that's hypocritical to say.

HavePassportWillTravel: Where r u?

HavePassportWillTravel: Are you blanking me?

HavePassportWillTravel: R U OK?

Exhausted and in no mood for another round of push pull with his infuriating girlfriend, whatever she liked to call herself, verbal or otherwise, he texted back a short reply.

SoldierPrince: Fine. TTYL

He wasn't surprised when his phone dinged with an incoming text.

HavePassportWillTravel: Are you punishing me?

SoldierPrince: No.

He stripped and climbed into his rack. Tor hadn't slept in over thirty-six hours. He was barely awake when the next chime sounded.

HavePassportWillTravel: Glad U R ok.

Was he okay? Tor ached in every muscle. He was so tired his eyes felt filled with sand and he had a couple scrapes that would sting for another day, or two.

SoldierPrince: I am alive. Tired. Need sleep.

HavePassportWillTravel: Pleasant dreams. TTYL

Yes, he had no doubt she'd text him later, because the woman who claimed they had no relationship apparently fell apart when she did not hear from him for a day.

That truth followed him into his dreams making them more pleasant than they might have been otherwise. Because they were filled with her.

Blythe watched at Tor greeted his family for his November visit.

Wearing tailored slacks and a dress shirt, no suit jacket or tie, he looked almost the same as when he'd left for his final military training before being deployed.

Except his eyes. The humor that used to lurk there was gone.

Had that happened before he embarked on his two-year stint as a soldier?

She could not remember.

Sterner he might be, but he still fit in with his surroundings perfectly. The opulent palace décor that Blythe even now found uncomfortably *royal* sometimes, was such a natural backdrop for her prince. His family had waited to meet him at the palace in their private reception room.

Not noticeably more casual than the rest of the palace, it was nevertheless where they gathered for holidays and moments like this.

She had wanted to go to the airport and wait for his plane to arrive, but had known she could not. Not without giving away their secret.

Hungry for every glimpse of the prince, she found it even harder to look away now than it had been to stop herself showing up on the tarmac in advance of his arrival.

But that is exactly what Blythe had to do. Look away.

Janice already suspected Blythe had a thing for Tor. She couldn't afford to give the sister of her heart more evidence to feed that suspicion.

And knowing that, Blythe still watched as Tor shook hands with his father and brothers, gave a one-armed, sideways hug to Janice and a charming, but formal partial bow toward Janice's mom, Lady Ingrid, who was now married to Prince Canute.

Tor's reserved greetings for the adults shifted to something far more natural when Bjorn toddled up and lifted his arms toward him. Tor's gorgeous face transformed with a welcoming smile as he lifted his nephew for a hug before setting him back down.

"Bjorn, I have a gift for you."

The two-year old's face lit up. Tor made a motion with his hand and one of the security detail stepped forward with a large brightly wrapped box. Bjorn tore into the wrapping and cried with delight when he saw the building blocks designed for little hands that had been custom made so he could build a rudimentary replica of the palace he lived in. There was a stable and horses and little figures that represented the royal family, too.

"My house!" the toddler exclaimed with delight.

Blythe laughed softly at the little prince describing the palace as his *house*.

He was such a little sweetheart. She'd never really considered children before meeting Tor and then the sister-of-her-heart giving birth to a little boy Blythe could not help but love. Her own homelife hadn't leant itself to a desire for emulation, but something in her longed-for family in a way she never had before.

A family she could not have with Tor.

Her prince dropped to his knees and pointed out the different figures and asked Bjorn if he knew who they were. The toddler named every single one of them, including the one meant to be Blythe.

"What a smart boy you are, Bjorn," Tor said with more warmth than he used with any of his other family members.

Bjorn's grin was huge. "Thank you, Uncle."

Then the little boy gave Tor a spontaneous hug.

Which the prince returned without hesitation despite the physical distance he had maintained with the adults in his family since his arrival.

"You will make a good father yourself, one day," Prince Canute told Tor, his voice laced with approval.

The affirming words sliced into Blythe's heart with the precision of a stiletto.

Any children Tor had would not be with *her*.

The longer their casual relationship lasted, the less casual it felt. And the more grief she felt at the prospect of losing Tor to his destiny.

CHAPTER FOURTEEN

That night at dinner, there was one guest Blythe had not been expecting. Janne had told her it would be a family dinner, which usually meant exactly that: family.

The only exceptions there had ever been at these more intimate meals had been Blythe herself and Tor's friend, Else.

Else was not here to see Tor because she was preparing for her wedding. Tor had told Blythe in one of his texts last week that he probably wouldn't see the other woman until his next trip home.

If then.

Apparently, Else's parents had demanded she and Tor cool their friendship so as not to feed the continuing speculation about them.

Blythe could not tell if Else submitting to the dictate had hurt Tor, or not. She'd asked but he'd said no.

The problem was, Blythe wasn't sure Tor would have admitted it if he had been hurt.

Regardless, it *wasn't* Else at the dinner table tonight, it was the daughter of one of Lady Ingrid's. A member of the English nobility, Lady Angela was a beautiful young woman with impeccable manners and who was completely at ease amidst the royal family.

Blythe despised her on sight.

Lucky for him, Tor was polite to the other woman, but he didn't smile at her. And he did not look at her like he wanted to devour her body.

Like he looked at Blythe when no one else was around.

They had agreed to be exclusive as long as they were together and Blythe had no intention of tolerating any aberration to that agreement.

She wasn't letting Tor go until she had to, and that day was not here.

Even if it was obvious Prince Canute was ready for his youngest son to settle down.

Tor had told Blythe he had no intention of even considering a future with a woman until his military service ended.

"Are you all right?" Janice asked Blythe partway through the meal.

Blythe forced a smile and turned it on her friend. "Of course."

"You're awfully quiet."

"Are you saying I'm not usually?"

Janice just laughed, but then she sobered. "When you meet new people, you normally ask tons of questions. It's that journalistic curiosity you hone with your travel Vlog, not to mention the show you're hosting. You usually struggle to rein it in."

"So?"

"So, you've barely spoken to Lady Angela."

"She wasn't brought here for me to get to know," Blythe said pointedly.

"I think my mom and Prince Canute are matchmaking." Janice gave Blythe an apologetic look. "I'm sorry."

"Why?"

"I know you kind of had a thing for him."

Neither said Tor's name and both spoke in undertones unlikely to carry to the others at the table.

"I told you I didn't."

"And you've never been able to lie to me."

Blythe nearly laughed out loud at that. Though the sound would have been more graveyard humor than comedic.

No, she'd never made a habit of lying to her sister-by-choice, but Blythe did not tell Janice everything. And she had been hiding her sexual relationship with Tor for almost three years now.

"It doesn't matter." Blythe did her best to infuse her tone with confidence and truth. Her words were true, after all.

Whatever feelings she had for Tor, they didn't matter because he had to marry a woman who could give him children, a woman born to fit into his world.

Prince Canute especially would expect Tor to marry another royal, or at the very least, someone of the nobility, like Lady Angela.

It was archaic and smacked of elitism, but Blythe had gotten to know the family patriarch well enough to realize the truth. Even if Blythe had been willing to deal with the whole "marry a prince" thing, Prince Canute would never consider *her* as a potential daughter-in-law.

He was nice to her, of course. But he was old fashioned and very entrenched in certain beliefs about how a royal family operates.

Add her infertility to the mix and she and Tor had no hope of a future together.

"If it makes you feel any better, I don't think Tor is taken with Lady Angela."

Blythe had to agree, if only inside her own head. There was no chemistry between the two of them.

And if Blythe was glad about that, that was her own business.

She knew she had Tor until he finished his military service, but not beyond that.

When he came home permanently, his family would expect him to start looking for a suitable wife.

Blythe would not be on their list of prospects.

For too many important reasons.

That night when Tor came to her room, she didn't even pretend to be surprised to see him. She had not invited him, but they hadn't maintained their *no touching in the palace* rule since she offered to break it the first time.

He was careful to be circumspect, telling her that he had access to the security tapes and erased the proof of his arrival and departure to her room before anyone else had a chance to see them.

He kissed her now, doing nothing else but holding her close for long minutes.

When he finally lifted his head, their gazes locked.

Molten with desire, his grey eyes drew her in. "I have wanted to do that since I saw you in the reception room."

"Me too," she admitted, though it probably would have been smarter not to.

Tor didn't reply with words, but with actions, pulling her back into a passionate kiss with full body contact.

She tugged at his shirt, pulling it out of his waistband so she could get her hands under the fabric. After months apart, she was desperate for the feel of his skin against hers.

Tor, on the other hand, seemed intent on relearning every inch of her body intimately.

Slowly and methodically.

Undressing them both a little bit at a time, as if teasing himself with what was coming next.

Blythe certainly felt tortured...with pleasure.

He touched, tasted, and teased her into a shivering mass of sexual need.

Only then did he make love to her, bringing them both to climax in too little time. She cried out her pleasure, even as her body insisted on seeking more and more and more.

It was her turn to use her lips and hands on his body, to bring him back to full erection. She grasped is oversized sex in both hands and put her mouth over the tip, tasting him.

He shouted, his big body jolting.

Blythe lost herself in giving Tor pleasure, but he refused to come without her.

"You're too self-controlled," she complained, even as she allowed herself to be moved into position for him to return the pleasure with his mouth on her.

His laughter had a dark, sexy quality to it before he set about bringing her to a climax, only to slow and lighten his touch until she was ready to climb to the summit of pleasure again.

Then he was surging up her body to thrust inside her and once again take them on a rid of ecstasy she knew she would never know the like of with another man.

They showered together and then returned to snuggle in her bed.

"This is dangerous," she said with a yawn as she curled into his big, muscular body.

Tor wrapped his arms around her. "I will leave before there is a chance anyone will see me."

"You can never be sure."

"I can."

"Your confidence knows no bounds."

"My confidence is entirely justified."

"Arrogant," she slurred in exhaustion.

Waking up alone should have made Blythe feel nothing but relief. Tor had left before his presence in her bed could be detected.

Only she felt let down.

And lonely.

She hugged the pillow that still carried his scent if not his warmth, inhaling the spicy masculine fragrance that she only ever associated with Tor.

Inevitable, if wholly unwelcome realization washed over Blythe.

Their *friends with benefit* deal was so much more than that her, but she could never admit it to him, or anyone else.

She might never be able to give voice to her feelings, but it was time she stopped lying to herself and acknowledged she was irrevocably, head over heels in love with the youngest Prince of the House of Asgersen.

Chapter Fifteen

Tor disconnected from his first call in three months with Blythe, surprised, but very glad that she'd agreed to meet him in Paris for his three days of leave.

She hadn't even scolded him about spending more time with his family.

The December Op had lasted three long months, every single day of which he and his unit had been on a no contact order.

No texts. No emails. No sat phone calls.

Nothing.

The Op itself had been grueling and costly to his team.

He'd lost a friend and seen another seriously wounded.

Tor wanted to see only one person.

Blythe.

It was not that he did not want to see his family, but that he did not want to see *anyone*. Except Blythe.

He booked the penthouse suite in a Paris hotel known for its luxury and more importantly, their absolute discretion.

Even so, he booked the room in Blythe's name, arriving a couple of hours after she'd checked in and sent him the room number.

He texted her from the elevator to let her know he was on his way up.

She stood framed in the door as he approached, her beautiful sapphire eyes focused on him, taking in everything about him.

"Hi." She spoke softly when he was only a few feet away, like that one word had been hard to get out.

Tor didn't bother to attempt a reply, just pulled Blythe into his arms and guided them into the room as he covered her lips with his own, kicking the door shut behind them.

Her hands were all over him, but not in a sexual way. It was like she was checking to make sure everything was there and accounted for.

He broke his mouth away. "I am fine."

He was not the one who had been wounded. He was not the one who had lost his life.

"Three months," she said. Like that explained everything.

"We were on a noncom order," he reminded her. He'd told her as much when he'd called her to ask her to come to Paris.

"I know, but..." She let her voice trail off, just shaking her head.

"I am here now."

"Yes."

They made love. It was inevitable. Tor needed the affirmation of life.

Blythe seemed to be equally determined to prove to herself that he was there and fine, in her arms.

Afterward, they lay without speaking, their bodies entwined as only two lovers could do.

"Will you have another op like the last one?" Blythe's soft voice finally broke the silence between them.

"You know I can't answer that."

"Especially to someone who makes her living in front of the camera." Her hands restively kneaded his chest, like an agitated cat.

But he did not want Blythe worried.

"Even if my brother was the person asking, I could not answer."

"Oh. Really." She sat up and looked down at him, her brown gaze filled with curiosity. "But he's your king."

"And I my unit is currently deployed under orders from an ally country's military."

"Still, you're a prince. There shouldn't be secrets between you and your king."

"My king would never ask that question," Tor pointed out gently.

Blythe frowned. "He should. Three months without word. I'm sure King Holger was really worried."

"He did not sound particularly concerned when I spoke to him."

"You called him? When?"

"After I called you." Tor let that truth about his priorities sink into his *friend with benefits.*

"After, but...I can't pretend I'm upset you called me first. I was climbing the walls."

Did she have any idea how revealing her words were?

"Now you can climb me."

She rolled her eyes. "Very funny."

"I am not joking. I can think of nothing I would like better."

Blythe cast her gaze toward his sex, her eyes flaring with surprise at his renewed erection. "But we just finished."

"Has it been so long you do not remember how frequently we make love, given the opportunity?" He surged up to steal the answer right from her lips as he pulled her flush against his body, her breasts pressing delightfully into his chest.

He slid his hand between her legs, caressing her wet heat, building her pleasure back up until she was the one pushing him on his back to climb on top of him just like he wanted.

The beautiful column of her neck stretched as she let her head fall back and rocked her body at a leisurely pace, keeping them both on the edge of climax.

He touched her all over, every bit of silky skin he could reach, remapping his woman's body and storing sensations for memories to pull out when he was thousands of miles away from her again.

Her luscious breasts drew him like a beacon and he slid both hands up to cup her generous curves, rubbing his thumbs over the engorged tips.

Blythe moaned, increasing her pace. "You know just how to touch me."

"If I have not learned after all this time, I would be ashamed to admit it."

"You knew from the beginning," she told him without hesitation.

The words stroked his ego almost as nicely as her body stroked his.

Wanting to see her come apart, he reached out and grabbed one of her wrists, guiding her hand to where their bodies met.

"Touch yourself." His voice was husky with need and she had to hear it.

Whether it was that, or just because she wanted to, Blythe obeyed and slid a single finger down to press against her clitoris.

They both groaned and shuddered, their bodies moving faster against each other.

Needing her to come first, he touched her in that intimate place too, his fingers brushing over hers.

Blythe cried out her pleasure, her face set in a rictus of ecstasy.

Tor joined her only a moment later, his entire body bowing up off the bed and lifting her too.

They collapsed together, Blythe allowing herself to simply lie on top of him, his sex slipping out of her body naturally and with a final throb of pleasure.

"It is always so good with you," she said, like that was somehow inexplicable.

He did not tell her that was because they had been made for each other. The time was not right for that revelation, or the fight it would surely entail getting her to admit that truth as well.

He said nothing at all, just tugged the bedding over her, knowing from past experience that she chilled easily as the sweat dried on her body after lovemaking.

"I don't want you to go back," she whispered like offering up a shameful secret. "What if it is you next time?"

Her reference to his fallen comrade did not sting like it would have from someone else. He knew she didn't want anyone to lose their life to war, but especially him. And while she was still insisting on hiding their relationship from his family, he would take what proof of her care for him that he could get.

"Shh." He rubbed her back, turning his head to kiss to top of her blond head. "For the next three days, the future does not exist. We will pretend I am just a prince and you are just my lover."

She hugged him, nuzzling into the join of his neck and shoulder. "Not lovers."

"I said pretend." He ignored the twinge her continued denial gave his heart.

"Okay," she said. "For these three days, you are just a prince and I'm your lover." She giggled. "Just a prince. Right. Why not just a man?"

"I can stop being a soldier, I can never stop being a prince."

"Well, I like you as you are and if that means you're always a prince, then I guess that's okay."

She said that, but he suspected the fact he was a prince was one of Blythe Whitney-Jones, intrepid travel vlogger's, primary reasons for refusing to consider their relationship in any serious light.

One thing she'd never made any bones about, Blythe did not see herself as princess material and not because she felt unequal to the task.

But because she did not *want* to be a princess.

The view from the visiting platform at the Eiffel tower took Blythe's breath away. She'd been to Paris before. Of course she had, she made her living sharing her travels with an appreciative audience.

But this was the first time she'd been in the amazing city with a companion that was not a coworker.

Surprisingly, Tor had never been and he wanted to do all the touristy things.

Hence their trip to the Eiffel Tower. Yesterday, they'd gone to the Arc d' Triomphe and tomorrow they would spend the morning at the Louvre. Not enough time, he assured her to see all they would want to, but they could come back.

Like that was going to happen.

A small sigh she couldn't quite stifle puffed out of her lips and her shoulder sagged before she even realized it was happening. She straightened her posture immediately, hoping Tor had not noticed.

She peeked over at her prince to check and found Tor watching her, rather than the view.

"You're supposed to be looking at the city," she instructed him, chagrined.

His smile was tinged with something like concern. "I like the view I'm looking at just fine."

Blythe just rolled her eyes. "Stop trying to be charming and look at the gorgeous view."

"First, tell me why the sad little sigh."

Blythe just shook her head and turned her own gaze on the city skyline.

Tor's arms came around her from behind, his body pressed along her back. His head close to hers, he whispered intimately, "Tell me."

"You shouldn't hold me like this in public." Someone could recognize him and snap a picture and then the cat would be out of the bag in screeching, clawing fury.

Tor made no move to let her go, or step back. "Remember, for these three days, you are my lover."

"*Pretend*," she stressed. "Pretend lover."

"So, pretend it is okay if I hold you like this."

"Tor." Her voice held warning.

He had to know this little tableau was dangerous.

For all the notice he took of her tone, moving not one iota. "Why the sigh, *min skatt*?"

"I was just thinking." About how impossible it was going to be to let this man go, but their time together was dwindling by the day.

"About?"

"How much I don't want to let you go back." It was part of the truth, if not all of it.

When he finished his military service, Blythe knew she had to break things off and make it possible for Tor to find his future princess.

Just thinking about that not too far off day made it hard to breathe.

Her prince's strong arms tightened around her. "No thinking about tomorrow today."

That was good advice. If she could take it. "I'll try."

He turned her in his arms and kissed her. Right there, in front of all the other tourists. And Blythe didn't even yell at him. She just took his hand and followed him off the visitor platform.

CHAPTER SIXTEEN

That night they had dinner in a rooftop garden, the view rivaling the one they'd had earlier.

It was romantic and special. He was urbane and sexy.

Blythe reveled in being the sole focus of Prince Tor of the House of Asgersen's attention.

They talked about his family, about other trips they would like to take together, places she'd always dreamt of seeing...the sort of things real lovers discussed.

They did not mention the next evening when he would be leaving. They did not talk about the end of his military service and what inevitably came with that.

They talked about her vlog, her show and her next trip.

They did not talk about what he would be doing when he returned to his unit.

They touched and smiled and got intimately close across the table to talk, but it was safe.

Tor had made sure their table was secluded, the only people they saw the waitstaff.

After they had eaten a truly scrumptious five-star meal, Tor stood from the table and put his hand out. "Dance with me."

"Where..." she started to ask, but stopped as she realized waitstaff were quickly moving the table and chairs from their private alcove as the volume of the ambient music increased from background to more prominent.

Blythe let Tor pull her into the Viennese waltz hold he'd taught her. The dance lesson he'd given her at Janice and Holger's wedding had been the first of many over the years when dancing at official events was their only excuse for touching each other in public.

She followed Tor's lead seamlessly now, her body moving fluidly to the soft strains of classical music. They'd never club danced together, but she'd come to appreciate just how sensual traditional ballroom dance could be.

She loved the gliding touches, barely there caresses and movement of their bodies in tandem to the music. The full chiffon skirt of Blythe's royal blue, 40s inspired cocktail length dress by an up-and-coming designer swirled around their legs.

Tor's arm pressed against her back, his other hand against hers in a perfect hold that felt more intimate than she ever did dirty dancing with a male friend at a club.

Why?

Because she knew what that hand felt like on her body. Knew how those arms felt holding her up while he made love to her against a wall. Knew what the rock-hard thighs only inches from her own, felt like against her bottom while she rode him to completion.

Tor smiled down at her, his molten gaze heated. "You are my favorite dance partner, *min skatt*."

Pleasure zinged through her core, even as they moved so smoothly and demurely to the music.

"You dance with some beautiful women who are much better at this than I am." Blythe wasn't arguing, or even questioning, simply pointing out a truth.

"I measure other women's beauty by you, *min skatt*, and *no one* feels as good in my arms."

"You're so adept at saying the right thing."

He swung her into a turn and then brought her back into his body. "Truth is truth."

"You're my favorite dance partner too."

"I've seen your newsfeed." His tone said maybe he hadn't liked what he found there. "The way we dance together must feel very tame."

"Does it, to you?" she challenged.

His expression turned thoughtful, like he hadn't considered that angle. "No."

"It doesn't to me, either."

"And the other?" he asked, referring no doubt to the dirty dancing she'd been thinking about just moments ago.

"Does nothing for me."

His gaze locked with hers, like he was trying to read her sincerity.

Something in her expression must have convinced him because he gave her that devastating smile he saved just for her. Full on sincerity, no tempering. "Nothing with you feels tame."

"Not even chatting across the family dinner table in your brother's palace?" she teased.

"First..." He swung her in until her back was to his front. "It is our country's palace. It does not belong to Holger, but to the House of Asgersen." They waltzed to the left, but he dipped his head down so his mouth was practically kissing her ear. "Second, there is nothing tame about the thoughts I have about you even at my family's dinner table."

Blythe shivered as desire washed over her. "You think about me...like that...then?" she asked in a husky whisper.

"Yes."

"There's something perverse about that." She meant to tease, but her tone was still breathless and soft.

"I disagree. There is nothing more natural than the way I think about you, the way I touch you, the way you touch me...the way you feel in my arms."

"You're really getting into your lover role, aren't you?"

"Yes." Then he spun her in his arms and kissed her with all the passion building between them.

In the back of Blythe's mind, she knew this wasn't smart. No matter how secluded they were, it was still public, but she couldn't make herself break the kiss, much less step out of his embrace.

Of its own volition, her body strained toward Tor's solid muscles, her need for him going from a low simmer to a full, raging boil in seconds.

Tor was the one that stepped back, his gaze dark with sexual desire. "Are you ready to go?"

She nodded, her throat too tight with passion to form words.

"But dessert?" one of the waitstaff inquired when Tor indicated their readiness to depart.

Tor gave Blythe a naughty smile. "I had something special planned, but it can't be packed up to go."

"I'm sorry, but we'll skip dessert," she told the waiter.

His understanding smile morphed to professional blandness in only a second, but it had been there.

Blythe didn't mind. This was Paris. The city of lovers. That she and hers wanted to leave for increased privacy would shock no one.

Tor's face looked set in granite as he drove the sleek sports car he'd rented for their time together.

"You look angry," Blythe said, knowing she sounded more intrigued than worried.

He shifted the gears on the powerful car's engine, and sped through a light about to turn red. "You know better."

"I do. And you know better than to handle this thing like a Formula One driver," she reproved him mildly.

"The light was still yellow."

She couldn't deny that. "But it was close."

"You know what is close? My body combusting with need."

She laughed softly, loving the effect she had on him. "I think you will survive waiting to get back to the hotel."

"Maybe." He shifted down, taking a corner just a little tight. "Maybe not."

Deciding he didn't need distraction while he was driving like a man on a mission, Blythe did not reply.

The next twenty-four hours were incredible. They made love often and continued to play the tourist in the City for Lovers.

But Tor's departure came with the inevitability of everything else challenging in life.

Blythe blinked back tears as they kissed for the final time inside in their super luxurious hotel suite. "I want to take you to the airport."

"You know we cannot do that and keep our relationship under wraps."

"We haven't been as careful on that front as we should have been already," she agreed, trying to keep her voice even.

He shrugged. "It was three days out of time."

It would be more like a nine day wonder in the press if anyone had caught photos of them kissing or dancing, but Blythe didn't let herself worry about that.

It was true that Prince Tor was less well known than his older brothers and even less so in Europe, which had plenty other royals for their paparazzi to follow.

They would never have gotten away with their pretend lovers weekend in New York, or even Boston, but Paris? Most likely yes.

It was that *most likely* that worried her, but Tor seemed unconcerned and Blythe wasn't putting any unnecessary stress on him before he returned to his military unit.

That leave set a pattern for those to follow. Tor managed to meet Blythe in Athens twice, Istanbul once and Paris twice more for three-day leaves over the rest of his deployment.

Each time they acted like lovers with nothing more to do than explore each ancient city. They did not stifle their affection in public like they did in Tapt Oyer or the States, though they were careful to protect their privacy as much as possible and respect each city's culture in regard to any sort of PDA.

Her prince returned to the Palace in Tapt Oyer once each year to visit his family and Blythe always made it a point to be there for the visit, but they had to hide their intimacy and how well they knew each other. Though he insisted on their friendship being known and recognized.

Janice seemed happy that Blythe and Tor had become friends. She'd also, thankfully stopped teasing Blythe about having a thing for the youngest Asgersen prince.

Tor stepped off the plane in Tapt Oyer, a sense of coming home welling over him.

His official two years of deployment was over, but he had yet to decide if he would make the military his career.

With his brothers running Tapt Oyer Global as CEO and COO, he wasn't sure he was needed at the company at all. Wasn't sure he *wanted* to work there.

Two years ago, the concept of wanting to work someplace would never have occurred to him. That was before he'd seen death the way he had in the last two years. Up close and personal. The concept of blind duty in the face of the ephemeral nature of life did not gel.

He owed it to all the soldiers that fought for freedom to live free.

While Tor had no intention of dismissing duty as unimportant, neither would he allow the perception of his duty to the Crown dictate his every life choice.

Tradition dictated that Tor take an active role in the military, eventually taking his rightful role as the Commander in General. He was sure everyone expected him to do exactly that.

But he wasn't making any decisions about his future without talking to the woman he planned to make that future with.

Blythe was supposed to be at the palace when he arrived. He would have liked her to be at the airport to meet him, if only so they could have a moment of privacy now rather than later.

Though he was pleased no one else, besides the security team he would have to grow accustomed to again, was there to accompany him to the palace. Tor was glad to be home, but he wasn't looking forward to having to interact with people once he reached the palace.

The last two ops had been harsh.

Tor slid into the back seat of the SUV that would take him to the palace, his thoughts centering on Blythe, as they often did.

Too many nights, his very sanity had seemed to hinge on the image of her smile he kept forefront in his mind.

His lover and closest friend was still set on secrecy.

Tor was done with hiding however.

He'd given her time to get used to his life, to come to terms with telling Janice. Now his war zone deployment was over, Tor was done waiting.

He was ready to embark on the rest of their life together.

He was ready to go to bed every night with his woman and wake up every morning next to her. Tor wanted a family, children like his precious nephew and newborn niece.

Chapter Seventeen

The palace was lit up, glittering against the evening sky, the sound of music floating out the open double doors into massive foyer, people in formal dress milling around the front and visible through the open doorway.

It was a party. No doubt to celebrate his return.

A surprise for him that Tor would have much preferred not to be surprised with. Blythe had realized that of course and texted Tor of his family's plans as soon as she'd learned of them.

He'd been able to mentally prepare and was grateful.

He found it much harder now to don the air of civility and charm he used to wear like armor in his role as the youngest Prince of the House of Asgersen.

Tor's family were standing together in the Great Hall when he entered, their faces wreathed in welcoming smiles.

Drawing on years of training, Tor returned a smile of his own. If it did not quite reach his eyes, he wasn't worried about it.

This moment was about appearances, not reality.

Reality would have been asking him what he wanted and respecting his need for quiet so soon after another operation that had seen him lose a fellow soldier and friend. Again. Reality would not be a ballroom full of dignitaries, high profile business associates and their country's elite welcoming him home when all he wanted was a private evening with his family.

Reality would absolutely not be the very obvious attempts at matchmaking several party guests were.

Blythe seemed to be the one person who understood what Tor needed. Breaking with past behavior, she stayed close by and ran interference for him with overly enthusiastic partygoers.

He understood that his people were celebrating his safe return to Tapt Oyer. However, some, especially single women of a certain age, wanted to *personally* welcome him home.

He was a prince, but that didn't stop a few forward souls from trying to grasp his hand, or even *hug* him.

What had the world come to?

He had never hugged his father without an invitation, would still never even consider doing so.

Not that Tor voluntarily hugged anyone anymore. It was a behavior he'd left behind in his teens.

The exceptions being his nephew and infant niece.

And Blythe. He hated not being able to just reach out and touch her when that was all he wanted to do.

Blythe practically vibrated with the need to be alone with Tor, but they had this interminable *celebration* to get through before that could happen.

Blythe was glad she'd had the chance to warn Tor what his family planned. She gave an internal shudder at the thought of how he would have felt being blindsided by such a loud and pressing homecoming.

It shocked Blythe, but his royal family didn't seem able to grasp that he'd seen real combat. He'd lost friends and seen others seriously injured. He'd participated in dangerous ops that could very well have ended his life. Tor had never told her exactly what his special unit's ops were about, but he'd let slip once that retrieval of at risk targets was part of it.

He wasn't coming home from a two-year long jaunt around the world. Only that was how the rest of the royal family acted.

Blythe knew that Holger and Geir had had very different experiences in their two years of military service, acting more as liaisons and diplomats than active soldiers, but still.

They all knew that wasn't the type of service Tor had signed up for. Or gone into.

He hadn't come home the same man who loved parties and crushes of people.

Didn't anyone else see how much Tor had changed?

He'd grown more taciturn, less apt to crack a joke. In fact, he rarely smiled in any genuine way unless they were alone together.

Or with his beloved nephew and niece.

Blythe knew she should not be gravitating toward Tor, but she could not help herself. Her prince needed someone to play buffer between him and the people she knew he would much rather not have to greet on his first night home.

So, she overheard his father tell one of the ladies, no doubt invited specifically to meet the youngest Asgersen Prince, "Naturally Tor will continue his role in the military."

"No." Blythe may have spoken quite loudly and inserted herself into a conversation she was *not* party too.

And she did not care.

"You aren't reenlisting, are you?" she asked Tor, begging him with everything in her to say no.

The past two years had been torture as his elite unit went on one dangerous mission after another. Most of which, did not allow any sort of communication with the outside world.

"It is tradition," Prince Canute said before Tor could answer. "Naturally, my youngest son will keep his place in the Tapt Oyerian Military."

"As a prince, it would be a nominal role, I'm sure." This from the other woman, who Blythe may or may not have been introduced to.

She could not remember, nor could she make herself care. The woman simply had no idea. Tor did not understand the concept of nominal service, much less have any inkling of adhering to it.

"To...Prince Tor?" Blythe asked the man himself for confirmation, stumbling over his name like she never did in company.

"If I were to remain an officer in our military," Tor said in a tone that said nothing about which way he was leaning in that regard. "It would be in the same capacity as before I left for active service."

"If?" His father asked, his brows beetled. "There is no *if*. It is your duty."

Tor did not direct his reply to Prince Canute, but kept his gaze locked with Blythe's, though it was clear his words were meant as much for his father as for her. "My duty is to the Crown as a prince. How I live out that duty is between me and my Sovereign. King Holger."

The addition of his brother's name had been unnecessary from the point of view of feelings, but Tor no longer had the habit of leaving any room for misinterpretation of his words. Unless he had a specific agenda in doing so.

His father should realize that, but Prince Canute blanched, clearly wounded by the reminder he was no longer the king.

Tor's eyes narrowed, like the older man's reaction surprised him, but he made no effort to soften the effect of his words.

And Blythe didn't think that was because he still held resentment for the way Prince Canute had abdicated parental responsibility for Tor long before abdicating the throne.

Tor just wasn't that man any longer. He wasn't the charming, affable peace maker he'd been when they'd first met.

The change had been happening all along, but the last two years had cemented it.

Tor did not indulge in other people's drama. He said what he meant and he expected others to accept his words at face value.

Blythe was fairly certain that whatever role he would be asked to fill in his duty to the Crown, it would not be as a diplomat or ambassador.

Not if King Holger wanted to maintain smooth relations with his allies and business associates.

His father made an excuse and left, the woman who had been hoping to catch Tor's interest following suit moments later when it was clear she had failed completely in that endeavor.

"Dance with me," Tor said, putting his hand out to Blythe.

She wanted to take his hand more than anything, gripping her own together to stop herself. "But no one else is dancing."

"They will, if we do."

"It's not that kind of party."

"There is a live orchestra. Of course it is that kind of party."

But it wasn't. And they both knew it.

It was a welcome home reception. Being held in a ballroom with plenty of floor space for dancing for those inclined.

Blythe skimmed the room, seeking insight into what to do. Tor's hand remained reaching out to her.

Chandeliers glittered over a room filled with partygoers dressed to the nines. Blythe herself was wearing a floor length designer gown in russet silk. Janice had said that it complimented her curvy figure, that the men at the party wouldn't be able to keep their eyes off of Blythe.

The only eyes she cared were on her were Tor's. Blythe wanted to look beautiful for him, and him alone.

She'd worn her hair in a half up, half down style she knew he would like, her natural brown waves touching her shoulders. The only jewelry she wore was a locket he'd given her, bought in the marketplace of Istanbul. Inside was a picture of Tor and one of Janice.

The two most important people in Blythe's life. Not that she would allow him to see the photos and he had no idea she wore his picture so close to her heart on a daily basis.

Gorgeously dressed tables were set around the perimeter of the room, over the top flower arrangements giving an elegant but celebratory aspect to everything.

But the center of the room was empty of furniture, if currently filled with guests standing and talking. The live orchestra played at one end of the room, the volume of the music not overwhelming, but not so quiet it could not be heard to dance to either.

Tor made a hand gesture in the direction of the conductor and suddenly perfect waltz music was playing.

Unable to do anything else, Blythe laid her hand in his.

His hold was perfect as always, his smile not as big and unfettered as he offered her in private, but it *was* genuine.

They danced in silence for several moments before other couples joined them. By the end of the song, the middle of the ballroom was filled and they continued to dance as the next one began.

"You won't really stay in the military, will you?" she asked him, unable to forget his father's words.

"Not doing what I have for the last two years, but there is value in having the leadership influenced by those who have actually served in hot zones."

"So, you would be an officer."

"I already am an officer."

"What would be different then?" she asked, her heart in her throat.

"I have been in the reserves since I turned eighteen."

"I know." He used to have one weekend a month for training and two weeks every summer.

She'd found out the first time he had to go away after they started their friends with benefits thing and wasn't going to be in Boston for a weekend she'd planned to see him. Blythe had been unaware of Tor's participation in the small island nation's military before that.

"I would continue with training and teaching one to two times per month as well as being part of the decision making process for our military."

"But no more dangerous operations."

"Unlikely."

"But not impossible."

"I have specialized training that could be called upon."

"But you are a prince."

"Who serves my country, not the other way around."

"You *want* to take the traditional role waiting for you."

"It depends."

"On what?"

"I think this is a discussion that should wait for later."

Looking around her, realizing how close the other dancers were, how easy it would be to overhear their discussion for someone determined to do so, Blythe nodded. "You're right."

His brother tapped Tor's shoulder a few minutes later and suddenly Blythe found herself dancing with Prince Geir while Tor partnered another woman.

"My brother is taken with you," Geir said as he expertly led Blythe around the dance floor.

It felt so different dancing with Tor, no matter how good his brother was at the traditional steps and cadence.

"We are friends."

"More than that, I think."

Blythe refused to comment. Over the years, she'd learned that when dealing with the royal family, silence was more effective than explanation at times.

Geir frowned. "I don't think Tor was happy with the surprise party."

"Did you think he would be?" Blythe couldn't help asking with some censure. "Even if he was just getting out of the military, the adjustment would be hard enough, but he only got back from his latest mission a few days ago."

"You are very perceptive and protective of him."

Blythe chose silence again.

A small sigh escaped the prince. "Holger and I tried to tell our father that this party would be better served happening in a month's time."

"He wouldn't listen." Blythe was not surprised.

Prince Canute made no secret of his desire to see his youngest son settled in marriage and this party was one big attempt at matchmaking.

For all the good it would do the former king and his plans.

"No, he wouldn't. And it's clear Tor has no interest in socializing."

"He has been an exemplary host," Blythe disagreed. If not flirty with the women brought to his attention.

That was as much her fault as Tor's need for some downtime. She'd kept his attention on her and knew soon the time would come to let it go.

"Like I said, protective."

"And you aren't?" Blythe had noticed she wasn't the only one running interference for Tor tonight. She wondered if Tor had.

"He's my little brother."

"Hardly little."

"But he'll always be younger."

"I know." Blythe couldn't keep the wistful tone out of her voice.

"Eight years is hardly a barrier between two people meant to be together. Holger is seven years Janne's senior."

"It's different though, isn't it?"

"I do not think so. If I do not miss my guess my brother does not either."

He was right about that, but Blythe had already strayed dangerously close to deep waters that could drown her. She backpedaled. "Well, it hardly matters for two friends."

"Does my brother know you see him as nothing more than a friend?" Geir asked, his expression less than pleased.

"Is that really any of your business?" Blythe found herself asking, surprised at her own temerity, but she would be darned if she would discuss her relationship with Tor with anyone but the man himself.

"Don't hurt him," Geir instructed in a tone that left no doubt how serious his edict was.

"Of course not." They were having sex, not involved in the love story of the century.

Even if she had fallen in the love with her prince, he'd never given any indication he felt the same.

Chapter Eighteen

Tor did not make it to Blythe's room until the wee hours of the morning, long after the last partygoer exited the ballroom.

Blythe knew he'd had to wait until all the guests staying in the palace were tucked safely into their rooms so they would not see him making his way to hers. But each minute she waited for him had crawled by in slow motion.

Uncaring of the enthusiasm she revealed, she flew into his arms the minute her door shut behind him.

One kiss led to another, and to another, and finally to making love in a frenzy of need up against the wall of her sitting room only to be followed by more lovemaking after he carried her to her bed.

Afterward, Tor wanted to talk. Blythe didn't mind. She didn't want him to leave yet and if that meant talking, she was happy to chat.

Until she realized what Tor wanted to talk about.

"But we've discussed this." Blythe stared at Tor, panic making her breath come in short gasps.

"That was three and a half years ago, Blythe." He sat up, unconcerned that the bedding pooled on his legs, revealing his semi-erect sex.

Did the man ever go completely soft?

Shaking her head at her thoughts, she said, "But..." only to trail off, unsure what she could say without sparking an argument.

"It is time to either go forward, or stop." Tor's expression lacked any semblance of humor.

He was not joking. Not teasing. He meant business.

Blythe could feel the cracks forming in her heart. "You want to break up?" she asked, unable to modulate her voice to hide all the pain that idea caused her.

Even knowing it was time. Even knowing she was the one who had planned to have this discussion with him.

Soon.

Just not yet.

"According to you, we cannot break up," he said, his tone unreadable. "Because we aren't officially together."

Yes, that was what she said, but they both knew the truth. "I haven't been with anyone else since Janice and Holger's wedding."

"And that does not tell you something?" he demanded, sounding more impatient than loverlike. Though his eyes roamed over her nudity with the warmth of a caress.

She shifted into a sitting position too, tugging the sheet and comforter up her body in a belated attempt at modesty. She needed armor for this conversation, not just some bedding.

"Can you say the same?" she asked, rather than answer his leading question.

"Yes."

He didn't elaborate, but what else did she need to know? They had agreed to make their friends with benefits deal exclusive and they'd both stuck by that agreement.

Which meant what? That the relationship she'd worked so hard to deny could be labeled as nothing but that.

A relationship. They were undeniably lovers and she'd been a fool to think she could maintain an emotional distance with this man.

"I wasn't ready for this." She gazed at him appealingly.

Unmoved, he said implacably, "I find that hard to believe."

"And yet, it is true," Blythe insisted. "You're still in your twenties," she said, like that in itself was an argument for her point of view.

Even though she didn't really believe it anymore. Prince Tor of the House of Asgersen might be twenty-six, but he had the maturity and life knowledge of a man much older. Over the years she'd come to see what it meant that he'd been raised to be a prince.

Maturity and control had been expected of him when other children were throwing tantrums and learning how to respond to social cues.

"We are back to that?" he asked, clearly unimpressed.

"Not really," she admitted.

No one could say this man did not know his own mind, or had living to do before he settled into his future.

Which didn't mean *she* was ready to break up so that could happen. Not even a little.

He shook his head, his gorgeous face cast in harsh lines. "You are highly intelligent, Blythe. You must have expected that I would want to take our relationship public at some point."

"I thought you'd want to end it." Or that she would. Out of necessity, if not desire.

"Really?" The mockery in his tone lacerated her. "More than three years of fidelity didn't convince you that wasn't the likely scenario?"

Put like that, but those years hadn't been normal ones.

"It wasn't like you had all that much chance to find someone else," she pointed out. "First you were in school and then you were serving oversees."

"You don't think I had opportunity? If nothing else, my father and his new wife have made sure I am surrounded by eligible women whenever I came home on leave."

"I know," Blythe said, feeling unaccountably cranky.

"You did not like that."

"No." She felt far too possessive of him to take the matchmaking with equanimity.

But Blythe had to let that feeling go. She had to let Tor go. Blythe had no choice.

And the longer she let this conversation go on, the more it would hurt when she said the words that needed saying.

"We have to break up," she said baldly, if quietly.

Forcing the hated words from her throat had taken all her will. There was nothing left over for volume.

Tor reeled backward, like she'd landed a powerful blow even the soldier prince found hard to shake off. "You do not mean that."

"I *do*." There were no choices.

Tor deserved to find someone he could spend the rest of his life with and that woman was not her.

"Why?" he asked. "Are you still that worried Janne will not accept a relationship between the two of us?"

"No. That's not it." Blythe wished it was. "You and I don't have a future and it's not fair to either of us to keep seeing each other like we have been."

Once again she spoke her truth, as she'd done on that long ago night she'd invited him into her body without protection. And she knew, just like then, that he would hear the truth without truly understanding it.

"Why don't we have a future?" he demanded, anger flashing in his grey eyes like lightening in a cloud laden sky.

"You know I don't want to be a princess."

"Snap." He snapped his fingers for emphasis. "My future wife will not be a princess unless my brother wills it."

"You're mincing words. I don't want to be married to a prince. I'm not made to be part of a royal family."

"You already are part of my family."

"But I don't have responsibilities for behavior or social obligations I would have as your wife."

"So, you've thought about it?"

Of course she had. Once she'd realized she loved him, Blythe had thought of little else. Could they make it work? But further tests had confirmed that even IVF would not give them a chance at having children together.

"I can't be your wife."

He stood from the bed, his glorious, naked body stiff with affront. "I don't recall asking you."

"No, of course you haven't. It's just talking about the future. We can't have that one."

"Because you don't want to be married to me."

Why did she have to answer that question when he'd never asked her if she *would* marry him? It was not fair.

He just stood there in silence, waiting for her reply.

"I didn't say that," she said finally, her voice barely above a whisper, emotion wracking her body. It was all she could do not to fly apart.

"You as good as said you *will not* marry me. You see no future for us."

She nodded, unable to force another word out of her tight throat.

"Which equates to you *not wanting* to marry me," he pointed out, his tone glacier cold and just as immovable.

She didn't want to marry him and be unable to give him the children a prince required.

And now that moment was upon her, Blythe realized how very much she did *not* want to tell him the truth of her lack. It hurt too much.

It shouldn't. She knew in her head that it should not.

The inability to have children did not make her less.

Only that was not how it felt to her heart, no matter what her brain said.

Blythe had never even thought of having children until she started sleeping with Tor. Now, her inability to get pregnant felt like her femininity, her very value as a human being was diminished.

It made no sense, but the feelings persisted, always hurting.

A hollow area in her soul had opened up and it left her feeling empty and useless.

Telling herself that she was not defined by her ability to procreate didn't help.

Because deep down, where that little girl who did not understand why her parents did not love her, resided, deep, deep down...Blythe did not believe it.

She was defective.

She was not enough.

She had never been enough.

If Tor loved her, Blythe might feel differently. But in three and a half years of sharing their bodies, he'd never spoken a word about love. He'd never even called her by an endearment that could be interpreted that way.

He called her a *treasure*, not *darling*, not *beloved*, not even *sweetheart*.

He might not love her, but there could be no denying that this conversation was hurting him too. His set expression wasn't revealing much, but his eyes? Those grey eyes were filled with emotion and none of it positive.

Even so, Blythe hurt too much to try to make Tor feel better about what had to happen. Her heart was hemorrhaging with loss.

She said the only thing that would end this painful confrontation. "Yes."

Tor bit out an ugly four-letter word.

He dressed in silence, his movements precise, emanating a fury that battered against her already bleeding heart.

He paused at the door to her bedroom. "I won't bother you again."

He waited a moment, like he expected her to say something, but Blythe had no words.

He left her then, his posture rigid, his expression as closed as she'd ever seen it.

Everything in her screamed to call him back, but she didn't.

What would be the point? Blythe had let their *friends with benefits* thing go on longer than she should have. Looking back, she realized it had not been fair to either of them.

Anything that led to this much hurt had not been a good idea.

It was time to let him go.

For both their sakes.

Blythe collapsed onto the bed, pulling his pillow into her body as a poor substitute for holding him. She buried her face in the ultra-soft Egyptian cotton case, his scent triggering the tears that she'd held back so hard while Tor had been in the room.

But she was alone now. Blythe could cry if she needed to.

Alone again. No hope of that solitude being broke by a meetup with Tor tomorrow, next week, next month...ever.

An awful sound, like that of a wounded animal, came out of her.

And no one was there to hear. Just like when she'd been small.

Just like then, she had no one she could call. Blythe could not tell Janice about this pain. She's spent too long lying to the sister of her heart and was just now realizing how impossible that made it to go to the other woman for comfort when she needed it most.

And the worst thing was, that Blythe had no one to blame but herself.

She had fallen in love with the man she could never have. She had set herself up for this heartbreak and to have to face it alone.

CHAPTER NINETEEN

A year after his return from deployment, Tor looked up to find Geir standing in his New York office.

"This is a surprise." His brother's visit was not on Tor's calendar, but calling it a *surprise* might be stretching it.

Geir and Holger had contrived to visit him unexpectedly at least twice since Tor's move to New York. It was odd.

Considering how busy they both were, their visits were an excess of family obligation.

Geir settled into one of the sleek black leather chairs facing Tor's desk. "It was a last-minute change in my itinerary."

Tor did not call his brother a liar, but he doubted that change had anything to do with business.

Neither his father, nor his brothers had been happy when Tor had announced his intention to take up a management position for Tapt Oyer Global in New York.

However, neither had his brothers refused Tor the position.

"Everyone is well?" Tor asked. "The children are thriving?"

Tor hadn't seen the little prince or his sister in too long.

"Janice is making sure their childhood is just that." Geir's tone said he approved of their sister-in-law's break from family tradition in child rearing. "They both miss their Uncle Tor."

"I will schedule a trip to Tapt Oyer soon." In the past year, Tor had managed to arrange all his trips to home to avoid seeing Blythe.

Which meant he made fewer trips than he might have otherwise and missed more than one family event. He'd gotten surprisingly little flack for that from his brothers, but they each called him at least once a week. Another odd new behavior.

Having experienced the ultimate in loss while deployed, Tor appreciated this new attempt at closeness between the siblings rather than eschewing it.

Which did not mean that any of them talked about their emotions, or the like.

Sarcasm and business were their language currency.

"That is what I've come to talk to you about."

Ah, their father wanted Tor to visit Tapt Oyer, with plans for more matchmaking no doubt. "A phone call would have done," Tor chided his brother.

"Not in this case."

Tor went on full alert, his body tensed for action. "Janne is all right?"

His sister-in-law had had a miscarriage a month after Tor's return to Tapt Oyer. He hadn't even known she was pregnant.

Still in the first trimester, Janne and Holger had shared the news with no one.

Except perhaps Blythe, but Tor was no longer in a position to know what the travel journalist knew about their family.

"She is fine," Geir answered, his expression saying that was not the whole truth.

Tor waited in silence for Geir to continue.

"Someone close to the family is leaking sensitive information to the press."

Tor sat up straighter, barely holding himself back from leaping to his feet.

He was careful not to reveal too much of his inner thoughts or feelings, even to his brothers. The practice was so ingrained, it came as second nature to him.

"Personal or business?" he asked Geir in an even tone.

"Both."

Tor very deliberately bit out an expletive.

"Exactly."

"You do not know who it is?"

He framed it as a question, but Tor had no doubt he was right. If Geir knew the name of the culprit, he would have named him.

"Not as such, no."

"What does that mean?"

"The leaks happen after Blythe has been to visit Janne."

Something inside Tor seized painfully. "Impossible. Blythe would never betray the sister of her heart."

Or the rest of the Royal family. Blythe valued her place among them too deeply, even if she'd made it clear she didn't actually want to become one of them. Not if it meant committing to *him* for a lifetime.

Geir shrugged. "I would have thought not, but the timing cannot be denied. Either she's leaking information, or someone she trusts enough to talk about us, is doing it."

"Blythe doesn't have *any* friends that close outside our family." For whatever reason, Tor could not deny the now defunct friendship between him and the journalist.

"People change, Tor."

Tor shook his head decisively. "Not like that. Not Blythe."

"You haven't even seen her in a year. Have you spoken to her?" Geir look was speculative.

"Are you having me watched?" Tor should not be startled that his brother was aware he had managed to avoid Blythe that long, but he was. It wasn't as if the family never saw him, or her. Just never together. "And no, I have not spoken to her."

He let nothing of what he felt about that show in his expression or his voice.

"Of course you are being watched," Geir affirmed sardonically. "We all are. If not by our own security, then by the media or those interested in our country or business."

Okay, maybe that had been a stupid question.

"I do not need to speak to Blythe to know she would never leak privileged information to the media," Tor informed his brother.

"Her travel docuseries has been picked up by a large streaming service. The timing is suspect."

"You think she parlayed information in exchange for what? Entrée to the execs at the streaming service?"

"They are doing another docuseries, one on modern day royals. Our family is slated to feature prominently."

Tor had to agree that the timing was suspect, but Blythe wasn't. "What exactly is it you want from me?" Tor asked.

"Find out if Blythe is the leak, and if she's not, who is."

"Why me?" Surely this was a job for their security people.

"You and Blythe are friends. You should be able to figure out what is going on without ever letting her know you were looking into it. If she's not the source of the leak, we don't need the drama that would ensue if she realized she was suspected."

"She's your friend too. Why am *I* being tasked with this?"

"She's the dear friend of my sister-in-law, not *my* friend," Geir said.

"And you think it is different for me?"

"I know it is. Hell, Tor, she heard from you more often than any of us while you were gone."

Tor went still. *Did* his brother have him under surveillance? "How do you know that?"

"I looked at your sat phone summary."

"What? Why? When?"

"I was worried that you never called or texted any of us between the monthly calls to the palace."

"Why would that worry you?"

"Do you think I'm an idiot, Tor? You were deployed to a hot zone. You saw things during your two years of service neither Holger nor I ever have. You lost comrades, saw others permanently disabled by their wounds. Of course I worried. You needed someone to talk to and I'm just glad you found that person in Blythe."

That was a lot more personal observation than Tor or his brothers usually indulged in.

"So you checked my sat phone to make sure I had a friend I was talking to?" he asked, still finding that a little hard to believe.

Not that his brother would invade his privacy. Tor would have done the same to get answers he wanted. He was more shocked that Geir had been worried enough to do it.

"If I asked you if you had someone keeping you sane, would you have told me the truth?" Geir asked Tor dryly.

Tor didn't know the answer to that. If he thought telling Geir he was in frequent contact with Blythe would reveal their secret relationship, no. He would not have.

"That's what I thought. Do you think *I* wanted to talk about feelings?"

"No." Tor had no doubts about that one. "All right. We've established that you know that Blythe and I were close friends."

"Were?"

"We haven't seen much of each other since I got back."

"You haven't seen each other at all, but unless there is something you haven't told the rest of us, you're still close enough to find out what is going on without making her suspicious."

Tor frowned at his brother. "I think Blythe would be suspicious if I just showed up on her doorstep."

They both lived in New York now, but had managed to avoid each other for a full year.

"Surprised, not suspicious. They are not the same." Geir leaned forward in his chair. "Tor, we need you to do this. If the leak is someone else, security is the best option for finding them, but if it's Blythe..."

They both knew that would have to be handled much differently than someone else. Blythe was as good as a member of the royal family.

"Other than Janice, you are the best placed member of the family to find out if Blythe is involved." Geir met Tor's gaze levelly.

Neither of them said what they were both thinking. If Janice were approached to do it, she would refuse, but not before a lot of yelling and she would definitely tell Blythe they suspected her.

"I'll do it."

"Good." Geir stood and offered a document packet. "Here are the files we have on the leak and my preliminary research on Blythe."

Tor took the packet and set it down on his desk. He would have to clear some time this afternoon to look at it.

"I'm not flying out until later. Dinner?" Geir asked.

Tor agreed.

He looked forward to hearing stories about his nephew and niece. Geir was even better at telling them than their own father, Holger.

There had been a time not so long ago, when Tor had thoughts of having his own children.

With Blythe.

Pipe dreams that had no place in the present.

Chapter Twenty

Peremptory knocking interrupted Blythe's Saturday chores. She turned off the vacuum and went to answer, wondering what Janne was doing in New York.

The last she'd spoken to her friend, she'd thought the queen had no plans to travel.

Blythe had moved into a building, complete with doorman and private security, after her friend married into royalty. The king had insisted.

The only people on the list for the doorman to let up without calling her first were members of the Tapt Oyerian Royal Family and the only one of those who would surprise her with a visit was the sister of her heart, Janne.

Making no effort to tidy her appearance for her best friend, Blythe flung the door wide, her hair up in a messy bun, wearing a tank top and Yoga pants. "What are you doing in New York..."

Her voice trailed off, her voice failing. It wasn't Janne standing there with a bevy of bodyguards, but Tor.

Wearing a dark, perfectly tailored suit, his hair as short as he'd kept it in the military, his stance filled with royal confidence.

Blythe's heart surged with completely inappropriate joy, her body wanting to lean toward him. She hadn't seen him in a year, and she had missed him every single day.

Stifling the urge to throw herself into his arms and belatedly schooling her expression, Blythe stepped back in silent invitation for Tor to come into her home. "Tor...I mean Your Highness, what are you doing here?"

The prince put his finger to his lips in shushing gesture and then waved two dark suited men carrying some kind of equipment into her apartment.

One of the men came up to her and scanned her with a small handheld device before nodding silently to Tor.

Tor indicated the hallway with a tip of his head.

Blythe followed him, the door to her apartment shutting behind her.

She spun back, intending to knock and get it open again.

But Tor's hand on her arms stopped her. "Let them do their job."

What job? Blythe wanted to ask, but she couldn't make herself speak.

Every atom of her focus was on the feel of Tor's fingers against her skin.

He tugged her around to face him, but did not release her. "Come with me."

She didn't ask where. Blythe just nodded.

Tor's hold shifted to around her waist and she shuddered.

He cursed, but did not loosen his hold. In fact, it became all the more posses-sive, their hips brushing as they walked down the hall toward the elevator.

His security stepped onto the elevator first, pressing a button as Blythe and Tor stepped into the small space, the second security man following as the doors slid closed.

The first security guy tilted his head and spoke to someone else saying they were on their way down. The elevator doors opened to the parking garage where two black SUVs waited.

Diplomatic flags flew on either side and the doors were stamped with the Coat of Arms for the House of Asgersen.

Tor was making no effort to hide this meeting with her.

Blythe shivered in the chilled air of the parking garage. Tor shrugged out of his suit jacket and settled it over her shoulders, his warmth and scent surrounding her with aching familiarity.

The two security men split up, opening the backdoors on either side of the vehicle. Neither she, nor Tor spoke as the climbed into the car and did their seatbelts. One of the suited security men slid into the driver's seat and the other the passenger seat in front.

The other SUV pulled out first and then the one she and Tor were in followed.

They were in Manhattan before Tor broke the silence. "I am taking you to my apartment."

"Okay." Blythe had no other words.

She'd followed him from her own home like a lamb, she wasn't about to start demanding explanations now. Whatever was going on had to be important, or Tor would never have come for her. Blythe was positive about that.

He stared at her, shook his head and then uttered a four-letter word she'd only heard him use a couple of times all the years of their acquaintance.

"What?" she asked, emotions too close to the surface.

"We've wasted a year."

"What? I don't understand."

"You did not want to break up with me."

She opened her mouth, but he put his hand up. "Do not say anything if it's going to be another lie."

"I did not lie to you." Indignation gave her volume when maybe nothing else would have.

"You did." He glared at her. "I repeat, you did *not* want to break up."

"Of course not." Was he stupid, or something?

"We are not hiding our relationship anymore."

"We don't have a relationship."

"Have you had sex with anyone else in the past year? Have you even gone on a date?" he demanded, like he knew her answer before she gave it.

In that moment, she really wished she *could* lie to him, because Blythe so would. "No."

"Me either."

She knew that. His father was furious that Tor wouldn't even try dating any of the appropriate females he brought to his son's notice.

"You're supposed to."

"Am I?"

"You know you are. You have a responsibility to your family. You are a prince."

"The only woman I am dating is you."

"It's impossible."

"No, Blythe. We're done."

Her heart felt like it was in vise grips. "You just said..."

He shook his head. "How did I believe you a year ago?"

Before she could reply he leaned toward her, his intent clear, but he paused a breath away.

He was waiting for her consent. She wasn't going to give it. They could not kiss.

Her body and heart were in direct opposition to her mind.

Her brain had won for a year and all that had gotten her was loneliness and pain.

Unable to ignore the demands of her heart and body, Blythe closed the distance between them, pressing her lips to his. She fell into the kiss like a woman deprived of oxygen being offered life giving air.

Tor growled and kissed her back with atavistic passion.

It had been a year, but they were still perfectly tuned to each other and there was no fumbling to find the right pressure for their lips. Her hands were all over him before she even realized she'd reached out touch.

When they broke apart, she was panting and his gaze burned with need.

His short hair stuck straight up where she'd run her fingers through it, his tie was undone as were the top two buttons on his shirt. Her hands itched to reach over and press against the hardened bulge in his slacks.

Tor cupped her face with both hands, his grey gaze trapping her own. "We *are* dating and we *aren't* hiding it."

"But you live in New York." He was well known here. Everyone would know. "You noticed?"

"You know I did." Though, like him, she'd managed to avoid being in the same space together for the past year.

The SUV stopped and she looked out the window to yet another parking garage. Neither she nor Tor spoke while the security team escorted them to his penthouse apartment that took up the entire top floor of the high-rise owned by Asgersen's company.

He gave her a quick tour, like he wanted her to be able to easily find her way around.

"Your apartment has its own private gym, sauna and whirlpool," she said, impressed despite herself.

"It does. Are you looking for some time on the treadmill?" he asked with sexy humor. "Only I have another idea for getting some exercise."

"Don't tease. You know we can't do that."

"I think we can."

"You think we're dating," she said accusingly.

He gave her an assessing look and then led her into the living room, offering her refreshments without answering.

She took a bottle of water, needing something to clear her mind and realized too late, she might have been better off with a stiff whiskey.

This situation was surreal.

"Do you want to know why I kidnapped you from your apartment?" he asked as they somehow ended up next to each other on the large, elegant and surprisingly comfortable sectional facing a sleek gas fireplace.

There were other chairs in the room, but she had made no move to take one. Talk about giving mixed signals.

Feeling more frustrated with herself than she did with him, she said tartly, "You didn't kidnap me. I came willingly."

"Without any questions, your purse, or your phone," he observed. "I noticed."

"And you like that." Too much. It was all over the smug look on his gorgeous face. "Well don't get too conceited. I knew you wouldn't show up if it wasn't important."

"You do not believe I would have come simply to see you?"

"I know you didn't. The guys with their handheld scanners weren't there to get us dating again."

An arrested expression came over his features. "I wonder."

"What do you wonder?"

"How far my brothers will go to meddle with me and my private life."

"Your brothers are the reason you're here?" she asked, feeling let down.

"Yes." His eyes narrowed. "And you do not like knowing that."

"I'll take the 5th on that one."

"No. No more hiding between us. No more subterfuge."

"I don't lie to you." He had to know that.

"But you've lied about me."

"What do you mean?"

"Never acknowledging what I am to you to anyone else." His expression had gone hard.

Tor may have agreed to their *friends with benefits* deal, but she thought she was seeing for the first time how he really felt about that. She should have realized long before now that a man with his pride would chafe against being kept a secret.

"And what are you?" she asked, seeking clarification.

Yesterday they hadn't been speaking. A few minutes ago, they'd been kissing like they were both starved for it.

"I am your damn boyfriend, Blythe."

There was nothing left in her emotional reserves to deny that claim. "Yes."

"Finally, we make progress."

"Don't be so smug."

He reached out and cupped her nape, his thumb brushing along sensitive nerve endings. "Shouldn't I feel smug? I have you here beside me."

"And that's a good thing?"

"Very good." His dark brows drew together in a frown. "Don't you think?"

"Yes." No more denials. No more subterfuge.

She had spent the last year pining. She was done with the whole *giving him up for his own good* thing. He hadn't dated in the last year either. The way he acted, he'd missed her nearly as badly as she'd missed him.

A shiver of dread skated down her spine even as her heart rejoiced at the implication of that truth.

Chapter Twenty-One

"Someone is leaking sensitive information about my family and Tapt Oyer Global to the press."

It took Blythe a moment to realize they were talking about his reason for coming to her apartment, not their relationship anymore. "I noticed that. I brought it up to Janice, but she wasn't worried about it."

Janice's opinion was that there were too many ways to spy on people and businesses in their current age of technology, that it was an impossible hope to maintain true privacy in a family like the Asgersens, or even for their business Tapt Oyer Global.

Tor laughed, the sound harsh but still utterly gorgeous. "So much for my brothers keeping it from her."

"Why would they try to keep it from her?" Blythe's own brows furrowed in confusion.

His lips twisted wryly. "So, she does not get upset."'

Huh. Did they really think that Janice was such a fragile flower? "Well, she's not stressed about it," Blythe assured Tor.

"So much so that she has not brought it up to Holger. I gathered," Tor said dryly.

"What has that got to do with you rushing me out of my apartment without my phone?" Looking back, Blythe could barely credit she'd let him do it.

"The leaks coincide with your visits to Tapt Oyer."

"They do?" Blythe asked, surprised. But then horror washed over her. "*You* think I'm the leak?"

"No." A flat denial with no give.

Tor genuinely did not think she was the source of the leak? But why rush her out of her apartment then?

"Holger thinks I'm the leak?" she asked, still upset.

"He and Geir do not know who the leak is. They have tasked me with finding out."

"But—"

He squeezed her nape. "I think you've been bugged."

"What?" Another kind of horror crawled along her skin. "No, who would do that?"

"I do not know who, but if it's not via your phone, there will be an actual device attached to something else you have with you most of the time."

"Then it must be my phone. I change out purses for the season and my outfit. My computer and tablet get left behind too much and I don't have a piece of jewelry I wear every day."

As she said the words, Blythe realized they simply were not true. Her hand flew up to grab her locket in a protective gesture.

"Relax," Tor said. "If it was your locket, it would have triggered the scanner back at the apartment."

"You gave it to me."

"I know. And you wear it every day. You were wearing it the night you dumped me. I should have realized then..." He let his voice trail off, shaking his head.

"I didn't dump you."

"You most definitely did."

"I just pointed out that we cannot get married."

"Why is that, by the way?"

"No."

"No?"

"No, I'm not discussing particulars on that topic with you. You're the one who pointed out you never asked me."

"Fair enough."

"What does that mean?"

"I'll respect your wishes not to talk about it until if, and when, I ask."

"I'm not a fifteenth century damsel. If I want to get married, I could ask you."

"Are you going to?" he asked, humor lacing his tone.

"No."

"Then we will have to agree that the discussion in question will happen on my timetable."

"That's not what I said." Even as she argued, her heart was beating a rapid tattoo in her chest.

Was Tor saying he planned to ask her to marry him? Even after a year apart? Did she want him to? Funny that he had not even paused when she said she would not be asking him.

A less confident man would take that to mean she didn't want to marry him. Like *he* had last year. But Tor wasn't making those sort of assumptions now. Oh no, now he was all, when and if *he* asked.

"I missed you this year." No more hiding.

"I refused to think about you."

"That is kind of scary." That he could just shut her out like she didn't matter.

"I still missed you."

"Oh." She turned her head to nuzzle the hand at her nape. "I'm glad."

"Not nice."

"You would be bored with nice."

"Perhaps. You do not bore me." He tugged her until she was straddling his lap, her Yoga pants and his trousers no barrier to the heat between them. "I do not think I bore you either."

"Not a chance."

He reached around, both hands pressing on her bottom, kneading her curves. "I thought you did not want me anymore."

"We'd just made love. How does that make sense?" But she'd struggled too. Struggled with how easily he'd walked away. "You didn't fight; you just walked away."

"I was hurt."

"And you did not want me to see you hurt."

"Naturally not."

Maybe if he loved her, it would have been different. She'd wanted to talk about the breakup with Janice and lay the whole blasted relationship bare for the sister of Blythe's heart.

Only by the time Blythe had worked up the nerve, Janice was going through the worst experience of her life and needed support, not someone leaning on *her*.

"You look more thoughtful than you should straddling my hips, *min skatt*."

"Ooh, I missed you calling me that."

He tugged her closer so the apex of her thighs pressed down on his hard bulge. "Why so thoughtful?"

"You want to go public."

"Yes."

"Janice is going to be so hurt that I kept this from her for so long."

"You are so sure she did not know."

Blythe opened her mouth to say *yes* but closed it. Was she sure? How easy had it been to hide such an important element of her life? And if it had been that easy, had she *really* hidden it? "I'm *not* sure."

"Do you want me to ask Holger?"

"Yes."

"Okay. After."

"After what?" she asked before she realized what a silly question that was.

His laughter before he kissed her was Tor's only answer. Then his lips were on hers. They kissed like they hadn't just kissed down in the car. Like it had been too long and neither one of them could wait another second.

She rocked her body over his even as their mouths ate at each other. She didn't know which of them opened their lips first, and it did not matter, but their tongues rubbed against each other, sending pleasure coursing through her.

His big hands were everywhere, divesting her of her clothes even as she fought with the buttons on his shirt. He shoved her top and sports bra up, cupping her breasts while his pelvis thrust up toward her.

They got enough clothes off so she could take him into her body.

He stilled her hips, his face set in lines of strain. "Is it safe."

Emotion welled. Appreciation for his consideration. Grief at the truth, but she just nodded.

He surged upward even as she pressed down, both of them gasping as he seated fully in her body. How she had missed this feeling of fullness.

They went back to kissing, rocking together, his slacks only pushed down his hips rubbing against her naked thighs.

Erotic and intense, the pleasure built between them too quickly.

But it had been a year.

Every muscle in her body tightened as her climax washed over her, her womb contracting in ecstasy over and over again.

Tor shouted as he came, his hands pulling her tight into his body, like he never wanted to let her go.

Blythe let herself collapse against him, breathing harshly as her body shivered in the aftermath of such sudden and overwhelming pleasure.

"How did we think we could go without this?"

"It wasn't easy."

"No, it was impossible."

She could not deny his claim, not while their bodies were still connected and the joy was still thrumming through her.

Eventually they got up and finished undressing. Tor wanted to soak in the whirlpool and Blythe thought that sounded good.

The temperature was set lower than most hot tubs she'd been in. She asked him about that.

"I like to soak, but I get too hot."

It wasn't cold by any means, just not scaldingly hot. She nodded. "We could just lie here and soak, or..." She let her voice trail off.

"Or?" he prompted, already moving into her space.

"In three and a half years and several hotel stays, we never made love in a whirlpool."

"No, we have not."

"Want to?" she asked with a smile, but her heart was beating fast already, her body preparing for him.

"Oh, yes."

She thought she would ride him again, but he had other ideas, arranging her so she floated with her head on one of the cushioned corners. He stood and entered her, holding her thighs up and open wide for his possession.

The water muted sensations while enhancing others. It took longer for the pleasure to build, but when she climaxed, Blythe nearly passed out from the pleasure of it.

She had to lean on Tor afterward as they dried off and made it into the beautifully appointed bedroom. She teased him about being too wiped to carry her and found herself swept off her feet.

If Tor wobbled a little she wasn't saying anything.

That he could carry her at all just showed how strong he was.

Chapter Twenty-Two

T or talked to the security officer in charge of the sweep of Blythe's condo and phone while she slept. She was going to be livid when she found out that there had indeed been an app installed on her phone as well as bugs in her living room and bedroom.

Who had placed them and gotten the app on her phone was the real question as Tor had never doubted that technology, and not Blythe, was responsible for the leaks.

After he got off the phone with the security people, he arranged a conference call with his brothers. Tor was signing off that call when he heard the shower go on.

Dropping his headset, he headed to the bathroom. The sight that met him made something squeeze in his chest.

Blythe stood under the spray in the glass and marble enclosure, water cascading down her beautiful body. As she shifted to wash herself, he caught glimpses of her raspberry tipped breasts and the shadow between her legs.

Heat surged through him, but more than that, something inside him settled at the sight.

This was his woman. He was never letting her go again.

He'd made a mistake just accepting her desire to break up a year ago.

How had he believed she didn't still want him? He was not a man who suffered insecurity, so where had his willingness to believe come from?

Regardless, he no longer believed. The look on her face when she had realized he was the one at her door? He would never forget it.

Pure joy had lit her blue eyes with the power of a major city grid. She'd tried to hide it, but that one glimpse had been all Tor had needed.

This woman had not wanted to let him go any more than he had wanted to walk away.

Whatever her reservations about the future, they were not about how well the two of them fit together.

Tor stripped out of his clothes, leaving them in a heap on the granite tiled floor, and stepped toward the shower.

Blythe did not startle as he slid his hands around her waist, but leaned back against him. Like this, the two of them together naked and under the water, was the most natural thing ever.

Making a soft sound of pleasure, she let him take her weight. "I woke up alone."

The words and the chiding tone surprised him. She'd never complained before. Not once. Not when they had no choice about being apart upon waking and not when he'd had to leave her bed to handle something.

But they were an official couple and apparently, that changed things for her. He did not mind.

How could it bother him that she didn't like waking without him?

Tor filed that preference away for later. "I had calls to make and did not want to wake you," he said. "However, in future, I will try to stay in bed with you."

"I would like that," she said in a tone that left no doubt she told the truth. "But it was considerate this time, I suppose."

"That was my intent."

She turned in his arms and looked up at him, her blue eyes soft with emotion. "You're a good boyfriend, Tor."

Boyfriend.

That was not the right label and would be replaced by another more permanent one soon, but right now he accepted that they had at least progressed to acknowledging their relationship as one.

"I aim to please," he promised her.

Blythe's sapphire eyes glowed with emotion. "Only for me."

It was true. While Tor did his best to respect and care for his family, this woman was the only person he actively considered *pleasing.*

In and out of the bedroom.

Another truth he filed away to take out and look at later.

"Did your people find the bugs?" she asked, even as she slid her water slicked body along his.

"Later." He would tell her everything. After.

She wound her arms around his neck, pressing her soft breasts into his chest, tantalizing him with her curves. "Later?" she teased.

He didn't bother to answer, but kissed her instead.

They had already made love multiple times, but his need for her rose as a frenzy inside him and he took her against the wall of the shower, bringing them both to the ultimate pleasure before tenderly washing her body while she did the same for him.

They dried off and donned the thick Turkish robes provided with the suite before calling for food.

They were snuggled on the sectional, a gas fire burning in the fireplace when she asked about the bugs again.

"There was an app on your phone and bugs in your living room and bedroom." There was no point trying to soft pedal it.

The truth was too disturbing.

"My bedroom?" she asked, clearly horrified.

He put one arm over her shoulder, needing to offer comfort in a concrete way. "Whoever placed the bugs knows of your habit of working and talking on the phone while in your bed."

"That isn't all I do in my bedroom." Blythe looked ready to throw up. "That implies it's someone I know well."

"Sweetheart, if they got into your apartment to place the bugs, they have to know you well."

"You called me sweetheart."

"I have called you *min skatt* many times."

"That means treasure."

"It is considered synonymous with *kjæreste*." Which meant dearest, but his brother used that endearment with Janne.

He'd felt strange using it with Blythe, especially when she refused to acknowledge they were anything more than friends who had sex.

"It is?" she asked.

"Yes."

"Oh."

"Is this important?" He was never going to understand this woman.

"No, not really." She sighed. "It doesn't have to be someone I know, does it? They could have broken in."

"Unlikely."

"Or posed as a maintenance person and gotten the building super to let them in." She sounded so hopeful.

He hated to dash those hopes. "We are looking into that angle, but again, it is unlikely."

Her eyes filmed over with moisture. "Someone I know?"

Tor let out a frustrated sound, hating to see the pain on his woman's face and pulled her close, wrapping both arms securely around her. "It does not have to be someone you are close to, just someone you have had to your apartment."

Someone who had access to her phone.

"Casual acquaintances don't visit me here. I don't have parties. I don't invite work colleagues around that are not also friends."

"You're a private person."

She shrugged. "I struggle letting people into my life."

"I know," he said with meaning. "You kept me in the friend zone even after we started having sex. And even then, you never once invited me to your home."

"I didn't want memories of you there."

"What? Why?"

"They would haunt me after we broke up."

He shook his head. "You never thought we had a future."

"I had my reasons."

"Which you will share with me when the time is right."

She didn't answer, but he hadn't expected agreement. And the lack did not worry him. Tor was a stubborn man and he was not giving up on this woman.

If the last year had taught him anything, it was that they were better together than apart.

"No one like that, are you sure?" he asked her, knowing it would be useless to pressure her to talk about their personal relationship if she wasn't ready.

His Blythe could be stubborn. The past year apart was proof enough of that.

She went silent for a moment, clearly trying to remember such an event. Then she frowned. "I had a small get together so we could get to know each other when we took on new crew in the transition to the streaming service."

It was possible one of those people worked on both her show and the new docuseries about modern royal families. He asked her for a list of the new crew and texted the names to his security people.

"Will they be able to figure out who the leak is?" she asked like she couldn't decide if she wanted the answer, or not.

"The bugs can't be traced to who is listening, but they are hopeful the app can be." And the list of names gave them a starting place to look as well.

"Oh."

"You do not want to know."

"I *need* to know, but no, I don't *want* to know which of my coworkers betrayed me." Blythe bit her lip, vulnerability burning in her blue gaze. "I'm hoping it's not actually a friend. I don't have that many of them."

Fury at the person responsible for putting that look on Blythe's face simmered inside Tor.

"That's a scary look on your face," Blythe said.

"Not for you."

"No, I know, but you're really angry that someone infiltrated the privacy of your family through me."

"My family's privacy will always be under attack," he pointed out. "That you were used is unacceptable and when we discover the culprit, they will know it."

"Your brothers thought I was the leak." Hurt radiated off of her.

"My brothers knew only that the leaks coincided with your visits. Only a fool would believe you willing to undermine your relationship with Janne and my brothers are not fools."

"They asked you to look into me."

Tor considered whether to tell her of his suspicions and realized there was no choice to make. If believing his brothers doubted her hurt Blythe, Tor could not withhold the truth.

"I think they were playing matchmakers."

Blythe jerked, clearly startled. "What?"

"Janne knows you as well as you know her. There can be no doubt that she was well aware there was something between us."

"But how?"

"I do not think you hid your interest in me as well as you believed."

"She never said anything."

"Didn't she?"

"She said she thought I had a thing for you, not that she thought we were seeing each other."

"I'm not sure she put it together until this last year. But she and my brothers all wondered once I took the job in New York and we started avoiding each other, rather than seeing more of each other as two friends would do under normal circumstances."

"I..."

"I did not understand why my brother Holger did not simply call you and ask what was going on. Or send in his own security team to search for the bugs."

"You think it was because he was matchmaking?"

"He and Geir have both remarked in the past year that it seems like I was avoiding you." Which he had been doing.

Her brows drew together in an adorable pout. "They were right."

"Yes." He would not apologize. She'd broken up with him, not the other way around.

Blythe sighed and snuggled closer. "So, they interfered?"

"Yes."

"You don't sound very happy about that considering the result of their interference." The look she gave him wasn't a pout, but clear affront.

He gave into the urge he'd had since sitting down beside her and tugged Blythe into his lap, his hand sliding under the fabric of her robe to touch the silken skin beneath. "I am very happy with the results of their interference."

"But you don't like knowing they interfered."

"Exactly." Pleased with how well she knew him, Tor kissed Blythe.

After several pleasurable moments, she pulled back with a sigh.

"What is the matter?" he asked her.

"I have to talk to Janice."

"You are worried she will be hurt when you tell her the truth."

"Of course she will be."

Tor agreed, but he didn't say so. Blythe didn't need him fueling her already strong sense of guilt. "She will forgive you."

"How can you be so sure?"

"Because I know without a doubt that if the situations were reversed, you would forgive her."

When Blythe did not reply, he prompted, "Wouldn't you?"

"You know I would."

"So, why so worried she will not do the same?" he asked.

Blythe shrugged. "I should have trusted her not to judge me."

"For having sex with her brother-in-law without making any sort of commitment to him?" he asked, wondering what exactly Blythe thought Janne would have judged.

Blythe rolled her eyes. "You know that's not true."

"I do, but I wondered when you were going to admit it."

"It never was as simple as *friends with benefits* was it?" Blythe asked ruefully.

"No." If she had slept with another man, much less dated one during their supposedly no commitment phase, or possibly worse, during their temporary breakup, he would have been gutted.

Not that Tor was admitting to any such weakness.

"I would have hated it if you found someone else," she said with more emotional honesty than he was willing to express.

But then, he wasn't the one who had broken things off a year ago.

"I did not. Neither did you. That should tell you something."

The sad expression she gave him made no sense.

"What?" he asked with less patience than he probably should have shown.

"We're not exactly soul mates."

"How would you describe it?" he asked, not entirely happy with her dismissal of a concept he would have dismissed as a fairytale had anyone else brought it up.

"We're very compatible in bed."

"So, you only missed the sex?" he asked, his tone biting.

He was not impressed.

Maybe they had just been friends with benefits.

"No! I missed the texts and the emails and the phone calls. I missed seeing you."

"As I missed you."

"I just...we're not in love, or anything."

Something inside him twinged at the thought she did not love him. Even so, he said, "Love is not something I think about."

"No surprise there." Her wry tone was as good as an eye roll.

He ignored the sarcastic tone. "You know me well."

"None of you Asgersen men are what you would call in touch with your softer emotions."

"Is that a complaint?"

"No, just...why *didn't* you date anyone else?"

"I didn't want another woman."

"But you were really angry with me that last night."

"Should I have been happy with you? You broke up with me."

"Not because I wanted to."

"Because you thought it was inevitable."

"Yes."

"Twenty-four hours."

"What does that mean?" she asked, not sounding particularly worried.

"You have one day to reconcile yourself to telling me why."

"I told you..."

"That you don't have to tell me why you broke up with me unless I ask you to marry me."

"You're saying..." Blythe's voice gave out.

"That I have plans for tomorrow evening?" Did she really think he was leaving their future to chance after the last year apart? "Yes. Be ready."

"I could put the date in my phone, but I don't have it," she said pointedly.

"You will soon," he assured her. His woman did love her portable technology. "A phone anyway. I have arranged to have a new phone delivered preloaded with everything, including your pictures and videos."

"Everything but the spyware?" she asked.

"Yes, and it has superior security software."

"But..."

"The security team were not sure when they could return the compromised phone and I noticed it was an older model."

"So, you bought me a newer one?" she asked, her tone not easily decipherable.

He shrugged. "What? You think I should have gotten you a refurbished model?"

She rolled her eyes at him. "You're kind of spoiled, you know. Other people make do all the time."

"But in this instance you are not one of them. This is not a bad thing."

"Okay. Thank you." She kissed him, hugging him tight. "I'm not used to letting people buy things for me."

"Get used to it." Not that he'd never bought her gifts, but now they were going public with their relationship, he did not have to limit himself to items easily explained or tucked away.

He understood better now why despite her parents' wealth, Blythe lived frugally on the not terribly impressive salary of a Travel Vlogger. She'd produced her own show on the small cable network as well. No doubt she had more disposable income now her show had gone to the large streaming service, but she still deserved to be spoiled.

Blythe's parents felt no need to give their daughter gifts now that she was an adult and living a separate life.

Unless it impressed others, they did not do it.

And he knew Blythe had a very hard time accepting the gifts given on that basis.

Chapter Twenty-Three

B lythe stood on the threshold of her apartment, unexpected dread washing over her. But she'd been spied on while she thought she was in the safest place possible.

Her own home.

The bugs had not had video, but that didn't lessen her feelings of violation.

Someone had listened to her when she thought she was alone.

Working and talking on the phone weren't the only things she did in her bed. Neither was sleeping.

For the past year, especially, Blythe had become adept at finding stress relief with her vibrator. How many times had she cried out Tor's name when she came, thinking no one else would ever know?

"There are no more bugs," Tor said from over her shoulder.

He'd given his security team instructions to clear the apartment and then wait for them at either end of the hall. He was giving Blythe what privacy he could and she appreciated it.

"But there were." And that knowledge was really messing with her.

"Tell me what you want and I will grab it for you, and then we will go back to my place." No censure for her hesitancy, no criticism.

Just an offer to alleviate her stress.

Blythe turned to face him, feeling like smiling for the first time since arriving at her building's parking garage. "You are a pretty special guy, you know that?"

"Because I am willing to pack for you?" he asked, looking genuinely confused.

Her smile morphed to a full-on grin. "Because you are you."

Pleasure sparked in his grey eyes. "I'm glad you think so, because I cannot be anything other than who and *what* I am."

His emphasis on the word *what* was not lost on her. "I don't mind you are a prince. Not really."

"Dammed by faint praise. How many women have tried to get close to me simply because I *am* a prince? And you? See it as something you have to tolerate."

"What can I say? The whole concept of royalty feels really archaic to me."

"And yet, here I am, a modern prince."

"Offering to pack for me. That's sweet, but I can do it."

"If you are sure?"

"Yes." But she still didn't step into the apartment.

He didn't pressure her, just rubbed her shoulders. "Tell me what bothers you the most."

"For the past year, I've just had my hand and vibrator." It didn't bother her to admit something so personal to him, but it devastated her to know someone else was aware of it.

"Ah."

"They heard me. Pleasuring myself."

He made a growly sound. "Those sounds belong to me."

"Don't go all caveman on me." She didn't mention that the primal reaction was more a turn on than turn off.

It was also comforting that he took her privacy as seriously as she did.

"I think I would like to hear you get yourself off," he said with a sexy look.

And just like that the tension around her popped.

She smiled her gratitude. "With my upcoming *Caribbean Adventure* for the show, I'm sure we can arrange a phone call for just that purpose."

"You? Are a tease." He groaned. "We don't have time."

"We've done practically nothing but make love since the moment you spirited me away from my apartment. Don't tell me you're in the mood again."

"Fine, I will not tell you."

She was laughing when she stepped into her living room. He shut the door behind them and followed her into the bedroom.

They chatted about his family while Blythe pulled out clothes to wear that evening. Tor's phone rang and he went back into the living room to take the call. Blythe took the time to dress, then run a flat iron through her hair, creating waves with the technique her hairstylist had shown her. She made quick work of her makeup, going for the natural look she preferred.

Even so, it took her at least thirty minutes all told, and Blythe was surprised that Tor never came back into the room. After packing a case with clothes for a couple of days, she went looking for her prince to tell him she was ready to go. She found him pacing between the couch and the window, barking orders into the phone.

His gorgeous face was set in a scowl, his tone one she would not have ignored if she was on the receiving end of it.

Tor saw her and gave a clipped goodbye before hanging up and tucking his phone into his pocket.

"What is it? You sounded really mad when I came in."

"They have identified the culprit."

Just like that, all the relaxation she had achieved went up in smoke. Blythe went rigid with stress. "Who is it?"

"Your film editor." His expression said he understood just how devastating that news would be for her.

But Linda Jones had been part of her life almost as long as Janne, and Blythe had trusted the older woman almost as much as she did the sister-of-her-heart.

Blythe shook her head, unable to believe. "No." Her legs gave out and she collapsed into an armchair.

She'd worked with Linda since launching her Travel show on the cable channel. For the first couple of years, it had only been her and Linda. They were friends, not just colleagues.

"But she's a film editor." Leaking information about the Tapt Oyerian Royal family and Tapt Oyer Global wasn't going to advance her career.

"Who enjoys the finer things in life, not all of which are manageable on her income."

Which implied Linda had spied on Blythe and sold the information she got doing so for nothing more than money. How could that be possible? Even the juiciest stories wouldn't have netted her enough to risk her career and destroying Blythe's trust.

Could it?

"She spied on me. She used her friendship with me to exploit my relationship with your family." Blythe felt sick to her stomach. "She's the reason I got the show off the ground to begin with." Blythe was no film editor. "She was my friend. I thought she cared about me."

"I'm sure she does, but her own interests came first."

"But we all got a big payday moving to the streaming service."

"She got production role on the new docuseries about royalty because she brought inside information to the table."

"But..." Her show wasn't enough for Linda.

If she was honest with herself, Blythe would acknowledge she'd always known Linda wanted to do bigger things in the industry. She'd just never expected the other woman to use Blythe in this sneaky underhanded way to get them.

She could not hold back the sound of hurt.

"I am so sorry, sweetheart." Tor bent and lifted Blythe and then sat back down with her in his lap, his arms around her. "She will never be allowed near you again. I promise you."

Making no move to get off his lap, but not relaxing into him as she normally did either, Blythe looked up at Tor, tragedy written all over her beautiful features. "Do you know when she started?"

"The app was put on your phone eighteen months ago."

"But then she would have known about us."

"And she never sold that bit of information. She was willing to use you, but not hurt you."

"Should that make me feel better?" Blythe asked bitterly.

"It does nothing to mitigate Ms. Jones guilt, but only you know if it helps your feeling of betrayal."

Blythe's wounded eyes filled with tears. "It doesn't help. She hurt people I love. She has to be the reason news of Janice's miscarriage hit the scandal rags."

Tor agreed.

The miscarriage had made it into the tabloids before his family had announced their loss publicly, knowing that despite not going public with her pregnancy news of it would leak too easily. Janne had been kept from the media in those awful months, but Holger had not been so protected.

A king could not afford to me underinformed, even in the wake of such a terrible loss.

Tor had to stifle his fury toward Linda Jones. Right now, Blythe didn't need the stress of his anger added to her grief.

"Everyone is going to hate me." She sounded so forlorn.

"No, Blythe, they are not," he promised her. "Ms. Jones is at fault, not you, and our family knows it."

"I just can't believe she would do something like this."

"I am sorry."

"What will happen to her?" Blythe asked, though he could not tell if it was out of concern, curiosity or a desire to see the older woman pay for her actions.

Tor could do nothing but tell her the truth. "She will face charges and no doubt the loss of that coveted production role in the wake of her arrest. Not to mention, you will replace her on your own show."

"She can't work with me. I could never trust her again. But pressing charges?" She had such a tender heart.

He shook his head though. "No, Blythe. You are not responsible for the consequences of her actions. She is not getting away with hurting you like this."

"Surely you mean, hurting your family."

"I say exactly what I mean."

"But I'm not the important one."

"You are to me."

She stared at him in shock. "But you don't love me."

"I care for you. You know this." He planned to spend the rest of his life with this woman.

Didn't she realize that made her the priority in his life?

"Blythe, *min skatt*, come to dinner. We have things to discuss."

Shocking him, she burst into tears.

Tor immediately realized that their plans needed to be postponed. He sent a quick text for his staff to take care of changing the reservations and plans, and then took his treasure into his arms and held her while she muttered incoherently about babies, betrayal the impossibility of building a future.

Tor just let her vent, asking no questions and making soothing noises, but not using words that could be taken wrong. Finally, she seemed spent of emotion and stood up.

Looking away from him, she said, "I need to wash my face." She grimaced. "I probably got makeup all over your shirt.

Like he cared. "Go, wash your face. I will order dinner."

She nodded and turned to go.

While she was gone, he got dinner ordered and a comedy for them to watch queued on her television. He texted his staff and gave instructions to have some of his things packed and brought over.

He wasn't leaving Blythe and she needed familiarity around her right now.

They fell asleep without making love because that was what Blythe needed. She just wanted to be held and that was what Tor gave her.

Chapter Twenty-Four

Blythe woke up from a surprisingly sound sleep to pounding on her front door, then the sound of the lock turning and the door opening. The only other person who had keys to her door was Janice.

Blythe flew out of bed even as Tor was jumping up and barging toward the door. Naked.

"Stop," she shrieked at him. "It's Janice. She has keys."

Tor halted and then looked down at his nude body and grimaced. "I think I had better put something on."

"No kidding."

He gave her a significant look. "You too, sweetheart."

"Is that your new name for me?"

"You like it."

"I do." Because it implied tender feelings, even if they weren't love.

Blythe threw on pajamas and a robe in record time, not willing to risk Janice coming to look for her in the bedroom. Finger combing her hair with one hand, Blythe yanked open the door to the hall with the other.

She would have gone straight out but Tor stopped her by the simple expedient of grabbing the belt of her robe. "Hold up there, speedy. We do this together."

Blythe took a deep breath and let it out, then nodded.

They were holding hands when they walked into the living room.

"I knew it!" Janice crowed, her worried expression morphing into a smile. "Didn't I tell you, Holger?"

"Yes, *kjæreste*, you did," King Holger agreed drolly.

Tor frowned at his brother. "Where is your security?"

"Where are the children?" Blythe asked of Janice at the same time.

"They remained at the palace with our parents," King Holger answered Blythe's question first before he gave Tor a raised brow, looking very regal for the wee hours of the morning. "They are in the hall with your guard. My wife would be uncomfortable with others witnessing her tears."

"Janne is not crying."

"Not yet, but it's coming." The grim set of the king's features told Blythe he wasn't thrilled this truth, but his tone said he was resigned to it.

Janice patted her royal spouse's arm. "You're a very considerate husband." Then she turned toward Blythe, taking a step forward, but stopping, like she wasn't sure what to do, her expression full on tragedy mode.

Blythe couldn't stand that look on her heart sister's face and moved to pull Janice into a hug. "What are you doing here?" she demanded of the queen.

Janice returned the hug with interest, only pulling back after several long seconds. "You didn't call. When you found out about Linda. You didn't call."

Blythe hadn't been ready to talk to anyone except Tor. "How did you find out?"

"Holger told me. He knows better than to hide that kind of stuff from me. Why don't you?"

Blythe had no answer, mostly because she felt like the question covered so much more than just her current situation.

"You are the sister of my heart," Janice said. "You can always tell me anything."

There was definitely a message there that Blythe could not ignore. "I'm dating your brother-in-law." Though the fact he'd been in her bedroom with her in the middle of the night and they'd come out together holding hands had no doubt told Janice everything already.

The Queen of Tapt Oyer rolled her eyes like a sarcastic teenager. "That wasn't so hard, was it?"

Unable to respond to the humor, Blythe felt tears well and blinked them back.

Tor seemed to sense she was on the edge of an emotional melt down, because he gently disentangled her from Janice and pulled her into his body. "You two can talk in the morning. Right now, we all need our sleep."

Blythe could not miss the look of gratitude King Holger threw his brother. "Yes," he said to Janice. "Come, *min kjæreste*. You have seen for yourself that Blythe is all in one piece. Later this morning is time enough for hashing out the details."

"She hides her emotions," Janice said with a glare for her husband. "Don't assume anything of the kind. Her heart is in tatters."

"It's not," Blythe assured Janice. And was shocked to realize it was true.

Linda's betrayal had hurt her badly, but it had not shattered her heart.

"I don't believe you," Janice said baldly. "Linda was your friend. You trusted her and you trust so few people."

"Yes, and it hurts. A lot. Okay? But I'm going to be fine." Blythe knew that to be true.

Even if Tor had not come back into her life, she would have been okay. She was a survivor.

But he had come back and his presence was a soothing balm on her soul.

Janice's espresso gaze probed Blythe's, looking for truth and maybe more, then she turned her head slightly to give Tor a considering look. Finally, she nodded. "All right. We can all get some sleep, but I warn you I want answers tomorrow about *everything*."

Blythe didn't miss the warning. Janice wasn't going to get fobbed off and she'd want not only the *how long*, *how serious* and *how intimate* questions answered but a whole lot of *whys*.

"He gets answers first, then we'll talk, okay?" Blythe was not entirely convinced that after she told Tor the why of her insistence that they had no future that he would not end things.

She would need Janice's understanding and sympathy then. But she was done with hiding stuff from the people most important to her.

And not before time. Blythe could practically hear those words spoken in her heart sister's voice inside her head.

"Tor needs answers?" Janice asked and then shook her head. "Never mind. Tomorrow. You can tell it all to me tomorrow."

The queen suddenly seemed to deflate and went from looking fierce to exhausted. "I tried to sleep on the plane, but I couldn't." She covered her mouth as she yawned. "I really do think bed is a good idea."

It should have been easy after that. They'd all agreed on bed, but Janice didn't want to leave the apartment and tried to insist on sleeping in the spare room with Holger.

The king hadn't liked that idea at all, both for the sake of privacy and the security issue.

Proving she was too tired for rationality, Janice had dug her heels in and refused to leave.

Blythe had ended up agreeing to spend the rest of the night at Tor's penthouse, complete with multiple guest rooms well away from Tor's own suite, and state of the art security system as well as a bevy of guards on duty at all times.

Blythe threw a bag together, and once again left her apartment in yoga pants in less than two days. At least this time, she'd thought to grab a coat.

Tor took the time she was packing to dress, his own bags still packed from when they'd been dropped off the evening before. Blythe spent the drive assuring Janice that she really was going to be okay.

There had been a time that Linda, Janice and her mother, Lady Ingrid, were the only people in Blythe's inner circle. But that wasn't true any longer. She was part of the Royal Family of Tapt Oyer, even if she never married Tor.

Blythe had other friends, if not as close to her as Tor and Janne.

Linda's actions hurt, of course they did, but they didn't have the power to destroy Blythe.

Eventually, Blythe found herself in Tor's bedroom, the other couple tucked away in one of the guest rooms.

"It feels weird, doesn't it?"

"What?" he asked, pausing in the act of taking off his trousers.

"You and me sharing a room, with your brother and my BFF just down the hall."

"It's a long hall and each room in my apartment is soundproof."

Blythe laughed. "I wasn't talking about that!" She knew he was referring to sex, but she'd just been talking about being open about their relationship, being able to share the room until morning.

"Anyway, I'm glad they know. I like sleeping in your arms." Blythe shrugged out of her coat and went to climb into the bed with her yoga pants and t-shirt on.

Tor gave her a look, crossed the room, locked the door and then waited in silent expectation.

"I can't sleep naked with them here." He must realize that.

He gave a significant look to the locked door. "You can."

"But Tor what if there's a fire?"

"What if there's an earthquake?" he asked sarcastically.

"That' not as unlikely as you seem to think."

"You know what is unlikely? You keeping your pajamas on until morning."

She gasped. "We can't do *that*. Not *tonight*."

"I am not spending the rest of my life celibate when we are staying in the same residence as a member of my family."

"You make it sound like a done deal."

"What?" he asked in a silky tone that implied he knew exactly what she was talking about.

She answered anyway. "The *rest of your life* part."

"You are the only person who has any doubts on that score. My family knows you are it for me. I know you are it for me. And more importantly, I know that I am it for you."

It was time. Even if he hadn't proposed, he was going to. And he expected her to say *yes* because he believed she *wanted* to.

He was right.

She crossed her arms, taking a firm stance. "We need to talk and I'm not doing it naked."

"Right now?" he asked, clearly surprised.

"Why not now? I'm not going back to sleep for a while. Are you?"

"No." He gave her a heated look. "But I had planned to do something else."

"After." If he still wanted her once they'd talked.

"Plan on it," he said like he'd read her mind.

She settled in one of the two armchairs by the window. The curtains were drawn, hiding what was no doubt a lovely view of New York's skyline.

She needed all her wits about her and she never had that when she was in bed with this man.

Unsurprisingly, Tor only pulled on his silk knit boxers before taking the other chair.

The man had no issues with his own nudity. At least not when they were alone together. No doubt the shorts were in deference to her request not to have the discussion naked.

She appreciated his consideration.

His intense regard focused entirely on her, Tor waited in silence for Blythe to speak.

"I need to tell you two things," she told him quietly, having realized that only full disclosure would do. "Both could be deal breakers for that question you've implied you want to ask me."

Tor nodded. "I am listening, but I promise you there is nothing you could tell me that will change my opinion about it."

She wished she were as confident as he was. It would make telling him what she needed to so much easier. But despite years of hiding the truth and its consequence to *them*, Blythe was not a coward.

She licked her lips and then said, "Curing my leukemia when I was eight required both radiation and bone marrow transplant therapies."

"You have said."

"Those therapies can have lasting effects on the reproductive system." She twisted her hands together in her lap, tension crawling up her spine.

His brows drew together. "What are you trying to say?"

"You want children. I know you do." He loved his niece and nephews.

And he would be a wonderful father.

"And you do not?" he asked, still relaxed but paying close attention.

"I never used to think so."

"Because of your own dismal childhood."

"For the most part, yes."

"The other part?" he asked, like it mattered to him.

"Fear. Fear of having a child who could get sick like I did. Fear of not knowing how to be a good and loving mom."

"Are you still afraid?" he asked. "Because we both know that you would be an amazing mom."

He could have no idea how much those words hurt.

"It doesn't matter."

"Tell me why."

"The treatment that saved my life made it impossible for me to make or sustain the life of another in my body." There she'd said it. She'd told him the truth that had haunted her since realizing how much she *wanted* to make a life with her prince.

His brows narrowed, like he was thinking. "And this is why you believed we had no future?"

"Yes." Wasn't it obvious?

"But we never even talked about children."

"You're a prince, Tor. You are expected to provide heirs."

"No."

"What do you mean, no? Your father is matchmaking so hard because he wants more grandchildren."

"And if you and I want children, we will give him some."

"I just told you—"

"That you won't be carrying those children, but that doesn't mean we can't be parents," he pointed out in the gentlest voice she'd ever heard him use. "If we both want it."

"You mean surrogate?" she asked.

He shrugged. "That's one option, but not the one I like most."

"What do you mean?"

"There are so many children who have been orphaned by war, so many children abandoned by their parents, we could give some of them a home."

His words were so shocking to her, Blythe had to take a moment to really let their meaning sink in. He *wanted* to adopt? Since when? But like he'd said, they'd never talked about children or what the ideal family would like to either of them.

Because she never allowed them to delve into discussions of the future.

"Some?" she asked faintly. "How many is some."

"Well, no more than four probably, maybe five. Not a baseball team anyway." He said it like wanting to adopt any number less than fielding a baseball team of nine was no big deal.

"You and I both work." *Four,* maybe *five* children?

"And we have the means to hire help, but surely we can both cut hours if necessary to give the love and attention our children will need."

"You make it sound so easy."

"Because it can be."

"Adoption?" she asked, still reeling from the knowledge he didn't just see it as a solution to her infertility but as a desired component to building a family.

"It was always part of my plan for the future."

"Always?"

"Since seeing the ravages of war."

She believed it. Blythe, more than anyone else, knew the horrors he'd seen, and understood how those deprivations he'd witnessed had made him want to do something to continue to help the helpless.

Children left without parents, for whatever reason.

"You never said."

"You changed the topic every time the future or children or parenthood came up."

She had. She knew she had. "You know why now."

"Yes, but now *you* know that your infertility is not a barrier between us. It only makes you more perfect for me."

"How can you say that?" she asked in shock.

"Because I would rather adopt than have biological children. Another woman might see that as a detriment."

"I wouldn't have, even if I *could* have children," she assured him.

She was too moved by his desire to make a difference in the lives of children who had lost their families, or never had one to begin with.

Yes, there'd been moments where she fantasized what it would feel like to nurture life in her body. But that had never been what hurt her the most about not being able to have children.

And he'd removed the knife from the wound of her infertility by letting her know that while he wanted to build a family with her, how that family was built didn't depend on her biological abilities to reproduce.

"You're such an amazing man," she said with a catch in her voice.

Was it any surprise she loved him so much and so deeply?

"I am glad you think so because you are all that I want in a woman."

Did he have any idea what hearing that did to her?

In danger of melting into a puddle of emotional goo, Blythe girded herself for what else needed to be said.

Chapter Twenty-Five

"You said there were two things you had to tell me," he prompted into the silence.

She swallowed and nodded. After all the grief her inability to have a child had caused her, admitting what she needed to next still felt harder to do.

It made her vulnerable.

She locked gazes with him. "I love you."

He stared at her, like he could not parse what she had just said.

"I'm not sure when it happened. I've been drawn to you since the first time we met. No other man could compare to you, but you were younger," she babbled, filling in the silence between them. "I thought you needed time to date lots of women and get that out of your system."

"I am not wired for the playboy lifestyle," he said, sounding dazed.

"No, you really aren't. Despite the charm and smiles you used to get by when you were younger, underneath you're a really serious thinking guy."

"And you fell in love with that guy?" he asked.

"Yes. And well, I can't marry you if you expect me not to love you. Because I can't stop." The last year had taught her that.

"You can love me."

Inexplicable tears filled her eyes. "Good."

He was out of his chair and kneeling in front of her a breath later. "Do not cry, sweetheart. We love each other. That is a good thing."

"You love me?" she asked in shocked disbelief.

"How could you not know?" he asked, sounding less loverlike than angry. "I chased you like a lovesick calf from the beginning."

"No, it wasn't like that."

"It was exactly like that. I was a damned virgin the first time we made love because no other woman did it for me."

"You didn't make love like a virgin." *He'd been a virgin?*

"Thank you."

"Don't thank me! Why didn't you tell me?"

"Because you would have seen it as another reason to push me away."

He was right. When Blythe had still been hung up on their age difference, she would have had a meltdown if she'd realized she was his first and only lover.

"You told me the truth a long time ago and I never realized what you meant," he said, his voice laced with wonder and another emotion.

One she now had a name for. Love.

She nodded, tears spilling over. "I knew you wouldn't."

"But still, you told me."

"Yes."

"The only thing you've refused to tell me is how much you love me." He sighed. "But I think you showed it."

"Did I?" In her way of thinking, she'd been really self-protective bordering on selfish. How had that showed him how much she loved him?

"You put your relationship with Janne at risk so you could be with me."

"I hid our relationship to protect mine with Janice," she said, guilt flaying her.

"And you are smart enough to know that would hurt her when she found out. You had to spend the entire time we were together worrying in the back of your mind about the effect our relationship was going to have on the one you had with Janne."

"I did." He knew her so well.

"But you thought we had no future, so you created a way for us to be together that wouldn't end too soon. If you had told Janne, she would have seen your love for me and demanded to know my feelings."

Blythe had to agree. "She would have expected some kind of commitment."

"Which you believed I would not give you."

"Which I believed you *could* not give me."

"You were wrong."

Her lips twisted wryly. "Thanks for pointing that out."

"I'll have to work on my tendency to say *I told you so* before we start adopting." He didn't give her a chance to agree with him, but kissed her until they were both breathing hard.

She laid her head against his shoulder. "You're such an amazing guy."

"I am a prince."

Blythe was glad he couldn't see her expression, because really? "That's not the same as being a superhero."

"Isn't it?" he teased.

"Maybe for you, but not all princes are as special as you are."

"And there is not a single woman in the world as special as you are. Or as perfect for me."

Blythe couldn't believe that her biggest fear was gone. "Did you really say you love me?"

He said it in Norwegian and then again in English. And then in all of the other six languages he spoke. Finally, he said, "I love you, Blythe."

"But I made so many mistakes."

"You acted out of fear and that doesn't usually lead to great decisions. I saw it enough in combat."

She nodded, her throat tightening with emotion.

"You may not be perfect, but you are perfect for me," he promised her, his voice ringing with affection and sincerity. "I need you."

"I need you too."

He stood and led her to the bed, where they both undressed before joining each other under the covers and making love. For the first time, Blythe gave herself completely without any sense of impending loss, like she'd always had before.

They had the rest of their future together.

Later, warm and cocooned in the covers, while she lay on his chest, they planned that future.

"I don't want a long engagement," he said.

"Okay." She smiled. "I want to spend more time in Tapt Oyer together, with your family."

"Done."

She got up and he rose as well, their bodies moved toward one another.

She stopped when they almost touched and looked up into his beloved grey eyes. "I want to adopt sooner than later."

"Yes?"

"We've had our time to get to know each other." She wrapped her arms around his waist. "We don't need to cement anything before bringing children into our relationship."

"No, it is all nicely cemented." He sounded very happy about that.

Since she was too, Blythe wasn't even tempted to tease him. "Now, it's time to build our family."

"I like the sound of that."'

"So do I."

They would have to figure out the logistics of how to make her career work with being part of the royal family, but Tor made clear he expected her to continue her travel show, only he would be traveling with her when possible.

Blythe loved the sound of that. Almost as much as she melted hearing him whisper words of love in her ear as she dozed off to sleep.

Blythe talked to Janice the next day, telling the sister of her heart everything. Far from being angry with her, Janice reacted with compassion and understanding to Blythe's news about her infertility and how it had driven Blythe to keep up a façade of friends with benefits even after she realized her feelings for Tor were entrenched much deeper in her heart.

"That must have been really hard to find out. People say things so casually that must have really hurt."

Trust Janice to realize that immediately. "Yes."

"But you know that even if you never wanted to be a mom, you'd still be an amazing woman and the dearest sister I could ever hope to have, don't you?"

Blythe had some work to do to get to a place where she truly believed her inability to have children didn't make her any less, but she knew she wasn't doing that work alone.

Tor and Janice were firmly in her corner and always would be.

The rest of the Asgersens were just as supportive, even Prince Canute. He shocked Blythe by telling her he'd always hoped she and Tor might get together.

"I kept bringing other women around, trying to make you jealous."

Tor told his father off for putting him through that annoyance only to be told smugly, "It worked, didn't it?"

"Your dad is very impressed with his matchmaking skills," Blythe said to Tor later.

Tor grimaced. "Between him and my brothers, everyone is taking credit for us getting together."

Blythe smiled up at Tor, her expression brilliantly happy. "You and I know the truth."

"And that is?"

"Love brought us together."

He wrapped her up in his arms, leaning down so his lips hovered right over hers. "And love will keep us together."

"Oh, yes."

The kiss they shared held all the newly admitted love and confidence he would never, ever let go of.

THE END

THE MAHARAJAH'S BILLIONAIRE HEIR

Lucy Monroe

Lucy Monroe LLC

For my brother-in-law Robby and his new wife, Brandy, two very special people who embody the genuine love which is the cornerstone of real romance.

And with special thanks to Mayurika and Mahvish for
taking the time to beta read this book and
make sure I "got it right".

With additional thanks to Mayurika for the substantive edit and for writing a forward for the book. You're the kind of readers every author needs. The best kind!

FORWARD

Lucy Monroe is one of my favorites. When I found out that she lives in my city and was having a meet and greet, I had to go and meet her. She is wonderful, grounded and full of humor.

When she realized that I am of Indian origin, she pitched the idea of me editing her first "Indian" themed novel. I was in heaven. Since my teenage years I have been reading these novels. Getting the opportunity to be a part of one of them for my favorite author is a dream come true.

Lucy not only writes mind-blowing romance, but she also works on the characters and the backdrop of the whole story. This novel weaves the rich India culture of family values, royal intricacies and the passion of the two main characters in a beautiful tale. "If we marry, we will have passion, not just friendship." This sentence just melts my heart, and there are many more in this book that will give that tickle in your toes.

The story is a kaleidoscope of colors from the US west coast to the Indian monuments. I am so lucky and proud to be a part of this book.

Mayurika Saxena

PROLOGUE

Her heart barely moving in her chest, the air void of necessary oxygen, Eliza walked into the private hospital room.

Her best friend and the man she was supposed to marry one day, lay in the bed, broken and battered. He'd survived the accident that had killed Adhip *uncle*, but just barely. His parents sat in chairs near the bed, their focus entirely on the man fighting for his life.

Only according to the doctor, Dev was destined to lose that fight.

Neither Veeresh, nor Mayurika, even looked up when Eliza walked in.

She walked to the other side of the bed from where they sat, laying her hand gently on Dev's forearm, a small patch of skin that was unmarred by the accident and not covered in bandages. "Fight, Dev. Please fight."

The only person she'd let have even a little piece of her heart since the death of her own family, Dev was necessary.

Silky black lashes fluttered and Dev's eyes opened only a slit. "Eliza?"

"I'm here." Tears choked her voice, but she didn't let them fall.

Eliza hadn't cried since she was ten years old. None of her tears then had brought back her family and tears wouldn't help Dev now.

His mother cried out his name, but Dev's head did not move, his gaze fixed on Eliza. "Take care..." His voice trailed off into gasping breaths.

Eliza said nothing, waiting for Dev to finish his thought. She would not risk talking over any word he might manage to get out.

"My family. Promise."

His mother made a terrible sound of grief. Dev's father, Veeresh, touched his son's brow, oh so gently. "All will be well."

But Dev's focus was still on Eliza.

"I promise, Dev. I'll take care of your family."

"Find..." His breathing grew even more labored. "Love..." Now he was looking at his mother.

And Mayurika *auntie* knew what he meant. She told him how much she loved him, how proud she was of him, the litany continuing even as Dev's breathing stopped and his heartbeat flatlined.

The doctors and nurses came running. Eliza got pushed out of the room. She didn't know how long she stood out in the hallway, but the sound of a Mayurika's wail told Eliza she had just lost her best friend.

At some point, Dev's parents came out. Veeresh had his arm around a sobbing Mayurika. Eliza stood dry-eyed, her grief a cement block inside her heart.

The only thing she had to cling to was her promise to Dev to take care of his family and she knew what she had to do.

They'd talked about it many times over the years. Dev wanted his cousin brought into the family. He wanted the firstborn cousin, the one who should have been made heir to the Maharajah, to come home to the palace.

He'd told Eliza that his cousin would have run their business interests with so much more acumen than Dev's father, or even the current Maharajah, the man Eliza called *grandfather*. Only one man could save the Singh family and the Mahapatras Dynasty.

Rajvinder Acharya.

The time had come to reunite the heir with his family.

Chapter One

V in looked down at the reminder for his next appointment, shock coursing through him and coming right out his mouth. In a bellow. "Jansen!"

The usually supremely efficient woman in her forties came rushing into the room, panic clear in her grey eyes. "Is something wrong? Are you all right?" She looked around his office as if expecting a gun wielding madman to jump out. "You shouted. You never shout."

"My next appointment."

"Oh, yes." She seemed to relax, back on familiar territory. "Mr. Singh is already here." She said it like that should be *good* news.

It wasn't.

In fact, it had been his plan to live out the entire rest of his life without once laying eyes on another Singh from the Mahapatras dynastic family.

"You did not think to ask me before giving part of my very busy day to *Trisanu Singh*?" he demanded, imparting all the loathing he felt toward his biological father's family into his grandfather's name.

"You do not want to meet with him?" Ms. Jansen asked, sounding scandalized. "He is a potential investor in the Asia clean energy project. He has far reaching contacts in India."

She'd done her job running background on Trisanu Singh's company, but she'd been unaware of the one connection that Vin never wanted to use. And that was the one between himself and *that* family.

"If that is what he told you to gain this appointment, he was lying." Even if the grandfather who had refused to acknowledge Vin at birth, or again seventeen years ago, *wanted* to invest, there was less than a snowball's chance in hell of Vin allowing it.

"I assure you, Mahapatras Enterprises is quite interested in the moves your country wants to make bringing clean and renewable energy technology to India." The upper crust Indian accent spoken in that even tone sent shards of disquiet running down Vin's spine.

He turned his body so he faced the man now standing just inside the impressive oversized double door entrance to his San Diego high rise business office. "Is it your habit to barge into another man's office?" Vin asked of the older man with disdain, cutting at the supposed adherence to etiquette of those who called themselves royalty, even those of the deposed Indian royal families.

Trisanu grimaced, stepping further onto the antique Armistar carpet. "Had I waited for an invitation, I suspected it would never have come."

"And that is an excuse for dismissing common courtesy?"

His grandfather sighed, suddenly looking older, his perfect posture slumping infinitesimally. "Forgive me. My grief has left me less than my usual self."

"I am sorry for your loss," Vin said automatically, as his mother had drilled in him to do, though he had no idea what he was expressing sorrow for.

Whatever dismissals of courtesy Trisanu might feel comfortable with, Vin refused to allow himself such luxuries. His loss of control moments ago was entirely out of character and he would not continue to give the older man any reason to believe his presence was anything but a minor annoyance to Vin.

"So, you have heard the news?" Trisanu asked.

"What news?"

"About your father's death."

Vin felt nothing. No grief. No *what might have been*. He was a thirty-five-year-old man with a life much too full, to worry about the biological father who had never offered anything beyond his DNA contribution. "My father is alive and well in his office down the hall."

Vin's stepfather, Jamison Latham, and Vin had become official partners, merging their two companies together nearly ten years previous, keeping their headquarters in San Diego.

Trisanu winced. "I am aware you are not happy to claim our family, but Mr. Latham is *not* your father."

"In every way that matters, he is."

"All but one."

Vin went back around to his chair and indicated his grandfather should sit before doing so himself. "The sperm donation is of no consequence."

Again, the wince, this time in clear distaste. "It is to our family."

"It wasn't seventeen years ago when I wanted to meet Adhip." Vin used his biological father's first name as a purposeful indication of his lack of respect, or familial ties.

Trisanu merely shook his head and sighed. "Adhip is dead."

"I was unaware, but again, I offer condolences on *your* loss."

"How could you not know? His accident was not unremarked in the press."

"I do not read that kind of press." He, in fact, made sure his daily newsfeed was curated in such a way as to exclude any mention of his paternal genetic family.

Trisanu adjusted his designer suit jacket, no traditional Indian clothing for him, but then that was usually reserved for the men of his mother's birth country only at special events and ceremonies. "You have no interest in the lives of the family of your birth?"

"Birth?" Vin asked with emphasis. "Adhip rejected my mother long before I was born and rejected me again eighteen years later."

Suddenly he realized his Executive Assistant was watching this exchange in goggle-eyed wonder. It was a testament to how shocked he was to have the head of the Mahapatras dynasty in his office that Vin had just noticed.

"You may go, Jansen," he dismissed briskly.

"Perhaps she could fetch me a cup of tea?"

Vin wanted to bark a denial, but again, that would indicate that the other man's presence bothered him. And his mother had raised him better than that, even if he hadn't grown up in a palace.

He inclined his head. "Of course. See to it, Jansen."

"Any particular type of tea, Mr. Singh?" Jansen asked, giving the older man a look filled with nothing but professional interest.

Finally. She remembered one of the reasons he'd hired her. She had a reputation for maintaining professional decorum during the biggest crises. And thus far, she had not let him down, her inadvertent eavesdropping on his private life notwithstanding.

"Perhaps my companion might be allowed in?" Trisanu asked.

Vin frowned. Who would have accompanied the dynastic head? "Your companion?"

Trisanu nodded, but didn't offer a name.

It couldn't be Vin's father, presuming Trisanu had not lied. Adhip Trisanu Singh was dead. Vin refused to express any false sentiment of grief at what, for him, was no loss. He'd never had an Indian father.

Only an American one.

And Jamison Latham had come into Vin's life too late for Vin to accept him fully in that capacity, regardless of what claims he made to Trisanu.

"By all means, bring your companion in. You have twenty more minutes of our scheduled meeting."

By his expression, Vin's biological grandfather didn't like the reminder of their time limit, but he did not balk. He merely went to the door and beckoned someone inside.

It was a woman. Though she wore an Indian *salwar kameez* with European influence in its styling, she was clearly a western woman. With blonde hair and blue eyes that glowed like sapphires with emotion Vin did not understand, she looked at him expectantly.

"Miss...?" She looked familiar, but he wasn't sure why. And then it hit him. She had been there on that fateful day, when he'd gone seeking connections that did not want to be made.

She'd been a child then. She was definitely a grown woman now.

"Worthington-Smythe," she offered her hand. "My name is Eliza, I would be very happy if you used it."

He squeezed a hand soft and small in his, shaking gently and then finding himself loathe to release. "We have met?" he asked, despite knowing the answer very well. He'd learned early in life that giving away information was never as beneficial as drawing it out of others.

"We have." She tugged at her hand, her lovely oval face tingeing pink. "I saw you in India nearly two decades ago. You were kind to me."

He remembered the shy, towheaded child. Even dealing with his own fury at how the visit had turned out for him, Vin had not been able to dismiss the sadness in the young girl's eyes. He had been gentle in tone and manner with her when all he'd felt was rage at the family that could dismiss one of their own so easily.

"I am glad you thought so. You seemed to need kindness at the time."

His grandfather made a sound, though Vin was unsure what it signified.

Eliza inclined her head in acknowledgement of Vin's words, her expression briefly shadowed by grief. He now knew that she had lost her parents not long before and come to live as ward to Adhip and his wife.

Images from their last meeting played through Vin's brain. By some gallows sense of humor, Eliza had been there to witness his ignominious rejection by the Mahapatras Singhs. His biological family.

Biologically related? Yes. Family? Not so much.

No longer rulers in India, as none of the royal families were, they nevertheless were incredibly impressed with their own importance and had had no place in their giant palace for a bastard son of the heir.

Using his hold on her hand, Vin led Eliza to a chair, waiting to let go until she was sitting down. "You were there."

"And you were kind," she said again. "Despite what you were dealing with." She smiled, those blue eyes glowing brightly in her lovely face.

Why did this beautiful and intriguing woman have to be with the despised Trisanu Singh? In other circumstances, Vin would have enjoyed getting to know the woman the girl had become.

"Why?" he asked as he settled against his desk.

Were it just his grandfather there, he would have returned to his chair, but he felt a strange loathing to put more distance between himself and Eliza.

"I do not know. You don't have a reputation, now, for being a kind man."

He dismissed her words with a flick of his hand. "That is not what I meant. Why are you here?"

"My parents were killed in an accident similar to the one that has taken Adhip *uncle* from us."

"I know, and I am sorry." And he meant the words in a visceral way he had not with his grandfather. He'd felt sorry for her then and understood her grief would always be a part of her now. "But I still do not understand what you are doing here?"

Even more confusing was how strongly his body was reacting to her. Vin's sex was growing hard just from her presence and, in spite of, that of his grandfather's.

Vin wanted Eliza like he hadn't wanted another woman in a very long time, if ever.

Trisanu cleared his throat. "I will explain." He gave Eliza a look. "We have only a few minutes to explain to Rajvinder the change in his circumstances."

Vin's instincts went on high alert, even as annoyance flared through him at the use of the name he only ever answered to with his mother. "My circumstances have not changed."

"Indeed, they have. You are the only surviving male heir to the title of Prince of the Mahapatras."

"I am not an heir. I was denied." He allowed his condemnation to narrow his gaze. "I am Acharya, not Singh." Not that his Acharya relatives had wanted to claim him either, at least not until his mother had managed respectability through marriage.

"That will have to change, of course."

Fury filled Vin, unlike anything he had known since that fateful trip to India, when he still had some stars in his eyes at eighteen. He had kept a tight lid on his emotions since, but right now he was in danger of blowing his top.

Standing, he let his voice go arctic cold. "Leave."

"Calm yourself. You have a responsibility to the family, to the dynasty. This is bigger than your singular life. We all have a responsibility now to let go of past prejudices and do what is needed for the sake of the family."

"To you? Whatever *this* is, may be worth it." He let the old man see just how much he meant the next words. "To me? It is of no importance at all." His jaw was so taut it hurt, but he managed to keep his tone even, if bordering on strangled.

Trisanu opened his mouth to speak again, but Eliza laid her hand on his arm. "*Dadaji*, perhaps we should use our time to request a dinner to discuss this further?"

She used the Hindi word for father of her father, no doubt Trisanu's preference since Adhip had been her guardian.

"Your accent is American," Vin said apropos of nothing, but curious.

"I was born in America and the one request my mother made of Tabish *auntie* was that I be educated at an American boarding school."

He should have guessed. Vin himself spoke with a British accent because he had spent his formative years from the age of six at English boarding schools. A requirement his maternal grandfather had made for funding their lives until his mother married Jamison Latham.

By the time his mother had remarried and could have kept him with her for the school months, Vin had established a life and friendships he was loathe to give up at school. And his mother, being the amazing woman she was, did not insist on it.

"There is no point in our having dinner," he said now. "I don't know why you are here, but I owe nothing to the Singh family."

"And to your mother, do you owe the woman who sacrificed her place in society to keep you?" Trisanu had the gall to ask.

"What the hell are you talking about, old man? If anything, the Singhs owe a great debt to my mother. I have always been a good son." Even if he was sometimes more American, and even British, in his thinking and behavior than she would have wished.

"Old is not an insult in our culture, as you well know."

Vin refused to respond, waiting in silence for Trisanu to make his point.

The older man sighed. "Perhaps you are right, and our family owes Badriyah a debt for her treatment at my son's hands. In any case, you can correct the past with your actions in the present. Once you are named Rajvindr Adhip Singh, your mother will be acknowledged as mother to the heir of our house."

"Your mother's stigma of giving a child out of wedlock would be minimized with such an official acknowledgement from the palace," Eliza added. "Having a son who is a prince would give her back her honor, in a sense."

Vin would not let that stand. "*Her* honor has never been in question. It was the men of her family and the one that took you in that were tarnished by the events surrounding my birth."

Trisanu scowled and Eliza gave him a worried look before nodding toward Vin. "I am sure Adhip *uncle* regretted the way he treated your mother."

"And me? Do you think he regretted rejecting the only son he would ever have?"

"He doted on his nephew," Trisanu said with obvious pride. "My grandson was the most estimable heir."

"And where is this paragon now?"

"Dev died in the accident." Eliza's expression cracked, showing a world of pain underneath her carefully controlled exterior. "He was my best friend and he's gone. They're both gone and the family is grieving. Please, just have dinner with us."

"I will have dinner with *you*," Vin offered, making a split-second decision. "Trisanu can stay at the hotel." He half expected a swift denial to his offer, or at least some posturing on the older man's part.

But after a speaking look between the two, Eliza nodded. "Fine. What time would you like to pick me up?"

"Who said I'm picking you up? This is the twenty-first century, surely you can make your own way to the restaurant." He realized he was being rude but refused to let it matter.

As Eliza had already mentioned, Vin did not have a reputation for being a kind man.

"Must you be so entirely lacking in manners?" Trisanu asked, exasperation finally showing in his perfectly modulated voice.

But Vin wasn't accepting censure from *any* Singh and particularly not this one. "Asks the man who barged into my office without leave."

"And you would have Eliza pay the price for the great sin you consider being connected to the Singh family?"

"I was unaware I was asking something onerous. If it is that important to you, I can send a car for her."

"I would prefer you had dinner at the hotel restaurant. She is an unmarried woman in my guardianship."

"She's not a Victorian maiden. She isn't even a teenage ingenue, if I remember our age difference correctly, she is twenty-seven years old, of an age by even the strictest standards to travel to a restaurant without chaperone."

"Of course I am. *Dadaji* is just watching out for me."

Vin shrugged. "I'll send a car. Be in the lobby at six-thirty."

He had to speak to his mother before the dinner.

His decision in regard to claiming his birthright did not only affect Vin, but it affected the woman who had given him birth, the woman who had done her best to raise him in love and with a respect for the Indian culture she'd had to leave behind when sent off to America to live in unmarried, pregnant disgrace.

How desperate had Trisanu to be to come knocking on Vin's door?

Maybe it was time Vin had the investigative company he had on retainer do a deep dive into the lives and finances of the Singhs. Did they truly merely want an heir, or were there other reasons Trisanu Singh was now willing to acknowledge his billionaire grandson?

He needed to remember that as lovely and charming as Eliza might appear, she had been raised for the last nearly two decades in the Mahapatras palace.

Vin could not trust her any more than he trusted any other Singh.

Chapter Two

Two hours later, Vin could in no way doubt how very much his mother wanted him recognized as the official heir to the house of Mahapatras.

Badriyah *Barbie* Acharya Latham's eyes positively glowed with joy at the prospect. "Oh, my dear son!" She clasped her hands before her, her beautiful, classic Indian features creased with a blinding smile, her dark eyes glowing with delight. "Rajvinder, to have you recognized."

There was that word.

Recognized.

He had taken the money settled on him by the Acharya family, who were no keener to *recognize* him than the Singhs had been, and he had built an empire. Vin was worth more personally than the whole Mahapatras dynastic clan and Acharya family combined. But his mother?

Still needed him to be *recognized.*

It hurt her that Vin was not. Equally as important, *she* still carried some of the stigma among her own family and her social set back in India of having been an unwed mother. It was one of the reasons she had not visited the country of her birth until after she married Jamison.

She went once a year now, and Vin always accompanied her, but he knew that there was still a reticence between his mother and her family. There was no question that none of them accepted him into the fold as they did his cousins.

Not even his meteoric business success had elicited Acharya family approval.

And now if Vin cooperated, after thirty-five years, she was being offered the chance to be *recognized* as the honorable woman she had always been.

"I despise the Singh family." It had to be said. He wasn't all that enamored of his mother's family either.

There were plenty American and British families he knew about that would still stigmatize a woman who had children outside marriage, much less thirty-five years ago. However, every family, regardless of culture, had a choice about how they treated those involved.

The Singhs had kept Adhip in their bosom as their heir, despite being fully aware of Vin's existence.

The Acharyas had treated his mother like she was an embarrassment and Vin's existence as the same.

His mother's face fell and she whispered. "No. They aren't all bad. Your father had an untenable choice."

"He had a simple choice. Marry you, or the woman he'd promised to marry. You were pregnant by him. His honor should have demanded only one course of action."

She shook her head, fiddling with the traditional veil she still wore over her shoulder like a scarf. "Things were different then. They probably still are. The royalty...you can't imagine how unthinkable it is for a prince to marry anyone but a princess. It just isn't done."

"Then he should have kept it in his pants." Adhip Singh had seduced Vin's mother, a naïve innocent, who to this day believed she'd loved that bastard *prince*.

His mother gasped. "Do not be crude."

"Sorry, *Maan*." He wasn't sorry for the sentiment in the least, and the look on her still youthful face said his mother knew him well enough to be aware.

He was only apologetic he'd let himself say it out loud in front of his sensitive and pretty conservative mother.

"Barbie, this isn't about you." Jamison put his arm around her waist, hugging her. "You know your son wants you to be happy, but correcting the mistakes of the past in both families should not be on his shoulders. You can't expect Vin to care what the Singh family might want, or even the Acharyas. Not after the way they have *all* treated him."

His mother twisted her lips at the use of his preferred name by Vin's stepfather. "But..." She let her voice trail off, waiting for what her husband wanted to say.

An ingrained trait that in no way diminished his mother's strength.

She might have the appearance of passivity, but his *maan* had a will of iron and was very good at getting her way. She'd managed to keep Vin despite the opposition of two powerful families.

Jamison smiled at her, his own corporate shark image softening for just a moment. "Your son has built a multi-billion-dollar business that I'm proud to be partner in. He doesn't need recognition from people too stupid to see his value from birth."

Vin wanted to agree, out loud and vehemently, but the look his mother gave Jamison stopped him. It was filled with such grief, such unfiltered disappointment.

She believed Vin *would* agree and was already grieving giving up what was apparently a long-held dream.

"You want this," he said to his mother, stating the obvious, but insisting on transparency.

She shrugged, belying her expression. "It is *your* life, as Jamison has pointed out. As much as I would like my family and the Singhs to finally accept you, you don't care about it." She sighed, giving him a reproachful glance. "I'm not sure *how* you can feel this way. Perhaps it was a mistake to raise you here in America."

"Barbie," Jamison chided.

But she just gave them both that look. The one that said she was disappointed. A look he was not at all used to be on the receiving end of.

And he didn't like it. He also didn't like how she pretended she maybe *could* have raised him in India. "You didn't have a choice about where you raised me, not if you wanted your family to help you financially," Vin pointed out implacably, his tone harsher than usual with his mother.

She did have a frustrating tendency to only see, or remember, what she wanted to.

"You told me your father refused to help financially unless you took your son to another continent to live." Jamison wasn't sounding any too tolerant of a less harsh viewpoint himself.

"But he didn't insist I give Rajvinder up. You cannot imagine what a concession that was for him." And once again she completely ignored the truth that she'd had no choice but to raise Vin in America.

Vin shook his head. "As long as you hid me away."

"You've hardly lived in the shadows," she said with gentle censure.

"Neither have I been a part of the Acharya family." He would have taken Jamison's last name after the marriage if his mother hadn't had a crying meltdown over the very idea.

She didn't want Vin to give up his *heritage*. A heritage that had left him a non-person according to two powerful families, but a heritage that he had embraced in many important ways regardless. He was proud to be Indian by birth, but that didn't mean he was proud to be part of two families he despised.

"I'll never understand your tolerance for your family's behavior toward you and Vin before we married," Jamison said in a more indulgent tone than Vin could have managed.

He was a thirty-five-year-old man with a life. "I'm not moving to India. I will not live in the Mahapatras seat."

Not that Vin never went to India. He'd spent a lot more time there since becoming and adult than his mother did. Vin had varied and important business interests in Asia and did most of his wheeling and dealing with India as his base.

"I'm sure they wouldn't expect that," his mother said with less conviction than the words implied. "We live in the twenty-first century, after all."

Vin wasn't convinced that either his mother's or his father's family had entered the modern age, but he wasn't compromising on his stance either. They didn't deserve the consideration. "I'm meeting with Eliza Worthington-Smythe to talk about what exactly the family wants from me," he informed his mother.

Both Badriyah and stepfather looked taken aback.

"I knew she was made a ward of Adhip and his wife," his mother said, sounding bemused. "But I did not realize she was so entrenched in the family."

Vin made no effort to hide his cynicism. "She is the child they never had."

That made his mother frown. She didn't like the idea of an interloper being raised in the opulence that should have been afforded her son.

"I hardly think it appropriate for you to discuss these things with *her*." His mother did disapproval as well as any royal.

"Because she's a woman?" he teased, knowing his mother had never held the more conservative views on that score as the rest of her family.

She wouldn't have struck out on her own if she had.

"Of course not, but she's not really a member of Singh family. She cannot speak for them."

"She's more a member than I am."

"That is not true. Acknowledged, or not, you have always been Adhip's son. You are their heir now."

"Only if I accept the legal trappings of such a thing." No matter how much his mother might want it, Vin wasn't sure he was willing to be a nominal prince.

Jamison frowned. "Technically, you could be named heir without your permission. It is more a matter of what the family is willing to acknowledge."

"And if they did that, I could then sell off all the assets and walk away." His mother's choices might have been taken away thirty-five years ago, but Vin would never allow his to be.

"You would not do such a thing!" His mother's shock and horror at such an idea was not feigned.

"I'll talk to Eliza." And that was all Vin would promise.

Dismantling the Mahapatras empire? That was a far too tempting prospect to simply dismiss on even his mother's say so.

Chapter Three

"Sit down, *Bitiya*," Grandfather Trisanu chided Eliza, calling her granddaughter in Hindi as he usually did.

She'd paced the lobby the last ten minutes, waiting for Rajvinder's driver to show up. If he showed up. She wasn't entirely convinced that incredibly angry man would keep this dinner date.

Appointment. Not date.

This was *not* a date. No matter how interesting and attractive she found Rajvinder Adhip Acharya and despite the fact they had to discuss, what for other people would be very private, intimate matters.

"Child!"

She sat, crossing her legs, uncrossing them. Clasping her hands, unclasping them, unable to sit still.

"Did you learn nothing at that university you insisted on attending rather than finishing school? I know my daughter-in-law has done a better job training you than this behavior would indicate. You must stop this fidgeting."

He was just being harsh because he was nervous too, she reminded herself. While Grandfather would never admit it, he was not nearly as confident of Rajvinder taking over the role as heir as the older man pretended to be.

Eliza might have been the one to suggest this move to the Maharajah, but he was well aware that he had no other options. Adhip *uncle* and Tabish *auntie* had remained childless until becoming guardians to Eliza sixteen years ago. His second son and wife, Mayurika had only had one child, Dev.

Who had been gone now for a year.

"Sorry, *Dadaji*."

"It will be all right, *Bitiya*. He may not have been raised to be one of us, but he is all the same. He will do his duty. His mother is a good, traditional Indian woman. She will have raised him mindful of his obligation to family."

"If you think so highly of her, why didn't Adhip *uncle* marry her?" Eliza would never have asked such a question a year ago, but a lot had changed since the loss of her guardian/father figure and the man she'd been promised to marry. Her best friend.

"She was from the Vaishnav caste. While from a respectable and quite wealthy family, she was not born to rule, or marry into royalty."

"But the royal families haven't reigned since the 1940s." Royalty had been a nominal title since the fight for independence from Britain and they'd lost even their remaining special privileges and income when the Privy Purse was abolished in the 1970s.

"It is still a different life, as well you know. Our family has a responsibility to lead in politics and the business sector. Our lifestyle is not one you can simply drop into. A woman should be raised to be a princess, to join the dynasty."

"If that's true then how can Rajvinder take over as prince?" Sometimes the more antiquated views of her surrogate grandfather were *very* hard for Eliza to understand, much less accept.

She knew that his remaining son, Veeresh did not necessarily agree with his father, though he rarely did that disagreeing to the Maharajah's face.

"Sometimes needs must."

It was such a simple viewpoint for a terribly complicated situation and did not in any way explain why Badriyah, who at least had been raised in a privileged household in India was not acceptable, but her Western raised son was.

Eliza said none of this however, knowing Grandfather Trisanu's patience would only stretch so far.

She noticed movement out of the corner of her eye and turned to see who was walking toward them.

Rajvinder, taller than any other member of the Mahapatras family at over six feet, crossed the lobby with a confident stride. He wore a different suit than the one in his office, but this one fit him just as perfectly and could be nothing but bespoke. The man might be a business tycoon, but he had the build of someone who spent time working out.

She shivered a little with the knowledge of what she had to discuss with this perfect specimen of masculinity. She'd never gotten butterflies in her belly over Dev, but Rajvinder reminded her that she was not just a research scientist, she was a woman.

Espresso brown eyes snapped with annoyance when they landed on Grandfather, Rajvinder's strong jaw looking hewn from rock.

Grandfather's lips thinned, but he stood and faced his estranged grandson. "Good evening, Rajvinder."

"I prefer Vin, but since we are not friends, you may call me Acharya." After offering that statement sure to offend Grandfather's sensibilities, Rajvinder...no

Vin, inclined his head. "Trisanu." There was no warmth in the business mogul's acknowledgment of the other man.

"I trust you will not keep Eliza out too late," *Dadaji* said, making no concession to, and surprisingly no argument against Vin's request to be called Acharya.

"Is she a child that she requires a curfew?" Vin asked sarcastically.

Annoyance flashed through Eliza. Why did *Rajvinder* (she purposefully gave him the name in her head) insist on making every concern Grandfather had for her wellbeing into some kind of insult? Did he have no concept of even trying to meet a person half-way?

"We are not having a traditional dinner. I'm sure I will not be gone too long," Eliza assured the older man, not wanting him to worry.

Rajvinder didn't bother to reply to that, but turned to go, leaving Eliza to follow along like an obedient dog. Was he just stressed? After all, he'd just found out his father was dead and the family that had rejected him, now wanted to recognize him as heir.

Or was Rajvinder just a boor?

The latter did not bode well for *her* future.

Frowning, she turned and offered Grandfather a smile. "Do not worry about me."

"I cannot help it, *Bitiya*. This discussion should be happening between his mother and myself. At least part of it, if not all, as you well know."

"In India, perhaps, but Rajvinder has been raised in America. I doubt he's even once considered the possibility of an arranged marriage. His mother didn't follow that path."

"She had no prospects once she chose to keep him."

"Surely it didn't have to be that way."

Grandfather shrugged and Eliza didn't have the time to press him. She doubted Rajvinder would wait patiently for her, wasn't sure he would wait at all.

Relief rushed through her when she found the man leaning in his perfectly tailored light grey suit against the wall near the doors to the outside.

He didn't smile when he saw her, his dark eyes flaring only briefly with something she had no hope of naming. "I thought maybe you had changed your mind about dinner."

"That's not likely, is it? I was saying goodbye to *Dadaji*."

"Implying I should have done so, only he's not *my* grandfather. He's not yours either, is he?"

"It's a term of respect." And Trisanu had acted as her *dadaji*, or grandfather, since the day she'd come to live with the Singh family.

"If you say so."

"Are you always this rude?"

He shrugged, stepping away from the wall. "I do not suffer fools."

"I am not a fool."

Surprise reflected in his gorgeous features. "I never said you were."

"Then perhaps you could extend me some courtesy?"

"And by you, you mean you *and* the man you call *dadaji*."

"Your mom was from India." Surely he'd heard, and even used, the familiar term or something like it. "You don't need to sound so mocking."

"I wasn't aware I was." And perhaps his mockery was not for the term, but the man. "My mother *was* from India. Now, she's an American citizen. She's lived in California since before my birth."

But although Badriyah had taken on some American traditions, she maintained close ties with the expat India community in San Diego. Eliza had done her homework and she was sure she knew more about Rajvinder and his mother than they knew about her.

That that would change if he agreed to her proposal caused Eliza a certain amount of disquiet. Rajvinder was not an easy man.

"That must have been frightening for her," Eliza said, commenting on the move Badriyah had made to California thirty-six years ago.

"What?" he asked, sounding startled, pausing in handing over a ticket for retrieving his car to the valet.

She waited for the valet to leave before saying, "Moving to America alone, raising a child without the extended family. I'm surprised your mother chose to do it."

Especially after being raised sheltered and pampered as Badriyah had been.

Rajvinder gave Eliza a censorious look. "It wasn't *her* choice."

"What do you mean?" Had she been forced to leave India when she wouldn't give up her baby?

That sounded so draconian, but after living more of her life in the palace than she'd live out of it, Eliza understood that draconian wasn't out of the realm of possibility for families like the Singhs and the Acharyas. Just like everywhere else, some Indian families, lived with one foot in the past.

"Is that really any of your business?"

"Probably not. I'm a terribly curious person." It's what made her a good scientist. Eliza cut her gaze away, not because she was embarrassed, but because she thought she maybe was supposed to be. "Tabish *auntie* is always reminding me to rein it in."

"Curiosity is not a bad thing," he said like his word was truth and there couldn't be another.

Eliza smiled a little. He was so arrogant, but she was used to arrogant men. Even Dev, who had a much more laid-back side than other men in his family had carried a certain level of arrogance.

"That was almost a compliment," she teased, wondering where the confidence to do so came from.

"Truth is truth." He made a dismissive gesture. "You're a beautiful woman, I'm sure you don't need compliments from me."

Eliza had never considered herself beautiful. Not even average height at 5'4", she had moderate curves, nothing to write home about. Her hair was a honey blonde now, but she used to dye it a pretty chestnut brown to better fit into the Indian household that made up her surrogate family.

"I'm hardly beautiful."

"You're trying to deny that there are plenty of men, and most likely women, in your life as well, that have verbally appreciated your beauty." He sounded disappointed in her.

But Eliza could not imagine why. "I look nothing like the princesses who have come before me."

And Tabish *auntie* did not believe in swelling a girl's head with praise. From the age of ten, Eliza had been raised to be a princess in the House of Mahapatras, but she had been expected to be a humble one.

"Anyway, until recently, I was too busy pursuing my doctorate in chemistry to notice how men saw *me*, much less if any of them liked what they saw."

Truth be told, Eliza was as introverted as it got. She didn't let people in. She'd lost too many to take the risk, but even developing casual friendships wasn't something she found a comfortable thing to do.

"None of the men around you even tried to break your academic concentration?" Rajvinder asked with clear disbelief.

"I was engaged to be married." She'd been promised to Dev since before going to university, but she didn't think that was something she needed to share right then. "I never pretended to be single."

"To the nephew that died along with my sperm donor?" Rajvinder asked, like he was trying to work something out.

"Yes."

Rajvinder touched her arm, his expression solemn. "I am sorry."

"Thank you. He was my best friend." Eliza surprised herself with how much his genuine offer of sympathy touched her.

"You said that earlier, I didn't realize there was more to your relationship."

And this was not a man with a high tolerance for only having half the picture. She was sure of that, which made his ignorance about his father's family odd. The only way he could have not known about his father and cousin's deaths was if he willfully avoided news of the Mahapatras Singhs.

That would imply that his bitterness toward his father's family ran much more deeply than Eliza would have expected from a man who had made such a success of his life.

And that did not bode well for her plans.

"An engagement would not stop all men from pursuing you," he said breaking into her thoughts.

"What can I say?" she asked, unsure why they were still on this topic. "If they pursued, I wasn't aware."

"If I had been one of them, you would have noticed," he said with unwavering confidence.

She had no doubt.

Chapter Four

A meticulously clean, dark blue Tesla Roadster pulled up, the valet jumping out almost immediately.

"Why are you here?" Rajvinder asked as he opened the door on the passenger side and then indicated she should get in.

Not sure what to say in answer to that question, Eliza slid into her seat, appreciating the leather interior and high tech, but beautifully designed dashboard and features.

Dev had loved cars and had wanted one of the limited-edition Roadsters, but Grandfather had said *no*. He wasn't indulging Dev with a two-hundred-thousand-dollar car, much less the limited edition. The Mahapatras dynastic coffers weren't as full as they once had been.

Adhip *uncle* had never pretended that they weren't all looking forward to the infusion of capital her inheritance would bring upon her marriage. Dev hadn't liked that kind of talk though, telling her she needed have her trustees protect her inheritance.

But money had never been something Eliza cared about.

As long as she could pursue her academic endeavors, that had all been that mattered to her. And she'd fought to pursue those interests, unwilling to go to finishing school instead of university.

"Trisanu is not in need of a nurse, is he?" Rajvinder asked as he settled into the driver's seat, showing he did indeed have his own healthy dose of curiosity, because the question so obviously hadn't been prompted by concern.

"No." She clicked her seatbelt into place, appreciating the new car smell of the interior. "The family thought I should meet you."

Which was true, but such a small part of the truth, Eliza felt guilty not offering more.

Since this whole plan had been her idea, Eliza had insisted on seeing it through. It was always going to be her having this discussion with Rajvinder, despite both *Dadaji* and Tabish *auntie's* protests.

Grandfather had tried to say it should be him discussing Elizah's plan with Badriyah, not even Rajvinder. With what she knew of Rajvinder, Eliza had been sure that was a recipe for disaster. Tabish *auntie* had tried to say the discussion should be between Grandfather and Rajvinder, but again Eliza had refused.

She was an adult woman and she would keep her promise to Dev herself.

She'd thought her statement innocuous enough, but Rajvinder's gaze zeroed in on her like a shark sniffing blood in the water. "Why?" His expression demanded truth.

And it was clear the car wasn't leaving its spot in front of her five-star hotel until she gave it.

"Because as the heir to the Mahapatras dynasty, it would be expected that you marry me." The woman raised to be a princess.

Eliza knew that only with their marriage could she act as the bridge between the rest of the Singhs and the man they hoped would become the next Maharajah. He had not been raised to be prince, but he *was* a prince. By blood. She was not a blood relative, but she *had* been raised to be princess.

In marrying her, Rajvinder became part of the family in a more concrete way than even being made the legal heir could do.

Regardless of that truth, saying it so bluntly, she hoped she hadn't just destroyed any chance of his cooperation. But subterfuge was not her forte. Clearly.

Nevertheless, she didn't share Grandfather's certainty that Rajvinder would feel compelled by duty to take up his role as heir, including marrying the woman who was supposed to be his princess.

"Your fiancé just died a year ago, not to mention the man who acted as your father since you were, what? Ten?" Rajvinder asked, something in his tone she couldn't quite read.

She nodded and then realized his focus was now on the other cars and taxis filling the covered area in front of the hotel as he maneuvered his Tesla toward the street.

"Yes." She tried to keep the pain their loss still caused her from her voice.

She'd tried so hard not to let the family in, but Adhip *had* been her father for the last seventeen years and Dev had been not only her best friend, but the *only* friend she trusted with her secret hopes and dreams.

"And the *Singh family* expects you to marry a complete stranger." Unmistakable disgust laced Rajvinder's voice now.

"I probably know you better than you realize." She swallowed and admitted. "And the marriage was my idea."

Because she'd known that it was necessary. And Eliza had *never* expected to marry for true love. While Dev had been her best friend, she'd had no romantic feelings toward him. And she'd liked it that way.

She didn't ever want to love as deeply as she'd loved her family, not in a romantic sense. Not family. No one.

"You may know *about* me, but that doesn't mean you know me. I am a stranger to you, a man you met once for a brief moment when you were a child. And you just lost the love of your life," Rajvinder said, like the words didn't just disgust him, they bothered him on some other level too. "It's inhuman, but I should not be surprised. Their treatment of my mother and then me wasn't exactly lathered in compassion."

She didn't think this man really sought that commodity from anyone, but she didn't want him to think the Singh's were being that insensitive. It was obvious Rajvinder had not believed her assertion the marriage had been her idea.

"It's not like that." It hadn't occurred to her that Rajvinder might be offended on her behalf, but something moved inside her at the knowledge. "Dev wasn't the love of my life. His parents, my guardians, the grandparents, they all decided we would marry. It was a decision made before I even went away to university," she offered now, thinking maybe knowing that might actually help Rajvinder's perception of the current situation.

"But he *was* your best friend. Adhip *was* as close a thing as you had to a father."

"Yes." There was no disguising the pain Rajvinder's words were causing her.

She hadn't wanted to see Adhip *uncle* as a father, but he had been so good to her.

"Let's make one thing clear. Coming after you was *my* idea. This marriage? Was *my* idea," she told him again, willing Rajvinder to believe it. "I'm no pawn to the family."

"Your idea? Really?" he asked with skepticism. "Why?"

"I'm keeping a promise I made to Dev."

"To marry a stranger?"

"To take care of his family."

"That is not your responsibility."

"You do not get to tell me what is my responsibility," she informed the man who was way too used to bossing people around. "I am a twenty-seven-year-old woman. I make my own choices."

"Like you chose to marry Dev."

"Yes." She might have been sixteen when she'd first agreed to the marriage, but Eliza had never changed her mind about it.

She'd wanted the peaceful marriage she could have with him, but they'd never even kissed. Neither had particularly wanted to. Now she regretted she didn't even have a tepid memory to hold onto.

It seemed like a slight against Dev somehow.

"Dev was not your lover," Rajvinder guessed, showing an uncanny synchronicity with her thoughts.

"No." She didn't protest how that wouldn't have been expected of them, that the elders would have been very upset at any implication of impropriety.

Because that would have implied some kind of judgment toward Rajvinder's mother that Eliza did not feel. Honestly? If they'd been attracted like that to each other, Eliza wouldn't have finished her doctorate a single woman.

Instead, both she and Dev had conspired to use her education as a way to avoid the family sanctioned marriage as long as possible.

"We would have been happy together," she said more for herself than Rajvinder.

"And now you think you'll be equally happy with me?" Oh, the sarcasm was thick.

In that moment, Rajvinder sounded a lot like his father. Adhip did sarcasm better than anyone else Eliza had met, until now.

"I never said that."

"But you are willing to go through some kind of farce wedding?" he asked, disbelieving.

She glared at his profile, irritated he insisted on misunderstanding. "I don't expect my wedding to be a farce."

"You expect happily ever after with again, a *complete stranger*?"

"I don't expect happily ever after at all." She was no fairytale princess and she'd lost too many people to believe in stories of love and lifelong happiness. "My parents adored each other and doted on their only daughter."

Their love had been a tangible thing in her life until it was gone and then it had been a wound that never healed.

"Which is only another reason you should want the same thing."

"Or not. All that happy, all that love? It was no protection against death. Not theirs, not anyone I've cared for. I stopped believing in happily-ever-afters the day of the car accident."

Her mother had still been alive, in a coma, but ten-year-old Eliza had known, somewhere deep inside she did not understand, that her mom wasn't going to ever wake up.

She'd been right. She'd been told of her mother's death not quite a week after learning her father was gone forever.

Rajvinder made a noise of understanding. "I've never believed in them."

"Then we have that in common."

"I suppose we do."

Chapter Five

The trip to the restaurant was shorter than she'd expected. "I always heard California traffic was horrific, but it's a lot less congested than Mumbai."

"This is San Diego, not Los Angeles. We get our traffic jams but it's nothing like it is up there." She was surprised he offered the information without making her feel stupid.

But that surprise was nothing compared to what she felt as he pulled into a parking lot attached to a *mall*. There was a Bloomingdales right there, and several other stores she recognized.

"You're taking me to a mall for dinner?" she asked, unable to disguise her shock at the idea.

She wasn't a snob. She wasn't. But she'd never eaten in a mall.

She'd had snacks from street vendors in India, but never even that in a mall.

Malls were for shopping, buying clothing from the stores that carried her favorite designers. Not for eating.

Particularly not for eating dinner.

"The restaurant is in the mall." He cast her a sidelong glance that wasn't exactly condescending, but it was close. "Real life people eat here all the time."

"I'm just as real as you are."

"Are you?"

"Don't be rude."

His laugh wasn't mean, but it wasn't warm humor either. "You may not be a princess by blood, but there's no question you've been raised in a palace."

"I spent as much time at boarding schools." Her time away from the Singhs had helped Eliza maintain an emotional distance living with them would have made more difficult.

"As did I, but no question my mother had more influence on how I tuned out than the teachers at the school."

"She is your mother, of course she did."

"And were not the Singhs your *de facto* parents?" He pulled his car into an open spot not anywhere near the entrance.

Eliza couldn't quite believe he was just going to park there. She had to think back to focus on the question he'd asked. "They are (were in Adhip *uncle's* case) my guardians."

"So, this marriage of convenience has nothing to do with family duty?"

"You know that it does."

"So, the royal family of Mahapatras dynasty *are* your family."

"I never said they weren't."

"You claimed you were not a princess."

"I will not be a princess until we are married."

"You will like this restaurant." He opened his car door without addressing the possibility of marriage between them. "They serve farm to table, organic Asian fusion. It's very good."

She had no idea what that meant. Wasn't all food farm to table?

He came around to her side of the car and opened the door, offering his hand. She took it, feeling things she'd never felt with Dev at that one simple touch. How was that possible?

Eliza didn't know this man. Not really, no matter how much she might have read about him.

They started walking away from his car, like it wasn't a two-hundred-thousand-dollar vehicle that looked like he'd just driven it off the lot.

He saw her expression and laughed. "It's not going get carjacked while we're inside."

"Are you sure? Wouldn't it be better to use a driver?" They would not have had to park so far away from the mall entrance either.

Eliza didn't mind walking, but she was used to more care being taken with her safety. Surely the man who had built a multi-billion-dollar business should have his own security and be more cautious.

"I prefer to drive myself. Besides, I had a feeling we were going to discuss things we didn't need a driver witnessing."

"But surely your employees are accustomed to being circumspect." Servants gossiped, but they knew the topics that were off limits.

"You really were raised to see the world like a princess, weren't you?"

"I suppose." Because she would never have gone to the mall without a driver, and at least one guard to accompany her.

No wonder Grandfather had been so worried.

"Your parents were American," he pointed out.

She wasn't sure apropos to what? "They were."

"And despite being a foreigner and not a princess by blood, the Singh family find you good enough to be married to their heir? Heirs," Rajvinder corrected himself and acknowledged her commitment to marry Dev.

They stopped in the courtyard outside the restaurant. The parking lot had been full, but it wasn't crowded, though she noticed through the windows that several tables were occupied. The Christmas décor gave the mall a festive air.

Maybe all the people were busy shopping for the upcoming holiday.

She realized that Rajvinder was looking at her expectantly and she had not yet answered his question.

"I'm outside the caste system." Only, really, she wasn't exactly. Her role as ward to the Singhs gave her special status. Surely, he realized that and it did not need to be spelled out.

But Rajvinder frowned. "You're foreign. That's got its own stigma."

"It's the twenty-first century, not the eleventh."

"So everyone keeps telling me." He turned and headed toward the door to the restaurant.

She followed behind, refusing to rush. "You don't sound convinced."

"I'd say the way both the Acharya and Singh families reacted with medieval prejudices when my mother got pregnant with me would say otherwise. At least for those two families."

"But even that was thirty-five years ago."

He didn't reply, opening the door for her to precede him into the building.

"I'll take your word for it." But his tone said that was only until she proved herself a liar.

Chapter Six

The restaurant was surprisingly nice. Its open floor plan with beautiful wood tables and modern Asian influence in the décor felt like it could be any of the nicer eateries the family gave their patronage.

Eliza waited until the host showed them to a high booth style table in the back of the restaurant, after Rajvinder asked for something private and quiet, before adding further to their conversation. "Grandfather said Adhip *uncle* could not marry outside the caste."

"My mother may have been of the Vaishnav caste, but her family are not only better off than the Singhs financially, but also politically influential in the province. How was she not good enough?"

Despite having lived with her Indian surrogate family for most of her life, Eliza still found the caste system mysterious and often confusing.

So, she said what she could. The truth. "Grandfather admires your mother greatly. I don't think it has anything to do with *good enough*, more like hidebound restrictions they simply could not let go of."

"They were no better seventeen years ago."

"You shocked Adhip *uncle* with your arrival." She remembered well the time after Rajvinder had come to visit, so indelibly imprinted on her mind by being so close to her parents' deaths.

"He made that clear," Rajvinder drawled sardonically, sounding very American right then. "And he let me know there was no place in all of India for me to be his son either."

"I'm sorry." At the time, Eliza had been so lost in her own grief, what was happening with Rajvinder's visit did not really register. Only later had she realized that Adhip *uncle* had rejected his only biological child. "He always regretted his reaction to you. You refused any contact after that."

Rajvinder ignored the menu in front of him and waived away the waiter before he reached the table. "My sperm donor had two opportunities to do the right thing. He failed utterly both times. Life isn't baseball, he didn't get a third swing at the bat."

She wondered if anyone ever got a chance to let this man down more than twice, or more likely one time. She was beginning to understand that his arrival in India at the age of eighteen had been out of character for him and a chance Adhip *uncle* should never have expected.

"Tabish *auntie* was very angry at him for rejecting you back then." Eliza had never, in all the years she'd been their ward, heard her *auntie* speak sharply to Adhip *uncle*, except then.

"She told you that?" There was no mistaking the disbelief in Rajvinder's tone.

Eliza shrugged. "We are very close." Or as close as Eliza allowed them to be.

Over the years, her *auntie* had shared more of her heart than Eliza had ever been willing to do. "She wasn't able to give him children. Tabish *auntie's* own sense of failure would have been mitigated if he already had a son."

"And you claim *that* family lives in the current century and not the middle ages?" Rajvinder asked with pure sarcasm.

But in her mind, it was misplaced. "Plenty of modern women feel a sense of failure when they cannot conceive."

"Oh, really?"

"I have been studying science since my first year at university. You might be surprised what gets discussed among the scientists and pre-med students."

"Perhaps I would. I focused on business."

"To great effect."

They took a moment to look over their menus and she ordered a fish dish with ancient grains and vegetables. He got some kind of pasta with mushrooms and chicken.

She was a little startled when her dinner arrived to discover the fish was not cooked. Dipped in the sauce it came with, it was delicious though.

They'd eaten in surprisingly companionable silence for a few minutes, when he said, "You're more honest than I expected."

The approval in his voice was as unanticipated as how easy a companion he'd been thus far.

"Tabish *auntie* despairs about what she calls my terribly American blunt nature." Though privately, Eliza had always thought her *auntie* secretly approved her tendency to open candor.

The older woman reproving comments had always come out more teasing than anything else.

Rajvinder narrowed his eyes. "You seem very Indian to me."

"I've spent more of my life under the Singh's guardianship than I did living with my parents." The words still caused pain, but were true nonetheless. "It would be odd if my outlook remained entirely Western."

"Perhaps, but even dressed as you are, you have an aura about you." The look he gave her said the modest designer dress she'd chose to wear might not be as sedate as she'd thought, the heat in his gaze finding a corresponding, if unfamiliar, fire inside her.

"It's the attitude," he said, as if coming to a conclusion. "You remind me a lot of my mother. She's quietly subversive too."

"I'm a little more in-your-face, if not subversive." She might be introverted, but Eliza stood up for what she believed and wanted.

Hence her having this discussion with Rajvinder, rather than *Dadaji*.

Rajvinder deserved to know that truth. Because Eliza had no intention of playing unassuming, yes-woman, in her marriage, arranged, or not.

"Are you?"

"I'm here with you, aren't I?" Alone. Without Grandfather.

"You are, but you show what I consider a typical, deferential respect for Trisanu. At least outwardly."

"Because I do respect him. I show the same respect for the housekeeper." Which was also true, but in her heart, she acknowledged that she might express fewer of her own opinions with the older members of the Singh family. "When it matters, I speak my own mind."

"Do you?"

"Very much so. I told you I was the one who suggested to Grandfather, the time had come to invite you back into the family."

"To come back, I would have had to be a part of the family and have left. I was never accorded that opportunity."

"Well, you are being offered the chance now."

"If I marry you."

"Oh, I think ultimately, the family would come to accept you without the marriage, but it would cause a lot of hard feelings."

"Is that why you're willing to go through with it?"

"I'm willing because I think it makes a lot of sense and because I promised someone I cared a lot about that I would take care of the family. This is me doing my best to keep that promise."

"So, you say."

His words that put her motives into question shocked her. "You really are not very trusting."

"Few men in my position are."

"Because of your childhood?" she asked, trying to understand. Was he that bitter?

He laughed, the sound wholly amused. "I hope I'm not so molded by events I could not control. I'm talking about being the COO of a multi-national multi-billion-dollar business."

"I thought your mother's husband was your business partner?"

"He's CFO."

"My education is in chemistry. What do the acronyms mean?"

"A COO is Chief Operations Officer. I'm in charge of acquisitions, new projects and continued expansion."

Okay, that sounded impressive. "And CFO?"

"Jamison is Chief Financial Officer."

"Are you equal partners?"

"No."

"You have the bigger portion, don't you?" Even though the other man was older and a successful businessman.

"I do."

"You're not going to tell me by how much."

"It's not a secret."

But also something he wasn't interested in discussing. Good to know. He was a huge business success, but Rajvinder didn't feel the need to feed his ego spelling it out for her.

"Are all mall restaurants this nice?" she asked, prepared to change the subject.

His sardonic smile said he knew exactly what she was doing. "You've never been to a mall?" There was no mistaking the shock in his tone.

"Of course, I have. I've just never eaten in one." Didn't he realize it was far more shocking that a billionaire *had* done?

"Not even a snack?" he asked, still sounding ridiculously astonished.

Feeling uncomfortable as the recipient of his slide-under-a-microscope glance, she shrugged, but could feel the heat of a blush climbing her neck and warming her cheeks. "Does it matter?"

"Just how sheltered have you been? Your parents lived a pretty normal life, despite their wealth."

Her parents had been in his stepfather's league, not Rajvinder's. And they hadn't been Indian royalty. Even though the title of Maharaja, and more common shortened version Raj, had become nominal only, there was still an entirely different set of expectations for lifestyle that came with it.

Still, it stung that he was so dismissive of her life experience. "I went to university. In America."

"An all-female university, I bet. Are there still one sex universities in the USA?" he asked, sounding like he wasn't sure there were.

"Yes, there are several very good ones." Finding a female only institution with a good chemistry program had been harder. "I pursued both my Masters and Doctorate at a coed institution."

But she'd been too busy with her studies to do something as prosaic as date. Besides, she'd been promised to Dev.

"But you got your bachelors from an all-female institution." He said it like that was a bad thing.

"It was a very good university."

"I'm sure. Only the best for a princess in the making."

Eliza frowned. "Tabish *auntie* supported my decision to get a degree in chemistry rather than go to finishing school. I had no issue with her choice of university."

"How much of your life have you allowed them to control?"

"You sound very American right now," Eliza said with a small smile.

"I *am* American."

"You were born to a traditional Indian family. You can't tell me your mother didn't maintain certain norms." Hadn't taught him about duty to family.

"Of course, she did. I grew up appreciating and understanding my Indian roots, but *Maan* also allowed me to learn how to fit into the country I was born in." Rajvinder's handsome face turned cold and stern. "But I did learn one thing from my childhood and the circumstances of my birth, duty to family is not, and never will be, the deciding factor in how I live my life."

Disappointment rolled through her. "Grandfather believes you will ultimately be led by duty to the family, but he's wrong isn't he?"

"I feel no loyalty or duty toward the Singhs, or the Mahapatras dynasty. I love my mother, but what she wants for my life can only be weighed in my decisions, it cannot prompt them."

Chapter Seven

Eliza sighed, accepting his words, even as her mind scrambled with a way to convince him to accept his role in the Mahapatras palace. "I understand your lack of feelings of duty to a family that has never acknowledged you."

"But you feel that duty very deeply, don't you?"

There was no point skirting the truth, besides she wasn't ashamed to feel a debt of gratitude toward people who had given her a place of safety when her entire world imploded. "Very much so."

They'd given her a family when she lost hers, raised her to be part of royalty though she carried none of their blood, protected and cared for her.

She owed them so much, but even more, she owed Dev, the one person she'd trusted implicitly since losing her parents.

The substantial inheritance that became hers upon her thirtieth birthday, or marriage, whichever came first, was little enough to give. Money meant nothing to Eliza. A sense of family and belonging was everything.

Because while she might never want to love as she'd loved her parents, Eliza was mature enough to realize she had needed, and continued to thrive under, the security she found as part of the Singh family.

"To the point of being willing to marry a stranger?" Rajvinder asked, disapproval darkening his tone.

Words stuck in her throat as the reality that *he* was that stranger hit her in a new way, so Eliza nodded.

Marriage to this man would be nothing like marriage to Dev would have been. And Eliza wasn't entirely sure how she felt about that.

Unsettled for sure. But excited too. And that wasn't like her.

But he shook his head, his dark gaze probing hers, like he could read her mind through what he saw there. "I don't get you."

"Why?"

"You went to school here in the States. You were raised in America until you were ten. You attended university here, as well. You just said so."

"You don't think American women ever agree to arranged marriages?" she scoffed, wanting to laugh at his naivete. "We've already established that my outlook has been deeply influenced by the family I've lived with for the last seventeen years."

But Eliza found it particularly amusing that such a hotshot COO could be that naïve to begin with, that he could even suggest no American woman would consider a marriage of convenience. "Every country has its own unique culture certainly, but no way do you believe that *love* is the only reason for marriage here."

"No, of course not. But neither do parents arrange their children's marriages."

"You know that isn't true. I'm sure even among your mother's friends and yours, there are marriages that have been arranged by the families involved."

"Among the more traditional families, yes," he admitted, clearly grudgingly.

"But it's not just the Indian-American families that engage in the practice."

"I suppose."

Eliza rolled her eyes, more amused than irritated by his willful blindness to a cultural norm. "My parents loved each other very much."

"So you have said."

"Because it was true, but it was also true that they got married at the behest of both their parents. Two extremely wealthy families looking to merge through marriage as well as business."

Rajvinder said nothing, waiting to see if she had more to add.

She did. "Both my parents had coached me on not marrying someone who pretended to *love* me but was really just after my money. I was only ten when they died. That was such an important reality for them and people with wealth like them, that they started admonishing me about it from my earliest memory."

He stared at her for a second in silence and then nodded. "Point taken."

His easy acquiescence to her point of view surprised her, but then Adhip *uncle* always used to say that a truly intelligent man did not hesitate to admit when he was wrong. Rajvinder probably wouldn't appreciate her telling him that though.

"Where were your grandparents when your parents died?" he asked her, once again shifting their conversation.

To something that was still painful to her, but she wouldn't expect him to know that. "They had all died by the time I was ten."

"I am sorry to hear that. I know there's a certain loneliness in being raised without any extended family."

She could imagine that for him and his mother, it would have been particularly difficult. Because even living here in the States, his mother would have had a hard time building relationships among her countrymen. Her unwillingness to give him up would have cost her a great deal thirty-five years ago.

Eliza had been luckier. "The Singhs gave me back a family."

"And now you believe you owe them everything because of it."

His words were so close to her earlier thoughts, she couldn't deny them. But he made it sound like a weakness on her part.

She knew it wasn't. It took all her courage to give the family the trust and loyalty that she did after losing everyone else. "You don't know me."

"But you expect me to get to know you *very* well."

She drew herself up and gave him the look she'd learned at Tabish *auntie's* knee. "I do not appreciate your mockery."

"Who's mocking? You do realize that if we marry, the usual thing that follows is to share a bed." Something in his tone said he wouldn't mind that part of the arrangement.

Her own body responded to his with unfamiliar longings, desire that burned hot and deep.

"I know that." She hadn't been frightened of it with Dev. She hadn't been particularly keen either.

It was the opposite with this man. There was no denying she found him more than a little sexually attractive. And the fact she had no idea what to do with that attraction was just a little terrifying.

She and Dev could have stumbled through the wedding night together. With Rajvinder? Eliza didn't believe there would be any stumbling. At least on his part.

"It frightens you, doesn't it? The idea of sharing your body with me."

"Stop reading my mind," she blurted out, then covered her mouth, wishing she could pull the words back in.

They revealed too much. And she thought with this man, that would never be a good thing.

"You may not believe me, but I am not making fun of you. I'm trying to understand a situation that makes no sense to me. Have the Singhs threatened to disown you if you don't agree to the marriage?" he asked her, his tone devoid of compassion or criticism.

"They would not do that." Only she wasn't one-hundred percent sure that was true.

Doing one's duty to family was paramount to those of the Mahapatras dynasty.

While this plan had been Eliza's idea, there was no doubt that everyone in the family expected her to acquiesce to the marriage component.

"Don't lie to me. Not even to protect what you consider your family's honor." The look he gave her called her on her uncertainty. "We both know they are more than capable of rejecting blood family, much less a ward with no DNA ties, when it suits them."

"It's not the same." It wasn't, but if it was? She wasn't going to let it happen. Not this time around.

There would be reconciliation between the Singhs and their rightful heir to the Maharaja. Dev had wanted it, but Rajvinder deserved it too. It was past time that Rajvinder was acknowledged as part of the Singh family.

"They all made a mistake thirty-five years ago," she impressed upon Rajvinder. "We must believe they would not make the same choices today."

While Eliza felt real anger and sadness on Badriyah and Rajvinder's behalf, for the way both had been rejected, she couldn't personally be sad that Tabisha *auntie* had married Adhip *uncle*. Because that would make Eliza a hypocrite.

They had been very good together. And very good to *her*.

It was wrong that Rajvinder's mother had been so summarily rejected. Full stop. But thankfully, her life and that of the others involved had turned out well. Look at Rajvinder, self-made billionaire and international business mogul.

"They expect you to enter into an arranged marriage," he said sardonically. "They can't have changed all that much."

"It is still a very common practice, and not just for the Singhs. Children trust their parents to make the best choices for them." Most of the women and men she'd met in the Singh's social circle were either already married, or contracted to marry at some point in the future.

"I wouldn't trust even *my* mother to choose my lifetime partner."

Eliza had no trouble believing that. This man did not let others choose *anything* for him, she'd bet. It showed that ultimately, he did not trust anyone outside himself.

"If you had, you might be married by now," Eliza pointed out.

His gorgeous mouth twisted with sardonic humor. "You think thirty-five is too old for a man to remain unmarried?"

"You've been alone a long time."

"No one said I've been alone, just that I'm not married."

"Grandfather had you investigated. There is no evidence of a steady girlfriend."

"Perhaps I'm very private and good at keeping my relationships out of the press."

She almost believed him, but Grandfather's people were thorough. "The investigators did not rely only on what could be found in the society pages about you."

"Even so," he challenged.

"Are you in a relationship?" she asked, realizing that needed to be answered before they moved forward with any plans of marriage.

"I'm not sure it's any of your business, but, no, I am not." He gave her another one of those unreadable looks. "You do realize that most people would find the fact they were investigated a gross invasion of privacy?"

Relief not commensurate with the situation rolled over Eliza in a spine-tingling wave at his assurance he was not committed to someone else.

Ignoring an emotional response she'd rather not have, she said, "Tell me that you don't plan to do the same to the Singhs *and* to me before making any firm decisions about taking on the role of heir to the dynasty."

"Now you're doing your best to read *my* mind."

As if she could. This man had enigma down to a science. "Am I wrong?"

"No."

"There."

He shook his head. "You're very stubborn."

"It has been mentioned." She wasn't blind to her own faults and neither were the people she was closest to.

"And yet, you are willing to marry a man selected by other people."

"More by circumstance," she corrected and then added, "I'm the heiress to a multi-million-dollar fortune."

He nodded.

"I've been courted as a friend for that money already. I have had both women and men, colleagues and even professors, befriend me, hoping for access to my money. I cannot imagine a much worse situation than to believe someone loved me for myself, marry him and only then discover he wants my money, not me."

"So, you are saying you think it is better to marry someone whose motives while not romantic, are transparent?"

"Yes."

"And if I do not *want you* at all?" he asked.

She stared back, challenging him with everything in her. "Don't lie to me either." He may not want the marriage, but he was as attracted as she was.

She might not be an expert on human interaction, but she did understand chemistry and they had it on an explosive level. She was the spark to his tinder, he the fuel to her flame.

He laid his hand over hers, his thumb tucking under to rub against her palm, proving her thoughts with how the air between them fairly crackled with sexual desire from that small connection. "I have news for you, Eliza, everyone has hidden motives."

She didn't know what to say, and frankly her words were frozen in her throat, that touch to her hand short-circuiting her brain.

She had never known desire like she felt in this man's presence. Part of her, the craven bit that didn't want to take a risk, hoped that while he accepted his role as heir, he would reject the arranged marriage idea.

Her eventual marriage to Dev had always been this comfortable concept she relied on.

Marriage to Rajvinder? Would challenge the very fabric of her being.

She had no experience with which to combat the combustible connection between them.

Eliza had been courted by other men, yes, but she'd been promised to Dev for her entire adult life. She had never entertained another man's attentions for long enough to even experience her first kiss.

Rajvinder's lips looks so capable, so perfectly shaped. She couldn't help wondering what kissing this man would be like.

CHAPTER EIGHT

He made a strange sound and she let her gaze raise to his eyes.

There was amusement there, but something else too. Heat. And lots of it. "Do you have any idea what you are doing?"

She shook her head before she could think better of it. "I'm not doing anything."

"The way you are staring at my mouth is making me want to join you on your side of the booth." He sounded like he was about to do just that, his body tense in a way that implied he was ready for movement.

"I..." What could she say? She *had* been staring at his mouth.

And thinking about kissing him. How could he *know* that? Weren't men like him supposed to be unaware of the feelings and reactions of the people around them?

Adhip *uncle* had always seemed somewhat oblivious.

"I don't think you would be a comfortable husband."

"You assume I will go through with this entire farce."

She shrugged. "Not really." Her opinion stood, no matter who he married, but for her? She knew it was true.

Living with this man would be nothing but challenge and excitement. Terrifying. Intriguing.

She was seriously out of her depth.

Besides, if he said *no,* she'd deal with it, but she wasn't going into negotiations with a defeated attitude.

"Did you believe Dev would be a comfortable husband?"

That she could answer without hesitation. "Yes." Her best friend would have allowed her to live as independently as she wanted. "He had no problem with me pursuing a career in medical research."

"I thought your doctorate was in chemistry."

He had been listening. "It is."

"Wouldn't it be more natural to go into pharmaceuticals, or something?"

"Maybe, but the kinds of things I want to research are broader than that and it takes more than medical doctors to do the kind of medical research being done today."

Rajvinder nodded. "Laudable." He was silent, eating, for a little while. "Maybe too comfortable," he mused, searching her face in a way that made Eliza feel exposed.

"What are you talking about?" What was too comfortable?

"You and Dev."

No, it would have been perfect. "He would have been a very considerate, caring companion."

"He was your best *friend*."

"Yes." She didn't understand Rajvinder's emphasis on the friend part.

"Was he as uninterested *in* you physically as he was *to* you?"

"I never said that."

"Didn't you?"

Despite her avoidance of accepting certain truths earlier, Eliza was not one to lie. Even when it was more comfortable.

Stifling a sigh, Eliza shrugged. "Neither of us were particularly interested in the physical side of our relationship."

Rajvinder's eyes widened a little, less in shock at what she'd admitted, Eliza thought, than surprise at her honesty. "Did you plan to have children?"

"Of course."

"There's no *of course*. Some people choose not to have children for a lot of different reasons."

Was he one of those people? That would not work for his Singh family. Not at all. "We wanted children. Lots of them." Neither had particularly enjoyed being only children, and they had wanted at least three. Poor Dev, gone before he'd ever been able to see the fruition of the family he'd always wanted. "What about you?"

"I never considered having children. As your investigator revealed, I haven't had any long term, serious relationships, and no way in hell was I allowing any child of mine raised without his father."

"That's commendable."

"Too bad my sperm donor didn't feel the same."

"Adhip *uncle* was not perfect, but he was a good man." She thought maybe if Rajvinder could understand that, he might find some peace about his past.

"What made him good?" Rajvinder asked, making it clear he thought she wouldn't have an answer. Because he thought there wasn't one.

Eliza knew better. "He believed in supporting education for the masses. He believed that women should have equal protection under the law."

"And what did he do to back those beliefs up?"

"You're so sure it was all talk with him, but it wasn't. Your father actually held office for more than the last decade of his life. He fought to enact stricter laws guaranteeing children's access to education and protections for women, particularly in areas where a great deal of inequality still exists. Adhip *uncle* did his best to see programs put into place that made it possible for more girls especially, to attend school to completion. He funded scholarships for the poor who showed academic acuity."

"He sounds like a prince," Rajvinder said sarcastically.

"He *was* a prince, as are you. He had a responsibility to the people even if the family no longer rules. And he was aware of that every day of his life."

"He felt so much duty to the people, he refused to marry a woman outside the palace, even though she carried his child. He did nothing to make sure *I* received an education."

"Perhaps he knew he didn't need to." She had a hard time reconciling the Adhip *uncle* she'd known to a man who would, or even *could* deny his own son.

"Because my mother came from a wealthy family?"

"They did help her financially."

"With some very definite restrictions."

Eliza had no answer for that, so she said nothing.

"And you?" Rajvinder asked.

She was lost. "Me what?" Would she deny her own child? Never.

"Do you believe only royalty should marry royalty?"

"Patently *not* because I am not technically royalty, but I believe we should marry." Or she had before she realized just how devastating to the walls around her heart that marriage might be.

"You sound so confident of that."

"Do I?" She didn't feel confident. She felt restless. Uncertain. Achy with something she'd never felt before. Sexual need. "I was raised differently than you, I think. Both before and after my parents' deaths."

Rajvinder gave her an unreadable look. "What do you know of how I was raised?"

"I know you are more Western than Indian in your outlook." She wasn't going to deny any knowledge at all, nor did she think he would expect her to.

He shrugged. "On some things, yes, but that is a small, very obvious thing about me."

"I know more." A lot more. The investigator's report had been very thorough.

"You've read a report on me and now you think you know everything you need to, but how can you? Since I haven't been in a serious relationship, you have no clue how I will function as a husband. I may carry the same blood as the Singhs, but you can't know if I'll be kind, or cruel. Honest, or deceitful. Faithful, or have a string of lovers outside our marriage."

He thought he was being so smart, but she knew him better than he thought. "Your reputation in business is very telling. You are ruthless but not dishonest. You don't break contracts, even if doing so might make you more money. You show loyalty to your partners, your businesses, those who do business with you. A contract means something to you."

"That's not my personal life though, is it?"

"No, but if you're immensely different, there is such a thing as divorce." Did he think she would stay married to someone she found untenable?

This wasn't a love match, where feelings might drive her to stay married to a man who treated her with cruelty or even indifference. He would give her the same level of loyalty and consideration he did any business venture.

"You would divorce me if I turned out to be an asshole?"

"Yes."

"It actually relieves me to hear that."

And knowing he felt that way? Told her more about his character than she was sure he wanted it to.

He shook his head. "Let's finish our dinner. You know I'm not going to make a decision tonight."

"No. You have to have us all investigated first."

"I do, but I'm also going to insist on that old-fashioned concept of getting to know you personally before I make a decision."

"You don't expect to fall in love, do you?" she asked, making no effort to hide her horror at the thought.

He laughed. "Don't worry. We've both established I don't believe in fairytales, but I don't trust an investigator's report to tell me if we're compatible."

"So, you want to *date*?" she asked, nonplussed.

"You sound both shocked and confused by what is a very common practice." The laughter lurking in his dark eyes charmed her.

Though she was certain it wasn't supposed to. "For others, in different situations."

"I think for anyone in *our* situation."

Was he right? The idea of getting to know Rajvinder both excited and frightened her, a little. She already reacted so strongly to him.

"My mother likes the Christmas lights at SeaWorld this time of year. We'll take her to see them the day after tomorrow."

Autocratic, much? And a tourist attraction did not sound at all like how the tycoon usually spent his day. "But surely you are too busy..."

"I am never too busy to take my mother to view the Christmas lights."

"Oh."

CHAPTER NINE

Eliza tossed and turned that night in the luxurious bed that had felt nothing but comfortable the first night she'd stayed with Grandfather in the five-star hotel suite.

Rajvinder wanted to date.

Eliza had never dated.

Her life had been more sheltered than even she realized until the accident. Until her entire world was turned on its ear.

What had seemed like a natural follow through on duty, now loomed before her as a life-altering event. Marriage to Dev would have been easy, comfortable. They'd been friends, but nothing more. Eliza had known her heart would only ever be *so* involved.

And she hadn't felt even a little bit guilty about that. It had been the same for Dev. They'd talked about it, both a little worried about the other's reaction, only to be relieved when they had *both* acknowledged complete complacency with that situation.

She knew why she didn't want to be in love, but Dev had never told her why he felt the same.

Eliza realized now, she should have asked. Didn't she owe that to her friend? Shouldn't she have cared why Dev didn't *want* Eliza to be in love with him?

Dev had been her best friend, but there had been big blanks in his life she hadn't known about. Hadn't been interested to know. And now she felt badly about that.

They weren't even engaged yet, if indeed they were going to end up that way, and Rajvinder was already wreaking havoc with her thoughts and emotions.

Oh, she wasn't worried about falling in love with him. She'd cut off access to her heart and that emotion too completely. Eliza *was* concerned that the neat and ordered life she'd planned for herself had just become a lot less certain.

Rajvinder had said nothing against her working, and frankly, she wouldn't listen if he had. She may have spent the last nearly two decades in a privileged bubble, but her views on *how* to live were not in the least archaic. She was an adult and she got to make her own decisions.

That was something Rajvinder didn't understand.

Eliza had *chosen* to accept the first arranged marriage and it had been her decision to suggest this one. She didn't want to worry about things like love and overly deep emotional entanglements.

Her body's response to him was both encouraging and worrying.

Passion was not a bad thing. She'd been fully prepared to live without it as Dev's wife, believing their friendship and companionability made up for something so insignificant.

However, she had no doubts whatsoever that Rajvinder would *never* settle for a passionless marriage, even if, like her, he didn't want love. She wasn't even sure he believed in it.

Unlike her.

Eliza knew how destructive a force love could be and she wanted none of it. She'd lost too many people she loved to ever want her heart involved in a relationship again.

Eliza threw back the covers and got up, moving quietly so as not to bother Grandfather in the other room. He probably wouldn't hear her if she watched some television, but she wasn't taking any risks. So, she grabbed a book she'd been wanting to read and opened it, only to stare sightlessly at the page.

Grandfather wasn't happy about the dating.

He disapproved that her first outing with Rajvinder was to see Christmas lights, a holiday not celebrated at the palace. Though there were many in India who did celebrate the holiday, religiously if they were Christian and secularly, if they were not. But not in the House of Mahapatras.

Despite this truth, the Maharajah had expressed concern that Badriyah had *gone native* in her years living in America.

Eliza was kind of proud of herself for not showing even an inkling of her amusement at Grandfather's disgruntlement.

The investigative report had indicated that Badriyah was still a practicing Hindu, which meant her celebration of the Christmas holiday would have to be a purely secular one, with none of the religious overtones.

Of course, *Dadaji* probably had no idea that Christmas had been *the* holiday celebrated in Eliza's family. Nor, did she think, he would have cared.

If it wasn't part of life at the palace, it wasn't important to the Maharajah.

But Eliza's mother had loved decorating the tree and while they hired a service to put up lights and the other décor, it had always felt special and personal to Eliza.

She'd missed Christmas when she went to live in the Palace. Since one of the breaks from boarding school every year fell over the Winter break, which included the week of Christmas, she'd pretty much stopped celebrating when she was ten.

Oh, she'd always gone back to school with a passel of new gifts from Adhip *uncle* and Tabish *auntie*, but that happened every break she returned to the Palace. Winter, Spring and Summer always saw her spoiled with new pressies. It was Tabish *auntie's* way, but Christmas was not.

The little girl who had lost her holiday along with her parents was really excited about going to SeaWorld, no matter how nervous the woman she'd become was about spending time with Rajvinder.

Would he expect to kiss? He was such a sensual, confident man. Even so, he wouldn't expect to test their personal chemistry with his mother there, surely.

That thought should *not* disappoint her.

Chapter Ten

Eliza slid into the backseat of the luxurious town car and Rajvinder joined her on the leather upholstered seats.

"So, sometimes you do use a driver," she said to him as she clicked her seat belt into place.

Rajvinder shrugged. "*Maan* prefers it."

"Where is she?"

"At her home, waiting for us to collect her."

He might have been raised in California, but Rajvinder had picked up a barely-there British accent and a more formal way of speaking while away at boarding school. Or perhaps, his mother still spoke with that slight emphasis on formality that always charmed Eliza in Tabish *auntie*.

"Her home? You do not live with her?" Eliza asked.

"No. I've had my own place for a very long time. As I keep reminding you, this is not India. I prefer my independence."

"India isn't the only place families continue to live under a communal roof. Extreme wealth often leads to palatial type abodes and more than one generation living in them."

"You think my mother is extremely wealthy?" he asked with some mockery.

"I think she married a man who was moderately so until he went into business with you and now you're *both* in the extreme category, though because you own seventy-five percent of your ultra-successful business holdings, you are naturally richer."

"Is that why the Singhs want me to be recognized as the Maharaja's heir? They believe I will prop up some of their failing businesses with my money?" he asked with sharp cynicism.

"You aren't the one they expect to refill coffers that have shrunk over the years, but are hardly the result of failing businesses." At least she didn't think the Mahapatras empire's businesses were failing. Grandfather said they were all doing well.

"You told the truth about Adhip being involved in civic life and apparently he was good at it, but he was not so adept at business. Under his and his brother's helm, the Mahapatras fortune has shrunk almost in half and they have had to sell off several concerns."

"That can't be true." But why would Rajvinder lie to her?

"I assure you, it is. However good the Singhs investigators are, they aren't as efficient and accurate as Hawk Enterprises."

She'd heard of the multi-national security company. Who hadn't? Just recently they'd merged with a company that developed what was supposed to be the most advanced security software on the market.

"But Adhip wouldn't just sell off properties. People depend on the family for employment." They really did need the infusion of capital from her inheritance.

But if what Rajvinder said was true, then she could not be at all confident that it wouldn't just be throwing good money after bad.

Before there had been Adhip *uncle and* his brother running the businesses, now it was just Veeresh *uncle*. Grandfather had retired from the hotel business many years ago.

"Yes. Those same people whose children he was trying to get educated."

"How awful that must have been for him." It would have depressed Adhip *uncle* terribly to know he was letting down the very people he was so intent on helping. "He'd grown less jovial over the years, smiled infrequently...I didn't know why."

"I think it was worse for the people his incompetent management left without a job."

"Just because he sold off a hotel, or two, doesn't mean everyone got fired." It didn't work like that. Did it?

Her expert knowledge of chemistry and science in no way helped Eliza make sense of the situation Rajvinder described.

"Try four hotels and of those properties, only one was purchased by another hotel group. The others were torn down for other types of development."

"But all those properties were Mahapatras family homes at one time," she said with shock. The royal family had been large and lived lavishly. Once the privy purse was dismantled, they had turned many of their private homes into hotels, both to preserve a way of life in India for generations to come and to make a profit.

Grandfather often boasted of how successfully their family had weathered the privy purse crisis, but it didn't sound like that success had made its way to the next generation.

"They were indeed, but that did not stop Adhip from selling them."

"Can't you refer to him as father?" she asked, pained.

"No."

"You're very blunt. And stubborn." And a few other things she was doing her best not to say out loud.

"He was never my father."

"He wanted to be."

"I have only your word for that."

"Why would I lie to you?"

"To convince me that my family wanted me and therefore I have some kind of emotionally driven responsibility to step in and save them from themselves."

"That's not what Grandfather wants. He's looking for an heir, not a safety net." They had her for that. "He wants to know the next Maharaja will take care of the people that rely on the Mahapatras family."

"As well as his own sons have done?" Rajvinder asked with no attempt at diplomacy and a great deal of sarcasm.

"Adhip *uncle* did his best!"

"His best wasn't good enough then."

"I know *Dadaji* is not looking for you to give them money."

"Like you *knew* the hotel business was doing as well as it always had?" he asked with a raised brow.

How could she want to smack and kiss a man at the same time? And really...Eliza never wanted to smack people. She was a pacifist. Mostly.

"When I marry, I gain control of my inheritance. I've already promised to sign it over to Grandfather." There. Proof that the Singhs weren't looking for a monetary bailout from Rajvinder.

"Like hell you will."

"What? It's my inheritance and I'll do with it as I like."

"It won't be going into the Mahapatras coffers to be mismanaged like their own finances."

"Grandfather built the hotel empire. He's not going to mismanage it."

"The man you think of as a grandfather hasn't been in the family business for more years than you've been alive."

"He's still head of the family."

"And if he wants an heir, he'll give up designs on your money."

"What? No. You can't do that. I'm an adult woman and you aren't making my decisions for me."

"Neither are the Singhs." Rajvinder made a sound that was very much like a frustrated growl. "Listen, if they come to you with an offer to invest, you can look it over and decide if the investment is sound, but I won't be party to any more draconian decision making on your behalf by that family. They won't take advantage of you through me."

"What difference does it make to you? Are you worried I'll expect you to pay for things for me?"

"Don't be ridiculous. If I agree to the arranged marriage you seem keen to follow through on, you will be my wife. Do you honestly expect me *not* to look out for your interests?"

If she said yes, which was *her* honest answer, it was clear she would offend him. But it had never occurred to Eliza that Rajvinder would watch out for her. "Dev wasn't bothered by that aspect to our marriage."

"Dev was probably as hopeless a businessman as his father and uncle and believed all they needed was an infusion of capital to keep things afloat."

"It's not?" she asked, pretty sure she wasn't going to like the answer.

"If it were, selling the properties they did would have already seen them on the road to economic recovery, not continuing to slide down toward penury."

"It's not that bad, surely."

"Without some proper financial management and economic forecasting, the Mahapatras dynasty will be a family of paupers within a generation, two at the most."

"No. It cannot be that bad."

"Eliza, the Singh hotels are hemorrhaging money and the family continue to live like royalty with independent means."

"Can you help them?"

"Undoubtedly."

"Will you?"

"That's the sixty-four-thousand-dollar question, isn't it?"

It certainly was to her. She didn't want her adopted family to tumble into penury. She didn't care about her inheritance. It was the least she could offer them and Rajvinder would have to come to see that, but if it wasn't going to make things better, what could?

Looking at Rajvinder, self-made billionaire, she thought she had her answer. And she thought he might be right. Grandfather hadn't just come to California looking for an heir, he'd come looking for the one person who could reverse the family's economic downturn.

Chapter Eleven

Rajvinder led his mother and Eliza through the VIP entrance to SeaWorld, smiling at the way *maan's* eyes lit up at the sight of her favorite tourist attraction, indulging her desire to stop and check out the newest merchandise in the kitchy gift shop.

He had no doubts she'd drag him to every single one of the Christmas gift and décor kiosks erected only at this time of year and with special park themed holiday items, as well as all sorts of Christmas decorations. They'd had a different theme for their tree every year since those holiday décor shops had popped up at the park that first November.

SeaWorld was as much a part of Vin's childhood holiday memories as Santa Claus (at the mall, which would no doubt horrify Eliza).

One of the earliest times Vin could remember was of his mother bringing him to the aquatic park at Christmastime. Things had been different back then and changed a great deal over the intervening years, but it was still Badriyah's favorite way to *kick off the holiday season* as she called it.

They'd come in the later afternoon, so they would have time to attend a few of the shows and still be there when darkness fell early as it did this time of year, and the Christmas lights around the park were lit.

As he predicted, his mother wanted to stop at the first Christmas décor kiosk they came to. What shocked him was the delight, almost awe, with which Eliza handled each ornament.

"Oh, this is so beautiful." Eliza touched a silver and gold bauble reverently.

"You act as if you haven't seen a Christmas ornament before," his mother dismissed with something less than her usual warmth toward others.

She'd been silent in the car, barely responsive to Eliza's conversational overtures.

Vin didn't understand his mother's attitude. She'd made it clear she *wanted* him to take on the role of Mahapatras Prince, family's legitimized and recognized heir to the Maharaja.

Perhaps she thought that family would accept Vin without the trappings of the arranged marriage. Vin was not so naïve. While he knew the decision was entirely his, he also knew that if he refused to marry Eliza, it was entirely likely the Maharajah would look further afield in the family lineage for someone to name his heir.

And that would *not* suit Vin.

Besides, he'd never been in love, wasn't sure he believed in the emotion, so wasn't looking for it to justify his choice in a life partner. He would choose that life partner though.

Having Eliza brought to his attention by his grandfather and her own plans did not change the fact that he was very attracted to her. And the more time he spent in her company, the more Vin realized he liked the curious, but somewhat introverted young woman.

Eliza looked up from the glittery sphere in her hand, no embarrassment from his mother's words that Vin could see. "It's been a very long time. The Singhs don't do a tree."

"They wouldn't, would they?" his mother dismissed with a sniff. "Too hidebound."

Vin was shocked at this, the first criticism he had ever heard from his mother toward the Singh family.

Eliza frowned. "I'm not sure hidebound is the word I would use." She was sticking up for her family, but her tone wasn't so certain.

Vin got the distinct impression that Eliza had actually used that very term herself before.

"Really? And what word would *you* use? You, who are the child, Adhip raised with his wife in the palace, rather than his own son. A *Fhirangi*." His mother made the word for foreigner sound like an insult.

Utterly shocked at his mother's combative attitude, but even more so at her airing their family's past in such a public setting, he put his hand on her arm. "*Maan*, that is enough. Eliza is not your enemy."

"I'm sure in the beginning, you would have preferred Rajvinder had been given his rightful place from the beginning. But then you found love. Would you give that up so your son could have been raised a prince?" Eliza asked, her tone not at all combative, but genuinely curious.

So like her and Vin almost smiled.

But his mother wasn't smiling, so he held his in check. "No, I would not." *Maan* frowned at Eliza, sniffed and managed to look down her nose at the other woman, though at five-foot-three, she was about an inch shorter. "His father offered to make Rajvinder his official heir once and raise him in the palace, but naturally, it would have had to be without me."

Considering how Adhip had reacted to Vin's visit when he was eighteen, that surprised Vin very much and he said so.

"It was when you were a small boy. Adhip and Tabish had been told they would not be able to have children of their own."

"You never told me that. So, he asked you to give me up?" Vin asked with disgust, uncaring himself now about the people around them.

Though the kiosk was actually not busy and they were the only patrons.

"He did." His mother nodded, too complacent for the conversation as she handed a selection of ornaments to the kiosk clerk to ring up. "I said no, of course. But I have always felt guilty for doing so."

And suddenly he knew all this false complacency, the snippiness, it was because of that. Because of some unwarranted sense of guilt, his mother was the last person who should be feeling.

"I don't understand." Eliza put the bauble in her hand down with a look of longing before turning to face his mother. "If Rajvinder had been recognized then as the heir, your reputation would have been restored. Right?"

"Some things are more important than reputations. That was something my own family struggled to understand. I was never willing to give my son up."

No, she hadn't been. No matter the cost to his mother, she'd insisted on raising him herself. And now he knew it wasn't just her own family who had pressured her to give Vin up, he respected her even more.

The look Eliza gave his mother was pure respect and approval. She thought the older woman was *the boss* for making the choices she had.

Vin had to agree.

"They wanted to *adopt* me, didn't they? Pretend I was the orphaned child of some far-off member of the family."

His mother took her bag from the salesclerk and nodded. "Yes, exactly. I would never have seen you again. I could not live with that, but still—"

Vin would not let her voice a regret for doing the right thing. "You made the right choice, the best choice for *me*," he assured her.

She reached up and patted his cheek, like she used to do when he was young. "My parents were furious I refused, but I loved you, my son. I wasn't giving you into the keeping of a father you'd never known, a man who only wanted you, the best son anyone could ever have, because he could not have children with his *wife*."

"You were angry at my father for abandoning you," Vin said with as much wonder as Eliza showed for the Christmas décor.

His mother had finally admitted to feeling something she'd always denied. Vehemently.

Maan started walking. "Come, we must hurry, or we will miss Seymore's Christmas show."

"Who is Seymour?" Eliza asked.

"A sea lion."

"Oh."

"It's amusing and we watch it every year," his mother emphasized. Like she wanted Eliza to know that they had traditions.

Like just because she'd had to leave her home country and all those traditional moments with family behind, didn't mean *maan* had ever let him do without.

Clarity blast through Vin's facile brain and a great deal of his childhood made more sense to him now. Why Christmas, which had nothing to do with his mother's Hindu religion, was such a big holiday for them, why they celebrated so many of the American holidays that he always thought were odd for his mother to make a big deal over.

She'd had to give her own celebrations up in the early years, because until she married his stepfather, she wasn't comfortable joining the local Indian-American culture. She hadn't had a place a she felt she fit, so she'd made one. For herself and for him.

"You're a strong woman, *Maan*."

"I know that, son."

He smiled. "I just thought I should tell you that I know it too."

"Of course you do. You are my son."

He was and he would do anything he could to make her happy. Including entering an arranged marriage and taking over the role of heir to a family he despised.

If he got some of his own back on that family in the process? That would be okay too.

Chapter Twelve

Once again, Eliza found herself ensconced beside Rajvinder in his car, the driver up front. "I'm sorry your mother did not want to join us for dinner."

"She and my stepfather had plans."

"Oh, I thought it might be because of me." Though the woman had insisted Eliza use her American nickname, Barbie, she had made it clear she wasn't happy to have the younger woman butting in on her Christmas tradition with her son.

"She wants me recognized as heir to the Mahapatras Maharajah."

"But maybe she doesn't want you to marry me." Eliza didn't really understand the way Barbie acted toward her.

Resistance to the idea of an arranged marriage from Rajvinder was more understandable, considering he'd been raised with a strongly American viewpoint, but Barbie would have had her own arranged marriage had she not gotten pregnant.

And there might be Eliza's answer. The woman who gave every evidence of having traditional Indian values, had in fact been a rebel in her life's choices.

Still, Eliza probed further. "She's married to an American, isn't she?"

"Yes. She's not prejudiced." He said it like the idea was laughable.

Eliza wasn't so sure. "But the way she called me foreigner in Hindi." It hadn't been very nice.

"I believe she's more bothered by the fact that you, as a foreigner, are considered more worthy to be princess by the family than she was." The tense set of Rajvinder's jaw as he spoke said he wasn't too thrilled by that dichotomy either.

"Oh. I..." Eliza should have thought of that. It made so much sense. Thinking of it now, pierced right through the armor around her heart. She *liked* Barbie. "Their rejection must have hurt her a great deal."

"Until tonight, she never allowed me to see it."

"I'm sorry." Both that his mother had been so hurt by the family that had been so kind to Eliza, but also that she'd withheld those feelings from her son.

He shrugged, his gorgeous features dismissive, his focus on something out the window. "You weren't even born when they rejected her."

She craved those eyes on her, but that was silly wasn't it? "It wasn't her though, was it? Grandfather, even Tabish *auntie*, they only have good things to say about your mother and her family." When he didn't respond in any way, Eliza went on, "The real problem was that Barbie wasn't a princess. Thirty-five years ago, that was even more important than it is now."

And Adhip *uncle* had already been promised to Tabish *auntie*. Betrothal contracts were binding.

He looked at Eliza then. He didn't say anything, but he didn't have to. His expression called out the hypocrisy. Eliza might have been raised to the role, but technically? She wasn't a princess either.

Only it had always been her adopted family's intention she would be one day.

~ ~ ~

"How do you get away with going about the city without bodyguards?" Eliza asked, because all the other questions swirling in her head were too personal.

And really? She had no answer for why *she* had been chosen by the family to be their princess and his mother had not been considered for the role, even though she'd carried Adhip *uncle's* child. Only thirty-five years ago? That would have been a black mark against her too.

Unfair? Yes. But also true.

"Who said we didn't have security?" he asked, sounding amused.

"But, we didn't. Did we?"

"I always have security, as does *Maan*."'

Eliza's brows furrowed, filtering her memories of the day through her brain and trying to picture security personnel around them. "Where were they?"

"Nearby. My security detail travels in a car behind us at all times."

She turned around and sure enough an Escalade followed them, the driver and passenger dressed as tourists, vaguely familiar. "They blend," she observed.

"The most effective security do."

Was that true? She'd never thought about it. The palace's security detail wore uniforms and were always very visible. "The other night at the mall?"

"One waited out by my car while we dined, two were at a table kitty corner to ours."

"You never said." He'd let her think he was completely sanguine about leaving his limited-edition car in the unsecured lot. "You like to push buttons, don't you? I'll have to remember that about you."

"And you like to make assumptions."

"I don't." She was a scientist after all. She looked at evidence and drew conclusions. That was not the same thing at all.

"Don't you?"

"No. I just...it's only natural if I don't see security to believe they're not there."

"My driver is former special forces, as are most of the men and women on my detail."

"Women?"

His dark brow raised. "You would have me be sexist and only hire men?"

"No, of course not. I've spent years with my head buried in the lab, or my books. I knew I had security only because I was told I did. I rarely noticed them." But she'd been able to pick out who they were when she looked. Not only did they always wear their uniforms, but they'd stayed a lot closer than the people who had been watching over them today.

She hadn't noticed a single one.

Which didn't say much for her powers of observation.

"Why are you frowning?" he asked with a smile. Like he already knew the answer.

"I should have noticed them."

"They are paid to blend."

"But still, they were with us the whole time, weren't they?"

"Yes."

"And I never noticed any particular person that always seemed to be around, much less a team of them."

"That is not your job."

She refrained from rolling her eyes. Barely. "You knew they were there."

"I pay them to be."

"I mean, you knew where each one was at all times. I just know you did."

"So?"

"So, I need to be more observant." Security was there for a reason. And if she didn't notice them, it followed she'd been oblivious to any potential threat as well.

"Or you need looking after."

"I'm an adult," she said with more dignity than she was feeling. "I can look after myself."

His expression said he didn't believe here. "I think I'm learning that as beautiful as you are, at heart, you are an absent-minded academic."

"You think I'm beautiful?" He couldn't. She was average. Nothing like the women he could marry from India. Women with lovely golden skin, petite features and enticing curves. "I'd prefer you didn't resort to false flattery."

Beauty had never been a big thing to her, honesty was.

She'd been more interested in being recognized for the facility of her brain, but she was perfectly aware of how average her looks were.

One strong, masculine hand landed softly against her cheek, his dark gaze so serious she could not look away. "I do not know what you have been told, but Eliza, you are beautiful, and sexy, and I want you."

"You do?" she asked, suddenly breathless.

"Badly."

"I want you too," she said before she could think better of that level of honesty. "I...I can't..."

"What can't you do?" he asked, his thumb brushing along her cheek.

She gasped, her body's reaction to that small caress all out of proportion. She couldn't breathe...her heart was beating a crazy rhythm she could *feel*.

"You're touching me."

He gave a dark, sensual chuckle. "If we marry, I will be touching you, a lot."

"That's...I didn't expect..."

"To be touched?" he teased, his thumb brushing over her lips and sending her body messages she was not used to. At all. "To want me?" he added, somehow closer than he'd been only a second ago.

She shook her head. No, she hadn't expected to want him. She'd thought marriage to him would be even less a danger to her equilibrium than marriage to Dev would have been.

He leaned forward so their lips were mere inches apart, his gaze holding hers so she could not look away. "I'll tell you a little secret."

"Yes?" she asked on a barely-there huff of air.

"I wouldn't even consider this arranged marriage thing if I didn't want to possess your body so badly."

She should be concentrating on the first part of his comment because that was what mattered, but everything inside Eliza jolted at his admission of how much he wanted her.

Then his mouth came down on hers and Eliza wasn't thinking at all.

His mouth moved against hers with confidence and no hesitation as he coaxed her lips into a response she'd never given before. She grabbed his shoulders, the bunched muscles there testament to the fact this man did not spend all his days sitting behind a desk.

She kissed back, instinctively moving her lips against his. And that was just so incredibly amazing. She needed the feel of his lips more than she needed air. All thoughts of putting forth the Singh family's interest flew from her head.

Her only focus was on getting more of the amazing sensation of this incredible kiss. Her hands curled into fists against shoulders, her body thrumming with excitement, her lungs tight with the need for air.

He pulled away and she heard a whimper, realizing the desperate sound was coming from her and not caring, even as she sucked in much needed oxygen.

"Open your mouth," he instructed.

She nodded.

Amusement flashed in his dark eyes. Then his thumb pressed on her lower lip and she found herself doing as he instructed.

This time when his mouth covered hers, she could taste him in a different way and then his tongue flicked inside her mouth, shocking and exciting her at once.

It was only natural to slide her own tongue along his and she liked the way that felt. A lot. She moaned and did it again.

His hands skimmed along her shoulders, down her sides and everywhere he touched sparked with a completely alien, but magnificent sensual pleasure.

She remembered to breathe through her nose when she grew too lightheaded, and the kiss continued, her body straining against the seatbelt to get closer to him.

He pulled his lips away again, this time with a groan and a shake of his head. "You are dangerous."

She didn't know what he meant. She didn't care. She just wanted to kiss some more, leaning forward, trying to get his lips back.

He made a strange sound and kissed her again before pulling back and holding her away with his hands around her upper arms. "We're here."

"Here?" she asked, not knowing what he meant. She stared up at him, straining against his hold, her lips parted, wanting more of that delicious sensation.

"Stop, *sonii*. The driver is going to open the door any second."

The Hindi endearment was almost as good as his kisses. It took a second for his other words to penetrate her pleasure-addled brain. "We're stopped," she said, her brain sluggishly catching up with her surroundings.

"Yes."

She took a deep breath, forcing herself to lean back against the seat, away from him.

"If kissing is that consuming, I'm not sure I ever want to try sex," she admitted with a candor that shocked even her.

But right now? All her filters were offline.

"You've never enjoyed kissing this much?" he asked, with what was unquestionably deserved smugness.

"I've never kissed." She wasn't sure it would have made any difference.

This man had female kryptonite in his touch...heck, he made her knees weak just looking at her.

Chapter Thirteen

The door opened, but Rajvinder flicked his hand toward the driver, his other one settled on her thigh, stopping her movement. "But you were engaged to Dev."

"Since we were children. Yes."

"That's medieval."

"Can we not?" The last thing she wanted right now, while her body was in a turmoil she'd never known, was to discuss the whole cultural norm thing again.

"He *never* kissed you?"

"I never kissed him either," she pointed out with some aspiration.

"So, if you've never kissed..."

The driver cleared his throat. Rajvinder glared past her, but when Eliza turned in embarrassed concern at what the other man had overheard, the driver stood a respectable distance away, looking amused.

Eliza frowned at the man she knew also acted as part of the security team for Rajvinder. He was not supposed to notice what happened in the car, much less draw attention to it. Didn't he realize that?

Apparently not. The man gave Rajvinder a mocking glance. "You've got reservations, Vin. Did you want a few more minutes?"

Eliza gasped and glared at the driver, then she drew herself up and asked coldly, "Because we *want* to wait for our dinner?"

The driver's head jerked, like her words, or maybe it was her attitude, surprised him.

Before he, or Rajvinder, could comment further on the embarrassing situation she found herself in, Eliza unclipped her seatbelt, turned in her seat and offered her hand to the driver so he could help her from the car.

Which he did, a measure of respect showing on his features. "I wasn't trying to embarrass you, Miss Worthington-Smythe."

"You call Rajvinder, Vin. Is that usual?" she asked, rather than continue to focus on the unfortunate situation.

"I've worked for him since I left the military."

"And he doesn't stand on ceremony?"

The driver looked behind her at Rajvinder, who had followed her out of the car, like he wasn't sure what to say.

Rajvinder took her arm, insinuating himself between her and the driver. "No, excessive formality bores me and wastes time."

"You're going to find life in the palace tedious."

"No doubt I would if I intended to live there."

"But..." Was he saying after that amazing kiss that he didn't want to be the Mahapatras heir?

"If I agree to become the heir," he said, proving once and for all the man was entirely too good at reading her mind, or at least guessing what Eliza was thinking. "The arranged marriage, any of it, all of it, will be on my terms."

"What about my terms?" she asked, annoyed he thought she had no say.

Didn't the fact that she was doing the negotiating, rather than allowing Grandfather to do it on her behalf tell him that she wasn't a doormat to be pushed around?

"We will discuss your terms if it comes to that."

When it came to that, she mentally corrected. Because failure was not an option. And as in charge as Rajvinder believed himself to be, he would be a fool to dismiss her sense of duty and tenacity.

The restaurant that evening was *not* in a mall. In fact, it was as exclusive and upscale as any she'd ever been to with her royal adopted family.

Built with traditional Spanish architecture, there was a gorgeous fountain that would have been at home in downtown Barcelona tinkling with cascading water in the front courtyard. Gorgeous Christmas trees, decorated with stylish opulence nestled in the center arches on either side of the front door, welcomed patrons with elegant cheer.

She paused in front of the one the trees, taking in the holiday splendor before her. Pure white lights glowed amidst crystal ornaments and gold baubles that managed to look sophisticated rather than garish.

"It's so pretty," she breathed. "My mother did our tree all gold and crystal one year." This one brought back more memories she'd done her best to bury. Only instead of hurting, all she felt was a warm sense of nostalgia. She smiled up at him. "I thought fairies delivered our presents that year, instead of Santa Claus."

"That's quite a fanciful thought for a future scientist."

"If a scientist has no imagination, she can only live on the discoveries of the past, not build on them."

"You're a surprising woman."

"You think so?"

"Oh, you've been surprising me pretty much since the moment we met."

The maître d' showed them to a table, pulling Eliza's brocade upholstered chair out for her, offering both her and Rajvinder their napkins.

She spread hers over her lap, feeling just a little out of place in such a swank place dressed as she was, for a day at SeaWorld. She'd worn a skirt at least, but her outfit was hardly evening wear. "Tonight, you bring me here," she said with a shake of her head. "Wouldn't it have been the night for a less formal restaurant?"

The menu had no prices on it, the Christmas décor inside understated and elegant. She hadn't missed the Michelin Star plaque on their way in.

"Look around you. We are in San Diego; the dress code is nothing like Mumbai."

He could say that again. Several men were in short sleeved, stylish button up tops like Rajvinder wore with his slacks. His version of dressing down for the aquarium. Some women were dressed even more casually than Eliza in her designer skirt and flowy summer weight top.

There was even a man wearing khaki shorts, a t-shirt and flip-flops. The deferential way the waiters treated him told her he wasn't a poorly dressed tourist, but someone important.

"I went to school on the East Coast." And only now was she realizing how very unlike California the rarified atmosphere of her boarding school, university and post graduate alma mater were.

"You have a strange expression on your face."

"Is it like this on the East Coast too?" she asked, realizing she herself did not know, despite having spent nearly two decades in school in the Northeast.

"No, I do not think you'd find a billionaire dressed in shorts and a t-shirt at a restaurant like this one in New York."

"I suppose a billionaire feels he can dress as he likes."

"To a point. That level of eccentricity would not inspire confidence in the partners I take on for the big projects, regardless of the level of my wealth."

"You dress the part of success."

"I suppose you could say I do."

"It's not so different, living in the palace. We all have parts to play and how each of us takes on our role determines how much of an impact the royal family has on the people of India."

He nodded, like for once he wasn't going to argue how the royal family were just not enough.

She found herself smiling brilliantly at him for the small concession. "You have your own code of honor and commitment to the world in which you live."

"I do?" he asked, curiosity, not antagonism lacing his tone.

"Oh, yes, you do. You've made millions in the alternative energy field."

"That makes me a philanthropist?"

"It makes you someone who cares if we have a decent world to leave for the next generation."

"I'm more interested in living in one today that isn't smog infested."

"You've invested in areas few would expect because of their low ROI."

"You're talking about the farming cooperatives in Asia and Northern Africa."

"Yes."

"They are profitable."

"Only because you export half of what you grow, the rest you provide to the surrounding communities for a pittance."

"Your investigators are better than I expected, if you know that."

"I saw the names of the companies and I already knew what they did. Chemistry is a big part of agriculture and I did an entire master's thesis on that area."

His dark brows drew together, his espresso eyes keen. "I thought you wanted to work on medical research."

She frowned, wondering just how honest she should, or *could* be. She didn't want to damage his view of the family that wanted him to come in and take over the role of prince.

"Medical research is a more acceptable career path than feeding the world's hungry."

"I would think a princess-to-be would cultivate a lot of goodwill doing that."

"Perhaps, but Adhip *uncle* did not approve."

"The same man you told me cared so much for the non-rarified population of India?"

"He found it a laudable goal, but didn't want his daughter spending her days on a farm."

"Is that what you wanted to do, work on a farm?"

"With farms, to increase crop yields, to fight soil erosion, to..." She let her voice trail off, realizing she was getting lost on a tangent.

"Why did you stop talking?" he asked, no evidence of boredom in his tone or posture.

"Dev used to say I forgot I was talking with people when the chemistry of agriculture become the topic of conversation, that I slipped into talking at them."

"Perhaps, but when you are passionate about something, that is not always a bad thing. I'm interested."

"You are?"

"You know my secondary businesses. You know I am."

"You are," she said with wonder, realizing just how good it felt to have someone *want* to hear her views on this incredibly important topic.

Chapter Fourteen

They opted for the chef's tasting menu, a four-course dinner option that revealed they both liked being surprised and trying new things.

Eliza and Rajvinder discussed everything from what genetically modified wheat crops meant to the world's populations, to how to control pests, and even the best elements for certain types of crops. Rajvinder not only asked questions that proved he really was interested, he expressed clearly educated opinions.

She'd thought his kiss was heady, this level of interested and engaged conversation was sending all sorts of signals to her body Eliza would never have expected.

All three savory courses of dinner flew by, and they were sharing a dessert before she realized it.

He fed her a bite of the crème brûlée with raspberry coulis, something going hot and dangerous in his gaze as she took the bite and then moaned in a totally gauche way at how good it was.

"I don't usually like sweets," she offered by way of an embarrassed explanation.

But the creamy concoction was not overly sugary, and it had such an amazing flavor of, was that Madagascar vanilla?

"Me neither. Or rather, I rarely eat them."

"So you do *like* them?" she asked, trying to understand what he was saying.

"Maybe too much."

"But you don't allow yourself to indulge often." This made sense to her. Rajvinder was far too controlled to let anything rule him, even something as innocuous as a love of sugar had to be carefully monitored.

"No."

"You're a very self-disciplined person, aren't you?"

"I'm not sure my taekwondo trainer would agree."

"Really?"

"I only go through my forms and spar with him twice a week."

"But you exercise on the other days." She had no doubt about that.

"I lift weights and work through my forms every morning, but my security team and I spar, mixing all types of martial arts and hand-to-hand combat on my non-dojang days."

Because he liked doing things on his own terms. "So, how is that not self-disciplined?"

"He would prefer I worked in the dojang every day, like he does."

"But you allow nothing and *no one* to control your life, even to the point of setting your workout schedule."

"You think that's it? Not that it is simply easier and more time efficient to work out in my home?" he asked with some amusement, but not an out and out denial.

"Oh, I'm sure it's all that too, but you lost control of your life before you were ever born and once you learned what it would take to get it back, you've never given away even a small margin of say over what you do and how you do it."

He didn't answer...simply looking at her with those steady, dark eyes revealing nothing of his thoughts.

Realizing too late all she'd said and that maybe she shouldn't have been quite so honest, Eliza blushed hotly. "I'm sorry, I shouldn't have said that. I don't know you well enough to make those kinds of judgments about what makes you do what you do."

"And if you are right?"

She was fairly certain she was, but that didn't alter the fact that they didn't know each other well enough for her to have said it. "Are you saying I am?" Did he have no compunction about admitting something that to her would have been intensely personal.

"I think you are, yes."

"And it doesn't bother you to live your life controlled almost as much by what you won't allow as what you had no choice about allowing?" she couldn't help asking, despite knowing the question flirted dangerously with invasive curiosity.

"No."

That was definite.

Impressed, she smiled. "You're a pretty self-aware guy for a self-made billionaire."

"How self-made am I when I started with a stake provided by the family that always considered me an embarrassment?" he asked sardonically.

"Plenty children of wealthy families get money to live on, very few turn that money into a personal fortune and the kind of success you've achieved."

"My stepfather helped me."

Funny, she hadn't expected him to downplay his own successes. Or maybe it was that he didn't need anyone else's recognition. Rajvinder knew what he'd done with his life.

Still, Eliza couldn't let that comment slide. "You took him on as a partner *after* you'd built a hugely successful empire."

He shrugged. "He helped me in the beginning. Jamison introduced me to his connections and taught me a lot."

"But the student quickly outstripped the master." Eliza set her dessert away from her and took a sip of her after dinner cappuccino. "When you took him on as a partner, you were shoring up his business, weren't you?"

"He loved my mother from the moment they met and treated her like a princess."

"So, he deserved security of the type being your business partner could provide."

"Yes. Make no mistake, he's a damn good CFO."

"But he doesn't have your vision, or courage."

"Courage?"

"You've jumped in at the beginning of industries others are still waiting to see fail."

"Too bad for them."

"Oh, I agree. You're kind of amazing." And the more she learned about him, the more she realized this self-assured, self-made man didn't *need* the royal family that had rejected him at birth.

His love and loyalty for his mother were the only reasons he was considering stepping into his rightful role as prince. At the heated look he gave her, she thought maybe there was another reason, for the marriage at least.

And that both pleased and terrified her. She didn't want emotional entanglements. Though sex didn't have to be that, she wasn't sure sex with him wouldn't be the downfall to her heart.

"I am just a man," he assured her, sipping his own after dinner Scotch.

She smiled wryly. "I'm not sure that's true."

"Believe me, it is."

"Rajvinder, you've built the kind of life that takes you beyond the one percent and into the stratosphere."

His mouth firmed at the use of his full name, but he didn't take her to task for it. "And you became an Indian princess with a doctorate in chemistry. I think we've both traveled unexpected paths."

"I'm not sure the life I live now is so very different than the one I would have if my parents had not died." Their wealth had been a barrier between her and the rest of the world, just as much as the palace gates.

But Rajvinder shook his head. "I don't think you would have reached twenty-seven and never been kissed if your parents had finished raising you."

Hot, inexplicable embarrassment washed over her. It was like he was saying there was something wrong with her. That if she'd been raised differently, she would have been kissed, and more, by now. But she knew it wasn't about the way she'd grown up in the palace, and more about her own reticence to connect with others.

A result of losing so many people she loved so close together when she'd been way too impressionable.

So, maybe, yes...it was because her parents hadn't raised her, but not because of the way she had been raised.

And she wasn't about to say any of that. "I am not a freak."

"No, you are a beautiful, sexually desirable woman who has been sheltered as much as any novice in training to take orders."

She laughed at that, not because the words were funny, though they were kind of, but because of the look on his face that invited her to join in his amusement. And laughing was a better alternative than dwelling too much on the first half of his statement.

He was so frank in his admiration, and honestly, she wasn't sure what to do with that.

His approval of her brain, she took in stride, used to accolades for her academic prowess and critical thinking abilities. These compliments to her looks and feminine allure were so outside her experience, she was still figuring out how she wanted to respond.

"I have not been in training for a nunnery, believe me."

CHAPTER FIFTEEN

"**A**re you sure?" he asked, his tone not altogether teasing.

"Very." She grinned and told him, "Though my boarding school was run by nuns."

That surprised a laugh out of him. "That's right."

"It's kind of disconcerting knowing you have my whole life at your fingertips in a file." He hadn't seemed to be bothered knowing she'd had him investigated.

He was probably just too arrogant to worry what anyone thought about what they learned about him.

But though she'd expected the investigation, hearing how much he had learned disconcerted Eliza in ways she had not expected.

"I don't," Rajvinder said far too seriously to be joking. "I know only the trappings of what your life has been like, not how you responded to each different situation."

"I'm pretty sure your report told you I made only a few friends at each school, spending more time in the library than socializing."

"Why?"

Because she didn't want to let anyone into her heart. Because she never wanted to love another person, even a friend. Dev had slipped past some of her barriers and she'd lost him too.

She gave truth, if not all the truth. "I'm shy."

"And maybe you didn't want to let anyone get to close after losing your entire family so close together. But it wasn't just your family, was it?"

"What do you mean?"

"Tabish might have been your mother's best friend, but she was only an adjunct part of your life. Life in the palace would have been really foreign to you at first."

"I'm sure a therapist would have a field day with my past," she offered.

He cocked his head to one side and looked at her like...well she wasn't sure what he was thinking. "I think you've dealt with all the traumas of loss really well."

Would he say that if he knew how she still held her adopted family at arm's length? That her commitment to doing what they wanted in regard to marriage and her inheritance was motived by guilt as much as duty? Because Eliza had never allowed herself to grow as close to them as Tabish *auntie* had wanted.

The older woman had been devastated by her inability to have children and doted on Eliza. She'd wanted to be Eliza's mom, though she'd never said anything like that. But she'd treated Eliza like a daughter and Eliza had always maintained a safe emotional distance. Adhip *uncle* too.

"Did you always know your father was a prince?" Eliza asked Rajvinder.

"I did."

"Did it bother you, knowing you were a prince by blood if not by legitimate birth?" Was that another too personal question? She couldn't seem to stop herself asking them.

"I resented being denied my birthright."

"You did?" That shocked her. He acted like he wanted nothing from the Singhs.

"Very much. I still do, which is one of the reasons I'm considering this proposal of yours. I am the blood heir to the Maharajah, no matter what he would like to believe."

"Yes, you always have been, even when Dev was being raised as heir to the throne. It bothered him, that you weren't acknowledged."

"Did it?"

"Yes."

"Then he was the only one in the family that felt that way."

"I told you Tabish *auntie* was upset that Adhip *uncle* denied you."

"Yes, you did."

"Are you still doubting my word?"

"No, not doubting you believe that."

"But doubting she was sincere?"

"Perhaps. After all, she had you."

Eliza could not deny it. "It's so strange how life ends up." She'd grown up in the palace that should have been Rajvinder's home from infancy.

"You know that more intimately than most."

"Maybe." But so did he.

It scared Eliza to the bottom of her ice encased heart, how easily she found talking to Rajvinder. How the chemistry was a living and constant electric current between them.

"I think we've lingered long enough over our coffee." She needed some distance from this man.

Rajvinder didn't argue, simply took care of the check and led her outside. She expected the car to be waiting, but it wasn't. A horse drawn carriage was.

"I thought we could take a ride and look at Christmas lights. It seems to me you've been missing Christmas for nearly twenty years, and San Diego knows how to do the holiday."

Dark had fallen while they'd eaten dinner. The lights were colorful in some places, one spot every home and yard done up to reflect a childhood book. Downtown had lots and lots of white lights. She didn't know how long they rode in the carriage looking at lights, but the magic of the holiday swirled around Eliza in a way it hadn't in years.

It was a veritable Winter Wonderland. Without the cold, or the snow.

And after all her time spent living in a palace in India she'd become accustomed to sunny weather and did not miss that particular aspect.

Okay, maybe a little.

Memories of the trips her parents took her on to the mountains every year at Christmastime bombarded her and brought up feelings she'd long suppressed.

Rajvinder had slipped his arm around her shoulders early on and squeezed her arm now. "You're thinking about something very serious."

"My dad...he loved snow at Christmas." It was all she could make herself say. Emotions she'd thought she'd rid herself of were too darn close to the surface.

"Do you miss the snow?"

"I miss them." But yes, maybe she missed the snow a little.

"Of course you do. You always will."

She turned to him, looking away from the lights, though it was hard. "You're the only one who has ever acknowledged that."

"People expect you to get over the loss of your parents?" he asked in a tone that said he didn't understand that.

"Yes." Everyone did. They *all* said that time healed all wounds and equally inane things like that.

"Like hell."

"It doesn't bother you that I still miss them?" Even Dev had accused her of being needlessly maudlin whenever she'd said anything even remotely intimating that she wished they were still with her.

And he'd been her best friend.

"Why should it bother me?"

Because he didn't feel anything for her? No, she instinctively knew that wasn't it. "Your mom never stopped missing her family, did she?"

"No. Her grief shaped who she became."

"So did her love for you."

"Yes."

"You're so much more than the ruthless businessman your investigative file paints you as."

"If I wasn't, I wouldn't consider this proposition from Trisanu."

"Oh, you could consider it, but with an eye for revenge. That's not *why* you're thinking about it, are you?" Horrible images of him taking over as heir only to dismantle the family flashed through her brain.

"You are just now realizing that is an option for me?"

"I..." She didn't think in those terms. "I'm not the ruthless corporate shark. That's not how my brain works."

"But you're smart enough to realize it might be the way mine does. I wonder if Trisanu does?"

"I don't know." He'd never said anything to her.

"If he hasn't, he's lost more than his edge in business."

She went back to watching the lights as they travelled slowly through the streets in the horse drawn carriage. "I think Grandfather is not only intelligent, but very intuitive."

"And still he put his sons, who were abysmal at business, in charge of the family's fortune."

"He didn't have a choice." Who else was there?

"Oh, he had one, but he refused to break with tradition."

"What do you think he could have done?" she asked, genuinely curious what the super successful businessman would have done.

"Hired a manager with business savvy, and left the sons completely out of the picture."

"The business is the family's livelihood."

A short bark of humorless laughter sounded from Rajvinder. "And they've all but decimated it."

"It's not that bad, surely." He'd said something similar, but maybe not quite as grim before. She had already begun to wonder at her *dadaji's* real motives behind going along with Eliza's plan to bring the rightful heir back into the family.

She shivered slightly, the mild wind and loss of sun bringing with it enough of a drop in temperature that Eliza wished she had a sweater.

"Isn't it?" He slid his arm down until it was around her waist, pulling her in closer to him, warming her with his body, even as he snagged a lap blanket and spread it over her. "You think I was lying when I said that the fortune would be gone within another generation?"

"No." This man didn't lie. Of that, she was sure.

He also didn't exaggerate.

Ruthless? Oh, yes. Hard? Definitely. Dramatic? Unlikely. Dishonest? Never. He was too arrogant, and with cause, to think he had to be.

"Then don't you think it's time you stopped defending the indefensible?" He tucked the blanket around her.

Bemused by his consideration in the face of his clear intransigence about his family, she parried, "It's only indefensible if you refuse to acknowledge the role that family relationships had in the choices Grandfather made."

"You mean the man who willingly rejected his own grandson because I had the wrong mother?" His tone drew her gaze again and the unyielding expression she found there did not surprise Eliza at all. "*That* man was driven by family ties to make poor choices?" Rajvinder asked with heavy sarcasm.

She sighed. He had a point, but she knew the truth and honestly? She believed that Rajvinder did as well. "Yes."

"He's a hypocrite then."

She couldn't deny that assessment, so she said nothing, too loyal to the family that had taken her in to acknowledge the truth out loud.

"You're very beautiful with the Christmas lights reflected in your eyes."

"I wonder if I'll ever get used to how open you are with compliments?"

He pulled her to him and kissed her instead of answering. And it didn't matter that they were in an open carriage for anyone to see, that lots of other people were out looking at Christmas lights too.

Eliza responded with a passion she was helpless to resist.

This kiss was every bit as incendiary as the first, but it was Eliza who managed to break away, turning her face into his chest as she regained her equilibrium.

He rubbed her shoulder, silent and warm against her, giving her the time she needed to collect herself.

When she sat up, he didn't comment on the fact she put a couple of inches between them on the seat. "It's probably time for me to get back to the hotel."

He nodded and his car and driver met up with them minutes later.

Chapter Sixteen

The following days fell into a pattern. She spent the morning with Grandfather, many evenings with Rajvinder, and the afternoons shopping and getting to know the city with Rajvinder's mother.

Eliza had been shocked by the first invitation, but Badriyah (call me Barbie) had apologized for her lack of warmth on their trip to SeaWorld. She had gone on to say that she could not countenance a match between her son and Eliza without getting to know Eliza first.

Eliza respected that Barbie wanted to put her son's happiness ahead of her own. It was something she'd clearly been doing his entire life.

They were at an exclusive designer's boutique that specialized in Westernized salwar kameez and other clothing for the modern Indian woman. Eliza had noticed that Barbie dressed in a mix of Indian and entirely Western styles.

"You've found a way to thrive living here, haven't you?" she asked the older woman as she came out of the dressing room in a form fitting kameez in white, trimmed with coral, the silk pants underneath also fitted to the ankle, the complimentary coral veil casually worn over her shoulder. "That's gorgeous, by the way."

"I like it. I think Jamison will as well. I still wear the traditional Indian garb for him."

"He has good taste."

Barbie smiled. "There was a time I rejected everything from my homeland."

Eliza couldn't imagine it. "You're like the perfect blend of both cultures."

"I was very angry when I first went into exile."

"That's how you saw moving here?"

"How else should I have seen it?"

Eliza didn't have an answer. Her parents had died and while that had felt like a terrible rejection to her child's heart, she'd never had to live with the knowledge her parents did not want her around.

"Your parents probably thought you'd give Rajvinder up if they took the stance they did."

"Yes, they believed sending me to live in a foreign country, away from all those I held dear would make me resent and eventually let go of my son."

"They miscalculated your strength."

"Oh yes, they did."

"Rajvinder says you never expressed your displeasure with your family to him." That was something else Eliza couldn't help admiring.

This woman had a titanium backbone.

"He didn't need a reason to resent them anymore than he already did. I knew I could outlast my parents' disapproval and one day, my family would be together again."

"But not if your son hated his grandparents."

"Exactly."

"He's not fond of them, though." Rajvinder never pretended otherwise.

He held little respect for either of the families that had come too late to the table of his life. Which worried her a little about what he would do as heir to the principality.

Barbie sighed. "No, but for my sake, he has not rejected them completely."

"You're the reason he took the money from them to start his business."

"I told him it was the least my family owed me."

"And he agreed."

"He did."

"You're an amazing mom."

"Thank you."

Eliza found a sapphire blue kameez style top she could wear with leggings and went to try it on. When she showed it to Barbie, the other woman smiled her approval. "That looks lovely on you."

"I like it."

"I understand why I wear the traditional dress, but why do you?"

Eliza wasn't offended by the question and neither would she fob it off the way she did when her friends at school asked, saying only that she liked the styles. Barbie was someone that would play a key role in the rest of Eliza's life, if her son agreed to the arranged marriage. The older woman therefore deserved as much honesty as Eliza could give.

"When I first went to live with Tabish *auntie* and Adhip *uncle*, she insisted I dress in traditional clothes whenever I was in India." Tabish *auntie* had so wanted her own daughter. It had been her idea the first time, to dye Eliza's blonde hair dark brown. "She said I would find it more comfortable in my home."

"Did you?"

"I felt like the clothes helped me fit in, yes, but at first I felt like they were a disguise, camouflage so I didn't stick out and no one would notice me."

Barbie gave her a droll look. "I think, Eliza, that you will always stand out."

"You and your son." She shook her head.

"My son and I what?"

"You're both so complimentary."

"And the Singhs are not?"

"It's not their way."

"I believe that. I think I believed Adhip loved me because he was so vocal in his appreciation of me."

Eliza didn't know what to say to that. She felt like if she agreed, she was being disloyal to Tabish *auntie*, but if she disagreed, she wasn't being truthful.

"I never remember Adhip *uncle* giving Tabish *auntie* praise on her appearance." Even admitting that felt wrong.

But Barbie didn't look triumphant. Far from it, her lovely face creased with sadness. "Tabish is beautiful and she deserved to hear that from the man she married."

"Maybe behind closed doors."

"Perhaps."

"They were happy together." Should she not have said that?

But Barbie's smile dispelled Eliza's concerns. "I am glad. I grew to understand that as much as I might love the father of my beloved son, he was not a strong man, not someone who would ever buck tradition for the sake of another. That he managed to find contentment and happiness with his wife is something I am glad for."

"You are very forgiving."

Barbie laughed. "Not really. *I am* deliriously happy with my Jamison. I love him with a deep, abiding emotion I never knew with Adhip. It is easy to be glad for another's measure of happiness when I've had such a huge cup of it. Besides, Adhip lived without the most amazing son. I cannot help feeling sorry for such a tragedy."

"I think you might be the amazing one."

"Are you saying you don't see my son as larger than life?" Barbie teased with clear disbelief.

Eliza laughed, because? The older woman was right not to believe. "Who wouldn't see him that way? He's a self-made billionaire who cares about his mother."

"And done his best, which is a lot, to provide security for his stepfather," Barbie added.

"You saw that?"

"That my husband, who was marginally wealthy became incredibly so after going into business with my son? That Jamison was happier in the role of CFO than he'd ever been with the entire weight of his company on his shoulders? My son gave me and my husband a wonderful gift."

"He really is larger than life, isn't he?" Eliza said wistfully.

Because really, why would someone like that want to enter an arranged marriage with her?

"Oh, yes, and I'm glad you see that." Barbie patted Eliza's shoulder in approval.

They handed their bags to the driver before walking next door for lunch.

Sitting at the table outside was nice, the Christmas decorations downtown looked so festive, even in the daytime. Greenery shone in the bright sunshine, bright red and white striping in places, and bunting that would never have lasted in a true winter weather climate.

"You look like a child in a candy store," Barbie said with some amusement.

Eliza smiled self-deprecatingly. "I love all the holiday décor."

"It was one of the things I embraced with enthusiasm when I moved here. Celebrating Christmas as a secular holiday made it less depressing when I didn't have a family to celebrate Bhogi, Holi, or even Republic Day with. America has its own Independence Day though. I've always confused my friends and neighbors with joy in celebrating it. Of course, in my heart, I was celebrating my home country's far more recent independence."

"And because you'd never celebrated Christmas with anyone but Rajvinder, it was new and became something special for both of you."

"Yes."

Eliza smiled before looking at the single page menu with fresh specials for the day to choose from. Barbie really was an incredible woman.

And so strong.

Eliza wasn't sure she would have shown the same courage and strength in the face of similar circumstances.

She knew one area she wasn't the same. She absolutely would not have let herself love like Barbie did with Jamison.

"So, what do you think of our city?" Barbie asked as they ate their colorful salads.

Roasted beets was not a common vegetable in India. Eliza was discovering she loved them.

"I like the food," she said honestly. "And the feel of energy, the friendliness of people. I can see why you wanted to settle here with Rajvinder."

"It wasn't really my choice, not about coming to America and not about coming to California. I have cousins living in Los Angeles, close enough to keep an eye on me for my father, but not so close I would expect them to invite me to the family celebrations."

"That was their loss." Because Eliza just knew this woman would have made the two-and-a-half-hour drive to share family with her son.

"I think so too. I've made friends now to celebrate with, to share the culture of my homeland with my son and I learned to love my new home."

"I'm glad."

Barbie smiled. "So, you don't think you'll find it onerous to live here?"

"Live here?" They'd visit, of course, but live? "As heir to the Mahapatras dynasty, Rajvinder will be expected to live at the palace."

Barbie made a scoffing sound. "You have met my son, have you not?"

"Are you saying he's going to refuse to move to India? But that can't work. He'll be the prince. He needs to live in the palace."

"Perhaps you are right, dear." Barbie's expression and tone said the exact opposite. "But I have never known my son to allow anyone to set the terms of his life. I do not believe taking on the mantle of prince will change that."

"But tradition..."

"Is hardly a good reason for my son to do anything, in his mind anyway."

"Surely Rajvinder understands that one must go with the other." Didn't he? How could he not?

Barbie just gave a slight shrug. "I *am* surprised he allows you to call him Rajvinder. He barely tolerates it from me, but it is his name."

"Does he think it's too Indian?"

Barbie smiled sadly and shook her head. "As much as he has little use for either my family or the Singhs, my son has never blamed the country of my birth for the choices they all made in regard to him. Rajvinder is proud of his Indian heritage."

"But he doesn't like being called by his full name?" Vin wasn't exactly an American name, but it wasn't obviously Indian either.

"I made the mistake of telling him the Singhs have a tradition of naming the first born son with a name that means king or prince in some way."

"That's why he uses Vin and not Raj?" Because Raj would have been acknowledging the prince part of his name.

"I never told him that Adhip asked me to name our son Rajvinder if I had a boy."

"He did that?" Eliza asked in shock.

"He did. Letting me and our child go was terribly difficult for him."

Eliza had no trouble believing that. As content as Adhip *uncle* and Tabish *auntie* had been together, *uncle* had always had this underlying sadness Eliza hadn't understood. "If he'd been stronger, he wouldn't have let go at all."

"That was the conclusion I came to, yes."

"And still you named your son Rajvinder."

Barbie's gave her a look filled with dignity and not even a little give. "He was a prince even if the Singhs did not recognize his place in the world."

"You really want your son to be made heir, but not for your own sake."

"As much as it would be nice to have vindication finally, no, not for me. My son has always been the rightful heir to their nominal throne. He deserves the title."

"He doesn't know."

"Know what?"

"That I think of him as Rajvinder."

"How?"

"I avoid using his name."

Barbie laughed. "Surely you've had to say it at least once."

"Yes."

"And?"

"He ignored it, but he frowned."

"He did not lecture you?"

"No."

"Then you have found a soft spot in my son most would say he does not possess."

Chapter Seventeen

Eliza was pretty sure herself that soft spot didn't exist later when she met Rajvinder for dinner as she did nearly every night.

"But you can't be the Prince of Mahapatras and live in America." She'd brought up the issue, believing his mother had got it wrong.

"I assure you, I can."

She just stared at the intransigent man in front of her. "Grandfather will never agree to that."

"He already has."

"You've spoken to Grandfather?" Eliza asked with shock, and a little annoyance.

Dadaji hadn't said a word. Not before, or after, the meeting. Which might be typical for the Maharajah, but considering the fact that bringing Rajvinder back into the family had been Eliza's idea, it was still irritating.

"As much as you and I are the only ones necessary for the conversation of whether or not the marriage that was supposed to happen to my cousin goes forward, Trisanu is the only one who can negotiate the terms of making me his heir."

She couldn't argue Rajvinder's words. After all, Eliza had never taken an interest in the Singh's business, though they expected her to donate her considerable inheritance to bolstering said business.

And yet, being left out of the conversation she hadn't even been told about made her feel rejected on a level Eliza didn't really understand.

Being offended at Grandfather wouldn't change anything, but it would have made more sense than this emotional turmoil she felt right now.

Eliza snapped her napkin out with a brisk movement and then smoothed it over her lap once again. "He could have mentioned that you two met." Her voice was curt, exposing some of her disgruntlement.

"I mentioned it. Now."

She searched Rajvinder's handsome features, trying unsuccessfully to read his expression. The man probably made a killing at the poker tables. If he indulged.

"And he has no problem with you not living in India? At the palace?" she asked in disbelief.

"I have agreed to visit the palace twice a year. As you know, I travel to India more frequently for business." Rajvinder nodded toward her dinner. "Is the food not to your liking?"

"It's fine," she dismissed with a flick of her wrist. "Neither of you thought to discuss this decision with *me*?" What if she didn't want to live in India only part-time? Didn't her opinion matter at all? To either of these two stubborn, proud men? "What if I want to live in India?"

"Then I will see you twice a year when I am at the palace, perhaps more often if you wish to meet me when I am there on business."

The words dismissing her as a future component to his life hit her like a blow, all the air whooshing from her lungs and something painful squeezing in Eliza's chest.

Eliza told herself this visceral, over the top reaction to him as much as saying he didn't plan to marry her made no sense, but that didn't make the disappointment choking her any less keen.

Yes, she wanted to do her duty and follow through on her promise to marry the Mahapatras heir. And even more, she knew that marriage would make Rajvinder stepping into his rightful place as heir to the Maharajah easier for everyone in the family to accept.

The marriage was something she could give to the family that she'd been unable to give the emotional closeness she knew they had expected and Tabish *auntie* so clearly craved.

But it should not bother Eliza on any emotional level to realize Rajvinder wasn't going to fall in line with that aspect of him taking on his role as heir. In fact, she *should* feel relief.

"Is something wrong?" he asked, sounding like he honestly couldn't imagine what might be bothering her.

Probably because he couldn't. Rajvinder would have no reason to believe she would react with anything but acceptance to his decision not to honor his cousin's marriage plans.

Wanting the negative to be true, Eliza shook her head, no words coming to her usually active brain. She remained quiet through the rest of dinner, having little appetite and doing her best to hide it.

Since when had she started *wanting* to marry the self-made tycoon?

Eliza hadn't even really wanted to marry Dev.

Not for his sake certainly. As close of friends as they had been, Eliza knew without question she would not have been angry, or even disappointed, if Dev had backed out of the arranged marriage.

As she'd grown older, she had come to believe she did not have to marry Dev to keep her place in the Singh family. Adhip *uncle* and Tabish *auntie* saw her as their daughter, marriage, or not marriage.

Even now, as much as Tabish *auntie* wanted what she termed the stability of Eliza's marriage to the new heir, she had also told Eliza privately that if she didn't want to go through with it, Eliza should not.

Now that it looked like Rajvinder wasn't as keen on the marriage, Eliza couldn't hide from the truth that she *did* want the marriage.

And it worried her, because though he and Grandfather had discussed terms for Rajvinder becoming the Maharajah's official heir, she knew the old man was still laboring under the belief that his heir would be marrying the woman raised to be princess. Eliza.

Anxiety and disappointment created a negative maelstrom of emotions inside her.

Eliza and Rajvinder were in the car when she realized that as much as she'd looked forward to seeing the Nutcracker ballet, she was no longer in the mood.

"Would you mind terribly if I begged off on the ballet?" she asked, certain he wouldn't mind at all.

Rajvinder looked at her with an expression she might have been tricked into thinking was concern, if she didn't know better. "Are you all right? You were very quiet at dinner."

"I'm tired." Exhausted. A sense of defeat rode her while she told herself it didn't matter.

He'd agreed to be heir. That was what was important. Not only would Rajvinder be reunited with his father's family, like Dev wanted, but Eliza was sure he would fix the ailing business empire. Taking care of the family just as she'd promised Dev.

Rajvinder gave her another searching look, but nodded. He stopped in front of the hotel, going to unclip his seatbelt. But she stopped him with a hand to his wrist. "Don't get out. I'll see myself up."

He pressed the button and the snick of the seatbelt disengaging sounded. "I will see you inside."

"That's not necessary, really."

But Rajvinder was already getting out of the car. He said something to the valet before coming around to help Eliza out of the car, showing no compunction about stepping around the livery clad attendant that had opened her door.

"I will change our tickets for tomorrow's ballet," he said as he led her inside.

"Please, don't bother. I'll probably be packing. I'll look for a flight back to India tonight." She had some thinking to do, plans to make.

The marriage might not be going forward, but her time with Rajvinder Acharya and his mother Barbie Latham had made Eliza realize that maybe the time had come to stop living for other people.

That maybe it was time to start living. Full stop.

"What? Why are you going back to India?"

"I came over to negotiate your return to the family, but it looks like you and *Dadaji* have already done that. And since you're not interested in fulfilling the marriage contract, my presence is clearly surplus to requirements."

"Who said I wasn't interested in marrying you?" he asked, sounding genuinely perplexed.

Then before she could answer, he was guiding her to a couple of chairs in a secluded corner in the lobby. Without really realizing how it had happened, Eliza found herself sitting down, Rajvinder in a chair kitty-corner to hers.

His knee brushed her thigh as he leaned toward her. "We need to talk."

"Why? It sounds like you and *Dadaji* have everything worked out."

"Have you noticed that you refer to him as *dadaji* when you are feeling nervous, or emotional and Grandfather the rest of the time?"

"I'm not feeling nervous," she assured him. Nerves did not come into it. "And I'm not an emotional person."

"You really believe that," he said with some awe. Like her words were oh so ridiculous to him. "Are you backing out of the arranged marriage?"

"What?" Why would he ask that? "You said..."

"I never said anything about it, either way." He sounded very sure.

She was equally sure he had. "You did. At dinner."

"What did I say?" he asked. The confusion he exhibited would have been rather charming if she wasn't dealing with a maelstrom of unexpected feelings, that *did not* make her an emotional person.

In fact, her own shock at feeling them clearly indicated she wasn't usually emotional, but if she said that, she'd sound defensive and that would be self-defeating.

Instead she reminded him, "You said that I would see on your visits to India."

"If you chose to live in the Palace, then when else would I see you?"

"You meant as husband and wife?"

"Well, I'm not going to presume, we haven't actually agreed to marriage between us, but that is one possible outcome."

"And you don't care if we only see each other twice a year?" Married? As much as she'd never planned on falling for her husband, it had never occurred to Eliza that she and her husband would have such a distant relationship.

She stifled the urge to sigh, frustrated and confused by her own reaction once again. The idea should make her happy, not depress her.

"That's up to you. I can't say I'm keen to go months between sex, but I'm not going to force you to relocate to California."

"You plan to be faithful?" she asked, before thinking, but wanting the answer, so she didn't take the words back, or try to give him an out.

"Don't you?"

"I hadn't thought about it." She'd been pretty sure Dev had a girlfriend and Eliza hadn't been at all sure that he planned to give her up after marriage.

Considering her own attitude toward marriage, seeing it as more a joining of two friends in the united effort to continue the House of Mahapatras, than any kind of romantic connection, Eliza hadn't really cared either way. For some reason, the idea of Rajvinder taking other bed partners seemed entirely different.

Wholly unexpected and foreign rage surged up inside her at the idea. "No. No other bed partners. If I agree to this marriage, neither of us will take other bed partners."

Chapter Eighteen

"If you agree?" he asked with dry, near academic interest.

"It's my choice as much as yours."

"That's not the attitude you had when you first arrived in San Diego."

"I'm sorry if I gave you a different impression, but I assure you, it was."

Rajvinder inclined his head in acknowledgement of her words. "I told Trisanu that if he wanted me to take over the Singh's business interests and bring them back to profitability, he would accept that your inheritance would remain your own."

"That's not your decision. I never said that was what I wanted."

"No. You still have an unhealthy focus on doing your duty by the Singh family."

"Accepting one's duty is not unhealthy." But she supposed to a man who claimed to feel no responsibility toward his father's family, it might be seen that way.

"If it *is* your duty."

"Helping my family is my duty."

"And marrying me?"

"Duty plays a part in that, but I'm still not marrying you if I don't feel right about it." She'd never put that thought into words, but she knew it was how she'd always felt. "I came here prepared to an arranged marriage, but not if you'd turned out to be someone I could not see myself living with."

"Not like Dev." Something in his tone bothered her, but she couldn't place what.

"No. Marrying Dev would not have been the same as marrying you." She had no doubts about that truth.

"He was your best friend."

"He was."

"But he'd never kissed you."

"No."

Rajvinder brushed his fingertip along her lips. "I have."

"Yes." Many times. And she'd liked it more than she thought possible.

"If we marry, we will have passion, not just friendship."

She could not deny it. And something inside her was very satisfied at his acknowledgement of that truth, even while she feared what it could mean. "Yes."

"That scares you."

"Stop reading my mind." She frowned at him with exasperation.

No way did he know her that well, but then reading others was a skill he would need to be the successful businessman that he was.

Unrepentant, he gave her a shark's grin. "Friends understand each other."

"You want to be my friend?"

"I will be a better friend to you than Dev was." There was a wealth of implications behind those words.

"What do you mean?"

"For one thing, I won't allow the Singh family to take advantage of you."

"I never considered it taking advantage. Family does what it can." Besides, giving money was easier than giving emotion. Though Eliza had come to realize she'd probably invested a lot more emotion than she'd ever wanted to admit in her new family. It was apparently a night for inner revelations and not happy ones. "There's tradition in the royal lineage. Tradition that should not be lost."

"Perhaps, but it will have to change because I'm never making India my permanent home. I am an American man with an Indian heritage and I have no intention of changing that."

"But your child will be the heir to the throne as well."

"Are we going to have children?"

"Are we getting married?" she countered.

He stood up without answering, then put his hand out. "Come with me."

Bemused and still more than a little confused, she took the offered hand and let him lead her to the bank of elevators. He swiped with a card and then pressed a button that was marked private. When the elevator stopped, he led her out into a small annex and then through a door that led to rooftop garden.

"I didn't know this was here."

"It's reserved for special clientele."

"The ones staying in the penthouse?"

"Some of them, yes."

"Oh." Very exclusive then. She didn't ask how he'd gotten access. The man was a powerful billionaire. She doubted there were very many, if any, exclusive places he didn't have access to.

He led her to a spot where they could look out over the city, Christmas lights and the usual street and traffic lights mixing for a magical beauty she would not have expected from their vantage point. "It's so pretty."

"Eliza."

She turned to see what he wanted. Rajvinder had a ring box, in the distinctive blue of a traditional and very well-known jeweler. "I..."

"Will you marry me, Eliza?"

"You didn't have to do this."

"Ours is not a romantic match, and honestly? That works for me, but you deserve every trapping to make it special. The truth is, I enjoy your company. I'm insanely attracted to you and I'm very much looking forward to making you my wife."

What an old-fashioned sentiment for such a modern guy, but Eliza didn't mind.

"Dev never asked." His father had spoken to Adhip *uncle* and then *Dadaji* had told her she would be marrying Dev when she was done with school. She'd been sixteen.

It had all been very traditional and very much in keeping with how the family operated. Even though the Maharajah had told both her and Dev they were getting married, Eliza had known she could refuse, but she hadn't wanted to.

Dev had been her best friend and at sixteen, Eliza had only been too happy to agree to a marriage that would ensure her new family didn't disappear from her life like her birth family had through tragedy.

Rajvinder flipped open the lid on the ring box. The diamond ring inside glittered under the soft rooftop lights, twinkling like the clear Christmas lights strung around them. "I am not Dev."

"No, you aren't." Two men could hardly be more disparate in personality and life choices.

Rajvinder looked at her, like he expected her to say something else.

She didn't know what, so she gave him the truth. "I never thought I'd say this, but I'm glad." She had never been able to even imagine what a wedding night with Dev would be like. Had sort of dreaded it, but she didn't feel that way about Rajvinder.

At all.

"Is that a yes?"

"I don't want to live apart." Which was hard to admit. Because, really? It shouldn't matter. Not if their emotions weren't involved.

But she was too much of a scientist to deny the empirical evidence, which indicated heavily her emotions were indeed engaged.

"Do you have a suggestion?"

She actually wasn't tied to living in India full time. She never actually had. And maybe that was something he had already taken into consideration.

"Even since coming to live with the Singhs, I spent most of my year in school," she mused.

It was only very recently she'd moved back into the Palace fulltime. She'd finished her doctorate and they'd started planning the wedding. Then Dev had died and all those plans with him.

"I am aware," he agreed dryly. "I was surprised that even after marriage you expected to live there fulltime."

Well, she had expected the new heir to be taking up residence in the palace and herself, as his wife, to do so as well. "I just naturally assumed that was where we would be living if we married."

"I'm not a slave to tradition," he said mildly.

But she laughed. "No, you are not."

And of course, Rajvinder had considered her years away at school and drawn the correct conclusion that Eliza would be just as happy to visit the palace as to live there permanently. Rajvinder thought about everything.

Whereas Eliza could have acute tunnel vision at times, especially when she was working on her research. Speaking of.

In for a penny, in for a pound. And maybe some more besides. "I don't want to go into medical research."

Rajvinder didn't look even a little surprised at that pronouncement. "There's a place on any of my company's agricultural production projects for you, if you want it. But I think the one you might be most interested in is a new farming cooperative in India."

"Oh, yes." *She* was a little shocked by her own lack of hesitation, caring nothing in that moment for whether or not nepotism was fair, or even right.

His lips barely tilted on one side, but the amusement was there. "I'm not being generous. You will be an amazing asset to whatever research team is lucky enough to get you."

"You're saying I get to choose what project I want to work on?" she asked, enthusiasm for the idea, especially of the India based project, warring with her sense of guilt at abandoning the path Adhip *uncle* hand encouraged her to take.

And for the first time in a long while, her own desires won.

"Yes."

"Won't that offend the team leader?" she wondered.

"I've already sent your resume to all of them. The project managers have all expressed interest in having you added to their team, including the new India project." He once again showed he knew the direction her thoughts had gone.

"You're not serious."

"I'm not much for jokes."

"But you couldn't know I'd change my mind about what I wanted to do."

His brow rose, as if mocking her assertion. "You say I read your mind."

"But that's..." Crazy. Scary. Downright terrifying.

"I like California."

"I'm glad."

Living in San Diego would be no hardship. Eliza had been falling in the love with the city in a way she never had the East Coast. It felt like home.

"Each visit to India must last at least a month. If we have children..." And she wasn't at all sure she was ready for that kind of commitment. It seemed much more permanent than marriage to a near stranger. "I would want them to experience life in the palace in a very real way, not as a place they see for a few days a couple of times a year."

"So, you do want children."

"Maybe, some day. Not right away." She wrapped her arms around herself, pushing away the thought of what it might mean to her heart to become a mother. "Do you?"

"My mother would kill me if I said no."

"But do *you* want children?" she asked, realizing that if the time ever came, she didn't want to be a single parent inside of a marriage of convenience.

"I do, actually. I had excellent teachers on how to parent."

"Your mom and stepfather."

"I'm certainly not going to follow the example of either the Singhs or the Acharyas."

"They're not that bad."

"Says you."

She laughed. "Tradition is just really important, to the older generations especially."

"You don't think Dev was every bit as keen on tradition?" Rajvinder asked, his tone saying he didn't buy it.

She couldn't really say. They'd talked about some things and never discussed others. "He was really supportive of me finishing my education."

"Maybe he wasn't all that excited to get married."

That bit of truth didn't hurt like maybe it should have. "I don't think either of us looked at it as something to look forward to."

"But you were still going to do it."

"Yes."

"And now?"

"Now..." She paused, breathless for some inexplicable reason. She put her hand out toward him as her answer.

He didn't ask what she meant, but flipped the box in his hand to take out the ring and then he slid it carefully on her left ring finger. "You will marry me."

"I will."

"No lovers."

"None." If it came out a little vehement his statement hadn't been any less so.

"Children."

"Someday. Not right away." If they found the contentment in their marriage, a place of stability they could bring children into, then yes.

"I'll let my mom work on you, but honestly, I'm happy to wait for that as well. Children are a bigger commitment than promises between two near strangers," he said, reflecting Eliza's earlier thoughts.

The kiss that followed sent her senses reeling.

Chapter Nineteen

V in stopped his car in the circular drive in front of the Mahapatras palace, eager to see his intended bride.

Eliza had returned to India the day after agreeing to become his wife.

Trisanu had insisted on the wedding taking place immediately. Evidently, he didn't trust Vin not to back out of the deal of becoming his heir.

Considering the business and financial control concessions Vin had forced upon the Maharajah, he hadn't been surprised at the old man's need for some kind of assurance Vin would join the family as promised.

His mother had flown out with Eliza, intent on putting her own stamp on the royal wedding. She'd let both Trisanu and Vin know how unhappy she was to have only a matter of weeks to plan the type of Indian royal wedding celebration that usually took more than a year.

The ceremony itself was planned for December 24th. He wondered if the Singhs had even considered the fact, they were planning it for Christmas Eve? He knew his mother had, but more importantly, the date would matter to Eliza and Vin was determined that his fiancée's love of the holiday was taken into account in the traditional Indian plans.

He spoke to his mother frequently on the phone and at least daily to Eliza. Both women shared far more than he expected about the wedding plans, revealing a growing warm relationship that did not surprise him.

What did, was how well his mother apparently got along with Tabish Singh.

The two older women were, according to Eliza, two peas in a pod both bent on making the wedding a *ridiculously extravagant event,* also according to Eliza, who apparently was not keen on the whole ride an elephant in a parade procession thing, or coming to the wedding dais under a canopy carried by her ten nearest and dearest. Who were, in fact, Singh relatives she didn't know very well at all.

"You do not wish to have any school friends in the wedding?" he'd asked on one of their phone calls.

"No."

"Why?"

"I don't make close friends."

"None?" Though the investigator's report had said as much, he preferred confirmation of what he believed to be true from her perspective.

"None." She huffed out a breath. "And that doesn't make me pathetic."

"I never said it did."

"I didn't want close friends."

"I believe that."

"Do you?" she demanded testily.

And he smiled. "Yes. You didn't let anyone get too close after losing everything you knew of family within a couple of years."

She sighed. "You're so sure you know me well."

"Don't I?"

"Better than anyone alive," she admitted with her usual candor, if grudgingly.

"Better than Dev," he assured her. "He didn't know you were terrified of letting yourself love anyone."

"Why are we talking about love?" Oh, that was beyond annoyed and right into angry.

"We aren't."

"Good."

Vin didn't need her to admit that he was a better friend than Dev.

Vin knew he was. Not only had he protected her from having her inheritance sacrificed at the altar of Singh tradition and financial mismanagement, but he had taken time to get to know the things that were important to her.

Which was why he had called his mother to make sure that certain elements neither Barbie, nor Tabish would have even considered would be included in the wedding event of the year. Or decade to hear Eliza tell it.

"I don't remember things being this crazy with Dev," Eliza grumped.

"The family didn't have the same coffers to draw from when they were planning that wedding."

"You're paying for this wedding?" she asked in a tone that he actually couldn't read.

"I am." Anything important to his mother, he would provide.

And if doing so proved to both the Singh and Acharaya families that Vin hadn't needed either one to succeed well beyond anything *any* of them had been capable of achieving? So much the better.

"You don't mind?"

"My mother wants a *Royal* wedding, she will have every trapping." The fact that wedding would put a spike in it as far as both his Singh and Acharya relatives were concerned when it came to placing value on Vin was only icing on the cake.

Eliza huffed with clear exasperation. "She and Tabish *auntie* are exhibiting a level of insanity I had no idea either was capable of."

"Are you unhappy with the plans?" he asked, not sure what steps he would take if Eliza said she was, but knowing his mother's feelings weren't the only ones that mattered.

Which was natural he supposed. He intended to live the rest of his life with Eliza as his wife. Vin would be undermining his own future contentment if he started his marriage off with a genuinely pissed-off wife.

"Not unhappy, just overwhelmed," she admitted with a sigh. "I'd so much rather spend my days in a lab than trying on wedding finery, picking out fixtures and silks for canopies. Those two women have opinions on everything! They're even redecorating the main ballroom for the reception."

Considering the timing, it was ambitious, but not impossible. "I know." He'd had to approve the expenditure after all.

"It was fine the way it was!" she said plaintively.

"*Maan* said it was dated."

"It's a palace! The décor is traditional, not dated." There was something in her tone.

"You really aren't happy they redecorated?"

"It's just..." A sigh could be heard over the phone. "I used to hide in that room when I needed time to myself. A palace is surprisingly hard to find privacy in. Even my own bedroom suite had servants in and out of it throughout the day."

"So, you went to the ballroom and found quiet?"

"It's only used for the really big functions and kept closed up the rest of the time."

"Did you tell Tabish, or my mother, you didn't want it redecorated?" he'd asked.

"No, of course not. It was important to them."

"It sounds like it was important to you too."

"It's fine. I'm just focusing on little things because everything is so overwhelming."

It didn't sound like such a small thing to her. The ballroom had been her sanctuary. And now it wasn't anymore. But even if they didn't change the décor, the preparations for the wedding would have stolen her refuge for quiet.

"Tabish *auntie* has me on a diet!"

"What?" he asked sharply.

"She said I need to be at my best, but what that has to do with eating my favorite dishes at dinner, I do not know."

"You are fine the way you are."

"Thank you, but Tabish *auntie* is on a tear. I'm not going to tell her to leave the rice on my plate."

Vin had no trouble doing so, calling Tabish Singh the minute he got off the phone with Eliza and speaking to her for the first time since his disastrous trip to India at the age of eighteen. He let her know in no uncertain terms that he expected any efforts at limiting Eliza's diet to end. He also told both her and his mother that he wanted Eliza to have at least two hours a day of solitude.

Neither woman had been best pleased with his edicts, but as much as he respected and cared for his mother, Vin had no trouble reminding her, or Tabish, that he was the one paying for the Royal wedding and the free rein given them could end at any time.

Both women had promised to make sure Eliza had the time to herself she needed.

He hadn't told any of them that he was arriving today. He was a few days early, but even with the quiet time he'd negotiated for Eliza, she was sounding increasingly stressed out and exhausted with every phone call.

She'd spent most of her life in the world of academia and he thought coming face to face with the life of a real princess was not to her liking as much as she'd expected it to be. Eliza wanted to read her academic journals and spend time in the lab. She'd admitted how much she was missing her research.

Her texts were growing shorter and less frequent as well.

Vin found he didn't like it. So, he'd made a few changes in his own schedule and here he was.

"Rajvinder?"

CHAPTER TWENTY

H e looked up at the sound of his name and smiled. "Eliza."

She rubbed her eyes, blinked at him and then frowned, looking around the front drive to the palace, as if expecting him to disappear any moment. "What are you doing here?"

"I have it on good authority that our wedding celebrations begin soon."

"But you said you were coming in the day before the *Tilak*."

His mother and Tabish had been hard pressed giving up the *Sagai*, and truth be told Vin hadn't been thrilled himself. However, the ring ceremony had not been practicable in the rushed schedule they were on for the royal wedding.

Nevertheless, perhaps unsurprisingly, his mother had been particularly insistence on having the groom acceptance ceremony.

She wanted official and public recognition that Vin had been accepted as not only Eliza's husband-to-be, but was also the acknowledged heir of the Mahapatras Dynasty. Both would be formally stated during the *Tilak*.

"I changed my mind." He'd decided to fly in early and it was a good thing he had.

Eliza looked exhausted, purple bruises marring the pale skin under her eyes, her own smile not as vibrant as he was used to.

He put his hand out. "Come here."

"Aren't you coming inside?" she asked, her tone confused, her gaze latched on to him, but slightly unfocused.

"I'd planned to." He'd intended to put his foot down about the wedding plans that had so obviously gotten out of control. "But I have a better idea."

"What idea?"

"You need to get away."

Eliza came down the steps in front of the palace like she was in a daze, her movements almost jerky. "Get away?"

"Yes." He moved forward, worried in her current state of exhaustion, she might trip on the stone steps that wouldn't have looked out of place leading up to a state capitol building.

Or a palace.

Which they did.

Unimpressed by their stately appearance and impractical lack of any kind of railing, he surged forward to take Eliza's hand and bring her down toward the car he'd purchased for use on his trips to India. Unlike his vehicle back in the states, this was not a limited edition from his favorite electronic car maker.

It was in fact, even more special. A prototype of the luxury end model for the alternative energy car made at the India based facility he'd invested in the year previous. So far, *he* was impressed. If their mass production was anything like as pleasing, he would be adding more zeroes to his bottom line.

Eliza was protesting as he led her across the superbly smooth gravel of the extra wide drive that surrounded the entire palace like a dry moat. "But I have a fitting in fifteen minutes, there are arrangements."

"I believe having a bride that does not collapse with exhaustion when we are supposed to be exchanging our garlands would be the most important thing right now."

"What? I'm not going to—" Eliza tripped over nothing that he could see, making Vin's point for him.

Rather than argue any further, he stopped her at the car, leant down and pulled her to him. She stared up at him like she couldn't figure out what he was doing, both alarming and amusing him at once. His bride-to-be needed a break.

And Vin needed his lips on hers. Yesterday.

Pushing *that* disturbing thought away, Vin took the kiss he'd been missing since she left San Diego. It felt like Eliza had lost weight, her body too fragile under his hands.

But she returned his kiss without hesitation.

"Eliza! Rajvinder? What is the meaning of this?" a woman he knew only by picture demanded as she stopped and stared in shock at them from the top of the steps. "This kind of display is entirely unseemly."

Eliza went stiff and tried to pull out of his arms, but Vin held her gently, placing a comforting kiss against her temple. "Get in the car, *sonii.*"

The endearment meaning *golden one* fit her, with her honey blonde hair and even more so because of the light that so effortlessly shined out of Eliza. Even in her current state.

She didn't argue, didn't list the responsibilities she had, or the reasons she couldn't leave. Eliza simply nodded and, seemingly oblivious to Tabish Singh's squawking, Eliza got into the car.

That, more than anything else, confirmed to Vin just how important it was to get her away from the palace for a while.

Tabish was headed toward them, not rushing, because that would be *unseemly*, but the glare on her face said she was not happy with them kissing out on the front drive for the world to see. The litany of things Eliza was supposed to be doing hadn't let up either.

Vin shook his head. "Eliza will not be available for any of that. You'll have to make do without her."

"Make do? Without the bride? That's impossible." That was his mother's voice.

He smiled at her graceful walk down those same steps, confidence in every line of her body, like she belonged there. She always had.

But that didn't mean he was going to let her, or her cohort, run Eliza into the ground before the wedding.

"I would have been happy with a civil ceremony in San Diego," he reminded both women in a tone that had them stopping and looking first to him and then at each other. "I told you to give her time to herself. Eliza is an academic, not a wedding planner."

"We have a planner," his mother said with credible affront.

Vin wasn't falling for it. "I am willing to indulge your desire for a formal wedding—"

"Surely you understand that cannot happen in the timeframe allotted to us without considerable effort on the part of everyone involved," Tabish said. "As it is, this unseemly haste is already giving rise to gossip."

"The haste is on your father-in-law, not me." Trisanu wanted all the legalities done as soon as possible for Vin's taking over in the role of his heir, but had been insistent that the wedding happen before the final document was signed.

At first, Vin had surmised the old man thought his illegitimate grandson would be easier to control if he was married to Adhip's ward. However, after the latest information report from Hawk Global Investigations & Security, Vin suspected another motive. Whatever Trisanu's reasoning, Vin looked forward to disappointing the current Maharaja.

Vin would never be controlled by anyone, but especially a Singh or an Acharya.

And he would never allow the past to repeat itself.

The wedding that never would have happened if *both* he and Eliza had not agreed to it wasn't going to change that.

"I will have her back the day before the *Tilak*," he promised, with what he considered monumental patience, as he opened the driver's side door.

Tabish's eyes widened and then narrowed. "What? No. Absolutely not—"

"You're here early, we can put together a small ring blessing," his mother said, interrupting, giving Vin a look of parental appeal.

He might have been moved by it if he couldn't see Eliza out of the corner of his eye, slumped in the passenger seat of his car and looking far too fragile. "No. We agreed. There is no time for a *Sagai*."

"But that was before you were able to get here early."

"I put off important meetings because with every phone call, my concern for Eliza grew."

"Do not be dramatic, Rajvinder, all brides become tired coming up to their wedding days. There is much to do."

Vin gave his mother a look that he rarely used on her. She was after all, the one person in the world he acknowledged loving. But even she would not convince him to allow the current situation to continue. "You will have to finish the preparations for the event without her."

He took a breath and counted backward from ten.

Both older women must have realized just how close he was to losing his cool, because neither spoke while he did so.

"We have both given you free rein."

"As is custom," his mother pointed out.

"Really, *Maan*? You want me to get into a discussion about *custom* right now?"

His mother's lips sealed, her own expression not as friendly as it usually was.

"You may continue with the plans we have agreed to, but Eliza and I will not be here. Any truly important questions will come through me, but be warned if I don't think they are important enough to interrupt my time with my intended, my answer will be no. No to the elephant. No to the canopy. No to the pre-wedding rituals."

As much as he himself wanted those trappings, Vin meant what he said. He always meant what he said.

"Really, Rajvinder, I did not raise you to be so intransigent."

"You raised me to be strong."

His mother sighed. "I did that."

"To believe in my own value."

He got an almost smile for that.

"You also gave me a healthy dose of stubborn and there's no point denying it."

That wiped the smile from her face, but she didn't look angry.

"I have made only a couple of requests in regard to the wedding, but now I'm making a demand. Deal with it. All of it. If you need to hire more staff, do it, but my bride is coming to our wedding rested and relaxed."

"Taking her away for a honeymoon before the wedding is only going to feed the gossip," his mother pointed out, while Tabish nodded her head in agreement.

"I could make it a straight up elopement if you would rather?" He had no intention of anticipating his wedding vows.

His entire damned life had been marked by the timing and circumstances of his conception. There wasn't a single chance in hell of Vin allowing the same thing to happen to his own child.

Neither his mother, nor Tabish Singh had anything to say to his last sally, so Vin turned without another word and got into the car.

Chapter Twenty-One

"Are we really leaving?" Eliza asked.

With the press of a button, he turned on the car. "Oh, yes."

"Okay."

"You don't care where we are going?"

"Anywhere has to be better than here."

Considering the affection she held for the palace, those words said a great deal how truly overwhelming his academic was finding the preparations for a royal wedding.

Tabish Singh may have tried to raise Eliza to be a princess, but nothing was going to change his fiancée's basically introverted nature.

"We will go to one of my favorite places."

"Okay, but I don't have any clothes." She didn't sound worried, just tired.

The conviction he was doing the right thing taking Eliza away right now grew in Vin. "Call favorite number three on my phone, tell her your size, preferred colors and style of clothes you want. Tell her to have them delivered by tonight to..." He named the hotel he liked best in Agra with amazing views of the Taj Mahal from every suite.

"We're going to the Taj Mahal?"

"We are going to Agra and only the Taj Mahal if you are up to it." He wasn't sure how others responded, but he hoped Eliza would be like him and find just looking at the elaborate mausoleum destressing.

"I've always wanted to see the inside."

"If you're well rested the day after tomorrow, then we'll go." He negotiated the road, used to the craziness that was India's traffic. "Agra's not so far from the palace. Why haven't you ever gone to the Taj Mahal?"

"Too touristy." She yawned and then settled more deeply into her seat.

"For the Singhs you mean?"

"Yes."

He wasn't surprised. It was easy to take even national treasures for granted when you lived close to them and saw them as part of your home landscape. "When you speak to my Executive Assistant, have her arrange for my usual suite at the hotel too, if you don't mind."

"I don't mind," Eliza said on another yawn.

Vin wished he'd taken the time to pair his phone to the car, then he could be making this phone call on voice command. But he'd been in too much of a hurry to get to the palace.

Eliza pressed the phone to his fingertip to unlock it before doing as he'd suggested. Her discussion with his EA was brief, but he knew his instructions would be carried out without a hitch.

When she was done, Eliza put the phone down and asked, "You don't mind just buying me a bunch of clothes?"

"What I do mind is how exhausted you look."

"Your mother and Tabish *auntie* are indefatigable."

"They are doing what gives them joy, that gives them extra energy."

Eliza sighed. "I hate wedding preparation."

"I was beginning to get that impression."

"Does that make me abnormal?"

"No. It makes you Eliza, introverted academic who happens to also be a princess."

"Not officially. Not until we're married."

He smiled at her slurred words. He liked the thought of making her a princess. "Honestly? I know we both want to fulfill tradition." Which was a little odd for him, but Vin had never denied how proud he was of his Indian heritage. "But if I had been here, I probably would have exploded about two weeks ago and insisted on a civil ceremony with a very long honeymoon."

"We've never even discussed the honeymoon," she said in an unhappy tone.

"Did you want to?"

"Not really, no. I don't want to think about the wedding, or our wedding night, or anything else, right now," she said with more candor than he expected.

Her exhaustion had decimated her brain-to-mouth filters. And as much as he didn't really like knowing the wedding night was stressing her out, he couldn't fix something if he didn't know it was broken. He wanted her to rest.

"It's about an hour's drive to Agra. Sleep."

"I don't want to sleep. I want to talk. I haven't seen you in weeks." Her eyelids drooped even as she made that pronouncement.

He pressed a button on the steering wheel and soft jazz filled the car.

"Okay, maybe just a little nap."

She slept through the drive and arrival at the hotel. In fact, she never even woke up when he carried her inside and up to their suite. Vin laid Eliza on the bed and removed her shoes. The temptation to remove the rest of her clothes was strong, and later, when they were lovers, he wouldn't hesitate to make her comfortable like that when necessary.

But for now, he contented himself with looking his fill at the beautiful, if obviously exhausted woman fully clothed and sleeping on the bed.

In a matter of days this woman would be his wife. The satisfaction he felt at that knowledge was stronger than he expected it to be, but not unwelcome.

She was smart, kind, and loyal. Qualities he admired very much. She fit him in ways, he would not have expected, but even her bleeding heart was a good counterpart to his more ruthless nature.

His mother was convinced Eliza would soften Vin. If only *Maan* knew his plans for the Mahapatras Dynasty once he was married and his role of prince was legal and unassailable.

The old man was going to lose his mind, but it would be too late for Trisanu to continue his rejection of the illegitimate heir.

With one last glance at his sleeping fiancée, Vin went back into the living area to get some work done.

~ ~ ~

Eliza woke, light playing against her eyelids, warmth bathing her face from the wrong side of her bedroom.

Her brows drawn together in confusion, Eliza opened her eyes and blinked to adjust to the bright sunshine coming in from floor to ceiling windows across the room.

A room that was definitely *not* her bedroom back at the palace, though it was every bit as luxurious, if in a very different way. Looking around the swank, airy room, the bright colors she associated with India conspicuously absent, white the predominant color of the decor, she inventoried her situation.

Eliza was under a sheet and duvet covered, summer weight down comforter. Her shoes and jewelry were gone, but the rest of her clothes were rumpled from sleeping through the night in the strange hotel bed.

What was she doing here?

The louvered closet doors in one wall were no more familiar than the over-stuffed white chairs arranged beside a beautiful teak occasional table. What she had thought were windows were actually glass doors that led to a white plastered balcony with wrought iron furniture and greenery planted in large, elegant planters.

Where was she?

Where were Tabish *auntie* and Barbie? They should have sent someone to wake her hours ago and no doubt had dozens of tasks for Eliza to complete before nightfall.

Not least of which was the physical workout Tabish *auntie* insisted on to "make sure Eliza was at her very best" for her wedding day.

Memories of the day before flashed through her mind. Rajvinder showing up days early, that look of real irritation in his eyes when he saw how tired she was.

Weird. But sweet. And unexpectedly welcome.

Had they really run away from the wedding? Eliza's current situation said *yes*.

But where was Rajvinder now? The depression in the second stack of pillows on the oversized bed indicated he'd slept there as well.

Right next to her.

Even though she was fully clothed, indicating nothing untoward had happened between them, heated awareness washed over her at the thought.

She wasn't sure if she was relieved, or disappointed that nothing had happened last night, her first one alone completely with the man who would be her husband.

One thing she did know. Eliza felt better than she had in days.

She was hungry, but even more than food, she wanted a shower. Eliza got up and went into the bathroom, needing a good hot shower without interruption more than she needed answers. Besides, she needed some time to shore up her defenses before seeing her fiancée.

The man had made it past all the walls around her heart and had somehow become *important*. No one was ever supposed to be important to her heart again. Eliza had spent the last two decades keeping her every soft emotion in check.

She knew the crushing agony of loss, could still remember the pain that had finally drowned the girl who believed life was good and safe and right.

Losing the grandparents that had been nearly as close and every bit as doting as her parents had devastated her, but when her parents had been taken from her such a short time later, Eliza had known that loving someone came with a terrible price.

One she had been determined never to pay again.

Her world would never again be torn asunder by loss.

Only somehow, every phone call with Rajvinder had become increasingly necessary. Her days grey and dismal until that first text and brightened further when he called to check on her, as he always did.

Even worse, every time she talked to Rajvinder, Eliza revealed more of the true self she hid so completely from others. He knew how much she wanted children, but how terrified she was to become a mother. That the possibility of losing a child, like she'd lost her parents, was the specter that haunted her hopes for a family with ghoulish power.

How she was even more terrified of putting a child through the same loss she'd suffered.

Therapists would probably call the awful nightmares and terror she experienced something clinical and pathological, but all Eliza knew was that she'd *shared* those fears with Rajvinder. And far from dismissing her emotional concerns as unimportant, Rajvinder had promised her that they would not lose their children. That they would never leave them.

She'd told him he couldn't make those kind of promises.

He'd said, with his customary confidence, "I just did."

And no matter how illogical, or irrational, Eliza had found herself believing him.

It made no sense. Not in the face of her own past. But it didn't matter. She *did* believe him. Rajvinder was her hero and he would protect her from the pain of the past.

She'd never trusted anyone to do that.

Not Adhip *uncle* or Tabish *auntie*. Not even Dev.

Rajvinder had also assured her there was no hurry to get pregnant. That no matter how the Singhs saw life, they were not the English royal family and could wait for Eliza and Rajvinder to provide progeny.

That promise had made it possible for Eliza to breathe again and only then did she realize how incredibly stressed she'd been, how this specter of motherhood had preyed on her subconscious since her promise to marry Dev when she was sixteen.

If she didn't know it was impossible, because Eliza would never allow herself the emotional indulgence, she would think she was falling in love with Rajvinder.

Chapter Twenty-Two

After a very long shower that did nothing to settle her racing thoughts, Eliza came out to the bedroom, luxuriating in the thick hotel robe and drying her hair with a towel only to stop short at the sight of her fiancé.

He wore only a pair of pajama pants and nothing else. She was pretty sure those were for her sensibilities. His sculpted chest was on display and her mouth went dry as the desire she'd only ever experienced with him washed over her.

Despite the casualness of his apparel (or lack thereof), his aura was no less commanding than usual. Power and confidence exuded from him, inexplicably quieting her chaotic thoughts.

"Good morning." He eyed her critically. "You look better than yesterday, but I think you could use another day of sleep."

The words should have sounded critical, but they didn't. Eliza felt cared for.

When he said he wanted her at her best, he meant what was best *for* her, not the best she could give in any particular moment.

No one had cared for her with such single-minded intensity directed on *her* happiness since her parents' deaths.

It was both comforting, but also more terrifying than the prospect of jumping out of an airplane without a parachute.

Eliza sloughed off her thoughts and his concern with one raise of her shoulders. "Planning a wedding that usually has a year, or even two to prepare for, is not for the weak, or so your mother and Tabish *auntie* keep telling me."

"With the resources at their disposal, there is no reason for you to personally see to so many of the preparations," he said with a frown and a shrug that was more controlled power than negligence.

She wished it were that simple. "I need to go back." It was a matter of family pride, or so both women said, that Eliza play her part.

"No." He indicated the big glass doors. "Breakfast is ready on the balcony."

"What? You can't tell me no?" And why did that sound more like a question than a statement? She completely ignored his mention of breakfast.

She was so hungry, but Tabish *auntie* would be furious if Eliza ate like she wanted to.

His smile was deadly. To her common sense. "Usually, I would agree with you, but you have shown you are not going to protect yourself, so I will do it for you."

He was going to protect her? From their families? Dev had never even hinted at such a thing. If the relatives wanted it, he was right there telling Eliza she needed to agree.

Eliza wasn't sure how she felt about Rajvinder's attitude. "Is this going to be a thing with you?"

"I'm beginning to believe it is, yes. You need a keeper, *sonii*. You want to give too much of yourself away."

Did she? Didn't she owe it to the people who had taken her in during her terrible grief and never given up on her? "Surely that's my decision to make."

He reached out and touched her face, the barest touch under her eyes where a set of luggage had taken up residence. "I believe there is something about cherishing in our wedding vows. I cannot cherish you, if I do not take care of you. And I cannot take care of you if I do not make sure you take care of yourself."

"I'm not sure that's in the Hindi vows."

"It is, in fact, part of the first vow a man makes to the woman promising to be his wife," Rajvinder informed her.

"Oh."

He moved into her personal space, taking all the air out of the room. "We will speak all of the seven sacred vows," Rajvinder promised in a tone that was a vow itself.

"I thought you said you weren't a practicing Hindu." They'd discussed religion and spirituality, along with so many things Eliza had never realized were so important to know about another person, during their daily phone calls.

"I am not."

No, like her, he considered himself spiritual, but not at all religious.

Perhaps because religion condemned his mother's actions and the circumstances of his birth. Just as it had let Eliza down, offering complacent platitudes about God's will in the face of her parents' deaths.

Neither Eliza, nor Rajvinder had rejected spirituality all together, but she was relieved he was as uninterested in organized religion as she was.

She found herself smiling, because she knew exactly why they were speaking the seven sacred vows. For the same reason, Eliza had been running herself ragged since returning to India. "It's important to your mother and Tabish *auntie* that we observe the Hindi wedding traditions."

"Yes."

"Those two women are a force to be reckoned with," Eliza said with rueful honesty. One way, or another, they'd been ruling her life with martinet precision, all the while smiling and not raising a single voice.

And she'd let them have their way completely, to the point of debilitating exhaustion.

"In their element, yes, they are." One masculine finger played along the edges of her robe's neckline. "But you will be no less so in yours."

She wasn't sure force was the right word. "I can get lost for days in the lab when I'm chasing an answer. But this wedding stuff is a nightmare."

"Let the women who see it as fulfillment of their dreams plan it. They can bring in more staff if they need it, but you are off limits to them for the next couple of days."

"That's okay? I can do that?" Eliza asked, guilt warring with hope.

"We *are* going to do that."

"I've missed reading." she said with a sigh, looking around their beautiful retreat with renewed appreciation. Not a single wedding preparation in sight.

His frown was more ferocious than even Tabish *auntie* could manage. "They were supposed to give you two hours a day to yourself."

"Oh, they let me be alone for two hours a day, addressing invitations, making lists...stuff and more stuff." Eliza felt like she was tattling, but it was the truth and she'd never been any good at lying.

It was why she'd always told Dev not to confide his secrets in her. She knew she couldn't keep them from his grandfather, or the rest of the family.

She wished now she had. Eliza was sure there had been things in Dev's life he'd wanted to share and hadn't been able to.

He made a sound that left no doubt Rajvinder was not happy. "No more, Eliza."

"But it's our wedding too."

"Yes, and in all honesty, I want to make those sacred vows every bit as much as my mother wants to hear me make them."

"You do?"

"Yes."

"But..."

"The trappings aren't as important as the promises themselves. And we both believe in keeping promises."

"Yes, we do." She realized something she hadn't before. "But you want the trappings too. You want both families to look at you and really see you."

"Yes." He shrugged. "Their approval doesn't mean much to me, but I find I want them to be faced with the success I've achieved and have to acknowledge it."

"Which they will do attending a lavish wedding you paid for."

"Yes."

"And legally acknowledging you as the heir to the Maharajah adds to that."

"Yes, it does."

"I'm glad you are getting what you want out of this."

"Are you?" he asked, like it mattered, and she was beginning to understand that her feelings *did* matter to this man others saw as ruthless.

"Yes, I am." She was keeping a deathbed promise to her best friend, but she also wanted to marry this man. "I would be marrying you today, even if the rest of the family did not consider it my duty."

Rajvinder stepped back and turned away, toward the amazing view of the Taj Mahal beyond their balcony, taking all that wonderful heated sensuality with him. "What the Singh family knows about responsibility and duty could fit on the head of a pin."

"That's not true." Eliza reached out to touch Rajvinder this time, laying her hand on his back. "I know they let you down, but they take responsibility to family very seriously."

Her fiancé shook his head, making a disgusted sound. "I'm not the only family they've been happy to dismiss."

What was he talking about? "I'm sorry they didn't stand by your mom, but..." She really wasn't sure but *what*.

Eliza didn't think Rajvinder would ever forgive Grandfather for rejecting his mother as a potential princess.

"I'm not talking about my mother."

Then who was he talking about? "I'm confused."

Rajvinder shook his head. "Don't worry about it. I am not marrying the Singh clan. I am marrying you."

"But in a way, you are marrying the clan." Didn't he realize that? Their marriage wasn't only about Eliza and Rajvinder, but about the whole family. "Your child will be the next Maharajah after you."

"My child will *not* be the next heir."

"I thought you said you wanted children." Now she was *really* confused.

"And you said you wanted to wait. One has nothing to do with the other."

"You don't think it matters to me?" she asked more sharply than she'd intended. But her opinion mattered.

Maybe not to *Dadaji*, who had told her to butt out once they'd returned to India and she'd asked if everything was the way he wanted it to be. He'd said he would take care of the family as he always had done.

The Maharajah's old-fashioned views of a woman's place were more than a little chauvinistic.

The idea that her opinion might not matter to Rajvinder didn't sit well with her. At all.

Rajvinder turned back, his expression intent. "Does it matter to you?" he asked with a seriousness Eliza could not deny. "Do you care if your child grows up to be a prince?"

She didn't answer immediately, knowing he was asking for truth and consideration, not knee-jerk reaction. Finally, she said the only truth she knew. "I care very much if the Maharajah dies out."

She *didn't* care if her child was heir, but some things did matter. A lot.

Chapter Twenty-Three

Rajvinder's smile was all approval as was his nod. "Good. You don't need to worry; I won't let that happen."

"Then I don't understand."

He reeled her body in until his heat pressed around her, sending unfamiliar desire for physical intimacy rolling over her. "You need more days of rest and relaxation before we have this discussion."

"But we will have it."

"You do not trust my promise?"

"Of course I do." She wouldn't be marrying him otherwise.

She *did* trust him. More than she'd ever trusted anyone since her parents' deaths.

Suddenly, she *didn't* want to talk about their child being the next heir, or anything else that heavy. She was just a little terrified that she was already in too deep.

Rajvinder had said he would not allow the dynasty to die out. Rajvinder had made his commitment and she trusted him, however that played out. Whether he named a distant relative his heir, changed his mind about his own child, or something else, Eliza was keeping her promise to marry the heir.

She was repaying her debt to the family the best way she knew how by creating a bridge between them and the man they had rejected before birth, but who was their only chance at an heir of direct descent to the Maharajah.

"Come." He tugged her toward that amazing view. "Breakfast is on the balcony."

"Let me get dressed and I'll join you."

He gave a wry twist of his lips. "I would say don't bother, but that robe will be too warm outside of the air conditioning of the hotel."

She smiled. "You're very thoughtful."

"Don't tell anyone."

"That you have a heart?"

"Exactly."

She laughed as he left the room and she opened the wardrobe, certain the clothes she'd spoken to his EA about would be inside. She was right.

Rajvinder's people were nothing if not terribly efficient. Eliza chose a sky blue kameez and complimentary narrow legged pants, trimmed in a dark blue thread that looked almost metallic. She left the accompanying veil on the bed for later, in case they went out.

She noticed a blanket and pillow on the sofa as she walked through the living area and realized that Rajvinder had slept there. At some point he'd lain beside her on the bed, but the evidence of the blanket and pillow said he hadn't actually slept with her. The suite had only one bedroom and he had given it up to her.

She kind of wished he hadn't. She'd rather he wasn't so unexpectedly considerate and so obviously concerned for her, despite his ruthless business tycoon nature.

How could she help but have feelings for such a man?

Feelings she did not want, but had no nope of dismissing as she had in the past.

The round table on the balcony was covered with a full English breakfast along with a platter of fruit, juice, coffee and a teapot.

She went for the coffee before she even began to dish up her plate. While she doctored the liquid ambrosia with fresh cream and real sugar, Rajvinder put a bit of everything on the plate in front of her.

"Thank you." She smiled at him, inhaling the wonderful scent of her coffee before taking a thoroughly satisfying sip. "Oh, this is good."

"Don't they let you drink coffee?"

"Tabish *auntie* says I don't need the cream or sugar and I don't like it without."

"Is she the reason why you are nearly skin and bones?" Rajvinder asked forbiddingly.

"Hardly that."

He gave her a look.

"I doubt I've lost more than ten pounds."

"In two weeks?" he demanded, clearly unhappy.

"She wanted me to look my best."

"She promised she would stop taking food off your plate. And stop haranguing you about dieting."

"She did."

"But?"

"She can say more with a look than most could writing a book."

"You know, nothing about how she has treated you is endearing that woman to me." Rajvinder shook his head. "My mother *likes* her."

"They get along like sisters. It's sweet."

"You're saying they fight but present a united front to others."

"Exactly. And they stay up until all hours plotting and planning for the wedding. It's insane."

"I'm surprised *Maan* has not called her own family in to help."

"Tabish *auntie* asked her if she wanted to, but Barbie said *she* hadn't been invited to help with any of her nieces or nephews' weddings."

He smiled, like hearing that pleased him.

Eliza took a bite of fruit, reveling in the clear bright taste before remarking, "I don't think she's nearly as sanguine about the way her family has treated her as you think she is."

"I am beginning to see that."

"She didn't want you to hate your extended family."

Rajvinder sipped his own coffee, no cream, no sugar. She'd noticed. "I do not hate them."

"Are you sure?"

"Yes. I would have to care about them one way or another to hate any of them. I did despise my father for being weak. I was determined to never be like him."

"I think in some good ways you are a lot like him."

Again, that utterly charming, if slightly rueful, smile. "And I guess I'm old enough to hear that and not take it as an insult."

"I'm glad."

"However, I would never allow a child to grow up, particularly in this culture, without the benefit of acknowledgement." He said it like a warning.

"I hope you know that if the choice was mine, I wouldn't either," she assured him.

"I'm glad to hear you say that."

"Do you have a child already?" she asked, her brain rushing to conclusions she would never have guessed at.

He reeled back as if totally repelled by the idea. "No. I have *never* risked pregnancy."

"You wouldn't." Not with his background. She'd been foolish to even suggest it.

"Eat. I know you are enjoying your coffee, but you need food."

She smiled and did what he suggested, savoring every bite of her forbidden breakfast. If she wasn't careful, the final fitting for her wedding gown wasn't going to go well at all.

Chapter Twenty-Four

They spent the day like tourists, shopping the kitschy market stalls, laughing and talking about things that mattered, but weren't important to the upcoming wedding or the deal between Rajvinder and his biological family.

And there was touching. Oh, he was incredibly subtle. This wasn't a place that PDA would have been smiled upon, but Rajvinder found ways to keep her in a constant state of arousal throughout the day. She was shocked to find she liked the attention, liked feeling excited. It filled her with anticipation for later, even if it was so very far outside her experience.

To others, she knew Rajvinder was a super successful business tycoon, who could take over companies without breaking a sweat. But to her? The man was a *master* of seduction.

Having someone genuinely care about *her* wellbeing, above what even his mother wanted, *that* was incredibly sexy. And Eliza liked his take charge vibe, probably because she had absolutely no problem pushing back when she wanted to.

And he listened to her, like her opinion mattered, like what she wanted out of life mattered.

That was every bit as sexy as his incredible looks, or his superpower of touching in innocent ways and making it feel anything but innocent.

~ ~ ~

They were back in the hotel room when their conversation turned (surprisingly to Eliza), to her decision to marry Dev.

"You saw him as a brother?" Rajvinder asked incredulously.

"Not quite that, or I could never have married him. He was my best friend." She'd let Dev in closer than anyone else, but Eliza had still held back from him.

And she'd known he had a life she knew nothing about either.

"I have heard that friends become lovers." Rajvinder sounded doubtful.

"Haven't you ever had a lover who was a friend first?"

"No."

"Oh." She shouldn't be surprised by that.

"Do you have friends?"

He shrugged. "I have business associates."

"No friends from university?" Even she had a couple friends she stayed in touch with from undergraduate school. "No one who isn't related to business?"

"I have a friend from college. He and his family are coming over for the wedding." Rajvinder looked pensive. "He's never asked me for money."

And in his position, that was probably a good indicator of genuine friendship.

Rajvinder kicked off his shoes and socks, stacking them neatly to the side of the chair in the suite's living room, but not taking the time to put them away in the bedroom. Eliza found that action somehow endearing and more, the sight of his bare feet more intimate than she would have expected.

He sat on the sofa, his muscular arms stretched along the back. "So, you and Dev discovered you were attracted to each other?"

Rajvinder's posture was relaxed, but there was a curiously watchful quality about him.

Eliza kicked off her own shoes and went toward one of the armchairs, but Rajvinder made a come here motion with his hand.

She found herself settling on the sofa beside him, her feet curled underneath her. "The family decided we were to marry when I was sixteen. He was only eighteen. Neither one of us really thought about that side of things then."

"And later?"

It was her turn to shrug. "We would have made it work."

"You weren't attracted to him?" Rajvinder's tone was even, almost neutral.

But she could sense he was shocked, or maybe bothered, by the possibility.

"No. I'm pretty sure he wasn't attracted to me either." Dev had never indicated otherwise.

"That would have made for a damn failure of a wedding night." There was no doubting the disgust lacing Rajvinder's tone this time.

Who that disgust was for, she couldn't be sure, but the way he was softly touching her nape told Eliza it wasn't for her.

"People who aren't attracted to each other have sex all the time." She felt compelled to point that out.

He shook his head, something dark in his gaze.

He'd probably never even considered such a thing. She might be the one without any sexual experience to speak of, but in some ways, Rajvinder was terribly naïve. Especially when considering his wealth and privilege.

It was like he'd forgotten, or refused to acknowledge, that marriage for love was not the given. Even in the modern world.

There were still millions of people all over the planet who married for financial, social, or other practical reasons.

"It can be done quite comfortably with lubricant and taking enough time," she informed him.

Rajvinder made a sound that was a lot like a growl. "You said you hadn't had sex with Dev."

"I didn't. I looked it up." She found herself scooting closer to Rajvinder, powerfully drawn to his masculine sensuality. "The wedding night made me nervous."

He flashed her an irresistible smile. "So, like any good scientist, you looked for answers."

"I did. I learned I didn't have to find him sexually stimulating to have comfortable sex, but I would probably need some kind of lubricant as my body wouldn't naturally prepare for him like..."

"Like it will for me." He leaned forward, his mouth a breath from her own. "You're probably already wet."

"Don't be crass." But after a full day of his subtle seductions. He was right.

"Not crass. Honest." He kissed her. Just a soft press of his lips against hers, but it left her breathless.

He leaned back, his gaze searching her own. "You could have had boyfriends."

He wanted to talk? After kissing her? She made herself focus on what he'd said and replied, "I didn't want them."

"Why?"

She licked her lips, tasting him, wanting more. "You read my mind so well, you tell me."

He looked at her for a few seconds and then nodded, like he'd worked it out. "You already told me." He brushed his thumb along her lower lip, leaving sparks of pleasure in its wake. "You didn't want to care about anyone, but that still doesn't explain agreeing to marry a man who held no attraction for you. A man who wasn't saving himself for marriage."

There was that disgust again, and now she knew who it was for. Dev.

"I always suspected he had a girlfriend." Dev had spent a lot of unexplained time away from the palace. She'd heard him and his father arguing once too.

About discretion. About dignity. Not about fidelity.

"But you never asked."

She just shook her head. She hadn't wanted to know. She already felt badly for Dev, someone capable of feeling, someone who she thought probably wanted to love, but who had been as trapped by duty as Eliza.

"How did that make you feel?" he asked before leaning forward to place another soft, but nothing like chaste, kiss against her lips.

"Sad."

He reared back, apparently shocked again. "Why sad? Why not angry?"

"Dev was such as good guy," Eliza tried to explain. "He deserved love and I knew I would never give him even passion, but he was as trapped by duty as I was."

"And that made you sad? For him? Not for yourself."

"Yes."

"Because you didn't *want* to risk loving him."

She shrugged. Rajvinder knew her truths. She'd told him fears she'd never shared with anyone. And Rajvinder had never downplayed them.

Still, he looked unconvinced. "How were either of you trapped? You were both adults in the twenty-first century, not the nineteenth."

"The year we live in is not as important as the culture we are born to. You know that. Dev was raised to live by duty above all else. And to a lesser extent, so was I." Her parents' expectation that she would allow them a large say in who she married had been part of her family knowledge, even at age ten when she lost them.

It had been natural to her to allow her guardians the same privilege, as much because she hadn't wanted emotional entanglements as because the idea they would play such a role was *normal* to her.

"Archaic. Even the English royal family managed to marry for love this generation." Rajvinder's voice was thick with mockery.

But he couldn't dismiss Dev's heritage, or Rajvinder's own for that matter, so easily. "You say that, but the Mahapatras family is a dynasty."

"And that *dynasty* raised yet another generation to put duty to the title, to the station, above duty to their children."

"Dev didn't have children."

"And if he had, with the girlfriend you didn't want to know about?"

"He wouldn't," Eliza said with passionate certainty. "Dev wasn't like that."

He might not have had the strongest character, but Dev wouldn't have fathered a child he couldn't raise.

A strange look passed through Rajvinder's dark eyes. It almost looked like fury, but it was banked so quickly, she couldn't be sure.

"How was it *your* duty to marry him?" Rajvinder asked mildly for the tension she could feel emanating off him.

She looked away from him and admitted her guilt, her reason for seeing doing her duty as the one thing she could give the family that had taken her in. "I couldn't let them into my heart. I couldn't love them."

Tabish *auntie* had called Eliza her daughter, but Eliza had never felt like the woman was her mother. She couldn't give that loyalty and love away.

Rajvinder gently brought Eliza's head around so their eyes met again, his gaze filled with unexpected understanding and no judgment at all. "Of course you couldn't. You'd lost everyone who had ever mattered to your child's heart."

"How do you understand these things so well?" she asked at a loss. "You're not a touchy-feely guy."

His smile was gentle, but a tinge of the predator she knew him to be lurked in his espresso gaze. "If I didn't understand human nature, I would not be nearly as successful in business as I am."

She remembered him saying something like that before but hadn't realized how deep his intuitive genius ran. It was kind of scary.

She wasn't sure she *wanted* to be known or understood that deeply. "I guess that's true."

"So, because you couldn't give Adhip and Tabish love, you gave them obedience."

"Yes."

"And because Dev had no more backbone than his uncle, he was going to make the same kind of marriage."

"I'm pretty sure *uncle* and *auntie* had more chemistry than Dev and I ever did," she admitted, realizing only recently that her idea of marrying her best friend who she was not attracted to at all might have been more a recipe for disaster than the easy relationship she'd thought it would be.

"Perhaps. Perhaps not. But for myself, I am glad you are not grieving a lover."

She didn't know what to say to that, so Eliza said nothing.

Rajvinder, tugged her into his lap, his mouth hovering just above hers. "We have all the chemistry necessary to have a very satisfying marriage."

"Marriage isn't all about sex." But the more time she spent with him, the more she wanted Rajvinder, and the less convinced Eliza became in her certainty that good sex didn't matter to a good marriage.

His kiss forestalled anything she might have said. And she didn't mind. Not one little bit.

Her entire body jolted from the electric connection between their lips.

His kiss was masterful and questing at the same time. She could feel him holding back and her inexperienced sensuality was relieved.

They kissed until she was melted against him, his jacket gone, her top rucked up and her body zinging with every caress along skin no one else had ever touched.

Then, Rajvinder did the unthinkable. He pulled away, tugging her top down as he did so. "We have dinner reservations. We need to get ready if we are going to make them."

"I'd rather stay here," she said with more honesty than she would have ever given Dev.

Rajvinder's smile was devastating. "You are due for some spoiling."

"Dinner is spoiling me?"

"It is not about eating out at a five-star restaurant. It is about giving time."

"Which you don't have a lot of."

"I have made time for you."

And he had. This busy executive who routinely put in sixty-plus hour work weeks and used his weekends to wheel and deal, had taken time off to come and make sure Eliza was doing all right. To give her time.

"You're kind of perfect, you know?"

"I am far from perfect, but I saw the way Jamison treated my mother. She always said it wasn't the diamonds, or the elite vacations, but the fact he took time from his schedule for her."

And even though Eliza and Rajvinder were marrying for reasons of convenience rather than affection, he was committed to making that marriage work.

Feeling both elated and terrified by the feelings that thoughtfulness evoked, Eliza jumped to her feet. "Dinner it is."

She could use the breather.

Because if she wasn't careful, he was going to own her pieced-together heart.

CHAPTER TWENTY-FIVE

Dinner was amazing, and Eliza had loved having all of Rajvinder's attention.

He might have said it wasn't about the five-star venue, but that's where he took her. The ambiance was elegant, the service fantastic and the food superb. Their table for two located in a private spot created by a decorative screen and greenery, made Eliza feel like they were in their own little world.

And he'd made all this happen.

Rajvinder's attention to detail was astonishing. And a little intimidating.

She was kind of glad he *wasn't* taking a bigger role planning the wedding. With him as the driving force, as unlikely as she would have said it was, she now was sure that even their royal wedding could be bigger and more ostentatious.

"I feel like we're having the honeymoon before the wedding," she offered as they entered the suite later, making no effort to hide the approval she felt in her tone.

He kicked his shoes off like he'd done earlier, and she realized it was a habit.

Something warm unfurled inside her at the knowledge she knew this tiny idiosyncrasy.

He indicated the long white sofa they'd been sitting on during their make out session earlier. "I promise, I will not be sleeping on the couch during our honeymoon."

She made no attempt to flirt with him, or give him a come hither look. She wouldn't know what one was.

What she had given him was blatant honesty. "You don't have to sleep on it now."

He didn't ask if she was sure, didn't question if she knew her own mind. His eyes going dark with the passion that had simmered between them all day, Rajvinder guided her into the bedroom.

She didn't wait for him to kiss her. She'd wanted his lips all through dinner and now she could have them.

Sliding her hands up his chest, she pressed close and pulled his head down so their lips met. And it was every bit as good as every kiss between them had been.

Her fear of the wedding night and what came after the kissing was nonexistent in that moment. She wanted to touch him, to be touched by him.

~ ~ ~

Vin groaned as Eliza's hands mapped his upper torso, showing she wanted sexual intimacy as much as he did.

He'd been craving her all day, for the two weeks they'd been apart, if he were honest. The kisses they'd shared earlier only fed his hunger for her. Breaking off to go to dinner had been nearly impossible.

But it had been necessary.

He was done keeping his hands to himself now, though, and from her actions it was clear, so was the woman he would be married to in a matter of days.

He skimmed his hands down her elegant back and cupped her bottom pulling her up and closer for the kiss.

Eliza locked her legs around him, like it was the most natural thing in the world.

He moved to the bed, his own knees unsteady under the overriding lust racing through him.

Vin took his time undressing her and Eliza showed no reticence about sharing her nudity with him, though he knew he was the only man who had ever seen her this way.

And what that knowledge did to him.

Damn.

Knowing that not even Dev had ever seen her naked body, have ever touched not just her breasts and feminine sex, but her stomach, or her back, her bottom, her thighs.

Eliza's body was Vin's playground just as his would be for her.

She would only ever be his and he would be hers from now until death, the wedding vows a mere formality they had yet to get through.

Even amidst his lust, there was a tiny niggle of doubt about how she would respond to his plans for after their marriage, but he'd sounded her out. He'd made sure he knew what was important to her and that was not having *her* child become his heir.

Vin had made sure Eliza's future was set.

So was that of the Mahapatras dynasty, just not the way the Singh family expected.

And none of that was as important right now as the desire raging between him and the woman that would soon be his wife.

Once they were both naked, Vin stood for a long moment, just looking at her. Eliza's nipples were hard and berry red, her pert breasts not overly full, but he wanted to taste them like he'd never wanted to taste another woman, wanted to feel every millimeter of her satiny skin.

Vin would give her pleasure she didn't know she was capable of feeling and take the same from her body.

She didn't wax down below, like other lovers he'd had, Eliza's blond curls glistening enticingly with proof that he wasn't the only one turned on.

Not that her trembling limbs and panting breaths weren't a dead giveaway.

"You want this." He didn't make it a question because he didn't have any doubt.

"I do," she affirmed regardless, her voice breathy and low. "I never knew I could."

"You thought you were sexless?" he asked in a teasing tone, because his little scientist might be an introvert, but she was by no means lacking in feminine sensuality. "You excite me like no other woman ever has."

And didn't she look pleased by that fact?

He wasn't going to try to deny it, though. Vin might have a lot more experience than his virgin scientist did in the bedroom department, but none of his other encounters had affected him like a single kiss from Eliza's sweet lips.

"Then it's mutual." That admission didn't seem to make her quite as pleased.

Fear would be a better description of the look on her face.

"That's a good thing, *sonii*. Mutual passion should not frighten you. Even if it leads to emotions neither of us expects to feel." Vin had come to accept that even if they had met under entirely different circumstances, he would want to make this woman his.

"I don't want to love you," she told him baldly even as her hands reached for him.

"Don't think about that right now." He brushed his hand down her torso, loving the way her body undulated under the caress. "Think about how good this feels."

Love? Not something he let himself worry about. Mutual passion? That was something else and coupled with shared interests and beliefs, a damn good basis for marriage, in his estimation.

"I'm not on birth control," she told him, her voice soft and breathless, turning him on even further.

But her words gave him pause. "You said you were not ready for children."

"I'm not, but that was not the deal." Her tone said she was just starting to realize that maybe she should have worried more about what she wanted than what the family expected from her.

This marriage deal might have been Eliza's idea, but she had put herself entirely at the Singh family's disposal, with all their dynastic dreams.

However, Vin would protect her in this, as in other things. As her future husband and partner in life, that was his job.

Chapter Twenty-Six

"You having a child right away, or even at all, is not part of *our* deal," he assured her. "And what is between *us*, is all that matters."

"I don't think *Dadaji* would agree."

"Ask me if I care."

"You must care a little, or you wouldn't be going through with this."

"Trust me, this..." He trailed his hand down the inside of her thigh. "Has nothing to do with Trisanu Singh."

She bit her lip, something passing through her gaze he could not define. "But it does."

"No." Then he moved over her, capturing her lips in a kiss meant to convey just how little anyone else had to do with what happened between Vin and Eliza.

She responded with the passion that had quickly become necessary to him, opening her mouth to his questing tongue, moving her legs restlessly against him.

He did what he'd been craving all day and mapped her satin smooth skin from collar bone to ankles, reveling in the way she responded to his touch. Loving every gasped breath, every moan, every jerky movement of her body, as she sought more and more sensation.

And she had believed she was sexless?

She was living fire and he was happy to be bathe in her heat.

"Rajvinder!"

He lifted his head and met her beautiful blue eyes. "What do you want, *sonii*?"

"More."

He smiled. "Then I will give you more."

He started by following the path with his mouth that he had already taken with his hands.

He licked her ankle, mouthing the skin of her leg until he'd reached the apex of her thighs. He pushed her legs wider and pressed his tongue right against her swollen clitoris.

Crying out, she arched against him and he inhaled the sweet scent of her arousal as he tasted the very essence of her.

"Rajvinder, that's...don't stop...please, don't stop."

No chance. He was bringing her the ultimate pleasure and turning himself on past the point the reason at the same time.

He brushed his fingertips up her body until he found both of her breasts. Cupping them, he played over her nipples with his thumbs. Brushing back and forth, back and forth, until she was writhing on the bed, her most intimate flesh slick with her desire, incoherent mutterings spilling as a litany from her lips.

She climaxed with a scream, her entire body going rigid as he drew forth every bit of pleasure he could before she grew too sensitive. He wiped his mouth on the sheet and then moved up her body, loving how bonelessly she lay against the pristine white Egyptian cotton.

She looked hazily at him. "That was amazing."

"It was. You are."

"Are we going to..." She let her voice trail off, clearly uncomfortable naming the act.

His sex was so hard, it ached, but he shook his head. They would discuss birth control tomorrow, but until then, there would be no penetration.

"But..."

"Do you want to touch me?" he asked her.

Her eyes opened wider, her body going from boneless to alert in a breath. "Oh, yes."

He laid back, indicating his nakedness. "Then by all means."

Her gaze skittered to his turgid sex, but moved on to the rest of his body and he knew he wasn't in for a quick hand job.

He was right. She took her time, learning his body, touching him and tasting with untutored enthusiasm that was more exciting than the most experienced and adventurous lovers from his past.

Eliza paid close attention to his every reaction, so she learned just what affected him and what did not. By the time she touched his shaft, he felt like he could come with a single stroke, but she showed him otherwise, seemingly to innately understand the pressure that felt the best, the light touch that would excite but not give him completion.

When he came, he was hoarse with the shout, calling out her name as jets of pleasure shot from him.

She got up and he heard water running in the en suite. She returned with a damp cloth, which she used to wipe his excess pleasure from his groin.

"Be careful, or you will get me going again," he warned, not sure if he wanted her to be careful, or not.

"Can we again, that soon?"

"We could, but you still need to catch up on rest."

"You'll sleep with me, in here?"

"If that is what you want."

"I do."

They found a surprisingly easy comfort, his body curved around hers. It felt right in a way he would never have expected.

"This feels good," she said sleepily.

"It does."

"I've never slept with someone before. I thought it would be awkward."

"We fit. Now, go to sleep." But she was right. What should have been awkward was entirely natural.

And Vin found himself going to sleep hours earlier than he ever did, content in a way he had never been.

CHAPTER TWENTY-SEVEN

Eliza ate her breakfast looking everywhere but at the man she had spent the night with. Her fiancé, but more. Her lover.

Were they lovers if they hadn't actually done the deed?

"You seem preoccupied this morning, *sonii*." Rajvinder's deep masculine tones broke into her reverie. "I would say you were embarrassed if I did not know that was impossible."

Her head jerked around, and she stared at him. "Impossible?"

Because she was so embarrassed by the intimacy they'd shared, she felt like her skin was too tight and she could not meet his eyes without blushing.

Cue heat stealing into her cheeks as their gazes locked.

His espresso orbs were filled with certainty. "We have promised to spend the rest of our lives together. How could you be embarrassed by the natural expression of our joined lives?"

"The promises come later. At the wedding," she pointed out, unabashedly moved by his attitude about intimacy between them.

Entirely natural. Could anything that felt that good be normal, though?

"I disagree. While we will indeed speak vows at our wedding. You and I have already made our promises when we agreed to marry."

"I don't think that's how the world sees engagement."

"It is how we see it."

"You say *we* like you're sure I agree with you."

"Because I know you do. We are two people who take our commitments very seriously."

He was right. "You're so sure of yourself."

Dark eyes glowed with nothing short of approval. "I am sure of you."

"So then, why didn't we...you know?"

He chuckled warmly, the sound sexy and happy. "We didn't *you know* because you are not on birth control and you have expressed a desire to wait to have children."

"But the family are expecting an heir nine months from the wedding date."

"Even if we didn't use birth control, there would be no guarantee of such a thing."

"There is," she admitted with another load of embarrassment. "They had both me and Dev tested for fertility."

Grandfather had told her that he'd always regretted not insisting on such for Tabish *auntie*, which Eliza had thought was too cold.

Rajvinder's jaw went taut, his eyes snapping with unmistakable anger, but all he said was, "Regardless, you and I will have children when we are ready. Our family will grow on *our* timetable."

"Grandfather will be angry."

"Trisanu's feelings on the matter are of no importance to me."

"I'm not sure that's true. I think you like the idea of making him wait for the next heir."

"He'll get his heir."

"But on our timeline?"

Again, that strange look she'd noticed before. "You said you do not care if your child inherits the title so long as the House of Mahapatras does not die out."

"You're going to name a distant cousin as your heir?" she guessed. *Dadaji* would be livid.

He'd specifically gone searching for Rajvinder because Grandfather wanted his own descendant to be the Prince in generations to come.

"Answer my question."

"You didn't ask one."

"Don't play word games." Rajvinder's expression turned as serious as she'd ever seen it. "Answer me."

"I still feel the same." No matter how angry the family might become, Eliza had come to see that Grandfather's wishes weren't always what mattered.

Rajvinder would keep his word to Eliza. He would keep the promises he had made to the Singhs, regardless of if it was the way they anticipated.

"So, we wait to have children?"

"You are just starting your career. We have time."

She was so happy she couldn't even smile, relief unlike anything she'd ever known washing over her body. "I would like to wait."

"You are terrified of loving a child."

Eliza didn't bother agreeing. He knew her better than anyone had since her parents' deaths. And he knew parts of her that had not existed until she lost those she loved most so close together. The dark recesses of her heart where terrible fear and old pain lived.

"You will learn it is safe to love me, then you will be willing to risk loving a child."

"You expect us to love each other?"

"I think you are very close to loving me, if you do not already."

"And you? What do you feel for me?" she asked with more emotional honesty and boldness than she thought she had in her.

"Your happiness and wellbeing are my top priority."

It wasn't love, but it was the kind of commitment any woman would kill for. A marriage of convenience to get it? Not a sacrifice.

~ ~ ~

Rajvinder made sure Eliza saw a highly respected doctor to take care of her birth control before they returned to the palace for the days-long wedding celebration.

He spent his nights in her bed, sharing pleasure, but he was waiting until their wedding night for full consummation of their relationship. He always left in the morning before he could be discovered by servants.

He would not have Eliza embarrassed.

~ ~ ~

Vin was in search of his fiancée now. He wanted to see the results of the Henna tattooing ceremony. The idea of the reddish-brown temporary ink staining her delicate skin in the beautiful patterns had him hard and wanting.

Vin certainly didn't mind the traditional kameez and loose-fitting trousers his mother had insisted he wear for all the traditional prewedding events. They were better at hiding his physical reaction to Eliza than a suit.

The sound of Trisanu's voice snapping in irritation stopped Vin. He turned toward the alcove outside the ballroom where he'd been going to search for Eliza. Though it had been updated, Eliza still went there for moments of peace in the hectic days of a traditional Hindu wedding.

His mother and Tabish had spirited Eliza away early that morning and Vin had calls to make, so he'd let it happen.

But he hadn't seen her all day and now the Henna ceremony was over, he had every intention of spending the rest of the evening together.

Trisanu's voice was mixed with the soft tones of Vin's fiancé.

Eliza stood with her back to him, her posture obviously defensive.

"I do not know what you were thinking, disappearing with Rajvinder," Trisanu barked. "You have duties to this family. And they do not include embarrassing us with your behavior."

Vin was ready to jump in and let the old man know just what Vin thought of his opinions on duty when Eliza spoke.

"I'm fully aware of my duty to this family, *Dadaji.*" She sounded more irritated than Vin expected, considering her patience with the family, and particularly the old man, to date.

"Adhip would have expected better of you," Trisanu said witheringly, angering Vin further. "Not to mention Dev, the man you planned to marry since you were sixteen."

Eliza drew herself up and Vin could just imagine the look she was giving Trisanu. "The man *you all* intended me to marry since I was sixteen."

"Naturally. Both of you had a duty to the Mahapatras dynasty."

"I think my willingness to marry not one, but two men to ensure the future of this family shows just how very aware of my duty I am," Eliza replied in clipped, cold accents.

Although Vin was confident she was in fact content to become his wife, he did not like hearing their marriage put in the same category as what she was going to do with Dev.

Trisanu nodded, his expression complacent. "As it should be."

"If that is all, Grandfather." Eliza moved like she was prepared to leave, but Trisanu's hand on her arm stopped her.

"Wait a moment, child."

She tilted her head. "Yes?"

"I am not happy that you ran out on your duties for the wedding preparations and engaged in behavior with such potential to embarrass the family. We are lucky no news outlet ran stories of your nights spent in a hotel with your fiancé in advance of your marriage."

When Eliza made no effort to defend herself, or agree, just stood there staring at the old man, her expression one Vin could only guess at, Trisanu cleared his throat. "Yes, well. You have always been a good daughter to this family."

"Have I?" she asked, like she wasn't sure that was the case.

Vin, his anger on a slow boil at the old man's words, knew better.

"Yes, of course. Which is why I know you will continue to do your duty."

"I have no intention of backing out of the wedding, if that's what you're worried about."

"No, of course not. You have given your word. I would worry that Rajvinder might back out, but we signed all the papers of inheritance this morning. He's too pragmatic to give up all the family can offer him," Trisanu offered in what Vin thought showed a truly ignorant excess of confidence.

"If you say so." Eliza didn't sound entirely convinced.

And Vin smiled despite his anger at the old man.

She knew him better than anyone else, and how that was possible, he wasn't sure. But he knew it to be true.

Even if she didn't know that Vin had far more to offer the family then they could ever offer him, something she had finally come to accept, Eliza would know that what the family *could* do for him was a negligible consideration for Vin.

"It should go without saying," Trisanu said, his tones pompous. "But your recent aberrative behavior has inclined me to spell the family's expectations out."

"Expectations?" Eliza asked, her tone curiously flat.

"Once you are pregnant with the legitimate heir, you will return here to live at the palace full time."

The wily old bastard. Vin had expected something like this from the old man, but he was surprised he was showing his hand to Eliza before she even got pregnant. Trisanu's overweening arrogance would be his downfall.

Vin had his own plans already set in motion, plans that might not rectify the mistakes of the past, but would definitely make sure they were not repeated.

Now that the inheritance documents had been signed, no machinations on Trisanu's part could stop Vin from following through on his intentions.

"You expect me to take Rajvinder's child from him?" Eliza asked, fury lacing her low tone.

"Of course not."

"Good," the relief in her tone warmed Vin even as his fury at Trisanu mounted.

Because he wasn't fooled. That was exactly what the old man wanted to do, and his next words confirmed it.

"He will visit, as has already been agreed."

"But you want me to raise our child here without him?" Eliza asked, her tone incredulous.

Vin could have told her that Trisanu's ruthlessness was nothing to be surprised by.

"He will be busy with his business. Where you and the child live will not matter to Rajvinder." Trisanu spoke his despicable lies in a tone as if saying it to small child trying to understand. "Besides, I have connections in our judicial system. Once you are here, I have already arranged for a judge to sign full custody papers, giving you legal right to keep the child in India."

Eliza gasped. "You never had any intention of Rajvinder taking over as Prince."

"He is Prince. Now the papers are signed, nothing can change that."

And Maharajah Trisanu Abirhaj Mahapatras Singh would learn just how many friends in the judicial system of India and this very province Vin himself had if the old man tried.

"But he's just a means to an end to you."

"I have this family's best interests at heart. Can you say the same?" Trisanu asked with censure.

"Rajvinder will never let you take his child away," Eliza said with conviction, ignoring the other man's question about her loyalty.

"I am not taking his child, merely making sure the legitimate heir is raised within the palace's walls. And I think you overestimate Rajvinder's interest in his child. He's a billionaire business shark, not fatherhood material."

Eliza shook her head. "You don't know him at all, do you?"

"I understand him better than you do, child. He's a man of the world. You're naïve, as it should be."

"Grandfather, I think you have some very outdated ideas about men and women."

"Keep a respectful tongue in your head."

"Expressing my opinion is not being disrespectful."

"Have you forgotten all this family has done for you? How we took you in and raised you as one of our own when your parents died?"

Several seconds of silence reigned, then Eliza drew herself up. "If that is all, Maharajah?"

The old man winced at the formal address, but he nodded.

Eliza spun on her heel and headed toward the doorway outside which Vin stood. Her grandfather left through another doorway, into the ballroom.

CHAPTER TWENTY-EIGHT

V in made no move to conceal his presence from Eliza.

She stopped when she saw him, her eyes snapping with a fury her calm demeanor with her grandfather would have belied. "Did you hear all that?" she demanded.

"Yes."

She glared up at him, as if Vin had been the one to make the atrocious demands on her. "And?"

"And there's no way in hell you are raising our child without my fulltime participation." But she already knew that.

What Vin was unsure of in that moment was how far Eliza's guilt and sense of duty would take her.

"And you couldn't come in there and say so?" she demanded, clearly incensed.

"You were handling your own just fine. Besides, I wanted to hear what you said."

Her brows drew together, confusion mixing with her anger. "Why? You already know how I feel about that."

"I thought I did."

"Are you doubting it now?" she challenged him, now clearly as hurt as she was angry.

"No."

She jerked her head in angry acknowledgement. "Good."

"Why did you let him believe you would acquiesce then?" He'd been waiting for her unequivocal denial and had been disappointed not to hear it.

"The Maharajah will believe what he wants to believe. He has always been that way. Nothing *I* say will change that."

It wasn't what Trisanu believed that concerned Vin, but what Eliza would do. But in a flash, he realized those thoughts were ridiculous, born of a heretofore unknown insecurity.

The realization that anything could make him irrationally insecure was both unpleasant and shocking.

She shook her head. And he realized that she had been expecting him to say something, something he obviously had not said.

"I've got things to do for your mother. Excuse me." Eliza turned away.

"Wait."

But she was already heading the way Trisanu had gone, her gorgeous henna covered hand flicking back in a dismissive wave to Rajvinder, the set of her shoulders in no way inviting him to follow.

Hell. He could have handled that whole situation better and now his fiancée was both hurt and angry.

And it wasn't Trisanu's fault.

Even if the old bastard had instigated the situation.

Taking a deep breath and reminding himself that he could handle entire boardrooms filled with hostile people, Vin followed Eliza with trepidation he wasn't about to acknowledge.

He caught up to her in the great hall. He thought he'd heard the vast expanse of marble tile referred to as the Royal Reception Hall. It was a giant foyer with portraits of Maharajas and their wives going back several generations, is what it was, all royal pretensions aside.

Vin reached out and stopped Eliza with a hand on her shoulder. "Wait, *sonii*. I am sorry I did not step in and express our solidarity in no uncertain terms."

She spun around to face him. "You should have! You heard what he thinks. That you don't care."

"What he thinks has never been important to me."

"But it's important to me," she said with pain filled honesty.

"I will remember that in future."

She took a deep breath and let it out slowly. "Okay."

"Okay?"

"I believe you."

"I like when you say that."

"Because you are so arrogant you want me to think you are larger than life and infallible."

"Well, I do try very hard to be." He wasn't joking entirely. Vin had never been able to settle for average. In anything.

She rolled her eyes. "I know you do. And for the most part, you succeed."

"For the most part?"

"Perfection would be boring."

"I would not like to bore you."

"No worries on that score."

"There you are, the designer is here for the final fitting of your dress." His mother smiled at Eliza warmly.

"I wanted to spend some time with my fiancée," Vin said with a frown.

"Do not whine, son. You'll have plenty of time with her after tomorrow."

Vin drew himself up with dignity. "I do not whine."

"I did tell you I had things to do with your mother," Eliza chided with a teasing lilt to her voice.

"I will see you later then."

"You will both be far too busy." His mother stepped closer so her words could not be overheard. "And you will stay in your own suite tonight, no sneaking down the halls in the early hours. It is your wedding day tomorrow and you will hold your libido in check."

Vin felt heat crawl up his neck and realized he was blushing, but what grown man wanted to be having this kind of discussion with his mother?

"Fine." What his mother didn't know wouldn't hurt her.

"Rajvinder." His mother's tone was far too reminiscent of his childhood.

"Yes, *Maan?*"

"I will sleep in her suite if I cannot trust you to stay out of it."

A snort of laughter sounded from the fiancée sized peanut gallery and he glared at Eliza. She blinked back at him innocently.

"I promise, *Maan.*"

"Good. You always keep your promises."

He did. Damn it.

~ ~ ~

Eliza woke the morning of her wedding and realized it was also Christmas Eve, her sense of nervous anticipation inexplicably doubled.

There was no reason for the extra excitement.

After all, the Singhs did nothing to mark this day or the next, but the holiday was still special to Eliza.

Her last memories of her family all together was Christmas. And for whatever reason, only happy memories of them assailed her this time of year. Longing, yes, that too. And loneliness, but that she'd long since grown used to.

As she climbed out of bed, she promised herself this was the last year Christmas Eve would be just another day. And since it was her wedding day today, it wasn't anyway.

But next year and every year after, she and Rajvinder, Barbie and Jamison, would all celebrate the holiday.

And they would make more good memories to add to the best from her childhood.

Rajvinder hadn't come to her bed last night just as he'd promised Barbie he wouldn't.

Eliza had loved the look of consternation on her fiancé's face at being taken to task over that sort of thing by his mother.

She hadn't missed the heated looks he gave her since the Mehendi Ceremony. He liked the Henna tattoos very much. Eliza had gone to sleep warmed with the knowledge that leaving her in peace hadn't been easy on the man she was about to marry.

She had a surprise for him he would see on their wedding night. The idea had come to Eliza after seeing his anticipation of the Mehendi. She'd asked her soon to be mother-in-law for a favor and Barbie had been only too willing to do a private intricate Henna tattoo that covered Eliza's entire back.

It would wash off eventually, but Eliza had no doubt that Rajvinder was going to love it while it lasted.

She was not at all surprised when a knock sounded on her door just as she was crossing the room toward her en suite.

Eliza opened it to find the beaming faces of Barbie and Tabish *auntie*.

And so it began. Amidst giggles far too girlish for women of their age, and jokes way racier than Eliza would have thought the two women capable of, she was poked, prodded, powdered and pushed into her wedding finery.

And against every one of her own expectations, she enjoyed every single minute of it. Their exuberance was infectious, feeding the deep well of excitement Eliza had in no way expected to feel on her wedding day when she embarked on this plan to reunite the rightful heir with the House of Mahapatras.

After the umpteenth veiled comment referring to some surprise Rajvinder had arranged for her, Eliza threw up her hands. "So, spill already! I already know about the elephant."

And that had been at Barbie's insistence, not Rajvinder's.

"Don't mess up all my hard work." Tabish *auntie* fussed with Eliza's hair.

Barbie straightened the folds of the traditional red wedding gown embellished with real gold thread, twenty-four carat gold beads (as she was informed by Barbie) and only the finest Austrian crystals. "Be patient, Eliza. You will see soon enough."

"You keep hinting."

"You need to eat something."

"Maybe we should have thought of that before getting me all trussed up in finery," she grouched and realized she really was hungry.

Darn it.

Then Barbie fed her pastries while Tabish *auntie* tutted and protected her dress with a fine linen cloth.

But Eliza felt much better after she'd been allowed to drink a cup of tea and finish her breakfast.

Her improved mood went into the stratosphere when she stepped out of her room and saw a palace transformed.

Not by the wedding decorations, but by Christmas.

Poinsettias were everywhere and garlands of red velvet accented with shimmering crystal snowflakes at every gather between the swoops of fabric lined the walls on both sides of the hall. She stopped and gasped in delighted shock when she reached the Royal Reception Hall.

The biggest Christmas tree she'd ever seen indoors was right in the center and decorated elegantly to match their wedding colors.

"Wait until you see the ballroom," Barbie said.

Grabbing up the skirts of her gown, Eliza flew down the stairs and ran to the room that had been her sanctuary since arriving to live at the palace. Inside she found the wedding décor as Barbie and Tabish *auntie* had discussed, but there were no less than six Christmas trees and poinsettias replaced the traditional wedding flowers everywhere.

Eliza spun in a circle, her hand over her mouth, tears threatening her eyes.

Tabish *auntie* smiled. "I didn't know what to think when Rajvinder insisted on incorporating a Christmas theme with the wedding décor, but I believe it turned out all right."

"It's beautiful." Rajvinder had done this for her.

She wanted to see him so badly in that moment, her heart ached like it hadn't since it shattered from loss.

But this time the ache was a good one, if no less profound. And it was in that moment she could no longer deny the truth that had been staring her in the face.

She *loved* Rajvinder.

Loved him enough that it would destroy her to lose him.

Chapter Twenty-Nine

Terror washed over her and her knees nearly buckled. Her walls had fallen, leaving her barely mended heart vulnerable to love for the man she was about the marry. She could not catch her breath as she acknowledged emotions she'd been so sure she would never allow herself to feel, but even a broken heart was stronger than the mind's will.

She could barely stand. Her heart raced so fast, Eliza could feel it pounding in her chest and pressed her hand against it, making a soft sound of distress.

"Are you all right?" Barbie asked, her voice filled with concern, her beautiful face creased with worry.

Tabish *auntie* looked around and then back at Eliza. "Do you not like it? I do not know if we can change the décor this late."

And suddenly the one thing she needed was there, strong arms coming around her, Rajvinder's voice in her ear. "This was intended to delight, not terrify."

She turned in his hold until she could see into dark eyes, what she found there so perfect, so necessary. "I love you," she blurted with all the fear and devastation roiling through her.

Rajvinder did not smile, but she saw he wanted to. In his eyes. Instead, he leaned down and did the unthinkable in front of Tabish *auntie*.

Rajvinder kissed Eliza until the fear had to take backseat to passion. Then he lifted his head and met her worried gaze. "Listen to me, *sonii*."

She nodded.

"Tragedy happens. I cannot promise our life will be without it, but I promise you there will be great joy too."

"Do not die." Again, she demanded the impossible.

Again, he promised it. "I will not."

And she believed.

Had to believe, or she would lose her sanity in fear. And Eliza was stronger than that.

"Your mom said you weren't supposed to see me before the wedding."

"I do not believe in superstition. We make our own luck." He smiled that devastating smile. "Besides, I had to see your reaction to my surprise."

"It's amazing. One of my best Christmas memories ever." She waved her hand toward all the trees and poinsettias. "It's all so beautiful. Thank you."

"Nothing is as beautiful as you are today."

She ducked her head, embarrassed by the compliment. "Barbie and Tabish *auntie* did their best."

"They had perfection to work with."

She rolled her eyes, but didn't dismiss his words. They made her feel good. "I'm glad you think so."

"Are you ready to get married?"

"It will be a long day."

"I am aware."

"I'm ready for it."

"Then it is time I saw to the elephants."

She laughed and hugged him before Rajvinder let her go.

He stopped on his way out and turned back to her. "I have one more surprise for you. I know you will be very happy, but others might not be."

She gave him a smile, wobbly, tinged with emotional tears, but there all the same. "I am looking forward to it."

His expression was all approval. "I believe you. I believe in you."

"And I believe in you, Rajvinder. You keep your promises."

He nodded and left.

"What was that about?" Tabish *auntie* demanded.

"I don't know."

"But you said you trusted him."

That wasn't exactly what she'd said, but Eliza supposed it could be taken as implied. "I also told him I loved him. I can't believe I blurted it out like that."

"I thought it was beautiful." Barbie was crying without shame, her smile so lovely, so very welcome. "I cannot tell you how happy I am that you two are so well suited."

"You must not worry if he does not say the words," Tabish *auntie* assured Eliza. "There are things far more important in marriage than the love of your husband."

Barbie's look said she didn't agree, but the look she gave Tabish *auntie* was filled with understanding. "My son will realize his feelings when his stubborn brain allows him to do so, but he may never actually admit to them."

"Does Jamison say the words to you?" Eliza asked Barbie.

"Eliza! That is hardly an appropriate question," Tabish *auntie* admonished.

Barbie smiled at the other woman and then Eliza. "It is all right. Yes, Jamison does say the words."

"In front of his son?" Eliza didn't use the term stepson, because in all the ways that counted Jamison Latham had been the only father Rajvinder had ever known.

Barbie's eyes widened, acknowledging she'd noticed the deliberate use of the term *son*. "Yes."

"Then I trust that one day Rajvinder will say them to me. No doubt with a lot more aplomb than I used, but he learned many important life lessons from the man who became his father."

"I've always thought so; Jamison is a very good man."

"His real father was a good man too," Tabish *auntie* said, her own eyes washed with suspicious moisture now too. "He would have been so proud of you today, Eliza."

"Rajvinder got some of his best traits from his biological father, but don't expect him to ever admit it," Barbie warned the other woman with a commiserating smile. "He'll never accept the duty that dictated my exile to America."

Tabish *auntie* sighed. "I'm not sure he should. We cannot change the world for the better if we are not willing to change how *we* react to the world."

"Don't let Trisanu hear you say something like that," Barbie said with a laugh.

Eliza found herself joining the older women in their mirth, her fears for the future dissolving just a little around the edges as she let warmth in to melt the ice around her heart.

And she realized she owed those three little words to someone else. Someone who had patiently waited to hear them, who had earned them just as Jamison had earned the moniker father.

Eliza grabbed Tabish *auntie's* hands and smiled. "Thank you for all you have done for me. No one could have been a more loving mother to me. I..." She swallowed and took the leap. "I love you, *Maan*. You are my family."

Tabish *auntie's* eyes filled with tears. "You bad child, making me cry." She belied the admonishment of the words, tugging Eliza into a tight embrace and whispering, "I love you, daughter." And then repeating it in Hindi. *"Mein tumse pyaar karti hoon, beti."*

Barbie's smile was gentle and approving when Eliza stepped back. "You will make a very good wife for my son. I could not have planned a better match for him myself."

Coming from the woman who still held some very traditional beliefs despite her Americanized ways, it was as sincere and encompassing compliment as could be.

Eliza, who had spent nearly two decades eschewing relationships, found herself being hugged again, by a woman she knew she would be as close to in the years to come as she was to Tabish *auntie* now.

***

Eliza had been raised with all the trimmings of being a princess of the House of Mahapatras since she was ten years old, had known she was to marry a Prince since she was sixteen, but she felt like a princess for the first time riding an ornately decorated elephant to her wedding.

It should have been over the top. Totally naff. But it felt like she was sharing in millennia of tradition.

A little while later, tears burned the back of her eyes as she approached the Mandap and saw that it too had been decorated with poinsettias and beautiful crystal snowflakes dangled with glittery gems from the corners of the silk canopy.

She approached the traditional sacred fire burning in the center of the Mandap, the berobed officiant on the left side.

Rajvinder, his gaze fixed firmly on her and nothing else, stood to the priest's left, across the fire from where Eliza stopped.

She'd seen him earlier, but unlike her, Rajvinder had not been dressed in his wedding finery.

He was now.

And seeing him in the traditional Indian garb of a prince on his wedding day fairly took her breath away. He should have looked uncomfortable in this style of dress so different than the bespoke suits he wore most days.

But he looked entirely natural and very powerful in his silk Kameez and trousers. The color of the House of Mahapatras, it was embroidered with thread a darker shade of burgundy that was almost black.

He even wore a turban, the impressive ruby broach worn by every man marrying in this family for the past several generations pinned in the center.

The officiant started speaking and she could not deny that each word held the gravitas of lifelong commitment. And love.

Love she may not have wanted, but now filled every crack in her heart.

She met Rajvinder's espresso gaze, her own probably revealing everything she'd thought never to feel. His expression subtly changed, going from intense to something even deeper, his gorgeous eyes making her promises that the wedding vows would not require.

And she soaked every single one in, letting those promises fill in emotional fissures almost two decades old, healing ragged edges to finish making her heart whole.

She had no brother to offer the three fistfuls of puffed rice to signify a wish for her happy marriage.

Emotion welled inside of Eliza when Barbie's husband, the man who had taught Rajvinder by example how to be a good partner, stepped forward and offered the rice to her.

Eliza threw each handful into the fire, offering her *homan* and feeling that with such genuine hope for her and Rajvinder's happiness, their marriage could not be anything but a good one.

Later, as Rajvinder placed the traditional floral garland around her neck, she was sure of it. This man got what he wanted and he wanted their marriage to succeed.

Everything he'd done to make this day special for her was a promise of that. Even her garland had little tiny Christmas balls mixed amidst the flowers. A subtle reminder that they were getting married on Christmas Eve, something neither of them would ever forget.

She put her own garland on him, unable to resist brushing her hand over his shoulder after she'd done so.

He smiled and she found herself returning the expression, moisture glistening in her eyes.

Their exchange of rings came next as she'd been told it would and the tears of joy spilled when she slid her ring on his finger. Against tradition, Rajvinder reached forward to brush the moisture away from under her eyes and she felt cherished.

Grandfather performed the tradition of pouring water through her hand to drip over Rajvinder's giving her away in the way of the *kanyadaan*.

Unexpected and unwelcome grief washed over Eliza in that moment. She'd lost her father and then the man who had raised her as his daughter had been taken from her too.

She sucked in air, trying to push the grief away on this day of all days, only to hear Rajvinder's voice cut through the pain as nothing else could have. "They are with you now, *sonii*. Believe it."

She looked up from where Grandfather's hand still hovered above her own and met Rajvinder's gaze. And in that moment, she felt the presence of not only her father, but her mother and the grandparents she'd loved so much, as well as Adhip *uncle*, the man who *had* been her father for seventeen years.

Smiling through her tears, she nodded.

"And now you are mine," Rajvinder said in a way that was not at all traditional.

But she nodded again. "And you are mine."

The vows that came after were profound, but only an adjunct to that truth, the rest of the wedding rituals touching deeply into her soul.

This marriage might have originated as a business deal, but it would be what she and Rajvinder made of it.

And against all expectations she'd had that day in his office, Eliza had every intention of making this marriage everything her parents' had been. And more.

Chapter Thirty

The reception, held in the Christmas tree bedecked palace ballroom, was lavish and everything Barbie and Tabish *auntie* could have wanted.

Barbie's entire Acharya family were there, dancing attendance on the woman they had once exiled. The Singhs were there en masse as well.

Rajvinder had invited both business associates and a couple of people she realized were the friends he'd spoken of. Eliza noticed even people she'd attended school with whom she'd wanted to invite were here, along with distant relations she barely remembered.

Really all that mattered was that Rajvinder stayed by her side, though, even as every tradition observed felt amazingly intimate and happiness inducing.

Most of the speeches had been made, or so Eliza assumed, when Rajvinder stood to make his own.

This was not part of the wedding agenda they had decided on.

He stood and waited to speak until the entire ballroom was silent but for the random sound of cutlery clattering and a few stray whispers.

He smiled down at her. "I told you I had another surprise for you."

"Now?" she asked, feeling trepidation for no reason other than Rajvinder would never do the expected.

This wasn't Christmas decorations in a palace that had never had them. It wasn't even a luxurious ruby and onyx necklace to take the place of the black and gold beads the groom was meant to give his bride during the wedding.

This was something more serious. His expression said so, even if everyone else was smiling and acting like they couldn't see the intensity in his gaze and manner.

Maybe they couldn't.

Though Barbie had turned to give her full attention to her son, no apprehension on her lovely features, but a more serious expression than she'd worn earlier.

Rajvinder nodded to one of the servants/security standing at the far entrance to ballroom.

The man opened the door and a woman stepped inside.

She was dressed traditionally in an ornately embroidered dress, like many of the guests, but unlike most of them, it was the burgundy color of the House of Mahapatras. Holding her hand, was a small boy of two or three and he wore an outfit almost identical to Rajvinder's.

Gasps could be heard throughout the ballroom and the buzz of shocked whispers.

"I present to you all the mother of my cousin Dev's son, Haya Anand Singh and my heir, Prince Devam Veeresh Singh. He will be Maharajah after me."

"She is not a Singh," the Maharajah said dismissively. "They were never married. I saw to that."

A gasp sounded from the direction of Veeresh and his wife's end of the table.

"She is a Singh. We have had her name changed legally and I have drawn up all documents necessary to not only recognize her as my family, but Devam as my heir."

Grandfather surged to his feet. "Stop this outrage! You signed contracts!"

Rajvinder met the older man's gaze, no evidence he was bothered by the Maharajah's anger. "That stipulate I will name as my heir a direct descendant to your line. Prince Devam is your grandson. I have the DNA results to prove it, if you think to challenge me on this."

And suddenly Eliza understood all the cryptic things Rajvinder had said about *his* child being heir to the Mahapatras Dynasty.

Her heart hurt terribly to realize that Dev had a son he'd been prepared to abandon for the sake of duty, but joy at Rajvinder rectifying not only the past but the present with his actions overshadowed any pain.

She turned to her new husband. "Thank you."

"What do you mean, thank you?" Grandfather demanded. "He's denying your own children their heritage."

She smiled gently at the man, who she genuinely did believe wanted the best for his family, but might be terribly blind to what that should be. "My husband has a worldwide empire, beyond the influence of the Singhs. Our children, *if* we have them, will inherit the legacy *their* father built."

And what a gift that was, to suddenly feel *no* pressure to provide the next heir to the House of Mahapatras.

"If you have them..." Grandfather spluttered, but the arrival of Dev's parents, forestalled any more words.

Mayurika *auntie* reached out and touched the little boy's face reverently. "You have given us back a piece of our son. How can we thank you?"

Veeresh *uncle* offered his hand to Haya. "Daughter, welcome."

Grandfather made a sound of anger, but no one paid him any mind. Rajvinder had brought new life to the Singh family, he had brought comfort in unending grief for parents who had lost their only son.

And he had unequivocally given Eliza all the time she needed to come to terms with the possibility of motherhood.

Eliza grinned up at Rajvinder. "You really are Superman, aren't you?"

"Superman could leap tall buildings but he could not run the businesses inside them. I can."

She laughed, delighted by her husband's arrogance.

~ ~ ~

They spent their wedding night in the palace, as every prince had done for generations.

When those plans had been made at first, Eliza hadn't cared where she was going to spend her wedding night. She hadn't anticipated it being anything special.

Now she knew differently.

Tonight was going to be very special.

But she was glad they'd opted to follow tradition, because that meant that she'd wake up Christmas morning to the amazing Christmas décor her thoughtful husband had arranged for.

He'd even had a tree put in his suite, and there were presents underneath. Eliza felt a thrill of anticipation for the morning, but no present could outshine the gift he'd given her at their wedding reception.

"Devam is a sweet child, and I really like Haya." She gave him a smile filled with joy as he carried her over the threshold in Western tradition.

Rajvinder kicked the door shut behind them, his expression one she couldn't quite decipher, but she liked it. "You were happy with my surprise."

"I was."

Rajvinder's lips twisted wryly. "Trisanu was not."

"He'll come around. He wants an heir with a traditional Indian upbringing. He's not going to get that with any child we might have."

"Exactly." Rajvinder let her stand, but kept her close with an arm around her.

"The Maharajah knew about Devam and not just his mother, didn't he?"

"I believe so, yes. With the strangle hold he's had on his family? He would have made sure he knew everything about Dev's life."

Neither of them commented on the fact that the Maharajah, as she was thinking of the man she used to call *dadaji* so easily, more and more, had said that he'd made sure Dev didn't marry Haya.

"Veeresh *uncle* did not know." His reaction had been too shocked, too delighted, to be anything but genuine.

"He and his wife were very happy when they found out," Rajvinder agreed.

"You did a good thing."

"I told you I would never allow a child to go unacknowledged in my family."

Eliza patted Rajvinder's chest in approval. "You're a good man."

"I am very glad you think so." He tugged her even closer. "But right now, I do not want to talk about family."

"What do you want to talk about?" she teased.

"You need to ask?"

"Maybe not." She stepped away from him, removing her veil.

In no real mood to dissemble, she lifted the flowers and necklaces from around her neck as well. She was as ready for this night as he was.

Maybe more so.

"Let me," he said when she went to start on the fastenings of her dress.

No further words were spoken for several minutes as Rajvinder unwrapped her like a present. When her back was revealed and the Henna tattoo there, he gasped and then groaned.

"You like?" she asked, nerves making her voice only a little breathy.

"Beautiful."

She smiled as she turned to face him. "You like the Henna."

"I do. All of it. I'm pretty sure I anticipated your Mehendi more than you did."

"I think you did too, but now that I know the effect the designs have on you, I think I would have looked forward to it a lot more."

"It's all you, but yes, they enhance your natural beauty."

"You are the only one that makes me feel beautiful."

"You should feel beautiful, because you are, but I am glad no other man has found his way past your reticence."

"It had to be you." Rajvinder was the only man she could imagine having a strong enough personality and character to draw Eliza out of her shell and get her past her fears. To heal her heart.

"Do I get to unwrap you now?" she asked, stepping close to him again, unembarrassed by her nudity.

"By all means."

She took her time, starting with his turban and working down until he was as naked as she was. His sex was rigid and pointing upward already, showing he was as keen to consummate their marriage she was.

Eliza couldn't help reaching out to touch.

He made a strangled sound. "Be careful or this will be over too quickly."

"Do you think I could make you lose your control?" she asked, genuinely curious.

He was such a put together guy. Nothing seemed to get to him.

"I know you can."

So, she proceeded to try doing just that. Eliza caressed his body, remembering the hot spots she'd discovered in their intimate time together and using that knowledge to her best advantage. When she dropped to her knees in front of him, he gasped as if shocked.

Although she hadn't done this yet, it was something she had been wanting to do.

She took him in hand, guiding the leaking tip of his manhood to her mouth. Eliza stuck her tongue out and delicately licked the pearl drops of liquid.

He tasted different than anything she'd ever experienced, salty and just a little sweet.

"Eliza," he said in a strangled voice.

And she took him into her mouth, her hands caressing him as well.

"Stop...please, *sonii*. No more."

She pulled back and looked up at him. "Don't you like it?"

"I love it. I love you, you little torment, but it is our wedding night and I have other plans for you."

Her heart swelled with emotion. "I think you're as good at making declarations as I am."

He laughed as he pulled her to her feet and then swept her into his arms to carry her to their marriage bed. "Because I told you I love you for the first time when you were on your knees with my dick in your hands?"

She laughed, all the joy and freedom this man had brought into her life spilling forth in the sound. "Not very romantic."

"I disagree. That is one of the most romantic things I've ever experienced in my life."

And that was what made Eliza blush. Not being nude with this man, not touching him so intimately, but having him say something so darn sweet about it.

"I really do love you, Rajvinder, my very own prince."

"And I love you, Eliza, keeper of my heart."

"I'll keep it safe," she promised with all the gravity such a vow deserved.

"And I will keep yours safe as well."

And she believed.

CHAPTER THIRTY-ONE

Their lovemaking was passionate and amazing, and yes, a little painful when he entered her for the first time, but even that was perfect. Eliza lost herself in the one man who could and had mended her shattered heart.

He stopped, their bodies connected at the most intimate level, and met her gaze. "This is ours. It is not about making a baby, though one day..."

"One day," she agreed. "I love you, Rajvinder, but if you don't start moving, I may resort to bodily harm."

He laughed, the sound going through her as he began to thrust.

It wasn't long before his powerful movements had driven her ecstasy to heights she had not hit, even with him. It was just too right. Too perfect.

And it was earthy.

And intense.

And physically so much more than she thought even this act could be.

"We are one."

Tears tracked down her temple but she wasn't sad, just overwhelmed. This intimacy was something so amazing, it washed over her heart even as her body sought the pinnacle of pleasure.

She moved with him, gasped, demanded, and wallowed.

In the pleasure. In the feeling of his body being connected so perfectly with hers. In the scent of them together.

In every aspect of this intimacy she never, ever wanted to do without again.

"I love you," he gritted out even as he increased his pace, his pelvis giving a little twist on the downward thrusts, sending sensation through her clitoris.

And suddenly that tight coil of ecstasy inside her exploded and she screamed, unable to hold back to the wash of pleasure.

"Yes," he shouted even as he kept moving, chasing his own completion and then he was climaxing too. "Eliza! Yes, *sonii*, yes!"

They collapsed together afterward, his body wrapped around hers in possessive, comforting strength.

"I think if I'd discovered sex earlier, I wouldn't have gotten my doctorate," she joked breathlessly.

"I won't pretend I'm not ridiculously pleased you waited to discover this kind of pleasure with me."

She snuggled into his body, kissing his well-defined chest. "Don't worry, I won't tell anyone what a throwback you are."

"A wife should keep her husband's secrets."

"I may need a little convincing," she offered.

He flipped her onto her back, his erection that had not gone down completely already sliding into her sensitized channel, his expression oh so sexy. "Your wish is my command."

And they started all over again, showing her just how true her joking statement might have been.

~ ~ ~

The next morning, he woke her just as the sun was sending its first rays through their balcony window. "Merry Christmas, *sonii*."

They exchanged gifts and then had an amazing Christmas breakfast with everyone except Grandfather, who was still in his rooms.

Devam and his mother came over later and Eliza took Haya aside.

"I just want you to know how glad I am that Dev had someone to love before he died," Eliza told the Indian woman.

Haya's dark eyes filled with tears. "He was such a gentle man, but..."

"Not strong enough to tell Grandfather no."   Eliza understood all too well. She'd been prepared to marry a man she did not desire, much less love, and enter a profession that was not her first, or even second choice, to make the Maharajah happy. "Maybe he would have in the end."

Haya's bittersweet smile said she didn't think so. "Prince Rajvinder has given my son, and me, a whole new life."

"He wants Devam to have his heritage. It's only right."

"And you? You do not mind? He said you would be delighted for Devam to be made Prince Rajvinder's heir, but..."

"I *am* delighted."

"But despite his business interests elsewhere, His Highness is still the Prince, and will one day be the Maharajah," Haya said, sounding a little confused.

"Yes, and we will always spend part of the year in the palace, but *our* home will be in San Diego. The palace will always be Devam's home, now, though."

"When the families exiled Badriyah, they did not know what they were giving up. I saw them all at the reception. Everyone wants to get close to him and he has no time for any of them. But he made time for my son." Haya sounded like she found that unfathomable.

"By naming Prince Devam his heir," Eliza tried to explain, "Rajvinder took him on as family, closer in his mind than any of his aunts, uncles, or cousins."

"Or Grandfather. I see why Dev was so scared of him."

"Rajvinder isn't though, and he'll teach Prince Devam not to be."

Haya smiled mistily. "We are very lucky."

"So am I."

Haya nodded. "I think that is very mutual though, Princess. He could not have a more compassionate or loyal wife. Dev told me a lot about you."

"I wish he'd told me about you," Eliza admitted without rancor, but feeling a little pain at the knowledge her best friend had hidden someone and something so important as being a parent from her. "I would have liked to know Prince Devam from birth."

"You really are a special woman."

"So are you. If Dev loved you, then you must be very special."

Haya's eyes glistened, but she blinked back any tears. "He said you were his best friend, and I can see now how true that was."

Eliza told Rajvinder about the conversation later and he nodded. "You were a very good friend to Dev and with one exception, I think he was a very good friend to you."

"He helped me find my way in the palace. It was so hard to be here at first, I was hurting too much to accept any of the adults around me, but Dev was different. And his son will find it very different than I did, making this place his home."

Both Tabish and her sister-in-law had doted on Haya and Prince Devam. And those two had soaked it up, making it clear they looked forward to moving into the palace.

The Maharajah might think he ran the family, but its strength was in its women and they were delighted to accept Prince Devam into their hearts and their home.

"Now you have me," Rajvinder assured her.

Eliza looked at him, letting every bit of love she felt for him show. "There is no comparison. I miss Dev's friendship, but you own my heart, Rajvinder."

"As you own mine."

"Life with you will always be an adventure."

"You have my word on that."

"And you always keep your promises."

"I do."

"My hero."

"You know you are mine as well."

"Your hero?" she asked, snuggling into his body, loving that this place of safety was hers, and hers alone.

"Yes."

"What did I save you from?" she asked him.

"A life without consuming and all-encompassing love."

"You are such a romantic."

"We'll keep that between us."

"I think your family figured it out when you gave me a three-week long honeymoon in Paris for Christmas."

He shrugged. "A woman should remember her honeymoon."

"I'm looking forward to Paris, but it's life with you I really look forward to."

"I love you, *sonii*, for this day and always."

She kissed him, giving the words back with her lips.

Now and forever.

EPILOGUE

"Should there be this much pain?" Vin demanded of the world's top obstetrician as she coached Eliza through delivering their first child.

They'd been married three years when Eliza came to him and told him she wanted to stop using birth control. She wanted children.

She'd been shaking with the fear of it, but her desire for a family was stronger than her fear, his very own personal heroine.

But this delivery thing was for the birds.

"We are adopting in future," he informed the room at large.

Eliza laughed and then groaned, her lovely face contorting in pain. "Just get over here and wipe my brow, Ironman."

She'd taken to calling him that because she said not only was he a superhero, but a superhero, executive billionaire.

Vin just shook his head and did as she instructed.

"You'd think you were the one having this baby," his mother admonished from Eliza's other side. "Pull yourself together son. Babies come with pain."

"But she has had the epidural."

His mother rolled her eyes. At him.

The doctor shook her head too, giving his mother a look that said, "Men!"

Then their baby was being born and he forgot all about his mother, the doctor, or anyone else in the room, but the incredible woman giving birth.

"It's a girl."

He cut the cord, all the while looking at the most beautiful face he had ever seen besides that of his wife, and fell deeply in love for the second time in his life. His daughter.

A child who would grow up with a loving mother and father, a child who would never have reason to question her place in her family or the world around her if he could help it.

He'd been very happy to see his uncle, Veeresh, develop a backbone with Trisanu. Apparently losing his only son, Dev, had given him the impetus needed to make sure his own grandson and the little prince's mother were treated with love and respect in the palace.

There was another child that, against the odds, would now grow up being certain of his place in the way denied to Vin.

New generations did not have to repeat the mistakes of the past.

"We're not done," Eliza told Vin.

He stared at her. And then looked at the doctor.

"The last ultrasound hinted at a second baby hiding behind the first. Their heartbeats were concurrent, but your wife is giving birth to twins."

He stared at Eliza.

"Surprise," she said with a tired smile before the ordeal of delivery started all over.

The second baby was a boy and Vin was not ashamed of the moisture in his eyes when he held them both in his arms thirty minutes later.

His gaze met Eliza's, "You have given me the world."

"That's fair, you made my world work."

"I love you, *sonii.*"

"I love you, Rajvinder."

Now and forever.

THE END

With more than 10 million copies of my books in print worldwide (Isn't that wild?), I'm an award winning and USA Today best-selling author with over 90 published books. My stories have been translated for sale all over the world and after a long career in traditional publishing, I've gone indie. I am loving the freedom to write the stories both me and my readers enjoy the most. My new steamy mafia romance series, Syndicate Rules features the morally gray alpha heroes and spice I love to write. I write contemporary, historical and paranormal romance. Some of my books have action adventure and intrigue. All of them are spicy and deeply emotional. I'm a voracious reader and love to talk about both my books and those I've read (or should read...good recs are always welcome) on social media. Welcome to my world where love conquers all, but not easily!

For info on my books and series extras, visit my website:
www.lucymonroe.com

Follow me on Social Media:
Facebook: LucyMonroe.Romance
Instagram: lucymonroeromance
Pinterest: lucymonroebooks
goodreads: Lucy Monroe
YouTube: @LucyMonroeBooks
TikTok: lucymonroeauthor

ALSO BY LUCY MONROE

Syndicate Rules

CONVENIENT MAFIA WIFE
URGENT VOWS
DEMANDING MOB BOSS
RUTHLESS ENFORCER
BRUTAL CAPO
FORCED VOWS

Mercenaries & Spies

READY, WILLING & AND ABLE
SATISFACTION GUARANTEED
DEAL WITH THIS
THE SPY WHO WANTS ME
WATCH OVER ME
CLOSE QUARTERS
HEAT SEEKER

CHANGE THE GAME
WIN THE GAME

Passionate Billionaires & Royalty

THE MAHARAJAH'S BILLIONAIRE HEIR
BLACKMAILED BY THE BILLIONAIRE
HER OFF LIMITS PRINCE
CINDERELLA'S JILTED BILLIONAIRE
HER GREEK BILLIONAIRE
SCORSOLINI BABY SCANDAL
THE REAL DEAL
WILD HEAT (Connected to Hot Alaska Nights - Not a Billionaire)
HOT ALASKA NIGHTS
3 Brides for 3 Bad Boys Trilogy
RAND, COLTON & CARTER

Harlequin Presents

THE GREEK TYCOON'S ULTIMATUM
THE ITALIAN'S SUITABLE WIFE
THE BILLIONAIRE'S PREGNANT MISTRESS
THE SHEIKH'S BARTERED BRIDE
THE GREEK'S INNOCENT VIRGIN
BLACKMAILED INTO MARRIAGE
THE GREEK'S CHRISTMAS BABY
WEDDING VOW OF REVENGE
THE PRINCE'S VIRGIN WIFE
HIS ROYAL LOVE-CHILD
THE SCORSOLINI MARRIAGE BARGAIN
THE PLAYBOY'S SEDUCTION
PREGNANCY OF PASSION
THE SICILIAN'S MARRIAGE ARRANGEMENT
BOUGHT: THE GREEK'S BRIDE
TAKEN: THE SPANIARD'S VIRGIN
HOT DESERT NIGHTS
THE RANCHER'S RULES
FORBIDDEN: THE BILLIONAIRE'S
VIRGIN PRINCESS
HOUSEKEEPER TO THE MILLIONAIRE
HIRED: THE SHEIKH'S SECRETARY MISTRESS
VALENTINO'S LOVE-CHILD
THE LATIN LOVER 2-IN-1 with
THE GREEK TYCOON'S INHERITED BRIDE
THE SHY BRIDE
THE GREEK'S PREGNANT LOVER
FOR DUTY'S SAKE
HEART OF A DESERT WARRIOR
NOT JUST THE GREEK'S WIFE
ONE NIGHT HEIR
PRINCE OF SECRETS
MILLION DOLLAR CHRISTMAS PROPOSAL
SHEIKH'S SCANDAL
AN HEIRESS FOR HIS EMPIRE
A VIRGIN FOR HIS PRIZE
2017 CHRISTMAS CODA: The Greek Tycoons
KOSTA'S CONVENIENT BRIDE

THE SPANIARD'S PLEASURABLE VENGEANCE
AFTER THE BILLIONAIRE'S WEDDING VOWS
QUEEN BY ROYAL APPOINTMENT
HIS MAJESTY'S HIDDEN HEIR
THE COST OF THEIR ROYAL FLING

Anthologies & Novellas

SILVER BELLA
DELICIOUS: Moon Magnetism
by Lori Foster, et. al.
HE'S THE ONE: Seducing Tabby
by Linda Lael Miller, et. al.
THE POWER OF LOVE: No Angel
by Lori Foster, et. al.
BODYGUARDS IN BED:
Who's Been Sleeping in my Brother's Bed?
by Lucy Monroe et. al.

Historical Romance

ANNABELLE'S COURTSHIP
The Langley Family Trilogy
TOUCH ME, TEMPT ME & TAKE ME
MASQUERADE IN EGYPT

Paranormal Romance

Children of the Moon Novels
MOON AWAKENING
MOON CRAVING
MOON BURNING
DRAGON'S MOON
ENTHRALLED anthology: Ecstasy Under the Moon
WARRIOR'S MOON
VIKING'S MOON
DESERT MOON
HIGHLANDER'S MOON

Montana Wolves

COME MOONRISE
MONTANA MOON